MUNDISIA

THE JESTER'S JOURNEY

OMUNDISIA

KYLE SORRELL

4 Horsemen
Publications, Inc.

Published By: 4 Horsemen Publications, Inc.

4 Horsemen Publications, Inc.
PO Box 417
Sylva, NC 28779
4horsemenpublications.com
info@4horsemenpublications.com

Cover & Typesetting by Autumn Skye
Edited by Kris Cotter

Library of Congress Control Number: 2025942287

Paperback ISBN-13: 979-8-8232-0956-4
Hardcover ISBN-13: 979-8-8232-0957-1
Audiobook ISBN-13: 979-8-8232-0959-5
Ebook ISBN-13: 979-8-8232-0958-8

DEDICATION

Dedicated to my loving parents, Gary and Patricia, my little brothers Samuel and Jacob, and everyone else who put up with my weirdness!

Tall
the
Minstrel

Fiddle
Cynkz

TABLE OF CONTENTS

Table of Contents

PART 1
GREETINGS

CHAPTER 1

Every star
Near and far
Waits for us
To just
Reach out
And accept them…

THE OVERWHELMING CHILL OF SPACE was something he had long since grown accustomed to. Even in Munderworld, what many would consider a realm separate from all others, the cosmos were easily within reach of any and all who had the courage (and the ability) to venture into it. He and Fiddle would regularly test their limits, daring to go as far as they could toward any starmatter, or nebula, or even far-off planets within view. Yet the result was the same every time—space was simply too big, too empty, and too boring, to bother with. And so the two spirits would return to the comforting, night-covered fields of Dulrot serving as the crown of Munderworld.

Yet now the jester spirit found himself lost in the universe, truly and thoroughly, for the first time in his entire existence. Not even recollecting the poem of old did much to alleviate his current worries.

Cynkz couldn't help but be amused as he thought about his predicament, and how he ended up there. Once again whimsical curiosity had propelled him forward into something he was not prepared for. He swore that he had once made the decision to think through his actions more carefully. To be fair—at least in his mind—the urgency of the shrinking rift in the sky above Potarium demanded a swift decision. For all its beauty, and for all the warm souls and boundless resources and art and meticulous architecture and open skies and lands between, the heavenly city was in a way unsatisfying. The path to something greater had been opened before him, and he had taken it without a second thought.

To say that Cynkz was ill-equipped would be an understatement of the highest order. The chill of space was easy enough to deal with, but the inverted nature of the realm was disorienting—debilitating, even. The once heavy, dark canvas of the infinite cosmos was now a pure white. The once beautiful, twinkling bright gems of the sky now glared through like black crystals. Far-off novas that would have, and most certainly should have, been soft, soothing shades of salmon caressing thin and dusty cerulean rims now appeared as harsh, vibrant gashes of deep emerald reaching out past an outer line of intense, almost metallic crimsons. Nebulas that would have sat as comfortable webs of calm strings of light and waves of natural hues now appeared as ruptured plates of uncanny waves of who knows what. Planets that should have been easy, bright orbs of smooth moon-grey and tawny sand-rock and herbal lime-green now shot back into the eye with sheens of near black and mud browns and unnatural violets.

Cynkz even caught glimpses of his own form as he looked about—his once dark cloak now flashed like a white flag. The deep crimson and violet harlequin pattern that was once so easy on the eyes now clashed with squares of silvered sky blues and near-white greens. Fortunately, for his sanity's sake, his physical body appeared to be unaffected. He caught glimpses of the occasional whip and flail of his now shortened, still jet-black ponytail at the edge of his vision, providing him some comfort. With enough time he was able to come to terms with the odd realm, and was finally able to make a startling realization.

I have been floating in circles, haven't I?

He knew the night sky well enough to know how to keep track of its starry formations. He did not recognize any constellations in his current place, but he knew for a fact that he had come across at least a few consistent shapes several times over. A new thought pierced his mind as he tried to map out his location.

I would consider myself lost—if I even knew what exactly I was looking for to begin with.

He possessed a vague idea of what he was looking for—Paithos, the Creator and the god of po and all living souls. The architect of the stars and the leader of Omun—those enigmatic, divine entities that watched over their lord's creation.

Yet all Cynkz had were names and titles, and nothing more. Thinking of names naturally brought with it images of faces he knew. He missed Kadd's wide smiles and grounded demeanor. He missed Pairne's bouncing red hair and the gentle lilt in her voice. He missed Fiddle's scruffy voice and fast quips and even his agitated, barely contained energy and expressions. He missed the welcoming huums and songs the good po would sing, filling the air like thick, warm honey. He missed the sharp chirps and trills of the humming-birds that would lull heaven to sleep in the dark hours of the night.

He missed it all, and yet he knew he didn't belong.

He remembered how he blazed through the realms of Munderworld. He remembered the portal that the Munder King himself forced open to allow Cynkz passage into heaven. He remembered Tuco, the prisoner who had been rotting away in a cell deep in the desert beyond Potarium's borders. He remembered that an entire city had been established underground out in the wastes, a safe haven for exiles and troublemakers. He remembered Harquin, the duplicitous entertainer and ringmaster. And he remembered the woman who led the ringmaster, and others like him—Yla.

Try as he might, Cynkz couldn't help but think of his most intimate experience with an Omun, fallen or not—the all-consuming eye of Eshra'Tel. He could recall the eerie feeling the eye gave of something far away watching closely. In fact, the feeling was so strong in his mind that it seemed as if he were experiencing it again, at that very moment. His thoughts went silent as he tried to quell his nerves.

The thread!

The thought cut into his mind swiftly like a dagger through cloth, and his hand dove into his chest pocket just as quickly. Yet what he pulled out and held before himself seemed to do little to help. The thread's once pure light had inverted, just like everything else. The celestial dust flaking off of the dark, wispy splinter resembled the twinkling black stars all around. Beyond that, it didn't appear to do anything notable. Cynkz stared at the thread for a moment, the way an expectant child might toward something they didn't fully understand, and huffed and sighed the same way said child might when frustrated when they failed to come up with a satisfying answer to what they were looking at.

With a languid flare, he pushed the thread back into his pocket and looked around once again. It was then that he finally noticed that the realm's icy air had receded, if just barely. Something warm in the distance seemed to catch his attention. A near impalpable aura seemed to tunnel his focus toward a single, far-off star. It was impossibly far away, yet when the jester held up a pale hand toward it, he could feel its soft, distant warmth. As predictably nonsensical as Munderworld could be, he never seemed entirely prepared for new, and equally improbable sensations. Before he could consider the thought of perhaps approaching the star, a new voice entered his mind—one that could be felt, rather than heard.

< Greetings, young Cynkz. I welcome you to Omundisia. >

CHAPTER 2

"U M, GREETINGS TO YOU TOO..." Cynkz tried his best to return the pleasantries, though he felt undeniably awkward as he tried to parse what—or who—exactly he was speaking to. Cynkz raised a brow and looked over the warm speck with curious eyes.

<You may relax, Cynkz, I am here to help you.>

"Well, that is reassuring." With a quick brush of his cloak, a soft breath, and a smirk, he gathered his bearings, feeling confident once more. "If I may be so bold as to ask, how should I address you? Are you … the star sitting in front of me?"

<Ah! I apologize.>

The voice's interruption was sharp and quick, enough so to catch Cynkz slightly off guard, chipping away at the slight veneer of confidence he had built up.

<Give me a moment, and I will address you in a more intuitive manner.>

<You'll have to excuse my manners—we do not get many visitors, particularly those of a mortal origin.>

"I can imagine," Cynkz said, his eyes squinting and a limp hand now raised to rub the pointed hairs on his chin. "But where are you exactly? Are you—"

<I am right in front of you.>

"Huh? But I do not—"

"There we go." The closeness of the voice this time surprised Cynkz, enough to cause his shoulders to spring up and his eyes to widen. It was a soft, warm tone undercut by a deep, almost guttural echo that seemed to bounce off of countless invisible walls all around him. Naturally, the jester looked around, trying in vain to keep track of the echoes as they rang into the void. He began to feel silly and remembered it would be best to just focus on the twinkling black speck ahead of him.

The voice continued, "I apologize once again. We Omun never address mortals directly, so our manners may not be up to par."

"Thank you, there is no need to be concerned," Cynkz said with a breath and a wave. "So, you have my name, but I am afraid I do not have yours."

"Ah yes, I am called Anim."

"Anim! Short and sweet—like many good things. I like it very much. To be honest, I would have imagined celestial beings to have much more, um—"

"More flamboyant names?" Anim responded. "Perhaps longer, more pompous sounding?"

"Y-yes, that is what I was thinking…"

"I apologize once again." The star's tone seemed downturned, as if now slightly tinged with shame.

"Here, in Omundisia, we Omun can see everything at once. All things are visible to us, even thoughts. I have been watching you for some time, and have peered into some of your memories, trying to make sense of the stranger floating through our realm—"

"Wait," Cynkz said, putting out a hand as if trying to soften the impact of his brash interruption. "You can see my thoughts? You can read my mind?"

"Yes." Anim's curt response was undercut by a certain childish sincerity, as if he did not even consider the breach of privacy of such an act.

Cynkz shrugged and smiled. "Well, I suppose I'll have to be extra careful then."

"You need not be concerned, Cynkz, as we Omun are not meant to judge. In truth, my view of your thoughts is somewhat involuntary. Even now, I can see parts of your mind expressing itself, the way the strokes of a brush leave imprints on a canvas."

"That is… huh." Cynkz couldn't help but break eye contact with the star, or at least what he believed to be eye contact, in order to scratch his chin again and contemplate Anim's words.

"What is wrong?" Anim asked. It was now that Cynkz noticed that whenever the star spoke its edges twinkled, as if its rays of light were reaching out to embrace him.

"That was just a surprisingly poetic way to interpret mind reading."

"Well, I only speak the truth."

"I believe you, trust me." Cynkz huffed, then looked around, as if trying to organize his thoughts—a now awkward gesture considering what he now knew.

"You know, the last time someone went rummaging through my mind, they commented on how much of a mess it was."

"Indeed, I too have noticed." Anim twinkled, then continued, "I cannot dig very deep into your psyche because of it. It seems that Krull himself struggled to do the same?"

"Who?"

"Krull, the Munder King, the first and most powerful of all Omun, now banished to the abyss."

"Ah, so he has a name." Cynkz, growing tired of scratching his chin to express thoughtfulness, merely resorted to resting his hands beneath his cloak. He had given up on adjusting his body language to his speaking partner. Would a star even care about such things?

Cynkz continued, "I suppose that explains what Eshra'Tel was screaming about as he was being crushed."

"Indeed, and I must say—it is quite the feat you pulled off. To orchestrate the destruction of an Omun—fallen or not—is no small matter. Some here may even see you as a threat because of it—"

"I swear to you, I do not wish to be a threat." The jester couldn't help but throw forth his hands from his cloak, reaching out to appear as open as possible.

"I know, Cynkz. I can see your intentions and your heart as clear as day. I know you mean no harm."

"Well, that's good, but," Cynkz looked around, trying to take note of many of the other stars dotting the pale void, "what of them? Do they agree with you?"

"Who?" Despite appearing as little more than a twinkling black speck in the void, quite a bit of character could be gleaned from Anim's tone, and the cadence of his sparkling edges.

"The other stars? The Omun?"

"Ah, I should clarify—not every star you see is an active Omun. Only stars with worlds destined to harbor soul-bearing life awaken as an Omun."

"How interesting! Does every Omun come with a name? Do they all have their own personalities?"

"Yes. We are ultimately born with all of the abilities and knowledge we may need to maintain our worlds. The Creator himself used to interact with us regularly to ensure things moved in a suitable direction—"

"Wait... the Creator? Paithos? And he 'used to?'" Cynkz's shoulders seemed to lower, as if a great weight were slowly burdening them. He dreaded Anim's response, but knew he had to inquire further.

"Yes, and unfortunately your fears are accurate. The Creator—or Paithos, as the po call Him—has been reclusive for eons. In fact, it was not long after His confrontation with Krull that He saw fit to retreat to a place that even we Omun cannot see into. In truth, we have been lost ever since, and much of the universe is in some form of disarray because of it."

"I see..." Cynkz couldn't help but lower his head. Instinct spurred him to rub at his temples. He did so for long enough, and with enough force, that he had to readjust his pointed cap and his hair afterward. Anim seemed more than willing to wait patiently while Cynkz performed the gesture.

"I can see you are disappointed,' Anim said. "I know that you were hoping to meet Him. Unfortunately, we currently have no means of re-establishing contact with Him."

"Ugh…"

"I sense a feeling of familiarity within you, Cynkz? The Munder King, too, had secluded himself within your realm, and it took quite the adventure to get to him and get answers, correct?"

"Yes, yes, but I suppose I should not have expected things to be easy. Nothing ever is, is it?"

"Well, it may not be easy, but I do not believe it is hopeless."

"R-really?" Cynkz perked up, once again gesturing with enough force to knock his hat out of alignment. Though this time he didn't care enough to immediately readjust it. "So you believe there's a way we can speak to Him? Do you have a plan?"

"Well… not a plan, but an idea of something…" Anim went silent for what felt to be a moment too long. It was long enough that Cynkz even grew anxious and was on the verge of fidgeting, and perhaps looking aimlessly around the void before the star spoke back up. "The thread… You still have it, correct?"

"Of course! Here, just a moment—" Cynkz excitedly threw his hand into his coat pocket and pulled out the now dark splinter. He held it up ahead of himself, between his forefinger and thumb, displaying it proudly. The dust of dark starmatter emanating from the thread looked not unlike the stars themselves in this space.

"That is amazing, truly," Anim continued. "The fact that it still exists in a corporeal form, and stays calmly in your possession, may be a sign."

"A sign?" Cynkz said, his incredulity accented by a subtle lowering of his hand and raising of his brow. "Why do you say that?"

"Apostles are … interesting creations. After the practice of Omun directly assisting one another was abolished after Krull and Eshra'Tel's rebellion, mindless, celestial automatons were created to handle some of the more mundane of our ethereal responsibilities. New apostles are constantly created, each one born to fulfill a single, specific purpose. Once their duty is done, they are returned to the Creator to be reformed into something new."

"So the apostle we took this thread from no longer exists?"

"Presumably, yes. Though nothing is normally left of an apostle once they return. All matter serves a purpose. No energy is wasted. That thread should have disappeared as soon as the apostle returned to the Creator."

"I see! So this thread could perhaps lead us right to the Creator?"

"Perhaps… I only figured it may be possible because of how the thread was tampered with."

"Tampered?"

"Krull has touched the thread. I can see the lingering shadow of his influence on it."

"Ah, yes, he did do something to it when I met him. Can you tell what precisely he did?"

"Yes… and no."

"Hmm?"

"Krull left a message, seemingly for the Creator himself."

"A message!" Cynkz's eyes grew wide, and he nearly dropped the thread in his excitement. "What does it say?"

"That's the problem, young one. I cannot decipher it. Whatever Krull did, it is beyond me, and likely any other Omun. He truly meant for the Creator—and *only* the Creator—to see it."

"Ugh! I swear, Fiddle was absolutely right to find his father frustrating! Nothing can be straightforward with him, nothing can be easy..."

"Yes, one would think he would wish to be more forthcoming with his own son."

"Well," Cynkz shrugged, playfully, "even Fiddle's charm seems unable to get his father out of his usual cryptic and grumpy mood—"

"I do not speak of Fiddle, Cynkz Alabaster Krullowski II."

"That's ... my full name..."

"Yes. Surely you can make the connection I am trying to elucidate?"

"So, that vision... of my mother embracing the sun... that was—"

"Your conception, yes."

"My ... conception..."

The void proved to be a less-than-desirable space to come to grips with things. Cynkz could feel his thoughts racing, yet he couldn't force out a single word. Emotions ran rampant through him, yet he felt paralyzed, unable to express any of them. If not for the fact he was currently floating through empty space, he'd have surely fallen back. With nothing else to hold on to, he merely raised a languid hand to his head to rest it.

It was then that he finally noticed a slight hum echoing through Omundisia. It was soothing, if nothing else.

Anim gave the strange visitor a moment, but eventually felt the need to fill the empty air with something, anything to take the poor boy's mind off of the revelation.

"You know,' Anim said, "I always found Krull strange. Unlike most Omun, he enjoyed playing fast and loose. Yet he always followed the Creator's guidance perfectly and without issue. He despised getting lost in 'little details,' yet he found great pleasure in watching and observing the po as they performed the most mundane of activities. He took great pride in his position, as the first among Omun, given the responsibility to watch over the first of the Creator's children. Eshra'Tel's world had yet to give birth to new life, and so he would assist Krull with Peara."

"What could that have possibly looked like?" Cynkz felt exasperated, and his tone said as much. He nearly whispered the words, yet were perhaps the heaviest he had ever spoken.

Anim continued, "It could be nearly anything— from things as minor as reflecting an extra bit of moonlight on certain nights to affecting the tides themselves to promote the growth of certain sea organisms. These organisms could, say for example, go on to provide a bountiful harvest for that year, promoting a boost to certain populations, and allowing for important individuals to be born."

"I see… I can understand why even beings such as yourself would need guidance. That such seemingly minor things could have such long-lasting consequences—it must be a tough job, being an Omun.”

“Indeed,” Anim twinkled. “Yet the worst part is having to sit back and watch tragedies unfold.”

Cynkz perked up, now having something else to focus on than his previous revelation. “Why must tragedies of any kind be allowed to occur? If Omun are meant to watch over and aid in the development of their worlds, then does that not run counter to your mission?”

The two sat in silence, or at least what silence Omundisia allowed. The soft hum of the void seemed to grow heavy in Cynkz’s ear, to the point where he wondered if it was actually Anim just giving a prolonged “hmm,” expressing himself as he gave himself time to think of a suitable answer.

Anim finally responded, though now in a much sterner, sharper tone. “As horrible as such things can be to witness in the moment, such hardships are often necessary. The living are meant to learn to take care of themselves, and to eventually grow to a point where they can decide what their lives are worth, and what paths they will follow. If we Omun—or even the Creator— were to merely come in and solve every problem, the living would grow decadent, and ungrateful, and such souls would be destined for a burdened afterlife. Also, preventing a current tragedy could lead to who knows how many more souls being born, many of whom could go on to be the source of even greater tragedies. All these things must be considered in every action we perform.”

"Managing such things seems impossible, if I am being honest."

"Normally it would be, if not for the Creator's constant guidance."

"Yet He has secluded Himself—"

"And lost are we, His loyal servants, as a result."

The distraction did little to help, and Cynkz lowered his head as his thoughts were burdened once again with the truth of his lineage. Yet, for some reason, a light flickered within, and the jester let loose a swift chuckle at another realization.

"Hmm? Are you okay, Cynkz?"

"I am, it is just… I suppose Fiddle and I are technically half-brothers, aren't we? How odd."

"Not necessarily," Anim continued. "In a sense, all living things are brethren, as all things originate from the Creator."

"Well, that's one way of looking at it, I suppose, though that makes procreation seem a bit… awkward…"

"Speaking of which… Cynkz, you, as a child of a true Omun, carry countless implications."

"Such as?"

"You should, in theory, possess the genetic information of your father Omun, and thus should be capable of many things. Perhaps this is why you can shapeshift so thoroughly into things you would or should otherwise know little about?"

"I suppose. In truth, I never put much thought into it."

"The fact that, of all things, you would settle on merely shapeshifting, is interesting. Would you mind showing me? Your shifting ability?"

"Well!" Cynkz puffed his chest and flared his cloak, and couldn't help but smile. "If you insist, I would love an excuse to show off a bit."

Cynkz held his arms out and drifted back into a burst of colorless smoke. From the cloud emerged a great bird, wings wide and black as night. With a quick flap followed another burst of smoke, from which an impossibly long serpent slithered forth. A quick curl of its iridescent body led it into another burst of smoke, and from it, another creature emerged. Again and again, this process repeated, to the point where Cynkz began to get more creative with his transformations. One moment he emerged as a magnificent stag, and the next as a cloaked hunter. In another moment he was a large, simple boulder, and the next he was an even larger sentinel, complete with billowing, dusty robes and a crude, impractically long spear. Another burst and another form emerged—a large choir of humming po children, a spindly oak, an elegant whale, an ominous obsidian orb, a rainbow feathered serpent with wings—nothing was off limits.

"That will suffice for now, Cynkz."

Cynkz, now sitting as a mere squirrel, looked up rather disappointedly at the star, as if he had been interrupted just before enacting some performance. The small, reddish-brown critter shrugged, and with a final puff of ashen smoke, the familiarly cloaked figure emerged.

"Well?" Cynkz wondered if he pushed himself a bit hard. It took him a moment to catch his breath.

Silence filled the air, and though for only a few moments, it was enough for Cynkz to begin growing anxious. He could feel the star judging him. He almost felt like a lab experiment of some sort.

The star's usual, amicable tone broke through. "What do you feel when you transform? Do you notice anything odd?"

"I, um, not necessarily," Cynkz said, instinctually reaching up to scratch his chin and look around the pale void. "Why? Is something wrong?"

"Well, I didn't expect your technique to be so … crude…"

"Crude?" Cynkz perked up once again, this time raising a curious brow toward the black speck ahead of him. "In truth, I have never been criticized for my shifting ability. Is it that bad?"

"No, not 'bad,' just … crude. When you shift, your body's entire mass collapses, and then bursts outward, rearranging itself in a new form."

"So… that may explain the smoke…"

"Yes. Fortunately, the process is near instantaneous, and thus is not noticeable to you."

"Wait! Does that process occur when I transform things beyond myself? Such as, well…"

"Such as other po? Yes. They too undergo the exact same process when you transform them."

"That is … concerning… I am grateful that I never used that particular ability too often. I wonder what Fiddle would think of it, though."

"As far as I can tell," Anim said, "you have no issue returning things to their original form. You have a real talent it seems. It appears effortless."

"Well," Cynkz shrugged, "if I am to have a single skill, I suppose it helps to be proficient at it."

"You should be capable of much more, however."

"Really?" A wry grin began to press hard lines into the jester's face. "Such as what? Perhaps if I learn a thing or two I could actually be of some use to you, perhaps repay you for telling me so much."

"I actually have an idea—a way of beginning you on a path to learning more about yourself and your capabilities, as well as assisting me, but… I have a final question."

"Ah, of course, Anim, whatever you need."

"If you do meet the Creator, you would, in a sense, have access to a power beyond all others. If, by some miracle, you could even speak with the Creator, per-haps even convince Him to assist you… What would you do? What is it that you seek?"

Cynkz's expression flattened. Once again he found his eyes looking around, as if searching for answers in the void. Thus far he had no one to answer to but himself. There was something calming about letting mere whimsy and curiosity spur him forth. Yet now he was faced with a greater responsibility. Rather than let heavy thoughts weigh him down, he merely chose to speak plainly and honestly.

"I wish to ask the Creator some questions. About the po, about Peara, and about myself. I suppose Paithos has no obligation to justify His actions to me of all po, but… I would like to know why Peara's time was cut short, and if there is perhaps a better way of doing things."

"I see." Anim sat quiet, with even his occasional twinkling settling into a calmer rhythm. Cynkz didn't need to see a face to read that the entity was in deep thought.

"Is that okay?" Cynkz asked. "I mean no ill will. I do not seek power, nor even to disrupt Paithos's plans. I merely seek answers."

"I know, Cynkz. I know you mean no harm, and in fact can see that your intentions are pure. But it does much to hear you reaffirm them. Now, if you are ready, we can go to my world and begin—"

"Um, how will I get there? I imagine your world is too far away to merely fly there."

"Ah, of course!" Anim's excited tone invigorated Cynkz. For a while, he wondered if he was the only one greatly anticipating whatever may come next. "We Omun can travel effortlessly through light. You should be capable of doing such as well."

"Fascinating! How do I do it?"

"It … may not be something you are capable of doing independently. Here, I will assist you."

The black star flared its edges, and a bright flash of light overtook the cloaked figure, and the two were gone, as if they were never there.

CHAPTER 3

A BURST OF LIGHT FLASHED UNDER A gray, clouded sky, and from it emerged a darkly cloaked figure hovering above.

The shift in perspective and his physical state provided enough of a shock that the jester nearly keeled over. With a quick breath and a hand on his chest, he was able to recover, at least.

"Are you alright Cynkz?" Anim asked. His voice still seemed to ring through Cynkz's mind, as opposed to echoing out physically around him.

"Y-yes, yes, I am fine," Cynkz responded, finally gathering himself and straightening his posture. "I suppose it is only fair that I experience a bit of what I have put others through, through transformation."

A quick look around didn't reveal much. The first thing Cynkz noticed were the constant, fast-moving winds. They were warm and heavy, and unrelenting. Despite being several miles above ground, and able to see ahead for many more in every direction, there was not a single thing to obstruct the wind. There were no trees, or mountains, or anything really to protect oneself from the turbulent air. The ground itself was little more than a massive, flat plane of dark brown soil. It was surprisingly flat and even, perhaps a result of being constantly windswept. The sky itself provided a nice contrast, appearing as an almost silvery sheet of gray clouds that covered the entire sky and moved quickly.

"What is this place?" Cynkz asked. "Does this world have a name?"

"No, not yet," Anim said. "No souls have been born here, thus no one has named it."

"How is any life meant to subsist here?" Cynkz couldn't help but flare his arms out slightly, as if gesturing toward the wasteland itself. The harsh winds dragged against his cloak, now returned to its original color, hard enough to pull him forward.

"Well," Anim continued, "that is why I have brought you here. Directly below you, buried beneath the hard soil, lie the components necessary for a sapling to form. I have witnessed the same process countless times— the wind gathers certain materials, they come together to form a would-be sapling, yet as soon as it grows, the wind sweeps it away, ripping up its very roots only to be ground to dust."

"What do you need me for? Could you not merely whip up some cover for one of the saplings?"

"Hmm…" Anim seemed to be thinking of something. It was only then that Cynkz finally realized that he was essentially talking to the sky. Fortunately, the two were completely alone. He still couldn't shake the awkward feeling.

Anim finally continued, "We, Omun, as I stated earlier, must work as indirectly as possible. Even something as small as 'whipping up some cover' could have grand, unforeseen consequences. Certain compounds and materials being displaced, or forced together—especially at such a delicate stage—could affect a burgeoning species in countless ways."

"But…" Cynkz paused, thinking over his next words carefully before continuing, "My intervention will surely have a similar impact, will it not?"

"Perhaps, but you are, somehow, not bound by the same laws we Omun are. You are free to act swiftly and independently. I believe you have been given a gift, that perhaps the Creator has allowed you into our realm, and the greater cosmos, to do something. I believe you are meant to help us, and perhaps even to help the Creator, whatever that may entail."

"Well!" Cynkz puffed his chest and flared his cloak, stumbling just a bit as he forgot about the harsh winds once again. "I am glad that you believe in me so much, Anim. I could not have asked for a better guide."

"Thank you, Cynkz. Now, let us begin."

Cynkz smiled, then looked to the ground beneath him.

Anim continued, "If you lower yourself directly to the ground, you should find an odd lump of soil. That lump contains the materials for a future sapling, with the potential to grow into a great tree, capable of producing more seeds, and providing the cover necessary to allow them to grow naturally."

"So I'm merely planting a tree?"

"Cynkz… these trees will go on to provide a home for this world's future people. These trees will potentially go on to become great symbols of stability, of culture. Perhaps they will be linked to their worship of the Creator."

"I see, I see, Anim. I meant no offense."

"I know, but… You must remember Cynkz, every action you take will likely affect so many things, things even I cannot foresee. We must be careful and consider the weight of everything we do."

"Of course," Cynkz said with a slight bow. He turned his attention back to the ground and slowly lowered himself. He wondered how he would potentially look to someone from the ground—his cloak waving violently in the harsh wind as his dark, pointed silhouette descended upon them. Before he could get too lost in his own head, he noticed a faint shadow in the soil below. Handfuls of grains could be seen rolling down its side.

Ah, there it is, Cynkz thought to himself.

"You are correct, Cynkz. That is it right there," Anim responded.

Cynkz chuckled just as his feet landed on the ground. Anim seemed to take notice.

"Ah, I apologize again, Cynkz," Anim said.

"It is fine, Anim. I will just have to get used to my thoughts being out in the open," Cynkz responded.

Anim continued, "An important ability we Omun possess is time compression. Essentially, we can 'compress' our perception of time at will. This allows us to witness the passage of many years very quickly while remaining alert and aware all the while. We natural Omun normally do not need to make much use of the ability, as we have the patience to watch every step of time's slow march, but I would imagine that a mortal-born being such as you would appreciate it."

"Well, I am rather patient," Cynkz said, "but yes, even I have my limits. How will I accomplish this?"

"All you need to do is kneel down, and provide ample cover to the sapling-to-be."

"How long will I need to do this?"

"I would guess, around 25, maybe 30 years—"

"*30 years?!*"

"Well, remember, you will be compressing your perception of time…"

"Y-yes, yes, but… It just seems like a long time to be sitting still."

"To one such as yourself, mayhaps. But worry not, Cynkz! I will be watching over you."

"Well alright then, I will trust in you then, Anim."

"Splendid! I appreciate your amicability. Now, kneel down, and provide cover to the mound of soil beneath you."

Cynkz looked below at the lump of soil sitting between his feet. He gently sat himself down, sitting himself back just enough to avoid sitting on the precious mound, and flared his arms out, using his cloak as a curtain to drape around himself. As a final measure of protection, he rested his hands at the side of the mound, using them as a final layer between the collected grains and the harsh wind. His pale hands stood out within the shade his body and cloak now provided.

"Good! Good," Anim said excitedly. "Now, relax. Try to hone your senses. Focus entirely on the space between your hands. Try to imagine that nothing else exists beyond that space. When all of your senses come together, the effect should begin to take hold."

Cynkz took a deep, comforting breath and began to clear his mind. The shade reminded him of the dark nights of Dulrot. He thought of his time spent sitting out in the open air, resting upon his own cloak as he looked at the stars. He could remember the feeling of the world beneath him almost vanishing as the universe swallowed up his vision, and the motionless stars gave the feeling that time had stopped. He could remember the feeling of resting somewhere high above, far enough away from the wind rustling through the trees below, but not so far that the infinite chill of space became distracting. He considered it resting on the perfect point of the horizon—that perfect line between two spaces where neither interfered with the other. As if a warm blanket had been cast over him, the world itself seemed to move in a way beyond his perception. The many sounds of the world, its winds and the grains of sand dragging across the ground—everything began to settle as one in his mind.

"Good! Just like that!"

Cynkz's psyche snapped back to the present. The stillness faded, and the growing whistle of harsh winds returned to his ear. He couldn't help but squint as he looked over his shoulder, though his expression seemed to convey a more perplexed emotion than a frustrated one—something Anim seemed to take note of.

"Ah, um, I apologize. Please continue."

The jester couldn't help but smile as he returned to the task at hand. Something about the entity's excitable outburst—that such beings would share in such relatable emotions—was reassuring. Though perhaps such freedom of expression could lead to mistakes being made? The Munder King already proved that, though exceedingly rare, it was possible for an Omun to act irrationally, and in a manner that could even endanger the lives of the po they were meant to watch over. Such pondering only served to distract him, and Cynkz focused once again on the lump of soil in front of him.

He didn't even need to think of Dulrot this time—quick, soft breath, and a moment to focus, and the effect took hold of his senses once again. Everything seemed to darken, and all of existence may as well have been an infinite void surrounding his two pale hands and the small mound of dark brown soil between them. Despite this, he could sense something moving around him. At the edges of his vision, he noticed the light shifting between light and dark. From his peripheral, he could see clouds moving at such speed that they appeared as mere streaks, whose lines merged with the arcs of stars passing by in the night, before quickly disappearing before the day's light. Again and again, this process repeated. Before long, the process seemed to merge unto itself and became little more than a smear of impossibly rapid information. What should have been violent storms and world rending hurricanes registered as little more than slight trickles of rain pelting the jester's cloaked back.

And then something new appeared, nearly breaking his trance. Something small, and spindly, and an odd shade of green and blue, closer to turquoise than either color on its own. What little light could reach it beneath the cover provided allowed it to shine brilliantly. As the days went by, the sapling grew. As it stretched out, the speckles of starlight whizzed by and danced off of the plant's perpetual dew-covered hide. Cynkz couldn't help but remain transfixed on the comparably slow-moving plant slowly growing and moving upward. It almost appeared to be reaching for him, rather than the sky. Just as the plant began to exhibit a new, lavender hue in its shine, and the buds of new leaves began to form, Anim finally spoke up once again.

"There! That will do, Cynkz."

Everything stopped, and Cynkz's senses came to a screeching halt. It was midday, and a surprisingly sunny one at that. It was only then that he noticed the plant had grown nearly wide enough to touch his hands on both sides, and it was tall enough to where Cynkz could lean forward only a few inches and touch his nose to it. Before he could marvel at his success, he felt a deep pain in his chest and took a desperate breath. It felt as if he had been holding his breath for far too long, and he stumbled over to lean on one hand as his other reached up to grip his chest as he desperately gasped for much-needed air.

"You did it!" Anim cried out. "You did it! You did marvelously! I knew you were capable!"

"Thank you, Anim." Cynkz finally gathered himself and pressed himself up onto his feet. He took great care not to step anywhere near the new plant sitting defiantly against the wind before him. He took a final, comforting breath and rested his hands beneath his cloak before looking back up to the sky.

"Did 30 years truly pass just now? It barely felt as if a few minutes went by."

"Well," Anim said, somewhat coyly, "more precisely, it was around 31 to 32 of your years. The orbital cycle of this world is a bit longer than Peara's was."

"I hope Fiddle and Kadd will forgive me for being gone for an extra few decades."

"Well, about that…"

Cynkz didn't even need to say anything. He felt that his curious brow, now pressing hard lines into his forehead, was more than enough to show his worry.

Anim continued, "Time moves differently in different places. Surely you have noticed this when moving between Munderworld and Potarium. We are such a distance away, however, that much more time has passed than a mere 32 years…"

Cynkz frowned, as if his lips and face were growing heavy to keep him from asking the obvious, yet he knew he must, and forced the question out, "How much time has passed in Potarium, then?"

"Well, an exact number is difficult to give, as even now time moves quickly there, but…"

"But?"

"No less than 200 years went by while you were—"

"*200 years?!*" Cynkz nearly stumbled back, though this time he at least had solid ground to stabilize himself on. It did little to help him come to grips with the news.

"I apologize, Cynkz. I failed to fully consider and explain the implications of our actions, or even the time you spend in Omundisia, so far away from your home…"

Cynkz stood quiet, keeping his eyes fixed downward. He stared at the strange plant that had been the focus of his attention for decades—decades that flew by in seconds. It wasn't often that he was forced to consider the slipping away of time. Most in the afterlife considered it meaningless, after all. Yet here before him stood defiant proof that the old way of thinking may have been flawed. Perhaps it was not so much that time was meaningless, but that those who had lost time's value were seeking a justification for it? What if calling time itself meaningless was little more than a manner of coping with its value, having been lost on them—the damned and the dead? Life moved on without them, those who now reside in the afterlife, whether they be in a dark pit in Munderworld or a prison cell in Potarium. Cynkz was beginning to understand the frustration of those who felt dissatisfied with heaven, and with the fact that their people, who were now technically extinct as far as the rest of the universe was concerned, in a sense had no greater future to look forward to.

Perhaps it was selfish, but there was another thought that seemed to weigh even heavier on the jester's mind—that of remembrance. In the grand scheme of things, 200 years was not much, but it was certainly enough for someone to be forgotten.

I hope that they will still remember me…

"They do, Cynkz," Anim said quietly, or at least as quietly as a voice in one's head could manage.

"Huh?"

"Potarium," Anim continued. "I can see glimpses of it now, and can see that they do remember you."

"So you can keep an eye on them, then? Are the good po doing alright? I know I left the place in quite a mess…"

"Indeed, and in fact, they have taken great pains to rebuild. They seem to be taking their time with that golden tower, however. As well as a number of statues and other pieces of art now decorating the pearlescent streets."

"Pearlescent?" Cynkz said as he turned his head upward, bringing a smile with it. "The streets merely consisted of cream-coated stones and bricks when I was there. It is good to see they have upgraded."

"Yes. There are also many more po there now. It seems many more have ascended from Munderworld?"

"That is good. The Sisters of Elm seem to be continuing to do good work."

"Also, many of the imps are living among the po now. They seem to have grown quite attached to one another."

"Really? I suppose it makes sense, but the imps did not make the best first impression, from what I remember. I wonder if they all learned that they were behind the puppet incident?"

"It appears they have moved on from that," Anim said. "I can even see glimpses of Fiddle and Kadd walking openly through the streets. They seem to be constantly talking and laughing."

"Yes, well, Kadd is a good conversationalist, and I know Fiddle is quite the chatterbox…"

"There is another on your mind, isn't there?" Anim paused for a moment, seemingly giving Cynkz time to look up and stare with wide eyes. "I can see a woman with blazing red hair bouncing around in the back of your mind as well. I can also see her spending much time with Kadd and Fiddle. The two seem to be making sure she spends much of her time laughing as well."

"Ah, Pairne…"

"Cynkz, I do not think they have forgotten you. It would take more than a few centuries of leave for anyone to forget what you have done for them. Fiddle, in particular, would never forget a friend he had accompanied for eons. Your time together in Munderworld was not meaningless, I assure you."

Cynkz looked back to the ground once more, though his thoughts were elsewhere. He never thought that he would be feeling homesick so soon after leaving. Though he struggled to consider if it really had been a short time or not. Who ultimately gets to judge the value and weight of time? Rather than weigh his mind down anymore with such questions, he merely chuckled and looked back at the sky.

"Thank you Anim," Cynkz said. "That means a lot."

The two shared a warm, silent moment with one another. Even though Anim was little more than a great ball of light, Cynkz wondered if he was smiling back at him. The day's warmth was quite comfortable too, he noticed.

The tranquility was cut short as a new, sharp voice pierced the veil between them.

<Anim! What are you doing? Who is he, and what is going on?! Explain this at once!>

The voice pounded at the edges of Cynkz's mind. Its tone was harsh, and the way it seemed to scratch at the edges of Cynkz's psyche instantly reminded him of Eshra'Tel. His heart felt as if it were pulling itself down into his stomach as the dread set in.

"Be not afraid, Cynkz," Anim said, doing his best to comfort his guest. "That is merely one of my brethren—another Omun."

"He does not seem happy," Cynkz responded, doing his best to keep a calm, stable tone.

"Ah well, Siar'C is… well, I suppose it was only a matter of time that others would notice, and you would have to meet them at some point."

"So what now?" Cynkz asked.

"It is time for you to meet some of my brothers and sisters, Cynkz. Let us return to Omundisia."

CHAPTER 4

A BURST OF LIGHT EMERGED IN THE pale void.

Above a massive black star, a cloaked figure came into view, drifting relaxedly through empty space. Cynkz couldn't help but wonder if he would ever grow accustomed to the constant shifts in perspective and light.

Before he could get too lost in thought, the same sharp voice from before cut through, and began bombarding Cynkz's mind with questions:

<*Who are you? What are you doing in Omundisia? How did you even enter our realm, intruder? What secrets and worlds do you seek to plunder?*>

"Siar'C!" Anim shouted, his voice emanating from the great star taking up much of the void just below Cynkz. It was the first time he had heard Anim assert himself, a stark contrast to his usual accommodating air. "Cynkz is no intruder! He is a rare guest, and the least you could do is address him normally. You do not need to shout into his mind from halfway across the cosmos."

<*Hmph. Fine. Give me a moment and we can speak more comfortably.*>

Everything went quiet for a moment, save for the constant, soothing hum of the void. Cynkz, unsure of what to do, or even where to look, began to graze his eyes over the odd plane of existence. Despite the inverted colors and lights, he was beginning to grow fond of the realm. Seeing the countless dark specks of light twinkling in the distance put his mind at ease. It was not as pleasant as stargazing in Dulrot, but it was close enough for the time being.

Cynkz looked at Anim below him, and then to the planet far behind him. It seemed to be the same world he was just in. He wondered if, being this close to Anim, and if he sat between Anim and his world, he would appear as an eclipse of some sort.

"I am here," Siar'C said, his tone as bitter as ever.

Cynkz, caught off guard, whipped himself around and looked about. Nothing appeared different, at least as far as he could tell.

"Look above you if you wish to address me directly, stranger," Siar'C said.

Cynkz looked above and could see a new, faint star fading slowly into view. It was safe to presume this was Siar'C, making himself visible.

"Ah," Cynkz said. "It is a pleasure to meet you—"

"What is all of this?" Siar'C interrupted. "Who are you, truly? What do you want? I expected better of you, Anim. An intruder bursts into our delicate, holy realm, and you decide to coddle them? Going so far as to bring them to your own world—still in its infancy—and you dare to teach him our ways? How foolish."

"Siar'C, he has a name," Anim said. "He is Krull's son, as I am sure you already know. You could at least address him respectfully, as an Omun-born?"

"Tch, fine." Siar'C's scoff was almost charming, in a sense. That such entities could express themselves in such relatable ways was a constant source of amusement to Cynkz. "Greetings to you, Cynkz. I am Siar'C."

"A pleasure to make your acquaintance, Siar'C," Cynkz said, making sure to bow as well as he could manage while drifting in the void. "It is an honor to meet yet another great angel. We po hold you all in high regard."

"Hmph. I appreciate the gesture, but you may find it tiresome to repeat the action for every one of us that you meet. Also, your confusion as to what you even are worries me. You consider yourself a po, and Anim calls you Omun-born. Yet you are also seemingly free from the restraints that even we Omun must contest with."

Cynkz, in an attempt to steer the subject in a more amiable direction, chimed in, "I would love to meet as many of you as possible."

"Most of the stars you see now are merely dormant Omun, those whose worlds have yet to bear proper souls," Siar'C said. "Though there are indeed a number of conscious, active Omun watching us right now, yet they are too cowardly to say anything. Each one is too afraid to come forward and defend their realm, without the Creator here to hold their hands and lead them forward—"

"Siar'C!" Anim yelled once again, catching Cynkz off guard. "You know better than that. You know that all Omun mean well and that they are merely being patient, watching, and observing, as all good Omun do. It is the Creator's way."

"You are correct Anim," Siar'C said. "We are meant to follow the Creator's way, but we have been without His guidance for so long. If He were still with us, I doubt a single one of us would have even allowed the intru—Cynkz—to even get a single foot in our realm."

"True perhaps, but…" Anim paused, thinking over his next words carefully, "the Creator has been silent for eons. Many of our worlds are struggling. We need something—or someone—capable of coming in and effecting change."

"You do not yet know true struggle, Anim," Siar'C snapped. "When your world finally bears life, and you have countless, conflicting souls to watch over, you will understand how delicate our existence truly is. And you will understand the danger present right now in allowing a mortal soul to gallivant about in our holy realm. Speaking of which—"

All went quiet. Cynkz felt tense, as if the stars themselves were now looking him over, judging him. He wasn't sure of what to do, or even what to look at. He noticed a certain cadence in Siar'C's twinkling— it was quick, as if each ray were an arm feverishly stretching out to twist and turn a curious object for observation.

Siar'C continued, "Do you realize how much of a threat you pose, Cynkz? Do you realize how much chaos and disorder you could potentially bring upon the universe through your mere presence?"

"I do not wish to cause trouble," Cynkz said. "I only wish to help, and perhaps speak with the Creator—"

"Ha!" Siar'C's shrill interruption nearly caused Cynkz to jump out of his own skin. It was not unlike the odd outbursts Yla expressed whenever she was amused. "How do you plan to help anyone here? Have you not caused enough trouble already? Blazing carelessly through Munderworld? Nearly bringing Potarium to its knees as Eshra'Tel brought ruin to your heavenly city?"

"You know full well you are being unreasonable, Siar'C!" Anim said, raising his voice to match Siar'C's tone. "You can see just as well as I do that Cynkz's intentions are pure!"

"Hmph. 'Intentions' mean nothing. Their execution—and the incentives that drive them—is what matters. Incentives drive our actions—all of us—even us Omun, Anim." Siar'C's twinkling paused for a moment. Cynkz could feel the star looking him up and down, the way a royal or king might sneer as they look over a peasant in disgust. "I can see it, memories caught like dust in the web of your fractured mind, mortal. I can see that you, too, are capable of darkness. I can see that through your own carelessness, you nearly brought Potarium to its knees as that ambitious fool Eshra'Tel nearly wormed his way back to Omundisia. The Creator has been reclusive for eons now, and shows no signs of re-emerging anytime soon. Do you know what havoc Eshra'Tel would have brought upon the universe had he escaped? Your little city of po would be nothing compared to the countless worlds and countless souls that may have been devoured by him. You barely made it through the ordeal intact, and yet you immediately—and foolishly—barreled forth into a new realm? You childish, negligent, inconsiderate, impertinent, clumsy little—"

"Siar'C!"

Anim's voice boomed through the void, echoing both off of the ethereal walls of Omundisia as well as Cynkz's mind. While more than grateful for Anim's defense, and relieved that Siar'C's ranting was cut short, he couldn't help but feel vulnerable. It was difficult for him to speak up for himself in such a position. Despite floating in an infinitely open space, he felt more confined than ever. It was not unlike the oppressive feeling he would often feel when tiptoeing through tight caverns or sitting anxiously inside a small room. Worse still was a single niggling thought gnawing away at the back of Cynkz's mind like a locust—is Siar'C wrong? Cynkz struggled to think of an argument against some of the accusations. Even he himself had admitted to barreling forth on little more than curiosity and whimsy, never staying around long enough to have to deal with the consequences of his interference. Though he knew better than to think of it this way, he did in fact leave Potarium in ruins. He did not cause the chaos, but he left it in its dilapidated state.

It was then that Cynkz noticed how quiet everything had become. He looked anxiously to each star—down at Anim, and then up toward Siar'C, whose edges were stretching out sporadically in frantic twinkles. It appeared the two were arguing amongst themselves, out of earshot of him. This realization only made him feel more anxious, as he sat by in silence like a child waiting for their parents to finish quarreling.

Fortunately, Cynkz did not have to sit alone for too long, as the calm hum of the void was interrupted by a bitter huff.

"Fine then," Siar'C grumbled. "We shall invoke the input of some of our brothers and sisters then. I will begin."

Invoke? Cynkz thought. *I hope the others are more—*

"Sihl!" Siar'C called out. "Join us, if you will."

Another moment of silence sat heavy between them. Cynkz could feel himself beginning to feel dreadful about each of these moments, the more that they occurred.

Another star slowly faded into view, high above Anim and appearing a little to Siar'C's right.

"Y-yes, Siar'C? What is going on?" Sihl's stammered and unclear speech only instilled even more anxiety within Cynkz.

I never figured an Omun of all things could be so unsure of himself... Cynkz thought to himself.

"I-I assure you I am just as capable as any other Omun, sir," Sihl said.

Cynkz's eyes shot wide, then settled as he smiled and let out a sigh in defeat. "I will probably never get used to that," Cynkz muttered, going so far as to scratch the side of his head, a nervous tic he rarely expressed.

"I a-apologize, Cynkz," Sihl said. "I do not mean to peer into your mind so carelessly. I would better respect your privacy if I was able to."

"Nonsense," Siar'C said. "You have every right to go poking through the intruder's mind. We must vigilantly filter his intentions, in case he ever decides to become a potential threat, and we have a reason to expel him immediately—"

"Do I truly appear as a threat to you, an Omun of all things?" Cynkz asked, leaning forward, hand on his chest and his face expressing deep concern.

"Yes, you do," Siar'C replied in such a curt, straightforward manner that it nearly hid his usual bitter tone. "Don't you agree, Sihl?"

"I… hmm…" Sihl seemed unsure, though whether his concern lay with himself, or with how his answer may be perceived by Siar'C, Cynkz could not tell.

Sihl continued, "I must agree that it may not be a wise decision to allow the stranger to go fumbling about our realm, or the greater universe. The Creator may be hidden away for the time being, but He could return at any time, and it would be horrible if He returned to a cosmos in even greater disarray…"

"I respectfully disagree," Anim said, his voice echoing soothingly from below. "Though I feel as if this conversation may not progress well without invoking another. I would like to bring in Hel—"

<Wait! Wait, wait, please let me join! I can stay silent no longer. This is too interesting!>

Another voice, and another star emerged. It sat evenly between and above Siar'C and Sihl. Together, they formed a perfect triangle.

"Well, this is a most unwelcome development," Siar'C huffed. "I suppose we have no choice but to hear what the boisterous oaf thinks of this situation."

"Greetings, fellow stars! And greetings to you, Master Cynkz. I am Jio-Mol."

"A pleasure to meet you, Jio-Mol." Cynkz gave another bow as he finished his greeting.

"Well, it is good that you are so intent on being a positive force!" Jio-Mol shouted. At least, it seemed loud enough to be considered shouting. Cynkz struggled to grow accustomed to the new star's spirited demeanor.

Jio-Mol continued, his words flying forth at a worrying pace, "I see you have already helped Anim with his world. I would love to enlist your assistance! You see, on my world, the good citizens have become addicted to an edible insect they call illymites, and—"

Siar'C snapped, "Hold on, you fool! We have not even come to an agreement on what to do with the intruder. Don't get ahead of yourself."

"Ah, my apologies!" Jio-Mol, even in his deference, projected a forceful air. Not even Siar'C's abrasive presence could chip away at his gregariousness. "I agree with Anim—I too believe the newcomer would be nothing but a force for good. And his intervention would do well to eventually get the Creator's attention. I see no issue with letting him remain with us."

"All he will manage to do is make a greater mess of things!" Siar'C shouted, as if trying to match Jio-Mol's energy.

"Heh-haha! I disagree!" Jio-Mol bellowed.

"You still agree with me, do you not, Sihl?" Siar'C asked.

"W-well, I do think that he is more of a potential threat than anything," Sihl said. "There are so many delicate things in the universe, and particularly on our worlds—his involvement would prove a monumental risk."

Anim began to speak once again, "Well, I think we should—"

"But this could be big!" Jio-Mol interrupted, seemingly unknowingly. "The possibilities are too great to ignore! In fact, we should try to get everyone's input. Let us invoke every Omun in the universe! Let everyone give their piece, and then let's tally them all!"

An immediate thought burst into Cynkz's mind: *Oh Paithos… I am quite patient, yet I do not think that I could stand to sit here and bow and greet every star in the universe… Having to listen to infinite voices, all chattering over one another, arguing over me…*

"I don't think that will be necessary," Anim said calmly. "I have yet to invoke an Omun, and I believe I know the perfect one to help us decide—her wisdom has yet to fail us in a debate."

"You speak of Helon?" Siar'C said, softening his usual tone just a bit as he said the name.

"I do," Anim said.

"Helon is a great mediator," Sihl murmured.

"I must agree. She has a good handle on these sorts of things," Jio-Mol said calmly, for the first time since introducing himself.

Just as the conversation quieted down, a feminine voice broke through the veil.

<Fear not, brothers. I have been listening, and I am here now.>

Her voice was a nice change of pace from the others—far less forceful, almost humming along with the void itself. It was almost motherly in its tenderness.

Another odd detail stood out to Cynkz as he pondered the new voice—each star was not actually black, but an exceptionally dark and unique hue. Perhaps it was the stark contrast between their dark lights and the bright void that made them appear so dark at a quick glance.

Anim responded to Cynkz's observation immediately. "An Omun's age can be determined by their hue. Though it may seem paradoxical, 'cooler' colors show a younger, hotter star. 'Warmer' colors reveal a duller, more aged star."

"Speaking of which, h-has anyone heard from Guro lately?" Sihl asked.

"Guro has been quiet as of late," Helon rescinded.

"Guro?" Cynkz raised a curious brow, and a light hand to his chin. He wondered if his gesturing meant anything to the Omun, but such habits are stubborn, and he would rather not waste time obsessing over such minor details.

Anim, again, was the first to respond. "Guronimhal— or Guro, as most refer to him—is currently the oldest living Omun in the universe. He is fast approaching the end of his lifespan, unfortunately."

"How much time does he have left?" Cynkz asked.

"It is difficult to say," Anim continued, "but we estimate he has no more than a million years left."

"A million years?"

"A million years is not much to an Omun, Cynkz. We can persist for billions upon billions of years.

Though to a mortal soul, that can seem like an unfathomable amount of time. Though… heh…"

"Hmm?"

Anim continued, "Well, it's just that. We refer to beings such as yourself as 'mortal souls,' yet you can technically persist for an eternity. In a way, you are destined to outlive us, even though it is in an afterlife. An apostle, depending on its purpose, may only exist for a few moments, and we Omun may go on to live for a billion-billion years, and yet, in the grand scheme of things, there is little difference, isn't there? What difference does it make to an eternity whether or not something persists for a few seconds or a few billion years?"

"I suppose even Omun must face the existential dread of their own limited existence," Cynkz said.

"Well, it is not so bad," Anim said. "We Omun take great pride in serving a holy duty. And as with everything in existence, nothing is truly wasted. Though an Omun may physically perish, our mass is then able to go out into the universe, and the material used to create new things—be it planets, life, or even other Omun. Even in death, we are returned to the Creator, and our bodies are used to create the basis for new life. It is a beautiful cycle."

Siar'C chimed in, his voice sharp as ever, "Unfortunately, the death of an Omun can be catastrophic. Whatever worlds they were overlooking now have nothing to tether them. Without the light and warmth of an Omun, what life is left—if there is any—is doomed to a swift death. The planets themselves are then vulnerable, as they aimlessly begin to drift randomly through the cosmos. Their destruction is inevitable."

"But even in destruction, it is not all for nothing, correct?" Cynkz asked. "Their material goes on to help create other things as well?"

"Yes," Helon said. "You catch on rather quickly."

"It is well known that Guro cares greatly for his people," Jio-Mol added calmly once again.

"All Omun care for their people," Sihl added. "Though Guro is particularly loving. It is tragic to have to witness not only your own death, but the death of those you love."

"We are beginning to get off track," Siar'C snapped. "We have a more pressing matter to attend to."

"Indeed," Helon said. "Anim, you may have acted a bit impulsively, bringing the newcomer so soon to your own world and affecting change."

"Ah, well… I apologize," Anim muttered.

"That was exactly my assessment," Siar'C said, taking an opportunity to bolster his own position.

"I would not say you are much better, Siar'C," Helon responded.

"What?! How so?"

"I, too, can see potential in the newcomer's assistance. If the Creator truly found his presence a blight on Omundisia, He would not have allowed Cynkz into our realm to begin with. Cynkz, as it seems, is a free agent, one who could do much good for us in lieu of the Creator's absence."

"Tch." Siar'C's scoffing cut through the open air like a knife through silk. He put extra emphasis on the sound as if meaning to drive it into everyone's ear with force.

Siar'C continued, "The intruder is nothing but a risk. He is a clumsy child, and will only make things worse."

"Siar'C, I know your world has been going through a lot recently. I can only imagine the pain of having to watch your beloved people war with one another nearly to the point of extinction. But we are all struggling without the Creator's guidance. Perhaps you most of all could use Cynkz's help?"

"Hah! The child is soft! My people would tear him apart!" Siar'C said, seemingly taking glee in the thought.

Cynkz, seeing an opportunity, interjected, "If I may, great Siar'C, I am quite swift, and some would even say crafty. I may very well be able to keep up with your beloved people, and am sure I could assist your world? I am rather good at getting a productive dialogue going."

"How well did that work with Eshra'Tel?" Siar'C snapped back.

"Yla was easy enough to get talking. The same with Krull. Even Sulmara, the world serpent who could have, and by all means should have, eaten me and Fiddle immediately."

"Ah, Sulmara," Anim said, his tone laced with a childlike curiosity. "The large, pink serpent in the grove? I saw glimpses of her in your mind. I'm surprised she didn't merely eat you."

"Well, that is the thing," Cynkz continued, "speaking with us and exchanging words and ideas, is far more interesting—and more productive—than mere combat. So long as you can make all sides see this truth, any outcome is possible."

"You share a similar wisdom to Helon, then," Anim said.

"As such," Cynkz continued, flaring his cloak and turning his attention back to Siar'C, high above and twinkling harshly, "I could apply this same technique to your world, Siar'C. If I could find the right people, and get them talking, who knows? I could end your war in a day."

"You naïve child," Siar'C muttered, almost hissing under his breath. "You see? This is precisely what I mean. This sort of naivete will do nothing but cause problems for all of us. He should be cast out immediately."

"We have no other means of potentially getting the Creator's attention," Anim said.

"While I believe we should exhibit caution, I cannot argue with Anim's logic," Helon said.

Siar'C snapped back once again, "You cannot be serious!"

"I am very serious," Helon said. "In truth, we have run out of options. We have nothing else to work with, unfortunately."

"Ha! I agree wholeheartedly!" Jio-Mol bellowed.

"B-but think of the risks!" Siar'C yelled, his voice quavering ever so slightly. "We only risk incurring His wrath! If we allow the newcomer to make things worse, who is to say the Creator would not merely cast us all to darkness as punishment for our foolishness? Do you all wish to follow Krull's example?! Eshra'Tel's?!"

"I believe the Creator is far more understanding than you give Him credit for, Siar'C," Anim said. "The Creator cannot truly blame us for merely trying to get His attention, as we only seek his help and guidance."

"B-but—"

"I agree," Helon said. "We mean no harm, and neither does Cynkz."

"You cannot—"

"Here, here!" Jio-Mol shouted. "Cynkz represents far too much potential—good potential—to merely be cast out!"

"You fool! You only wish to—"

"I-I must agree with Helon and Anim's wisdom," Sihl said. "I cannot argue with their ... reasoning..."

"Sihl, not you too..." Siar'C sounded nearly defeated.

"This is wonderful!" Anim said excitedly. Cynkz swore the massive star below him flared out as he said this, the way a child might swing their arms in excitement.

Anim continued, "I wonder if Jio-Mol's world would be a good starting point—"

"Wait!" Siar'C's shriek pierced the humming void, and all went silent for a moment. "I wish to invoke a final Omun, one who has been watching quietly this entire time. Though I doubt it will change much..."

Another? Cynkz thought. *I wonder who—*

"Carros! You may as well speak up now," Siar'C cried out.

A final dark speck faded into view, oddly a bit farther from the rest, above and to the right of the rest of the group from Cynkz's perspective. There were a few other distant stars not far from his position that, at a glance, Carros himself would have nearly blended in with had Cynkz not known any better.

"I am here," Carros said. His voice was deeper than the others, yet also quieter. The echo from the bass in his voice nearly drowned out his words.

"Opportunistic as always, I see," Siar'C said.

"I merely wished to wait and see how the newcomer would respond, and how everyone else would judge him."

"If you were more proactive," Siar'C continued, "then perhaps your people would be in better shape."

"You are not one to talk, Siar'C," Helon snapped. "We are all struggling, as are you."

"Hmph." Cynkz began to notice a tic with Siar'C—whenever he scoffed or quieted down, the edges of his star, the very rays of dark light reaching out from his center, would recede ever so slightly. Cynkz couldn't help but chuckle at the thought that this may be the closest an Omun could come to crossing their arms in defiance.

Siar'C continued, "In truth, I don't understand what makes you all think that the stranger would stand any better chance at getting the Creator's attention than us."

"You know full well why," Anim remarked.

"What do you mean?" There was a certain light disingenuity in his tone. Cynkz found it comical enough to where he had to turn his head down to hide his smile beneath the pointed rim of his cap.

Anim merely sighed, then addressed Cynkz, "If you would be so kind, please show everyone the thread."

Cynkz lifted his head, still smiling. "Of course, friend."

The jester playfully reached into his now bright cloak and pulled out the dark splinter of light. He held it up and ahead, and noticed that as its light sat near one of the stars, he could see the Omun twinkling their rays toward the thread, as if reaching out for it in awe.

A round of "oohs" and "ahhs" echoed from them all, save for Siar'C, who still had more to say.

"Whatever Krull did to the thread worries me. Why would he tamper with such a thing?"

"It is a message, obviously!" Jio-Mol bellowed. "That thread could provide a direct line to the Creator Himself! It is our duty to aid Cynkz."

"Regardless of what the message may say," Sihl said confidently for the first time, "we should at least try to return His property to Him."

"It is disappointing that you would go from supporting me to disagreeing with me, Sihl," Siar'C muttered.

"I believe the others are right," Carros said. "I would vote in favor of the newcomer, if he agreed to assist my world first. It is in a dire state."

"I see no issue with it," Helon said. "Though I understand that Jio-Mol technically asked for assistance first?"

"Eh, I don't mind," Jio-Mol said. "He can come to my world next."

"Indeed," Helon responded. "If Cynkz can prove himself on Carros's world, then there will be no doubt that his stay in Omundisia will be a positive one for us all."

"I agree," Anim said.

"As do I," Sihl said.

"Of course, I agree as well!" Jio-Mol said.

"Hmph." Siar'C merely scoffed once again.

Cynkz smiled, bigger than before, and shrugged playfully toward the difficult Omun. "Just give it time, Siar'C. Even if it takes me helping a hundred worlds, I will win you over, and take special care to assist you as well!"

Siar'C merely remained silent. Was it possible for a literal star to give someone the cold shoulder?

Helon spoke up once again. "It is settled, then. Cynkz will begin aiding Omun, and through his good deeds—and the undeniable change he brings about—The Creator will assuredly feel compelled to re-establish contact with the rest of the universe. I give the floor to you, Carros."

"Thank you, Helon."

"This is a bit unnerving," Sihl muttered. "Are you nervous, Cynkz? So many things could go wrong."

"Not necessarily," Cynkz said, patting down his cloak with a smile. "I have learned that things are never quite as bad as they seem, and it helps to keep a light heart and a lighter foot when facing challenges."

"Well said," Carros responded. "I look forward to whatever may come next."

Cynkz merely gave a bow and then readied himself. The final star stretched its edges outward, and in a flash, the jester was gone once more.

PART 2

MARN

CHAPTER 5

A FLARE CUT THROUGH THE CLOUDS and Cynkz found himself hovering above another world.

Carros immediately broke the silence. "Welcome to Marn."

"Marn? Is that this world's name?" Cynkz asked.

"It is. It is the name this world's people eventually settled on long ago."

Cynkz took a moment to look around. In every direction, there was nothing but ocean. He was immediately reminded of the dark sea leading to Potarium. Thankfully this particular ocean appeared normal enough. The waters appeared calm, and there was very little wind to disrupt them. For a moment, Cynkz began to wonder what problems such a place could be enduring that would require an Omun to seek external aid.

"Where do your people live?" Cynkz asked. "This place does not seem hospitable to po at all—"

"Ah, well, about that… There are no po here."

"Huh? Then… who resides here?"

"They call themselves Marnians, and they have adapted well to the ocean. In fact, they used to live nearly their entire lives underwater."

"…Underwater?"

"Yes. Mortal souls are not supposed to learn of this fact, but…" Carros seemed to need a moment—not necessarily for himself, but for Cynkz's sake. "Life exists on other worlds, and the form it adopts on each world is unique."

"So… they are aliens?"

"Well, if anything, Cynkz, *you* are the alien here. You are literally from another world, and another time, even."

Cynkz turned his head down, scratching at his chin mindlessly as he was lost in thought. He could ponder the implications of such knowledge. He could imagine the difficulties of dealing with another species, or even how the po would take such news. The po seemed to operate under the assumption that they were Paithos's only and most precious children. He couldn't help but liken the idea to a child learning they will have siblings soon. Rather than wrack his mind with such questions, he chose to begin with an obvious question.

"How am I meant to work with such beings, then? Surely I cannot merely fly by and introduce myself? I doubt we even speak the same language?"

Carros continued, "Ah, well, that is where I come in. Open your mind to me, just for a moment."

A peculiar light shone down from above, finding the perfect opening between a few of the large clouds above to hone in on Cynkz as if being focused through a lens. Before Cynkz could respond, the world seemed to disappear as countless visions began to run through his mind.

Strange creatures could be seen slithering through bright blue waters. Their leathery skin revealed every shade of blue imaginable. While pleasing to the eye, it did little to distract from their odd proportions—long and gangly limbs, webbed fingers and toes, and sharp fins pointing back from the backs of their arms and legs. Powerful joints connected everything and were the few things that stood out from their otherwise sleek, curved forms. They were impossibly thin overall, and they seemed to move in perfect union with the currents of the sea as they swam. If not for their snouts and long faces—not unlike the sentinels of Munderworld with their gnarled, extended maws—they'd have appeared more than alluring and approachable to the average po.

From afar, as they swam in great schools just beneath the ocean's surface, they looked not unlike a swarm of tadpoles. Glimpses of simple spears and beaded accessories revealed them to be a primitive people, perhaps tribal even. The vision followed them deeper, and the dark depths began to reveal countless new lifeforms that the people of Marn—or Marnians, they called themselves—seemed to have little trouble contending with. Neon slugs and asymmetrical crab-like entities scurried past spiky, leathery things covered in teeth hiding in the sand just below. Parasitic eels waved and writhed as they escaped much larger, more bulbous predators that almost looked like ghosts with fins. The Marnians seemed to have perfectly adapted to everything here, and never so much as flinched as they speared and clawed their prey.

More creatures revealed themselves, each one larger than the last, and each one seemingly commanding more of the ocean with their mere size and presence. Spider-like crustaceans sat below massive shark-like bodies, and these swam at full speed below whale-like creatures covered in what appeared to be crust and algae, or perhaps they were small and parasitic fish? It was difficult to tell, particularly due to its sheer size—they must have been at least several times larger than even the most opulent mansion in Potarium. Witnessing this world from below was quite the marvel—each unique body and shape perfectly swimming along, their silhouettes never crossing over one another as they cut harsh shapes against the light shining through the uppermost layers of the sea instilled the feeling that one was watching the momentum of life itself painting the world.

Finally, something else came into view—a last, gargantuan creature that had little trouble blocking out the light above. It had little respect for the delicate dance conducted by the rest of the sea, and its silhouette seemed to rampage through everything. Against the harsh light, and due to its frightening speed and writhing figure, as well as its dark, sludgy exterior, it was impossible to get a good look at the creature, but its impact was clear—it was terrorizing everyone and everything. A look back down to the depths revealed the lanky Marnians were fleeing, cutting through the deep water frantically as they tried to escape. Unfortunately, the beast was too quick, and it began to devour them in large numbers, no differently than it had the rest of the ocean life above. The Marnians split, their once unified group now dispersed, which only seemed to make them more vulnerable. The people of Marn were being devoured in massive numbers, with only a few stragglers escaping into the distance. With nothing left to eat, the beast turned its attention upward, toward Cynkz, and in the blink of an eye, his vision was engulfed in darkness.

As if knocked out of a trance, Carros returned him to the present. It took him a moment to readjust to the bright light shining off of the calm, flat plane of the ocean surrounding him.

A deep voice echoed in Cynkz's ear from above. "Are you alright, Cynkz?"

"Yes, yes Carros, I'm fine," Cynkz said. A few slow breaths and a quick shrug of his shoulders, and he was back to his senses. "That vision… the Marnians, that creature… You were filling my mind with information about this world, I presume?"

"Yes," Carros said. "I did my best to be efficient, but you should now have a basic understanding of the people here, and their plight."

"Are the Marnians close to extinction?"

"Yes. There are less than a thousand Marnians left. Most have sequestered themselves on a large island to the southwest. Unfortunately, the beast is capable of traversing land and continues to regularly terrorize them. Yet… there is another, perhaps more frightening, aspect to this situation."

"What could be worse than being chased and eaten by a monster?" Cynkz asked, almost jokingly. He did his best to rein in his tone but wondered if Carros could see through it.

Carros continued, "Each soul-bearing species has their own form of the afterlife. They too must be judged for their choices made in life and may be permitted to either struggle or ascend in death. Out of desperation—or perhaps madness—many Marnians have come to worship the beast. They have even given it a name—Marna-Muya—which roughly translates to 'The One Marn,' or 'The Godlike Marn.'"

"Oh, my…" Cynkz stroked the hairs on his chin once again, turning his eyes down toward the flat sea below him.

"Yes, as I am sure you can gather, worshiping a mere beast as a false god is a horrible proposition. I fear that many more Marnians than need be may be forced to suffer and struggle in the afterlife, having been spiritually led astray."

Cynkz released his hand from his chin and looked up curiously, holding his hand out as he addressed the sky. "But surely Paithos could understand that they are merely desperate? Is it right to blame them, and even punish them, for merely trying to cope with a horrible situation that seems to be out of their control?"

"Ah, perhaps," Carros said, his sober tone blending well with the low pitch in his voice. "But such is how faith is tested. One's faith should be resolute and unflinching. Life is sometimes hard and may seem unfair, but if one can hold on to faith properly, they can rest assured that they will be accepted into something better in the next life. Such is the purpose and process of faith."

"It must be difficult to hold on to faith alone when your very life is at risk," Cynkz said.

"That is the point. Life is short, and difficult, and limited, and thus carries real weight and risk. This is what pushes one's faith and morals to be truly tested. If one chooses to make use of their precious short time alive to do good, then that is a great sign of their character. If one falls to temptation and turns to vice or malice or bloodshed—perhaps even going so far as to cut another's life short—then they clearly have taken His greatest gift for granted, and, as you might say, need to 'learn the hard way' to appreciate what the Creator has given them."

"Bloodshed…" Cynkz furrowed his brow and nearly retreated into his own cloak as he sat hunched over.

"I can see that you, too, have struggled with such things," Carros said. "When you betrayed the duke, and even betrayed the assassin—"

"I would rather not talk about it, Carros."

The air stood still and silent between the two. The clouds, once bright bundles of cotton, now felt heavy as they slowly crawled over the sky, occasionally blocking out Carros's light.

"I understand, Cynkz," Carros said. "What will you do now? How do you wish to approach the situation?"

"Well," Cynkz flared his cloak, and smiled, "I suppose I will do what I do best—sneak in and find out who I should talk to. I wish to get a closer look at these people and their plight."

"Very well," Carros said. "I will be watching. Do as you will, Cynkz."

Still carrying his smile, the jester gave a bow, turned, and flew off toward the southeast, leaving nothing behind but the whip of his cloak in the wind. It wasn't long before the dark figure had disappeared into the horizon, leaving behind a quiet scene as Carros watched over the still water.

CHAPTER 6

THE PEOPLE OF MARN WERE NEVER meant to live on land. As their world consists almost entirely of water, their ability to adapt specifically to the ocean was crucial to their survival. Yet they always maintained some ability to operate outside of the water. Such things used to be considered little more than an oddity, but now these ancient vestiges of their evolution have proven to be crucial for their survival.

What Marnians remained were now hiding deep within the forests of one of the few large islands Marn possessed. These secluded hubs of life, despite seeming out of place, had much to offer—if there was a theme, it would have been variety. Insects of all shapes and sizes roamed free in both the air and on land. They fed on an impossibly diverse selection of fruits and berries and other things, which led to the spread of materials needed for other forms of life to emerge and thrive. Large, slow-moving, shelled beasts with long, ropey necks would stroll along as they munched on spiked brown leaves high above. Many of these leaves would carry little round things that would either be eaten and digested, or would simply fall off and become fertilizer for whatever scavenging things could be found on the ground below. Some of these round things would in fact be eggs, which could hatch into all manner of critters with shining carapaces and long, slow-moving limbs perfectly suited for exploring the strange and winding environment. Layers of trees weaved past one another, with nearly every trunk and every branch seeming to be of a different species, each one fighting for their share of what precious little soil the land offered. Despite their variety and incongruity, the Marnians seemed to have little issue learning how to break them down to use their bodies for materials.

In fact, the Marnians seemed to take quite well to land. They always possessed some capacity for crafting and invention, but had mostly resorted to disposable tools and weapons, as they were once a constantly migrating species. The ocean's current was their one true home. Yet now they found themselves forced to make do with simple, stable dwellings made of whatever materials they could manage from their new island home. Small huts and shacks—many of which were layered and connected to one another with small, makeshift bridges and ropes—seemed to have carved their way into a large, flat, and open area deep within the island. Countless thin, blue bodies could be seen moving back and forth as the people attended their daily duties. They moved well enough, though the awkwardness in their gait was undeniable, as they were forced to crawl on all fours in order to maintain any sort of balance. The many fins poking out from each limb were sensitive and needed to constantly retract as they moved in an attempt to keep them from rubbing against anything unpleasant. The way they slithered about was reminiscent of a snake swimming through water, a habit that not even the land and open air could deter. Another habit that could not be denied was their natural inclination for tribalism. They stuck close together, often in small groups, even as they went about foraging or gathering, and even hunting (or at least attempting to hunt). Still, it was impressive how well they had adapted to their new environment. If one did not know any better, from afar, it would be difficult to tell that these people were entirely out of their element.

One Marnian, who seemed to carry a perpetual scowl on his short snout, barged his way into a particularly large hut, the only one built onto a third layer as it overlooked the rest of the village. He was not alone, but it was clear that he was the one leading them along.

"Ekukhan!" the scowling Marnian barked. "Ekukhan! Why are we still here?! I thought you said we would be preparing to migrate farther inland?"

A taller, slightly wider Marnian slowly turned around from his makeshift window to address his uninvited guest. The long, purpled frills attached to the back of his head almost swayed like hair as he did so. "Valk, not this again—"

"Why are we still here? Just answer the damn—"

"Do not interrupt me, Valk! You know better." Ekukhan put his foot down with a mighty thump as he finished turning, as if establishing his position above the others.

"You're right," Valk said, whipping a webbed hand through the air like a knife through silk. "I *do* know better. If I were khan, I'd have moved everyone out of here already, so we may be safe from the beast."

"The people wish to pay another tribute to the Marna-Muya." Ekukhan kept a stern, beady gaze on Valk, completely ignoring the handful of other Marnians standing behind him. Valk, of course, returned the gesture with his own steely gaze. "Though, if need be, we could retreat to the large mountain farther inland, though I do not think that will be necessary. You know that moving the people around too much exhausts them, both in body and spirit. I see no issue with allowing them a release in the form of a night of festivities—"

"Festivities at a time like this…" Valk huffed, almost hissing as he forced the words out. "What good have these tributes and dances done? The Marna-Muya comes for us just the same, and never spares us in any way. This is a waste of time and you know it."

"I know how to lead my people, Valk," Ekukhan continued. "We would not have made it this far otherwise."

"We didn't all make it, did we?" Valk's eyes were now almost piercing as he leered at Ekukhan, and his voice had almost been reduced to a whisper. It was still clearly loud enough for all in the room to hear, however.

"Not this again…" Ekukhan tried to reach a hand up to his face, as if to rub his eyes or temples in frustration. Instead, the buzzing of an odd insect nearby prompted him to take a few swipes at it, shooing it away. Valk took visible pleasure in observing the pitiful gesture.

Valk continued, "The Marna-Muya sees us as no different than these insects, and you know it. He will dispose of us all the same."

"Marna-Muya only takes what he needs," Ekukhan said.

"Such as 'her?'" Valk hissed.

The two shared a hard glance, and for a moment, everything was quiet, save for the shuffling of bodies outside and the buzzing of insects inside.

Ekukhan crossed his arms and turned away, looking at nothing in particular outside his window. "She knew the risks of separating from the group. Trying to elope at a time like this… She knew that she would end up as little more than a sacrifice to Marna-Muya."

Valk, who was nearly on all fours, slammed the ground. It was enough force to shake the entire structure. Ekukhan even looked around worriedly, as if he feared the hut may fall apart from the shockwave. Valk kept his eyes straight ahead on Ekukhan the entire time.

"Some leader you are," Valk muttered. "You have always been like that, haven't you? Looking for excuses, ways of coping, always deferring and deflecting. You may as well have thrown her into the beast's maw yourself!"

Ekukhan merely sighed and refused to look at Valk. He kept his eyes on the world outside his window, watching the people move back and forth and gather things for the night's dance.

"If you do not appreciate how I lead, then you and your friends may leave at any time," Ekukhan said. "You are free to brave the waters—and risk Marna-Muya's wrath—all on your own."

Valk scowled once more, snarling under his breath, his frustration to the point of bursting out. Even a few of his associates, who had been silent and nearly motionless the entire time, leaned back in fear he may lash out at them. Instead, Valk merely stomped as he whipped himself around, making a hasty exit. The half dozen Marnians who accompanied him slowly followed suit.

Valk trudged slowly through the village, not so much going anywhere in particular as his mind was on other things.

That fool will have us all killed. But what can I do? I can hardly get this handful of idiots to listen to me. What can I really accomplish...

"I-I think I'm just going to follow Ekukhan's lead," one of the followers said meekly.

"I don't care," Valk grumbled. "Do what you want."

"I'm going with him," another follower said. "I'd rather stick with the bigger group."

Valk remained silent, keeping his gaze forward as the two slinked away toward the rest of the village.

Valk kept moving forward, paying little attention to the other Marnians as he made his way. He seemed to ignore the handful of angry looks and sneers of the Marnians he forcefully bumped into. His mind was somewhere else.

This is all pointless. These idiots would rather worship the beast, as if that will do anything. We've been cast out of our own sea and they choose to build these shabby huts and dance. Why do I even bother—

"Oof!"

Valk was knocked out of his trance as he finally noticed he had bumped into someone. They were strangely heavy, yet small and hunched over. It was an old Marnian woman it appeared. A strange sight, as ever since Marna-Muya began to terrorize them, most Marnians did not live particularly long lives. She was also covered in a number of leaves and other materials that were crudely stitched together. Most Marnians had no issue being completely exposed, so what was the deal with this one?

"Excuse me, ma'am," Valk said, for the first time in an accommodating tone. "Are you alright?"

"Yes, yes, I am fine," she said. "I was trying to get your attention anyway, and you were stomping forward in such a hurry!"

Valk looked the elderly woman over, noticing the strange shade of blue that comprised her skin. Marnian skin expressed itself through many different shades of blue, yet the elderly woman's was off—it had the slightest green tint added to it, making her almost appear teal. He couldn't help but look her over for perhaps a moment too long before feeling the need to speak up, his attempt at avoiding an awkward encounter.

"Your skin," Valk said, pointing toward her exposed arm. "Are you alright? Are you malnourished? Have you been out of the water for too long? How long have you been hiding out here on this island?"

"I am fine, worry not," she said, lifting up a thin, frail arm as she smiled. "In truth, I am more concerned for you, young one. You seem rather troubled. Also, you are asking me all these questions and you have yet to even ask me my name! How inconsiderate."

"Ah, uh, I apologize," Valk muttered. "My name is Valk. And you are?"

"You may call me Binx," she said. She clasped her hands together and wore an almost mischievous grin as she spoke. Valk couldn't help but think this strange old woman was up to something.

"Are you from another tribe?" Valk asked, his eyes now almost squinting as he looked down at the old woman. "Everyone that couldn't keep up with us fell victim to Marna-Muya, at least as far as I know."

"Ahhhh, the great beast!" Binx said, her pale eyes widening into near circles. "I have seen visions of the beast, of its ascension, and its downfall—"

"What?!" Now Valk's eyes grew wide, with ample light gleaming off of the large, near—black irises. He was loud enough to get the attention of a number of other Marnians, who seemed to once again want as little to do with Valk as possible and quickly went back to their business.

Valk continued in a hushed voice, "What do you mean you've 'seen its downfall?' How is such a thing possible? Have you gone mad in your old age, woman?"

"Well, maybe a little," Binx quipped.

"You elders play too much," Valk huffed.

"When you've been alive for long enough, you learn to deal with the slow, painful drag of time by having fun with it!"

Valk looked the old woman over once again. He thought endlessly about her words, about her supposed visions. The thought of Marna-Muya's downfall was a tantalizing one, to say the least. Even if the old lady was merely speaking nonsense, it had to be better than listening to Ekukhan and the rest of the villagers dance and worship the wretched thing.

"Come with me, old woman," Valk said. "I know a place where we can speak privately—"

"Ah, we just met, and you're inviting this young woman to your home so soon?"

Valk couldn't help but smile, even chuckling slightly in response. In truth, he couldn't remember the last time he laughed. Perhaps it was with *her*…

"Enough joking, and come," Valk said, stepping forward to place a hand on the old woman's shoulder to escort her personally. "I need to hear specifically about your visions. I want to know what you know."

"Of course," Binx said. "It would also be nice to sit down for a while. These old bones are tired."

"Any good Marnian knows the best way to stave off aching bones is to keep swimming, to keep moving," Valk said.

"I must not be a very good Marnian then," Binx said.

The two shared a hearty laugh and made their way forward toward the edge of the village, a fair distance away from the hustle and bustle gathering at the center of it all.

CHAPTER 7

THE LATE DAY'S SHADE BEGAN TO WASH over the small land. It wasn't long before the two Marnians had made their way to an inconspicuous hut on the far edges of the village. It was so far away in fact that it was difficult to consider it a part of the village at all.

Valk gave a quick order with a hiss and a flick of his wrist, and the other Marnians following him took up guarding positions and waited outside. It was clear that he wanted to speak to the old woman alone.

The inside of the hut was just as dreary as one would expect, but it at least possessed a few furnishings, such as a curved, spindly twine of bark that proved to be the perfect seat for the thin, serpentine creatures that could be seen near the back wall. The roof and walls had enough tiny gaps between the bark and leaves composing them that light shone through them, keeping the interior from being too dark. The old woman gave a sigh of relief as she hobbled quickly for the seat. Valk slowly walked behind and sat himself down as well on what appeared to be a stool, though it was little more than a roughly hewn stump.

"We are here," Valk said, moving ahead to hold open a shambled leaf curtain for his guest.

"Ah, finally! So tired of all this walking." The old woman scurried ahead, making her way for the larger seat near the back of the hut.

"I can agree with you there, old woman," Valk huffed. "We should be free to swim, not forced to walk and crawl."

"Your humble abode is so far away from everyone else," Binx noted. She finally climbed up and settled down, the edges of her dark sea-green rags brushing out under her weight. The chair itself even creaked and stretched as it adjusted to her.

"Yes, well, the other idiots would prefer to be at least somewhat near the water, so they can potentially pay tribute to the beast terrorizing us."

"Ah, yes, the infamous Marna-Muya…"

"Heh, well, infamous perhaps, isn't the right word for it." Valk turned his head down and rested his head in his webbed hand. The webbing provided a solid hold as it nearly cupped around the shape of his skull. "'Marna-Muya only takes what he needs,' some say. 'He has his reasons, and we should oblige.' 'He teaches us the meaning of sacrifice.' It's all a bunch of nonsense. Merely desperate coping mechanisms for the weak-willed."

"Well," the old lady took in a deep and weighty breath, "if the others could see its true form, perhaps they would be so disgusted that they would learn better."

"What?" Valk seemed to pull his head up slightly with the raising of his brow. The curious look he gave seemed to please the old woman. Whoever she was, she was not very good at hiding her emotions. The wry grin plastered across her short snout gave away everything.

"I have seen it—the beast's true form—beneath its slimy, writhing, dark and sludgy exterior."

Valk raised himself up to address the old woman more directly, though he maintained his skeptical expression. "How? What do you mean? There's something more to the creature underneath?"

"Yes, yes. Beneath the muck and mire and sludge, it is a creature like any other—a rather disgusting and off-putting one at that. I doubt anyone would want to worship such a thing if they saw it up close."

"What does it look like?" Valk asked.

"Limbs…"

"What?"

"Limbs!" Binx cried out and reached out with her tiny, teal arms, the frills and fins on each appendage swinging about as she acted out. "Countless limbs! Many thousands of writhing appendages, each palm a canvas of woe brought on by his victims! It's skin! Layers upon layers of sharp, scabby, warty leather that flakes constantly! And so many holes! Each one constantly opening and closing as if a mouth gasping desperately for air as it is smothered beneath the sludge itself! When nothing is there to cover them, they exude a most potent gas that, with a single breath, could suffocate a child! These things comprise its entire body to form a girthy mass of wriggling, slithering malice that knows nothing but hunger and suffering! In fact, if it does not constantly move, it struggles beneath its own weight as it begins to hinder its own breathing. It is truly an abomination that should have perished long ago."

"I see…" Valk rubbed curiously along the length of his lower jaw, each finger bumping against the tiny frills that lined the bony structure.

"As you can deduce, the creature is a detestable—"

"If we can hinder its movement, it could suffocate! If what you say is true, old wo—I mean … Binx… then we could finally be rid of the thing! All hope is not lost!"

"Yes, well, that is true," Binx muttered. "Oh! You finally remembered my name! How kind."

"How can we do it?" Valk leaned forward, his hands forming tight fists, as if he was trying desperately to contain himself as he literally sat on the edge of his stump-seat. "You must know of a way. Wait…" Valk leaned back, relaxing his grip and turning his attention away from Binx, looking around the dark of his mind as he pondered many questions.

Just as Binx raised a curious brow toward the young Marnian, Valk continued, "How do I know any of this is true? Why should I believe you? We are already at risk of extinction. Even now, Marna-Muya is probably circling the island, waiting for the perfect chance to strike and devour the rest of us. Why should I risk anything listening to you, old woman?"

"Oh, there you go again. But I know what it's like to be young and rash, so I will forgive it," Binx said as she playfully rocked back and forth in a seat that was clearly too big for her.

"I'm being serious, old woman." Valk sat himself back, keeping a stern glare on Binx all the while. The soft twilight peeking through the gaps in the hut reflected off of his eyes fiercely.

"Fear not, for I have another prediction, one that could actually aid us in subduing the beast, and will prove useful in convincing you that I am worth listening to! Killing two birds with one stone and all that."

"Two what?"

"Bir—oh, never mind. Do not mind this old woman's ramblings!" Binx cackled gleefully behind a light hand held up to her mouth. Valk merely stared, and raised his other brow at her.

"You are a strange one, old woman," Valk muttered in a heavy tone. It almost seemed to drag his head down as he spoke, though he kept his eyes up and facing toward Binx.

Binx leaned back, putting her hands together and waiting for her seat to finish creaking before speaking. "Before the night is over, it will begin to rain. It will begin lightly, but soon will pick up. Before noon tomorrow, the island will be enraptured in a fearsome storm that will continue on for another day after that. At the tempest's apex, the sky itself will growl with thunder, and strike with lightning! The tallest mountain will let loose a great wave of mud and rock, barreling down on much of the island below. Hopefully, the rain will be enough of a deterrent to convince the other Marnians to cease their dancing and get out of the way—"

"Marnians love the rain, though," Valk interrupted. "It's the closest we feel to being underwater, even when condemned to land. But you know this already, don't you?"

"Oh, um, well, of course! Of course…"

Valk stared curiously at the old woman. She could do little more than giggle and shrug. She was playing off whatever anxiety she was clearly feeling quite well. Too well, perhaps.

I have no idea what to make of this strange croon, Valk thought to himself.

"This is all nice," Valk said, finally breaking the silence, "but what are we supposed to do? Do you have a plan to capitalize on this supposed future knowledge, old hag?"

"Old hag?! Pah!" Binx threw one arm up in anger, yet had to catch herself with the other as she nearly fell from her seat. "How rude! I thought better of you, young man?"

Valk sighed and retreated his head to his hands once more as he leaned over.

"I'm sorry, Binx, truly I am," Valk said somberly. "I just haven't been in a good mood as of late."

"I can tell." Binx relaxed herself and looked on at Valk. He could see from his periphery that she was looking down on him in a motherly way. "You have lost something important, haven't you?"

"Tch…" Valk scoffed, though he couldn't bring himself to look the old woman in the eye just yet. "How can you tell? Is that a part of your powers, too?"

"No, but you are not exactly difficult to read. I have met others like you before—every expression, every action, everything you do and say is accented in a sharp way, as if lashing out."

"It's that obvious, is it? I figured as much, but… I preferred not to think too much about it and just move on."

"It does not matter how many times you tell yourself you would rather just 'move on,' but you are clearly holding on to something dear to you—a memory of something lost."

Valk still couldn't bring himself to sit upright and look the old woman in the eye. He hated it—so often he was used to speaking out and standing up when no one else would, and speaking out when no one else would—yet here he was, unable to lift his head the moment someone touched on a sensitive topic. He began to wonder if his anger and bravado were all an act.

Valk finally mustered the energy to respond, "Her name was Ghia."

"Hmm?" Binx cocked her head to the side, but did her best to maintain a respectful expression.

"My lover, and one of Ekukhan's many wives. It was a few years ago, but honestly, with how often I think of it, of my time with her, and of our final moments together… It may as well have been yesterday. She found herself separating from Ekukhan's harem. Normally she would not be allowed to mingle with a lesser Marnian such as I, but considering our dire situation, he looked the other way. Ghia wanted to escape, maybe break off from the remaining Marnians and travel far away. We spent many nights coming up with plans and dreaming up ideas—finding a powerful current to carry us to the southern sea, maybe settling into a reef near an island not unlike this one and claiming it as our own, that sort of thing. The green in her eyes shone like emeralds against the night's light, and it was particularly noticeable when she smiled."

Binx rubbed her chin as her eyes darted around. "A few years ago…" she muttered. "Maybe if we had gotten here sooner…"

"Huh?"

"Ah, never mind me. Please, tell me more about what happened, if you please."

Valk merely shook his head and looked back downward before continuing, "We started off slow, merely increasing the distance at which we would swim from the rest of the group as we migrated. We had a few close encounters, both with the Marna-Muya, and even a few other predators, but it was nothing we weren't used to. But then, one day, as we were all swimming along a smooth current in the Middle Sea. The sun was high, the sky was bright, and looking down into the ocean was like staring into the abyss—just a pitch-black canvas that seemed to reach out forever in all directions. Before we could realize the danger we were in, the beast attacked. In the blink of an eye, the abyss seemingly engulfed a third of our clan. It took us all a moment to realize that it was Marna-Muya. I swear he is a cunning, thinking thing—far too aware and smart for a normal beast—he knew full well that the bright sun would cast a deep shadow in the ocean below, and he used that to his advantage. He let us grow comfortable using the ocean currents to speed away, instilling within us a false sense of security. He had little trouble catching up to us and cleaning up whatever stragglers he could. Ghia and I decided to make a break for it and began heading south. We had to swim a fair distance away before we could no longer hear the screams, and we had to go even farther before we could no longer hear the constant snapping of Marna-Muya's jaws."

"What happened next?" Binx asked. "It seems as though you two made a rather clean getaway."

"Hmph," Valk scoffed once again, his eyes still down-turned as he now rested his head on his hands. "I told you the beast was cunning. He was perhaps merely saving us for later. Just as we thought the waters were still and quiet, the sound of heavy water breaking shot right past us, and could be felt sucking into something. Instinct forced me to swim as fast as I possibly could. I swear I would have broken my legs by pushing them so hard, whipping them back and forth against the water. In my frantic attempt to escape, I realized that I could no longer hear her. I turned, and all I saw was an infinite pit engulfing her entire body in darkness. I still remember it—the final harsh glint in her eyes as she looked into mine, disappearing instantly before a mighty, ear-splitting crack as the beast's jaws snapped shut. As if to taunt me, the beast opened its mouth again, and then shut it again. I figured the beast didn't need to chew, but I suppose I learned the hard way that day. Each time he opened his mouth, I could recognize less and less of my love. It was not long before all I could see were fragments of mush being sucked into the pit."

"How did you escape?"

"I didn't want to escape. I was ready to give up then and there. Yet something warm and fast caught my back, and before I knew it, a powerful current was carrying my listless body away. It did eventually take me to our destination. I landed right on top of the many reefs me and Ghia spoke of. Perhaps if Ghia had been just a bit faster, or if I had been less of a coward and taken her hand and pulled her with me… she could have enjoyed the many different colors of the reefs as well. I'd still be there, as would she. The rest of the world could be swallowed up by the damn beast for all I would have cared, because we would have had each other."

"You could have stayed though, correct? It seems as though it was safer there."

"Maybe. Maybe not. I could not stand the place anymore after that. All that it did was remind me that she was gone. I remember sitting there, dazed, though for how long I do not know. I eventually grew tired of it and just left, and eventually found my way back to Ekukhan and the remaining few Marnians that had survived. Part of me hoped Marna-Muya would have found me and eaten me as well before returning. Unfortunately, life is cruel, and seems to enjoy randomly prolonging one's suffering if it can manage it."

Things went quiet for a moment, giving Valk time to finally realize that his posture had tensed. He also noticed a warm stinging sensation in his hands as he slowly released his grip. He had his hands so tightly clasped from the moment he began speaking of Ghia, yet he never noticed it until now. His hands shook a little as he released them, and he noticed something else—some droplets of water on the ground underneath and near him. Was the old woman's foretelling coming true already?

With a slight creak and a bit of shuffling of her leathery feet, the old woman had already hobbled over to the young Marnian and placed a soft hand on his shoulder. Valk noticed her smiling and returned the gesture. It was then that he noticed tears as his cheeks pushed up into his eyes. Strangely, he felt more at ease than anything else.

"I don't know what it is about you, old woman," Valk said, "but there is a strange warmth emanating from you. You certainly stand out from the rest of us cold-blooded folk."

Binx didn't say anything, and instead merely smiled warmly as she gently squeezed Valk's shoulder. She eventually hobbled back to her seat, the same soft sounds of shuffling feet and sharp creaks of crudely shaped wood following suit as she settled in.

"If you wish to work with me," Binx finally said, "I will return to this very hut on the second day, as the storm begins to pick up. It will be the perfect opportunity to begin setting up a trap for the beast. By the third day, the storm will be enough to even wash away much of the beast's sludgy exterior, exposing its unholy form for all to see. Once the people are thoroughly disillusioned, and with the Marna-Muya properly incapacitated, we will be able to slay it, and finally be free from its terror."

"As long as the beast is dead, I don't care," Valk muttered.

"When did the other Marnians begin worshiping the beast? Surely it is not a good replacement for what came before?"

Valk seemed to finally gather himself and returned to his usual stern demeanor. He sat himself up, placing a wide hand on each knee, and took a much-needed breath before continuing, "It was before my time, but I know of the great Alsidra—he who created the world, and from whom all water, warmth, and light originates. Its form is said to represent many things, but ultimately he is supposed to resemble a heavenly seadrake, from which all Marnians are descended."

"Ah, so he is like the Marnian form of the Creator," Binx muttered to herself, rubbing her wrinkly chin as she looked around absent-mindedly.

"Yes, he is a creator—the creator of everything, according to the old stories," Valk responded.

"Oh, ah, of course." The old woman seemed caught off guard. Valk merely chalked it up to her not realizing how loud her muffled pontifications were. She was elderly, after all.

The night had finally come, yet faint lights—emerald and pearl specks moving about chaotically—could be seen poking through the many gaps in the hut's construction. An ominous chanting could also be heard from far away.

"Ah, the festivities have begun," Valk remarked.

"Is this how they worship the beast?" Binx asked.

"Yes. They gather as many insects as they can, usually those that emit light of some kind, and use them to mark an area where they will sing and dance. It is a half-hearted attempt to get Marna-Muya's attention, hoping he may be impressed with the display, and 'only take what he needs.'"

"Ah, Ekukhan's words…"

"You heard him? You were there?"

"Ah! No, no, I have just … heard the saying passed around before. I figured it must be from your leader."

"Tch. He is no leader of mine. The fool placates his own people too much. He is soft."

"I fear he may be an issue, then. He will perhaps not like the idea of slaying their new deity—"

"It doesn't matter what he thinks!" Valk slammed his fist into the stump. A fierce glare of the faint light bounced off of his wide eyes and harsh stare.

"Well, I am sure that once we—"

"We *will* slay Marna-Muya, and worry not—if Ekukhan gets in our way, or even disagrees with the outcome, I will slay him as well. Our people will have a future, one way or another. I will make sure of it."

As dark as it was, Valk could see the worried look on the old woman's face on the other side of the room. Her larger, paler eyes did little to hide her expression. He could see that she desperately wanted to avoid any unnecessary bloodshed, and yet he didn't care. Nothing mattered to him now. The thought of actually slaying the beast that had ruined so many of their lives, pushed their people to the brink, and taken the life of the person most important to him—it was too much. He knew it was perhaps a bit rash to be on board with the old crone's proposition so soon, but once again, he found himself not caring. His goal was set.

Binx finally broke the tense silence between them. "Well, we will just have to cross that bridge when we get to it. Try to get some rest, dear Valk, and do try to think things over. I will return to this hut in a day, and you can tell me then if you believe I am worth working with."

"In truth," Valk said, calming himself down just enough to no longer appear threatening, "I'm more than willing to work with you. I'm willing to assist anyone who—"

"Ah, patience, young Valk." Binx finally pushed herself forward and off of the seat, the usual creaks and scraping of wood on dirt following suit as she did so. "I have learned that time is a good resource, and is best used to allow feelings and ideas to marinate. When you are fully rested, and more clear-headed, I believe you will be more than ready to decide for yourself what path you wish to take."

Valk's expression seemed to compress. His eyes and lips flattened as if trying to hold in his usual stubbornness. Fortunately, all he did was sigh and scratch between a few fins on the back of his head.

"Alright Binx," Valk said. "I await your return. Though I still think it would be better if you stayed here, in this hut at least. I would never forgive myself if you too got hurt."

"Aw, that's sweet, but," Binx adjusted her seaweed-green cloak and smiled, "I'd rather keep moving. It's as good an excuse as any to get some exercise for these old bones, you know? And also…"

"Hmm?"

Binx continued, "You should consider trying to recruit some more Marnians to assist you if you are in fact serious. We could use as many extra hands and fins as we can manage. We will need to do quite a bit of work to set up a proper trap."

Valk lifted a quick, authoritative hand to the old woman, and nearly looked down his snout at her. "Worry not, Binx. I am not the most well-liked, but I do have some sway, at least. I can manage to get at least a few extra hands on board if things look well."

The two shared a look, though Binx was the first to break eye contact. She merely gave a slow bow before turning to release herself through the leafy curtain acting as a doorway. Her footsteps were oddly heavy, and she could be heard traipsing off into the distant night for a bit longer than one would expect.

Valk stood still, unsure of what to make of it all. He knew it would do good to be skeptical, but he also knew that there was nothing else he could think of doing. In truth, he had already come to terms with the thought of his own demise and his people's extinction. He had grown numb and angry. Yet the old woman's words, and her strange exuberance and optimism, seemed infectious.

Perhaps it is foolish to even consider such a wild idea from a stranger that neither I nor anyone else seems to know. Perhaps I don't care if it is foolish. Perhaps I am growing tired of not caring for anything beyond this damned beast and these damned fools I call my people. Perhaps we do have a chance at a future…

"Sir?"

Valk whipped his head up quickly. It wasn't often that he was caught off guard, but he thanked the dark for potentially concealing whatever humiliating expression he may have given his fellow Marnian.

"What is it, Coor?" Valk tried to regain his usual stern tone, but even he wasn't entirely confident he succeeded.

"What happened?" Coor asked. "I heard you getting upset, and I heard that old croon constantly squeaking in her seat."

"It went fine, Coor. But come. We need to get back to the village. There is much to look forward to."

CHAPTER 8

THE DARK OF NIGHT WAS IN FULL force. A world that should have been cloaked in absolute shade instead gleamed in a brilliant defiance as the moonlight cast an expansive layer of pearl white across the sea. The many glitters of the water came from countless stars twinkling between the numerous purple clouds that drifted across the sky as their reflections bounced off of anything and everything below.

Humid air wafted across the ocean and seemed to collect around the island. The heavy, damp air was perfect for the serpentine people of Marn—it was about as close as one could get to feeling as though they were back under the ocean's soothing embrace without any actual water being present. Many of the island's insects seemed to appreciate the atmosphere as well, and made for easy trapping and even easier crafting. Countless bright bulbs collected from the sacks of a variety of odd critters made for brilliant bulbs once gathered together.

Some Marnians merely stuffed them into loosely knit bags that, when shaken, would release the contents inside in small amounts, leaving a trail of dotted lights as it moved. Others had fashioned them into simple braids and bracelets that accentuated every movement with luminescent strings. At the center of the village was the largest collection of lights, consisting of so many different colors that they all melded together into a unified, pure white. A great pile of burning lights sat between everyone, tall enough to reach above most of the huts nearby. From deep within the island woods, it would look as if something alien, something alive, were pulsating, and its breathing coated the world with its radiance.

The hiss of feet dragging through, then the low hum from serpentine throats, signaled the beginning of the festivities.

Making full use of their long, thin bodies, each Marnian would lower themselves to the ground, then smoothly rise. This pattern would alternate between them, their shadows creating harsh silhouettes that moved along the wall of light in a wavelike motion. As they moved, the many crude beads and stringy vines they wore as accessories clacked and clashed against each other, mimicking the fluid motions of their wearers. Some of these accessories must have been filled with all manner of curious things, as many of them nearly jingled like metallic bells would. The slithering shadows began to pick up speed, as did the sounds ringing out from their accessories. What began as chaotic soon began to harmonize—if due to nothing else beyond the ever-increasing speed. At a glance, the ceremony may have looked like a mad scramble, if not for what came next—just as the sounds arrived at a manic crescendo, everyone immediately stopped, and for a moment there was complete silence. Not even the pulsating mass of light used in place of a bonfire interrupted this moment. What came instead was a deep, ominous hum coming from a single, unknown snout of one of the dancers. Then two more followed suit, and then five more. The humming quickly spread around the entire space before the dancing slowly began once again. The humming turned to chanting, and the chanting turned to singing; though what precisely they were saying was unknown even to the Marnians themselves. The entire ritual seemed to be an exercise in pure self-expression—nothing more, nothing less.

Their thin, wild shadows cast out onto the ground, painting the otherwise dull soil with waving lines not unlike the edges of a flame. Their tips nearly reached the edge of the sanctioned space, where Valk himself stood and waited as he leaned against a simple tree. He made good use of the dark shade it provided, though the piercing glint of light bouncing off of his eyes betrayed whatever he was trying to hide.

One Marnian woman noticed this and decided to break away from the ritual to address him, even bringing a sackful of dimly lit insects as a gift.

"What are you doing way over here? And why do you keep looking up at the sky?" she asked.

"I'm just minding my own business," Valk responded, keeping his eyes fixed forward and toward the sky.

"Why not join us?" she continued. "Life is short and—"

"I am fine… Thank you."

The woman, looking dejected, merely lowered her head and her shoulders as she slowly returned to the group. Valk watched her and took comfort in seeing her energy return as she began dancing again.

Another Marnian noticed this and took the opportunity to walk over himself, taking a moment to settle under the tree as well. He looked toward the festivities, but clearly, his mind was on something else.

"Do you really think that old crone knows something we don't?" Coor asked.

"Maybe, maybe not," Valk said, keeping his arms crossed and his attention forward. "In truth, I hardly care anymore. Even if she is merely deranged or senile, it is at least good to be in the company of another that does not take the easy way out and give in to the beast."

Coor sat himself up and away from the tree's trunk to look at Valk, though Valk seemed to pay no mind. "If I'm being honest, I don't think she's worth listening to. Perhaps we could just, I don't know, adjust to living on land. Maybe Marna-Muya will eventually die of old age, and then we—"

"We can finally slither our way back to the ocean? Like weak tadpoles that didn't have the strength to break from their mother's egg? We cannot survive on these strange land berries and land creatures, Coor. We were never meant to subsist for this long on these wretched things. We have been humiliated—forced to walk and crawl on dirty land and eat bugs while Marna-Muya gorges itself on the ocean's bounty. Marna-Muya grows stronger while we only grow weaker."

"It's not about being strong or weak, Valk, it's about—"

"It sounds like cowardice to me."

Coor squinted, his scaly hands pressed into tight balls as he stared directly into Valk's eyes. He knew Valk could see him, and even read his expression from the corner of his eye, yet Valk remained undeterred. Valk knew full well of Coor's anger, but in truth, he didn't care. As far as he knew, it was nothing compared to his own, and he no longer had room in his heart to deal with anyone else's nonsense. At least, not if it had the potential of getting in the way of dealing with Marna-Muya. Coor remained, his anger palpable, but it was nothing compared to staring into Marna-Muya's great maw.

A harsh buzzing flew in from above and immediately stopped. The two looked up into the pitch-black darkness at the tree's top to try and see what it was. After a moment of silence, a few sharp ticks and tacks could be heard making their way down the grainy bark. Soon something large and pointy revealed itself— another, unknown and large insect with a strangely iridescent carapace scurried forth. It seemed to take notice of the two watchers and immediately stopped. It twitched its antennae back and forth constantly as if observing the two.

"Filthy land pest," Valk muttered.

The three turned their attention back toward the festivities to witness something new occurring. The wriggling shadows cast by the dancers began to slow, as did their chanting. Many of them began to pair up and dance more slowly, and in proper rhythm with one another.

Valk hated mating rituals. He was glad that Ghia never cared for them, either. The two were able to just talk and swim with one another, and that was enough.

Ghia...

He couldn't describe what he was currently feeling. He could see everything in front of him perfectly fine, and yet he may as well have been blind, for his mind was somewhere completely different. On every fresh young face, he could see her. He could see Ghia smiling, laughing, chortling, puckering her lips to hum and chant. She could see her face on the many Marnian women who were slowing down to give their suitors time to embrace them. He could see her face being held in their hands, her eyes looking up at them, and her lips meeting theirs as they kissed. He knew it was foolish, but he couldn't help it. All of the moments of love and expression right there in front of him, now denied him, and were beyond him seemingly forever, just like Ghia.

"You know," Coor said, interrupting Valk's trance, "we could just take a handful of the women and make a run for it. Let these idiots get eaten while we go somewhere safe—"

"There is nowhere safe, Coor, you know that." Valk's tone was sharp and bitter. He may as well have spit his words out.

"But how else are we meant to repopulate? We can't merely stay here and wait to get eaten."

"All that splitting up has ever done is lead to further dwindling of our numbers." Valk turned his attention downward, his eyes fixated on the now slow-moving lines of shadows waving back and forth ahead of him amidst the near-white light. "Perhaps if we had been more unified from the beginning—if we were not all separate tribes, cast out to the far corners of the sea— perhaps we could have banded together and fought the beast. Perhaps we could have slain the beast early on, and perhaps she would still be here…"

"You can't blame yourself for Ghia, Valk."

"I will do as I please, Coor."

"You do not always get to merely 'do as you please.' That is not what being a leader is about—"

A whip and a crack in the sky stopped everything. The shadows shot still, and all eyes pointed upward. Valk, in particular, seemed caught off guard, but also seemed the most entranced by the interruption. A slow trickle began to pelt the world below. Drop after drop filled the air, cutting quick lines past the lights in front of Valk's vision. Everyone else began to dance and cheer, as they were soon covered in rain-water. The rain seemed to be dampening the pile of light, but no one seemed to care. The Marnians took every moment to embrace the water as they reached up and their chanting turned to outright singing. The water almost seemed to glide off of their scales as if they weren't even there, causing blankets of collected water to follow them as they moved about.

"Well, I'll be," Valk whispered.

"We should remain skeptical," Coor said. "It could just be dumb luck on the old crone's part."

"Rain is so rare though," Valk responded, finally pushing himself off from the tree, and slightly rubbing the finned shoulder he was leaning on.

"It is, but that doesn't mean anything," Coor said. "You know as well as I do she could have just gotten lucky."

"We will see," Valk said. As he stood still, significant pools of rainwater began to gather on him in every crevice and around every fin. It was not long before they overflowed, and he looked not too dissimilar to everyone else with their waterfall trails.

Before the night was over, the light pile had been completely drowned out by the rain. As its intensity increased, so too did the Marnian's response. By dawn, the serpentine people were practically jumping and diving through the air and swimming along the ground, taking full advantage of the heavy storm. They particularly seemed to enjoy sliding across the mud and dug out countless lines through it as they swam along. The village was an absolute mess, and no one cared, too caught up in the moment to worry about such things.

Everyone, except for Valk, who remained particularly restrained, and maintained his focus upward. Even he had to admit that watching the sun rising from above the water looked beautiful. The grayish-blue that coated everything early on quickly gave way to bright oranges and purples as the sun reflected off of the ocean like a great mirror. The many ripples in the water caused an almost hypnotic effect on the eye as the reflected colors and lights wobbled in response. Valk remembered the many sunrises he would watch with Ghia, as they would skim along the top of the water as fast as they could in the opposite direction of the sun, seemingly extending the effect of its rising for just a little longer for them to enjoy. He had not cared to watch a sunrise ever since her death, and knew that he would not be able to enjoy it. Yet now, with a new filled optimism, there was something greater that he could see within the spectacle.

The day continued, and so did the rain. Most of the village's residents, now exhausted, finally calmed down and decided to rest. Most merely fell asleep wherever they happened to be lying at the time. A few more forward-thinking Marnians had carved out little bowls in the mud for them to curl up into, with some even making room for their partners from the night before to join them. As these dugouts filled with water, tiny bubbles could be seen rising and popping from their snoring in the water gathered around them. Valk remained vigilant; for the first time, a wide smile beamed across his snout. Coor, despite being markedly fatigued, remained alert as well, though it took him an extra moment to realize that Valk had already begun making his way back toward the meeting spot. Valk could hear his associate trailing behind him, the wet slapping of their long, webbed feet hitting the mud nearly drowned out by the rush of constant rain.

"Valk, wait!" Coor cried out.

Valk remained silent, his mind focused on one thing—meeting the old woman again. He wanted to make sure he was there to meet her. He was nearly giddy as he thought of what else she might tell them, and to begin getting her grand plan underway.

Marna-Muya's death is within reach… Can it be? Is this possible? I can hardly believe it. I will avenge you, Ghia, one way or another.

He could hear Coor calling out to him, but the words were muffled. He didn't care anymore. It didn't matter. As far as he was concerned, he would personally force every single layabout to pitch in and help if it meant finally ridding themselves of this pest, this false god that had cast them out of their sea. The storm seemed to be picking up, and it was even enough to begin slowing Valk down. Still, he trudged on, and his hut was in sight. Strangely, he could also hear the buzzing of that insect from the other night. *Did it spend the whole night watching with us?* Valk merely shook his head and ignored the thought.

In a blur, Valk had barged his way through the waving, leafy curtain door. He stopped immediately, and a thin wave of water flew ahead, coating much of the ragged shanty's dirt-ridden floor. In fact, it had reached far enough to hit the creaking, curved wooden seat on the other end of the room, where much of the water bounced off of a familiar bundle of wrinkles and scales sitting in wait.

"Binx!" Valk called out in shock.

"I see you've returned," the old woman replied through a wide, cracked smile. "You're quite early."

"And so are you," Valk responded.

"Well, I wanted a little break from the rain," Binx said, going so far as to shake her hands and wave away some of the excess water that had splashed on her.

Valk merely stared for a moment, waiting for the old woman to finish.

"You really are a strange one," Valk said.

"Hmm?"

"What kind of Marnian needs a break from water of any kind?"

"Well, this old woman does," Binx grumbled. "Now, I assume you have returned to—"

"How do we do it? How do we slay the Marna-Muya?" Valk could hardly contain himself. This feeling was something he was not used to. He had grown accustomed to remaining reserved and apathetic since Ghia's death. He didn't like opening himself up, feeling vulnerable in this way, but something about the old woman, and her prospects, energized him.

At least until the old woman started laughing, going so far as to hold her hands over her gut and kick her feet as she expressed her merriment. Valk couldn't help but look puzzled and then felt a bit embarrassed as his furrowed brow allowed the small pools of water gathered above the spike cartilage above his eyes to release.

"I have never seen such a funny expression!" Binx cackled. "The look on your face! And all that water falling off! Ha!"

Valk merely sneered, then growled, "If you're done, old crone, I'd like to begin putting whatever wild idea you have for slaying Marna-Muya together."

"Ugh, you are no fun!" The old woman finally lifted herself from her seat. A series of squeaks and creaks followed, as well as a light tap as her wide, webbed, and leathery feet hit the ground. She took a moment to brush herself off, clasped her hands together, and took in a deep breath.

"Alright then," she continued. "Let us begin."

CHAPTER 9

THE STORM CONTINUED WELL INTO the next day. It at least appeared to plateau in terms of its intensity, but its force never abated. While most of the Marnians seemed to be enjoying the weather, relishing in a feeling second only to being in the ocean itself, a small group was hard at work.

Valk, Coor, and nearly a dozen other tall, lanky Marnians hurried back and forth in an area far from both Valk's hut and the village itself as the tiny old crone whipped her hands to and fro, barking orders all the while. She struggled to get her voice to carry as far as needed, so Valk often stood near to make sure the others received proper instruction.

The plan was simple: Marna-Muya would soon take advantage of the heavy storm to begin venturing on land in search of Marnians to devour. Coincidentally, as if being orchestrated by some higher power, lightning would strike near the top of the large, brown mountain deep within the island. This would cause a tumultuous landslide, enough so that even Marna-Muya could be crushed beneath its weight. All that they needed to do—according to Binx, at least—was to dig out a massive pit as a trap for the beast to fall into. Much of the debris from the stricken mountainside would run off directly into the pit, and Marna-Muya would be trapped. Binx mentioned that, due to the creature's excessive weight, it was not meant to stay out of the water for too long. In truth, the beast could perhaps merely be left to eventually perish on its own, but that was not enough. Binx wished to wait until the storm had washed away most of the dark sludge covering the beast, and let the Marnians see for themselves just what they had been giving such veneration toward. As the final nail in the coffin, one of the Marnians would slay the beast with a long spear, impaling it right in a tender spot that Binx knew of.

Binx knows a lot of things… And has a strange view of things… Valk thought to himself. He continued to dig, burrow, and scream out orders on the old Marnian's behalf, yet his mind was on something else.

Why should I care what the other Marnians think? Why should I care about their disillusionment? If this works, I will surely owe her a great debt, and yet… I refuse to take any chances… The moment Marna-Muya is vulnerable, I will slay him. I will pierce a million holes in his hide and cut him into a million more pieces. I know the old woman would not like it, but… She doesn't need to know that I plan to operate slightly outside of the parameters of her wild plan. I can apologize after the wretched thing is dead…

Valk couldn't help but stay in his own head. He knew full well that the second day had come and gone, and he didn't care. He noticed the next morning had arrived, and the sun had risen once more, and he didn't care. Strangely, he couldn't even muster images of Ghia during it all. He even noticed that Binx had run off somewhere, not that it mattered to him anymore. The trap was set, and apparently, all they needed to do was wait. If the beast was in fact going to take advantage of the weather to come on land, then he would personally see to it that it came to the trap, even if he needed to use himself, or others, as bait. He knew that he should be thinking of ways to perhaps lead the beast toward the trap, perhaps come up with some clever trick or tactics to make sure it occurred. Perhaps he could put the other Marnians working with him in formation, using their bodies to relay the beast as it rampaged. Perhaps he could fashion some sort of tool made from the same light bugs as the night before to get the beast's attention.

Perhaps I could wring Ekukhan's neck and drag his body along, using the stench to get the beast's attention...

"Valk!"

A familiar voice rang out from the brush. It came from the same direction as the shore, and his frightened tone was sharp enough to cut through the curtain of heavy rainfall.

"Valk! He's been spotted!" the Marnian cried out. "Marna-Muya is circling the island! He is coming!"

All eyes were on the Marnian, still panting and exhausted from running. Despite how ungainly they were on land, they appeared to be more than capable of moving quickly when needed.

Mumblings rose from the scattered crowd. Their murmurings blended in with the rain, making it easy for Valk to ignore. He kept his attention forward and his eyes wide. Part of him couldn't believe it, but the look in the worried Marnian's eyes said it all.

"Where did you first see this?" Valk said. "Where is Marna-Muya now?"

"I last saw him near the eastern shore, right past the village!"

"Show me!"

"I... I don't—"

Valk was already running forward, and he grabbed the Marnian's wrist as he made his way past him. He turned for just a moment to bark more orders. "Hurry up! All of you! Dig as far down as you can, as quickly as you can! Don't even bother covering it up! Just finish and then meet us at the shore!"

Valk moved so frantically that he was practically on all fours. He refused to let go of the other Marnian's wrist.

"V-Valk! You don't need to—"

"Tell me," Valk snapped. "What did you see? Will the beast take the bait?"

"I-I don't know, but I did notice something strange—"

"What?! What was it?!"

"I noticed some odd smoke just above the water. It was perhaps gray? It gave off no real color, and it dissipated quickly, but Marna-Muya appeared to be following its trail."

Smoke? Valk thought. *How peculiar... Is Binx doing this? Is that old croon capable of sorcery? Just what is going on...*

The crunch of crisp foliage breaking beneath them blended with the sharp tapping of raindrops as they hurried forth. Soon a new sound came into Valk's ear—a large group of Marnians scrambling amongst themselves. As they burst through the last remaining bushes and trees on the edge of the village, Valk saw Ekukhan giving orders, leading others around as they prepared to move.

They must have gotten wind of Marna-Muya as well... So much for "paying tribute," you fool. So much for being content with "the beast only taking what he needs."

"Valk!" Ekukhan's deep voice boomed through the rain. "What are you doing? We are missing a few others as well. And who is that—"

"Here, he's your problem now," Valk said. He twisted his arm and used the momentum from his mad scramble forward to throw the poor Marnian he had held on to right at Ekukhan. The bodies collided, and a small group gathered to help them up. Valk could see a few bewildered looks cutting his way as he continued forth. He made sure to pick up two long, crude spears that had been left on the ground as he darted ahead.

His mind was blank, and he kept his focus forward. He wanted nothing more than to see the beast for himself. He wanted to lure the beast himself—as far as he was now concerned, there was no other way to make sure things went smoothly.

The once-lightened sands of the shore, now dark and slick from the excessive rain, were in view. He could see the infinite horizon through the rainfall, and he felt relieved. He was finally able to stop for a moment and catch his breath. He looked out and didn't notice anything peculiar. He could see countless raindrops pelting the blanket of ocean, causing tiny, violent ripples on its surface. Something else could be heard rushing through the brush behind him, though he didn't even care enough to turn around to see what it was. A familiar voice soon carried through, however.

"Valk!" Ekukhan screamed. "What is going on?! Poor Rodolin is scared senseless. And you threw him like a sack of refuse at me! What on Marn are you doing?!"

Valk ignored him and kept his attention forward, as he always did.

"Word has spread that Marna-Muya is nearby," Ekukhan said, now assuming a much calmer tone. "We are planning to move inland toward the mountain—"

"I would not do that if I were you," Valk muttered.

"What do you mean?" Ekukhan squinted, the wrinkled, teal skin around his eyes pressing hard lines all around.

"The mountain will soon be struck, and much of the island below it will be smothered in mud and rock. Go in the opposite direction if you are looking for safety."

"How do you know that?" Ekukhan stepped forward and in front of Valk, blocking much of his view of the ocean. The two glared at one another for a moment before Ekukhan continued, "You still have not answered me—what are you trying to do?"

"I am going to lure the beast onto land and trap it." Valk took in a deep breath and turned his head slightly to look Ekukhan right in his eyes. "We will need to sacrifice a few Marnians to ensure it maintains its rampage inland, toward the trap—"

"What trap?! What are you talking about?! You never mentioned any sort of ridiculous plan to me before—"

"I don't give a damn about what you think or want, Ekukhan. You, the rest of the idiots in this pathetic village, Alsidra himself—all of you can burn for all I care. Hardly any of you care to even try to fight back, or manage any sort of counter to the beast. You all deserve to be devoured for tolerating it for so long."

Ekukhan appeared shocked. He put so much effort into maintaining a strong and stable presence, and yet, in that moment, he was forced to take a step back. For once, he was speechless.

"Valk..." Ekukhan muttered. "You do not mean that... I know you are merely angry, and you don't—"

"Either assist me or shut up." Valk held up the handle of one of his spears to Ekukhan, maintaining eye contact all the while. "Now is your chance, 'great leader.' Follow my lead, and help me slay Marna-Muya, or go cower with everyone else."

Neither rainfall nor storms nor lightning or thunder could interrupt the heavy silence that stood between the two. Ekukhan seemed confused, and saddened, once again nearly stepping back as he stared into the fierce and wild eyes of the young Marnian before him. Valk could see his own reflection in Ekukhan's wide eyes and could see very well his own expression—the furrowed brow, the tightening of the leathery skin and scales on his face as he grimaced, and the savage glint in his eyes being reflected off of Ekukhan's. Valk noticed the hand he was using to hold up the crude spear to his leader was beginning to hurt. His grip was far too tight, and part of him knew that Ekukhan would not take his offer, and another part of him hoped he would actually try to reach over so he could retaliate.

Valk could sense that he was losing himself in his pursuit of revenge, and worse still, he did not care. In his mind, if this did not work, then there was no point to anything else anyway, so there was no need to worry about such things. He was already willing to sacrifice his fellow Marnians in his pursuit. What difference did it make to add his very soul to the pile?

Another crash of thunder that felt too close for comfort caught their attention. Even the sands themselves seemed to rumble in response. The two looked out onto the ocean to try and peer through the wall of rainfall covering much of the horizon. At first, nothing seemed out of place, but then something faint in the distance caught Valk's attention.

Bursts of smoke! Valk thought. *Is it true then? Is that—*
The trail of odd smoke seemed to turn and was quickly making its way toward the muddied beachfront. It was then that Valk noticed something else following the smoke, something impossibly large and murky breaking the surface of the ocean as it sped forth. It had to be Marna-Muya, and it was preparing to break the island's shore. A great, black silhouette could be seen quickly carving a direct line through the storm. It was a sight that would normally strike fear into any rational being, yet Valk found himself

invigorated. Both he and Ekukhan began to backpedal and prepare to run ahead.

As soon as Marna-Muya was close enough to the shore where its size forced it to break the surface of the water, Valk and Ekukhan began to run back toward the village. The two resorted to all fours in order to move as quickly as they could. Valk even needed to hold both spears under one of his arms to allow each of his limbs to propel him forward. Despite the disadvantage, he managed to keep up with Ekukhan as they scurried ahead. Valk couldn't help but take a quick glance back behind him as he ran forward. Through a final burst of smoke, the beast revealed itself diving out of the water and under an excess of mud below it that seemed to come out of nowhere. A massive mountain of sludge and malice seemed to crash down and slide forward toward the island's center. Not even a moment passed before the beast settled on the ground and took note of the Marnian staring him down, and it began to dig its many limbs into the ground and propel itself forward, right toward him.

Valk couldn't help but grin wildly. The contrasting push and pull of his brow furrowing, his eyes widening, and his smile digging up into the rest of his face nearly hurt, but he didn't care. The beast's weight was enough that its footsteps could be heard from all around, even drawing out the sounds of the storm itself as it crashed forward.

"This is it!" Valk called out, before turning his attention forward to catch up with Ekukhan.

"What?!" Ekukhan replied.

"We can lead Marna-Muya straight ahead! Right into the massive pit we dug out—"

"But the village is straight ahead! There are still Marnians there—"

"Who cares?! They can be bait, then. I am leading the beast forward, no matter what."

"You have gone mad, Valk!" Ekukhan nearly tripped as he whipped his head around to snap at Valk.

"Then go ahead and get everyone out of the way! I am keeping the beast in my sight, and will make sure he goes where we need him to, no matter what."

"Tch! You fool." Ekukhan took the hint and finally put all of his strength into his gait. It was not long before he disappeared ahead.

Valk looked behind him and began to slow himself down just enough to get a view of Marna-Muya as it rampaged. It was only then that he noticed the beast did not roar—if not for its massive size and weight pushing the rest of the world out of its way, it may actually be difficult to even notice the beast was there. It was still covered in mountains of writhing sludge, but Valk was beginning to see glimpses of what lay underneath. He could see flashes of pale scales in the shape of countless little appendages. Those must have been the many limbs Binx spoke of. They looked not unlike the arms and hands of the damned reaching out from within the beast itself, desperately clawing for freedom from the beast. Valk couldn't help but sneer in disgust. The beast seemed to take note of Valk once again and increased its speed. It seemed to be taking advantage of the blanket of constant rain to "swim" through the land much the same way Marnians did. Whatever advantage Valk may have thought he could gain on land, it appeared to be nothing more than an illusion.

Hundreds of voices scurrying back and forth ahead caught Valk's ear. The village was close. Just beyond some thick bushes and trees a few hundred feet ahead. They seemed to have caught on to the beast's rampaging and were desperately trying to evacuate. Valk wondered if he could try to at least lead the beast at an angle away or through the village, but the risk of missing the trap immediately quelled the thought. Valk would barrel through with Marna-Muya in tow.

If the Marnians wished to dance in the beast's honor, then why not give them an audience with it? Let them get a close look at what precisely it was that had been terrorizing them for so long.

Valk broke through a prickly thicket, and the open, muddied area that was their village came into view. A number of their huts had already broken down due to the weather, and many of the Marnians were tripping over the materials as they gathered together to leave. A few of the villagers noticed Valk speeding ahead and parted. Ekukhan was at the far end of the village, trying to lead people out of the way. Valk could see many of their eyes growing wide and their faces growing pale as they witnessed the woods themselves being pushed aside as their greatest fear grew closer.

Valk finally stopped, for just a moment, to catch his breath and turn. Just as he did so, the beast's gigantic form broke through. The beast was surrounded by echoes—of its mighty feet and claws digging into the ground, of its massive body dragging through the dirt, of the trees and rocks breaking and crashing around it, and even its gigantic body crashing through curtains of rainwater. Finally came the echoes of Marnians screaming in terror as they tried to make their escape. The beast seemed to be overwhelmed as it witnessed so many vulnerable Marnians scattering about like insects. Worried that the beast would stop, or be drawn off course, Valk ran toward the beast and through whatever crowds were going against him, going out of his way to trip any Marnians that appeared weak or impaired. Valk left a short trail of immobile Marnians in his wake, and Marna-Muya took notice. The beast lowered itself to the ground and pushed forward with all of its might. The resulting shockwave seemed to trip up even more Marnians, to Valk's delight. Valk turned and began running ahead once again, toward the one single mountain the island possessed, where at its base the great trap lay. He could hear the many cries and gurgles of Marnians that were now falling victim to the beast. He had grown numb to it—he kept his eyes and his mind focused forward. He swore that he could almost feel something when he heard the sharper cries echoing forth—the women in particular who shrieked desperately for help. He thought of Ghia but remembered that she made no such sounds, the water muffling much of anything she could have possibly said as she was devoured.

The cool touch of sharp leaves brushing over his skin and scales brought Valk's mind back to the present. He had made his way through the village and was running through the forest on the opposite side. The beast maintained its rampage forward, just as Valk wanted. He caught glimpses of the mountain through the trees covering much of the sky above him. He was so close. His goal was so close. He could hardly believe it. He was so caught up in his own mind that he hardly noticed the lightning striking the mountain's top, just as the old Marnian had predicted. More echoes followed as the thunder faded off into the distant storm, and the rising grumble of rock and stone and mud began to slide down the mountainside. It was as if the island itself had melted, and succumbed to its own weight as it blew down the mountain like a dirty wave—a tsunami of boulders about to crush the world below it. Valk could feel his limbs giving out from exhaustion, but he didn't care. Everything within him pushed him forward, as he ran faster than he ever had before, faster than he ever thought possible of a Marnian on land.

Rows of mud and turf began to slide ahead of Valk. Hearing the mindless beast continuing its chase despite its inevitable downfall energized him. Valk had no issue jumping back and forth between loose boulders and uprooted trees as they slid down. Marna-Muya's steps as it chased began to grow more stuttered, lighter, and more clumsy. Just ahead, Valk noticed a great dip in the ground. The mudslide could hardly pass over it before falling into it, then being pushed out by more material behind it.

This is it. Now or never.

Valk finally stopped, choosing to leisurely ride along a giant loose stone. He looked behind him and could see the great beast struggling as it clawed its way forward. Its body was partially submerged in a constant wave of mud and rock. Still, it doggedly moved forward, seeming determined to devour the one morsel that had evaded him multiple times. Strangely, the beast never growled, screamed, or roared. Its dark, sludgy exterior was hardly distinguishable from the mudslide surrounding it. It may as well have been Marn itself, reaching out with the arms of the lost, crying silently for release.

Valk waited, and the beast closed in. Marna-Muya made a final reach forward. A great shadow loomed over the stalwart Marnian overhead as the massive limb slowly lowered itself toward its prey. In Valk's mind, everything may as well have moved in slow motion. He even began to twitch as he waited for the beast to finally fully commit to its swing. Just as the beast's claw hit its target, Valk was gone, dozens of feet away and making his way even farther. As the weight of the great beast pressed down, its mistake was made apparent— it had been standing right on the edge of the massive pit Binx had told the Marnians to dig, though it was now mostly covered in loose bedrock from the mountainside. A thundering crash, greater than anything the storm had produced thus far, echoed forth from the beast as it fell into the pit, now overflowing with sludge and liquified dirt. Gasps and whelps followed as it tried desperately to worm its way out. It perhaps may have found its way out if not for another strange occurrence—lightning struck once more, at the same spot at the mountain's top. From a billowing cloud of colorless smoke emerged a final barrage of material. The previous landslide had turned the mountain into a perfect, almost smooth slide for the rest of the earthy material to hurry down and crash into the trapped beast once more. Underneath its own weight, and the many layers of rock and mud, the once great Marna-Muya finally began to settle down, unable to muster the energy to writhe or flail or rampage as it once did. For the first time in perhaps its entire existence, the beast was vulnerable.

As the landslide slowed to a crawl, Valk picked himself up and took notice of the beast. Much of the mucous-like sludge that covered its body had washed away in the rain or been brushed aside by the grainy soil and rock from the mountain. Its sharp, pale scales revealed themselves once again, showing countless appendages of all shapes and sizes wriggling about. Valk instantly thought they looked like the arms of ghosts reaching out from within the beast. Its scales layered perfectly on top of each other, giving them space to first curve in and then out wildly, creating countless little bowls for material to collect. From afar, it gave the beast a slightly jagged appearance. The light did not seem to reflect kindly off of their surface, however—there were no signs of life or blood beneath them, giving it a sickly appearance. There were a number of algae-green splotches of discoloration that dotted much of its body, only adding to the effect.

It took a moment to find the beast's face amidst the constant, wriggling appendages and jagged scales that obfuscated the details of its appearance. As it whimpered, it hardly opened its mouth, and if not for the copious amounts of shining, silvered saliva oozing from its maw, Valk may not have even noticed its placement. He could see glimpses of the creature's yellowed, jagged teeth. Countless lines of small, sharp, and irregular shapes clamped down and tapped like hollow bark every time it opened and closed its mouth. Upon deeper inspection, he could see many things caught between these teeth—leaves, dirt, tree bark, bits and pieces of insect parts, the varying colors of these creature's guts, as well as even what appeared to be bone and pieces of Marnian limbs and hands and feet. Valk was startled at the sight at first, and then he couldn't help but wonder how many of those Marnian body parts were from the very people he had doomed to be devoured.

Valk refused to let such feelings affect him now. A quick shake of his head, followed by a gruff mumble, and he continued to thoughtlessly ponder over the creature's appearance. Despite its massive size, it didn't take long for Valk to finally find Marna-Muya's eyes. They were tiny, forward-facing beads that reflected the light more brilliantly than anything else on the creature. They were also situated nearly on top of the creature's head and were perhaps too close together. It gave off an uncanny impression. The ocean was filled with many strange and frightening creatures that defied initial logic, but the sheer scale and contrast of Marna-Muya seemed even beyond that.

Valk looked the creature directly in its eyes, and yet it refused to look him back. He knew it was ridiculous to expect such from the creature, but it frustrated him all the same.

Disgusting, he thought. *Pathetic. Worthless abomination. This is the thing that has terrorized us for so long? This was all it took to take down the "great Marna-Muya?" Ghia died for nothing...*

"Valk!" another familiar voice called out his name. Valk could only curl his lip in anger. It seemed as though anytime someone called out to him, it was not for anything good. He didn't even recognize the voice immediately, though he also didn't care. He wished for them to go away.

"Valk!" An old woman came scurrying across the messy terrain. For such a small, hunched body, she was quite capable of maneuvering across the rocky landscape. It was not long before she was at least close enough to not have to yell anymore.

Valk ignored the old crone. Part of him wanted to curse her and tell her to leave him alone. Another part of him wanted to thank her for what she enabled. Part of him wondered if he would get anything out of finally defeating the beast and if the old woman had unknowingly ripped away his sense of purpose. He chose to stay quiet, to avoid saying anything he might regret, instead choosing to keep his gaze fixed on the beast's beady eyes.

"Valk! Valk," Binx cried out. "You did it! You did so well. Just wait 'til the rest of the villagers see this—"

"I don't care what the others see or think," Valk hissed.

"What? Surely you don't—"

"I… do not… care. You can leave now, old woman. Thank you for everything."

"That's it? You can't just—"

"Who are you to tell me what I can and cannot do, old woman?!" Valk whipped his head as he turned to the old woman, who now looked more concerned than frightened. It didn't matter to Valk anymore, however.

"Valk, please, calm down," Binx muttered. Despite her frail frame and poor posture, she held herself up confidently as she furrowed her own brow back at the young Marnian. "You've already won. As soon as Ekukhan and the others see the beast in its pitiful state, you will be free to put it out of its misery with a bit of help—"

"I don't need help! And misery is all this blasted thing deserves!"

"Valk! Wait!"

Valk reared himself back, holding a crude, dark brown spear in each hand, and he thrust himself forward. The beast was still writhing and flailing about, though it had clearly lost a lot of energy. It was the perfect time to take down the creature in Valk's mind.

The Marnian landed on a large open area just above the beast's eyes. It was easy for him to dig his feet between a few of the large, scoop-shaped scales covering its body and stabilize himself. A few nearby appendages began to grab at his ankles, and he began his onslaught. They were easy to slice off, allowing Valk to focus entirely on making the most of each swipe. Instead of clean cuts and smooth thrusts, he took pleasure in swinging his weapons at odd angles, carving jagged lines across the exposed appendages. For the first time, the beast began to scream. This only galvanized the young Marnian—finally a proper response, a true sign that his vengeance was thus far effective. The beast's blood began to ooze everywhere as Valk continued hacking away, filling many of its scoop-shaped scales with a shining, dark green fluid that was as thick as mushed algae. It was not long before it combined with the constant rainwater and whatever remained of the brown sludge still on the creature. Everything soon melded together—the blood, the scales, the ripped skin, and plucked scales, the sounds of the storm, and the old woman's cries. He was blinded to the world around him as adrenaline took over and all he could feel was a spear in each hand flying back and forth into Marna-Muya's exposed hide.

The sight of Marnian blood popped out against the canvas of carnage like spilled ink on a blank page. Valk noticed this and his senses came back to him, informing him of his predicament—several unseen appendages had wrapped around him and were pulling his legs down! The scooped scales were now digging into his flesh, nearly deep enough to hit bone as the beast's movements caused them to flex and converge on top of him. Valk merely grit his teeth and began hacking away once again. Eventually, he was able to pull himself free, leaving behind a pile of carved flesh and a putrid mixture of both his and the beast's blood. Valk remained undeterred and merely pushed himself up and forward toward the beast's eyes. The beast slowly opened its maw, causing the front half of its face to rise, creating a massive uphill of dirtied scales. Valk merely climbed his way up to one of the beast's tiny, beady eyes and readied himself. Marna-Muya began to close his mouth, still slowly, and as its face leveled, Valk drove one spear into its skin to use it to hold himself in place. He could feel scales beginning to pinch onto his ankles once again. Valk chuckled, and merely hoisted himself up on the implanted spear. In a single motion, he used the momentum to pull himself up and swing himself back down, driving the other spear right into the beast's eye.

Marna-Muya roared for the first time. A guttural, spine-shattering sound echoed from its mouth. Its scream seemed to even push the curtain of falling rain out of the way. As the top of its mouth rose, it nearly blocked whatever light shone through from above, coating Valk in shadow. Valk couldn't help but smile wildly, feeling that he had finally gotten his prey.

And then, in the blink of an eye, the beast snapped its mouth shut! It did so with such speed and force that it nearly looked as if it had cracked its face in half and down into the ground. Valk found himself shaken, and his spears, once lodged so firmly into flesh, were now free. He maintained his grip, but nothing was holding him in place, and he slid down a mountain of blood and rainwater. He could feel his body bumping against each scale as he slid down at frightening speed. The steep slope of the beast's mouth and the speed at which he moved made it impossible for him to get any sort of hold. He worried about how hard he was about to hit the ground as his descent continued. Except he was immediately stopped. A gust of warm breath covered him, and for a moment Valk noticed he was suspended in the air. Before he could register what had happened, an ear-splitting snap descended upon him, taking with it his left arm and the spear it held.

He was not sure if it was the adrenaline, his anger, or the shock of the situation that caused him to feel nothing. Despite part of his body being held between rows of jagged fangs, Valk had no trouble mustering the strength needed to drive the other spear up and into a slick, fleshy layer just above the beast's teeth. Marna-Muya cried out once more, releasing Valk to finally fall free. The beast flailed and gnashed its teeth uncontrollably, which only drove the spear deeper and deeper into its gums. By the time Valk hit the ground, he was covered in so many different fluids that he couldn't keep track of them all. Everything had mixed together into a near-black substance that was not unlike the sludge that normally covered Marna-Muya.

As the world dimmed, everything also began to go quiet. As Valk closed his eyes, he couldn't hear much beyond the many taps of rainwater on his face and someone's footsteps scurrying frantically toward him.

CHAPTER 10

*V*ALK...
Valk!

Valk, stay with me!

The dark fog of slumber was pierced by a familiar voice calling through it. The young Marnian slowly returned to his senses as he was forced to take a moment to rest. He could hear a number of voices farther back, all melding together into a fuzzy haze in his ear.

Finally, light returned to him, and Valk could see the form of a small, hunched Marnian in a sea-green cloak sitting over him. The teal shade of her face stood in stark contrast to the dark gray sky above. Strangely, she didn't look directly at Valk but seemed to be transfixed by something just off to the side.

"Your arm..." Binx muttered.

Valk could sense something was wrong and could feel a strange, sharp sensation on his left side as the rain pelted it.

Ah, that's right... Valk thought, remembering Marna-Muya's final outburst against him. He knew he should have been more concerned, perhaps even frightened at the implications that losing a limb brought on. He should have been worried about how well he may or may not be able to swim, or if he could even hunt anymore. He should have been worried about the amount of blood he must have lost. And yet none of that mattered. A quick glance out of the corner of his partially opened eyes revealed the one thing that did matter to him—Marna-Muya's corpse. The beast had been slain, once and for all. He had finally gotten his revenge. And yet he felt unsatisfied. He looked at the instrument of his revenge, part of a crude spear that now sat leaning against a wall of sickly, drained flesh. Grainy black fluids could be seen slowly trickling down the instrument's rough handle. He felt just as apathetic as he had before. He glared into the very maw that had taken his beloved and watched as blood slowly trickled forth from it. He thought he might at least be able to relish the smell of the beast rotting away after its death, yet it brought no such solace. He had gotten his revenge, and now he was left with nothing.

He very well may have just stayed where he lay and let himself pass away peacefully, if not for another voice calling through the crowd, one that always reminded him of what he lost:

"Valk!" Ekukhan called out. His deep voice banged against the inside of Valk's mind like a battering ram.

He was getting sick of hearing his name. He also grew angry at the thought of Ekukhan living freely off of his own sacrifice. The feeling was palpable enough that Valk felt as if he needed to take in a deep breath so he could exhale and perhaps get the feeling out of his body. It was a foolish thing to think, and he knew it, but it was an excuse to get himself breathing, to fill his body with life and energy, which only fueled his anger. Rage seemed to be the only thing that stayed with him through it all. It was not a good feeling, but it was better than nothing—it was better than the agonizingly slow, trawling decay of apathy he felt moments ago.

"Valk, you… you did it," Ekukhan said, his heavy footsteps finally stopping as he finished making his way over to Valk. His tall shadow loomed over the hunched old woman and seeped over Valk, blocking out some of the light.

"Is there anything we can do for him?" Binx asked.

"No… such injuries are usually a sign that we leave the victim for dead," Ekukhan said, a solemn tone weighing down his already deep voice. "It does not help that he recklessly endangered so many of us in his mad pursuit."

"But he was only trying to help!" Binx cried out, nearly ripping herself away from holding up Valk to hiss at Ekukhan. "Your numbers are so few, you should be doing everything you can to save—"

"Y-you … do not speak for me, old woman," Valk muttered between heavy, pained breaths.

"Valk…" Binx mumbled in response.

"Thank you again… Binx… But I do not need you anymore, in fact…" Valk pushed himself off of the old woman and pushed himself up. He looked out onto a crowd of Marnians watching everything play out. He could see the many same scared faces and worried expressions that he had grown to hate. The anticipation of his next move seemed to fill him with adrenaline once more, dulling the pain. "There is only one more thing I wish to do… Ekukhan, I did what you could not. I cut down the very beast that terrorized us. I dove fearlessly into danger and confronted your supposed 'god.' Well, who will you pay tribute to now that the 'great' Marna-Muya is dead? Will the one and only Alsidra accept you back into his grace after you nearly gave in to the false god? You feared something enough that you were willing to abandon the ocean, and thus Alsidra. What kind of leader are you? Why do you still call yourself khan?"

"Valk! Silence! I have led these people for longer than you have even been alive!"

"And certainly longer than Ghia was alive."

"You dare bring her up again? In this manner? In front of everyone? Why not be satisfied in dealing with the threat and move on? Or at least attempt to move on—"

"There is no moving on from this! From Ghia! From your cowardice!" The flare of Marnian tongue was truly beginning to show itself as Valk hissed and spat every word. The treble of water and phlegm in his throat gave his words a frightening echo.

"What do you want then, you dangerous fool?!" Ekukhan was clearly doing his best to remain dignified, though even he seemed to be falling victim to emotion as his own watery, throaty voice rang out.

"I want to challenge you for the title of khan!"

A gasp flowed over the crowd like a soft wave. It was only then that Valk noticed the rain was finally beginning to ease up. Everyone now had a clear view— and an uninterrupted ear—to the drama unfolding before them.

Ekukhan flattened his lip and tensed his snout. He drew in another deep breath, forcing his wide chest to puff up and his shoulders to rise. He glared at Valk through a harsh squint that seemed to magnify the glint of light reflecting off of them.

"And why do you believe you could be khan?" Ekukhan said, flatly and sternly. "You are just as much a wild beast as Marna-Muya. You are mad, you are reckless, you are terribly injured. What do you have to gain from testing me—"

"I have everything to gain!" Valk screamed, leaning forward into a mighty stomp against the mud.

"You have nothing to gain, and everything to—"

"I have nothing else to lose. But I would at the very least like to expose your cowardice for all to see. I would like to expose your weakness. I will slay you just as I did Marna-Muya! I will be valkhan, and the rest of us will return to the sea without you! You can join Ghia in the ocean of the next world—"

"Enough!"

"No! It is not enough! It never was, and never will be!" Valk whipped himself around, and in a single motion, picked up the remains of his spear and tossed it directly at Ekukhan. Ekukhan flinched and moved just enough to allow the crude rod to land at his side. "Unlike you, I am at least brave enough to defend us."

Ekukhan stared at the spear, lost in his own mind. It was easy to see the conflicting thoughts carving deep lines in his face. Binx held her hands close to her chest and backed away from the two. The rest of the tribe created a huddled wall of shaded blue faces and fins several dozen meters away. For a time, everyone appeared to share a certain stillness and an uncertainty of what the next moment may bring. The weakening storm brought with it a delicate cadence of tapping water droplets against a mushy layer of mud.

"Let's get some decent weapons, at least," Ekukhan mumbled.

"What?!" Binx shrieked. "No! No one has to fight! No one else has to die! Why are you still—"

"You're awfully naïve for someone so aged," Ekukhan said, looking over his scaly shoulder. "Conflict comes in many forms, whether it be the ocean, great beasts, or even each other. Sometimes there is no other option than to confront it."

"Well said," Valk said.

Binx looked fraught with worry. She let out a few weak gasps as she tried to think of something to say, only to realize it was a fruitless endeavor. She stood and watched helplessly as Valk and Ekukhan made their way nearer to the crowd. Valk kept his attention ahead as he hobbled forth, but he caught a glimpse of the old woman from the corner of his. Her teal scales and saggy, wide snout brought out the many shadows in her wrinkles. Her sadness may as well have been carved in stone for how striking a visage it was. For the briefest of moments, a tinge of regret ran through Valk's mind. A draining, stinging feeling seemed to drag all throughout his body. As powerful as it was, the feeling had come and gone before it could fully register, and his resolve returned. It was easy then to ignore her and keep his attention focused on his final opponent.

A sea of Marnians now gathered in a large, loose circle in the muddied field in front of Marna-Muya's grave. At the center, two combatants stood, each brandishing a new spear and adopting a unique stance in preparation for the fight to come.

On one side was a taller, wider Marnian. Broad-shouldered, surefooted, and the deeper coloring of his scales made for an imposing figure. The light reflected a violet color off of his scales, accenting every movement with brilliant streaks. His greater weight could be seen in effect as his feet dug surprisingly deep into the mud as he assumed a wide, stable stance. All of this was offset by his calm, dignified demeanor. Despite his presence, he was restrained. A forceful discipline seemed to follow his every action and expressed itself through his physical form.

On the other side was what may as well have been his polar opposite. A thinner, shorter figure crouched low to the ground, partially to balance himself with his only three limbs as he gripped his own spear tightly. While not as large as his opponent, his ropey muscles made crisp contours into his figure. Everything about him was sharp as a spear's tip—his intense musculature, his thin and bony frame, his long snout that seemed to bear a perpetual sneer, and the harsh look in his eyes that barely restrained his discontent. In the light, his scales reflected an almost aquamarine color that would have been pleasing to the eye if not for his wild demeanor.

Even the sky seemed to be waiting in anticipation. The once relentless walls of rain nearly drowning the land had diminished to a mere trickle, giving the stage ample room to play its drama.

Valk's breathing seemed heavy and constant. It seemed to be a good strategy for ignoring the pain inflicted upon him by Marna-Muya. Ekukhan merely looked his opponent over and took a moment to ready himself with a deep breath of his own.

The brush of mud quickly being pushed out of the way caught everyone off guard as Valk used the opportunity to push himself forward, spear in hand, and pointed forward. He stayed low to the ground, nearly slithering along the slick surface and concealing the timing of his spear arm. Ekukhan tried to raise his own spear to retaliate, but Valk was too quick, already lunging his weapon's point right for his opponent's chest. Another brush of mud followed as Ekukhan pulled himself back and down, barely dodging the attack. A thin, grisly streak now sat along his ribcage.

"You always were an opportunist," Ekukhan said.

Valk gathered himself and turned, a wide smile plastered across his snout. "Call it what you want. I merely choose to act when necessary. It is how I was able to get to Ghia's heart first."

Ekukhan grit his teeth. He gripped his spear so tightly that the sound of flesh grinding against wood could be heard from a dozen feet away.

Valk continued, "You call me an opportunist, but in truth, it is just tenacity—having the will and the bravery to confront any challenge as soon as it arises. Your supposed 'patience' and 'discipline' is merely cowardice. I can see it, Ghia could see it, everyone can see it. The only reason you are khan is because everyone else is more cowardly than you are—"

"Enough!"

Ekukhan lunged at Valk, his own spear aimed directly at Valk's head. He could see the attack coming from miles away, yet Ekukhan moved too quickly for him to do anything elaborate. A simple crouch and angling of his spear would do. Valk braced himself against the thick mud and easily deflected his aggressor's attack. Ekukhan had put his entire body's weight into the attack, pressing Valk even farther into the mud. Valk's knees nearly buckled under the weight, but he held. Ekukhan was now nearly half past him, and his legs were exposed. Instinct nearly had Valk trying to get in a decisive cut with his other hand, only to remember that he had no such advantage anymore. A quick lift and blow with his heel to the back of Ekukhan's knee would have to do.

The large body buckled under the strike. What should have been an obvious opening instead led to Ekukhan using the momentum of his fall to spin along the wet ground. In a blur, he whipped around and cut a swift line along Valk's ankle. A streak of glistening blood was followed by a quick shriek as Valk threw himself back and away.

"I wanted to show kindness," Ekukhan said through a series of heavy breaths. "I knew of Ghia's affair for a long time. I could have banished both of you at any time, left you to fend for yourself. But I showed kindness. I tried to be understanding, despite your anger."

"Heh." Valk smiled through a heavy breath of his own and picked himself up with the help of his spear. He kept his eyes on Ekukhan through the entire motion, readying his response. "I'm surprised you bothered to even notice that one of your many wives was losing interest."

Ekukhan turned his head down and looked to the ground. The grayed, stormy light forced his furrowed brow to cast heavy shadows over his eyes.

"When our numbers began dwindling," Ekukhan continued, "I held back a lot of emotions, a lot of things, in order to keep everyone on track. I needed everyone to stay focused—"

"A lot of good that did," Valk interrupted. "So many of us died. So many of us were devoured by that wretched beast, most of whom perished without you even knowing about them. I was there in Ghia's final moments, unlike you—"

"What else could I have done?!" Ekukhan had risen and nearly stood over Valk, his great shadow looming over the young Marnian as he pressed his heavy feet into the ground and threw his free arm out in anger. "You two knew the risk you were taking! No one forced you to constantly test your limits, to test Marna-Muya by venturing farther and farther away from the rest of the tribe! You knew the risk, and you suffered the consequences. And now you sit here, lashing out at me like an angry, petulant child that your own foolishness cost you. This is why you could never be khan!"

Valk, in his rage, quickly released his spear to dig his hand into the mud. A foul combination of mud, his own blood, and whatever excesses were still oozing out from Marna-Muya onto the ground below, balled up in his webbed palm. A lumped ball of malice flew forward, hitting Ekukhan in the face. Ekukhan recoiled, even crying out as his eyes stung, and he clawed desperately at the material. Valk took the opportunity to pick his spear back up again and charged. Just as Ekukhan lowered his hands to try and brace himself, Valk drove his weapon straight into Ekukhan's shoulder. Another deep shriek followed. Valk couldn't help but smile as he relished the feel of his weapon in his prey once again. His euphoria was cut short as he felt the heavy grip of Ekukhan's mighty hand wrapping around his neck. Valk could only feel his entire body going limp as his larger opponent threw the entire weight of his own body against him. It took a moment for Valk's mind to register the pain after his body had been slammed into the ground.

Everything darkened as Ekukhan's looming shadow poured over Valk once again. His mouth began to froth as Ekukhan increased his stranglehold. Despite his best efforts, he couldn't break free, no matter how much he twisted and squirmed, the slick mud at his back making his movements slippery and wild. He could feel the warmth of Ekukhan's other hand nearing his wrist. In a moment of desperation, Valk slung his arm in toward his body to avoid the hold and swiped it again at Ekukhan's face. Ekukhan dodged the debris with ease, but this only left him open to another desperate attack. Valk drew in his breath and heaved forth as much saliva as he could muster into a shining glob, once again hitting Ekukhan in his eyes. Ekukhan's grip loosened just enough for Valk to get loose. He pushed himself off the ground with as much force as he could muster, flinging the bony part of his skull right into Ekukhan's snout. A deafening crack followed another shriek. Ekukhan brought up a single hand to his face as he thrust the other, now formed into a tight fist, right into Valk's chest, sending him flying several feet and sliding several more along the mud. A round of gasps cut into the combatant's ears, and everything went silent once again. Their heavy breathing nearly drowned out the trickling rain.

A hollow, bassy voice echoed across the arena, "How long?"

"Huh?"

"How long had she been pregnant for? When she died?" Ekukhan said. He took a moment to quickly pull the spear from his shoulder, resisting the urge to flinch as it released.

Valk, still breathing heavily, in pained, laborious spasms, took a moment to think. Slivers of yellow could be seen around his irises as he looked around the dark of his mind for an answer.

"One, maybe one and a half cycles," Valk grumbled.

Ekukhan looked to the ground as well and sighed. A tinge of defeat seemed to follow its trail. "We have no way of knowing precisely whose children they were—"

"I know... I know exactly who the father was! You're looking at him."

"It is unwise to pretend to be so sure of things you do not know."

"A true leader projects confidence, does he not?"

"Confidence, without wisdom or experience to inform it, is merely impudence."

"Bah!" Valk nearly spit in his retort. "Your talk of 'wisdom' and 'experience' rings hollow, Ekukhan! Face it—Marna-Muya drove fear into you, and everyone else, and you merely leveraged that fear to cling to your leadership!"

Ekukhan merely chuckled, though his eyes remained down-turned. Valk, growing frustrated, squinted fiercely at his opponent, curious as to what he was doing.

"One of my favorite things about being khan," Ekukhan continued, "is teaching the young. Teaching every member of the tribe from childhood everything they need to know—fishing, hunting, fighting, all of it. But the greatest thing about teaching is that, no matter how old you get, you can still learn a thing or two from your students." Ekukhan finally lifted his head and lightly held the wet, open hole in his shoulder. "Perhaps you are right, Valk. Perhaps I did let fear take me. Perhaps there is value in taking opportunities wherever, or whenever, one encounters them. I suppose such risks are something a true leader needs to be ready to take at any moment. Thank you, Valk, for giving me a final lesson."

"I'm tired of talking, and tired of your lessons. Let's end this already."

"Fine then, here." Ekukhan tossed the fresh spear he had kept in his hand since the beginning of the fight. A satisfying plop followed its landing just in front of the young Marnian. Ekukhan slowly leaned over to pick up the spear that had impaled him, its edge still dark and shining from his own blood. Valk found himself watching curiously but quickly snapped out of his trance and snatched the fresh spear in front of him and assumed his usual low fighting stance. Ekukhan assumed his own stance, and the two began to slowly circle one another.

The rain had nearly stopped, though the dark gray overcast remained. The light, filtered through sheets of ashy clouds, painted the muddied arena with an ominous flare. Nearly all colors became one as they blended together under the oppressive hue of the storm's remains. Still, the two, locked in combat, remained focused. The soft brush of slick mud being pushed aside as the two circled one another was all that could be heard. As the two began to slowly close in on one another, Ekukhan stayed upright and guarded. Valk, however, seemed to be lowering himself farther and farther, to the point where he was practically slithering along the ground by the time they were within reach of each other.

Ekukhan calmly took a final step to his left. Valk followed suit, sliding ever so slightly to his own left, only to spring into a wild kick! A thin wall of mud followed, concealing the low-sitting Marnian. Ekukhan remained steady but shot himself back away from the mud. The wall was pierced with Valk's movement as he lunged forward through it. As the curtain of muck reached its apex, the two fighters were concealed as the sound of flesh ripping and bone snapping echoed from behind it. The wall of mud seemed to take an eternity to finally descend, as if trying to wait until the very last moment to reveal its tragedy. Another satisfying plop quickly rang out as the mud hit the ground, and the bitter fight's end could be seen by all.

The Marnian tribe leader could be seen still standing in the exact spot he had last been seen before. He now stood hunched over, putting his full weight into his spear as it pinned down his opponent. The weight and force were enough to burrow a deep bowl into the mud where Valk's body now rested. The muscles in the stump where his lost arm sat had long since clenched together to stop any bleeding, and yet he now sat in a pile of dark blood, slowly draining from the gnarled gash in his chest. Strangely, Valk seemed calm. The tight muscles and deep wrinkles that had burrowed deep into his face were now loose and relaxed. He didn't even see the point in trying to act out, to try and get away. He accepted his defeat completely and without hesitation.

Ekukhan solemnly sat above Valk, his looming shadow as still as he was. Valk, for the first time, could see his own reflection in Ekukhan's dark eyes. It was the first time he could recall seeing his reflection after Ghia's passing. Despite being young, he noted the many dark lines that had been etched into his face. He noticed the glittering pool of blood concealing much of his head and neck, and noticed the edge of the tightened lump of muscle where his left arm once sat. For a moment he was shocked and didn't even recognize himself, and wondered who he was looking at. The shock was replaced with dread as soon as he realized who he was looking at—he finally saw himself as others now saw him, and as Ekukhan now saw him.

Valk coughed up a spurt of blood and merely chuckled from the pain. Ekukhan remained still and watched.

"Tch. Perhaps I will … now be reunited with her… With Ghia… Honestly, I'd rather her not see me like this…"

Valk felt his strength draining. He could no longer keep his snout pointed upward and allowed himself to lay his head on its side. He took a final look at the group that had been watching. He looked past countless frightened eyes, curious to see what the old woman would think. With his last bit of life, he turned his head upward and could see the old crone—her hands balled into tight fists, her head tilted slightly toward the ground as her wide eyes looked up at him, and the many recognizable lines pulling her skin into a mournful visage.

He wanted to properly thank her, and apologize a final time. Unfortunately, the gray overcast only seemed to darken, and he was truly exhausted. If the darkness hadn't finally taken his senses, and his strength, he very well may have done just that.

CHAPTER 11

A STRANGE, UNNATURALLY IRIDES-cent insect could be seen buzzing along the watery horizon. It wasn't long before it burst into smoke, its color not unlike the many gray clouds covering most of the sky.

A familiar, deep voice called out from the sky, "Cynkz! You did it! And all without exposing your identity or threatening the Creator's way! Splendid work!"

Cynkz merely hovered quietly, his head down-turned as he watched his own reflection in the ocean wobble and glitter in the light.

Carros continued, excitedly, "In truth, I didn't know if your plan was necessary, but I could see that the beast's true form, being exposed and being cut down no less, did well to disillusion my people. I doubt any more of my people will cast their souls away, worshiping the beast."

Cynkz remained still, almost transfixed, as his mind silently worked around a pressing question.

"What is wrong, Cynkz?" Carros asked, finally calming his tone.

"Do the Marnians have their own form of Munderworld? Of Potarium?" Cynkz asked.

"Yes, of course," Carros said. "All of the Creator's children must face trials and tribulations, and all of His children ultimately have salvation to look forward to in the next life."

"That is good. That is very good." Cynkz lifted his head, but only a bit, still seeming to refuse to look into the sky. "I suppose there is hope that Valk will find peace, and may in fact be reunited with his love."

"Yes, it is possible… Unfortunately, we Omun do not deal much with the afterlife. That is solely the responsibility of the Creator and His apostles."

Cynkz still seemed lost in his own mind. If not for the wind whipping his cloak sharply, the world would have seemed eerily quiet.

"I do not know if I should consider it a privilege or a curse to experience what you have for the first time. It is one of the hardest parts of being an Omun," Carros said.

"What do you mean?" Cynkz asked.

"Having to sit back and watch your people hurt each other. Despite possessing so much power, the sort of power most would consider unfathomable, and yet there are times when we can do nothing. Choice and will are some of the Creator's greatest gifts, and we mere Omun are to never impede a people's ability to express them."

"I see…"

"We must adopt a greater perspective. It is easy to get lost in the minute happenings, but consider what you have just done. An entire world has been given a second chance. In such a short time, you were able to save these people from extinction, and very well may have saved many of their souls from unnecessary suffering as well. They will now go on to give birth to countless more souls as they repopulate. Their future contains limitless potential."

"I wish we po still had such potential."

"Cynkz…" Carros's voice seemed to lower, and what warmth he provided seemed to intensify, as if a friendly hand had been placed on the jester's back. "I am sure that the Creator had a good reason for what He did."

"I sure hope so, Carros. It would be quite awkward if I finally met Him and He had no answer."

Carros seemed to need a moment to register Cynkz's words. "It is strange, truly. It is so rare that anyone speaks so… boldly about the Creator. We Omun hold His name and judgment in such high reverence."

"I know," Cynkz said through a weak smile. "I mean no offense by it. If Fiddle taught me anything, it is that a bit of harmless snark allows the heart and mind to cope with anything."

"The imp is perhaps wiser than he lets on."

"Perhaps. Or perhaps he is merely crafty with his excuses."

"Ha!"

Now Cynkz couldn't help but smile fully. Something about getting a laugh out of a celestial being did much to warm his heart. Even the salty sea air seemed easier to breathe in.

"Well, if you are ready," Carros continued, "we can return to the others in Omundisia. If you could, please look up to my warmth and open your mind once more."

"Um, about that…"

"Hmm? What's wrong?"

Cynkz's smile seemed to fade. It was an expression that he was not used to, and he couldn't even make it out in his warbled reflection in the still waters below. Carros remained patient, and Cynkz finally mustered the strength to speak.

"I think I hurt my back earlier. It was when I turned into the mudslide the beast slid on to break the island's shore—"

"Oh! Is that all?" Carros's excitement caught Cynkz off guard. He instinctively tried to look up with wide eyes, only to be met with a sharp pain that rolled down his spine like a roll of needles being pressed into it. Cynkz could hardly refrain from muttering some odd sound as he recoiled. He reached for his back and found himself curling over even more, giving himself a fuller view of his reflection in the water. The fact that he still couldn't read his own expression was comical enough to distract from the pain for just the right amount of time for the pain to subside.

"Just a moment, friend," Carros continued. "I may be able to assist you here."

A wave of unseeable warmth washed over Cynkz. He could feel it slowly working its way over him, or perhaps through him. In truth, he wasn't entirely sure what to make of the sensation. It was similar to the warm, honey-like sensation he felt from the huums in Potarium. The feeling seemed to overpower everything else, and he didn't even realize it when his back was healed. A deep breath brought his posture back upright, and he looked up happily toward the sky.

"Wow... um, thanks!" Cynkz said. He stretched and rolled his shoulders as he smiled. The wind was not particularly strong, but it provided enough force that it made performing the movements at least a bit difficult as his cloak tried to whip around his body.

"No need for thanks, Cynkz. In truth, I should be thanking you," Carros said. "Now, let's hurry back. I am sure the others would like to speak with you."

Cynkz smiled and bowed, and before long another wave of light peered through the clouds, and the jester was gone.

CHAPTER 12

"He's back!" Jio-Mol's boisterous enthusiasm could be heard from a universe away.

Cynkz had hardly settled back into the pale void, and his attention was already being directed to the court of stars now sitting in a pleasing arc above Carros's fiery body.

"That was quite the show," Helon said. Her gentle tone helped to counter Jio-Mol's disarming exuberance. It was useful to find anything to ground oneself in the void, even if it was just a calm voice.

"Cynkz!" A third voice forced its way into the void. It was Anim, though he was noticeably more excited than usual. Strangely Cynkz knew exactly where to look to address him—the twinkling black star in the center of the arc above Carros. "Cynkz, you'll never believe it! My people… they have grown!"

"Really?!" Cynkz's smile seemed to pull his body upward.

"Yes, and they have begun to adapt to the slowly changing environment. Here, I will give you a brief vision—"

Cynkz instantly felt a sense of trepidation, but before he could express it, Anim was already in his mind. Set before his vision was an endless field of trees, the grainy bark on each one shining a slightly different shade of lavender against Anim's light. Countless dozens of small, pale figures could be seen crawling up and down their many branches in search of cover.

"Look!" Anim whispered excitedly. "There they are! They have already begun to grow! Who knows what potential they harbor? What sorts of tribes or nations they will forge? The future cannot come soon enough!"

A quick release of Cynkz's mind brought him back to the present. Again, he felt the need to breathe deeply, to make up for having held his breath during the vision.

"Ah, I apologize," Anim said. "I let my excitement get the better of me."

"No, no it is fine, Anim." Cynkz lifted a light hand to gesture his acquiescence. "It is very interesting to see their progress, to see that my actions seem to be having a positive effect."

"Hah! You have done nothing to affect the greater cosmos, Cynkz." Siar'C's unmistakable, bitter tone cut through the void effortlessly, as it always did. "One, two, two hundred, it does not matter how many planets you believe to be 'helping,' it means nothing without the Creator's approval. Your 'assistance,' for all you know, could be doing great harm to His vision in the long run."

"Well, I am sure that if I assisted your world, you would be speaking differently—"

"Nice try, but no. I do not need your assistance."

Cynkz merely shrugged his sharp shoulder and smiled at the twinkling speck marking the leftmost end of the arc of stars above him. "Give it time. Maybe you'll eventually warm up to me."

Siar'C remained silent. Perhaps he was getting tired of Cynkz's persistence. Cynkz wasn't trying to get on the star's nerves, but he couldn't help himself from teasing him a bit.

Jio-Mol's voice rang out once again. "If you two are done, I would gladly enlist Cynkz's assistance next!"

"That would be ideal," Helon said. "I can see that he is beginning to use his abilities in interesting ways. Perhaps if he goes to more worlds, and gets involved in more interesting situations, he will grow. He will become more proficient and thus will be a greater help. This feedback loop could become such that the Creator is then forced to notice."

"So it is settled then…" Sihl muttered.

"Yes. We will continue along this path for now. Depending on how things develop, we can adjust course."

"I hope we are doing the right thing…" Sihl muttered once again. Everything went quiet, giving Sihl the floor, a rare occurrence if there ever was one. "While I do appreciate that we are able to take direct action toward getting the Creator's attention, we have to remember the risk we are taking. Think of the damage that could be done if something, anything, goes wrong."

"Yes... But I sense that Cynkz is not letting my words or our admiration go to his head," Helon continued. "In fact, I can sense a growing weight in his mind and heart. His concerns seem to lie elsewhere."

"I figured as much," Anim said. "Perhaps it would do us well to consider what Cynkz wants as well? It is not the Creator's way for any of us to selfishly use any of His children for our own gains, no matter how desperate we may be."

"I am fine, truly." Cynkz looked up, and a quick hand followed it as he held it forward. Every time he gestured toward the stars, he felt a tinge silly, but eventually, he quelled the feeling and accepted that his mannerisms were natural. The Omun never seemed to pay any mind to it, at least.

"Are you sure?" Helon asked.

"Indeed. You have done much already, and have come so far, and will more than likely only venture farther. If anyone deserves to be listened to, it is you," Anim said.

"Enough of this!" Siar'C called out through the void. "Just get on with it. Eventually, he will make a mess of things, and I will be proven right. None of that can happen so long as we stay here babbling."

"Fine then," Helon said. Her patience seemed to be getting tested, but she kept her cool. Still, the slight sourness in her tone was enough that Cynkz caught on to it immediately. "If you are ready, Jio-Mol, you may take Cynkz to your world and we can continue. That is, if Cynkz is ready?"

"Of course," Cynkz said, flaring his cloak. "I am as ready as I will ever be."

"Splendid!" Jio-Mol shouted. "This is going to be great!"

The other Omun faded from view, and Jio-Mol's edges twinkled as he directed another subtle wave of light to Cynkz. A bright flash left Carros to return to watching over his world in peace.

PART 3

HALIFELL

CHAPTER 13

THE DAY BEGAN WITH AN UNUSUALLY bright morning. What many would consider a beautiful sight instead filled a certain soul with dread as his tired eyes looked outside.

Ugh… I hate mornings…

The furred being laboriously lifted himself from his bed. He took great care not to awaken his still-sleeping wife. He was finally upright, though his slumped shoulders seemed to pull down on him with an unbearable weight. The morning always reminded him of his age, as he no longer woke up naturally full of energy or exuberance. He allowed his droopy eyes to close, but the light from outside was too much—there was no more comfort to be had, and it was time to get up. He stared blankly outside for a moment longer, trying to muster the energy to continue.

It was so cloudy yesterday… Why couldn't we have another day like that? Those gray clouds seemed to cast such a soothing shadow on everything…

He finally pushed himself from the edge of his bed, carefully moving each limb to make as little noise as possible. Despite the effort, as soon as his feet landed on the floor, something heavy landed on the smooth wood with a muffled thud.

Whoops… My tail… I don't know how I always forget about it. I've had the blasted thing my whole life…

A quick look over his shoulder revealed his wife, still asleep, still wrapped up beneath her blankets. He gave out a small sigh of relief, grabbed a simple tan tunic, and quietly continued out of the room.

The hallway was dark, but fortunately, Tarsers were a race well adapted to the dark. His large brown eyes made good use of every sliver of light that seeped in between the cracks of every door and wooden board. As he walked ahead, he couldn't help but take note of every door on the way. There were seven doors on each side—fourteen in total. He noted the first door to his right and all of the flowers and plant life that had crept in from the outside. Tarsers, being naturally dexterous great climbers, preferred to build their homes high up in the many large trees that filled the forests of Halifell. It was efficient then to let the trees themselves fill in the gaps of their homes. Regular pruning was required to keep the foliage from taking over the insides of their homes but most considered this a pleasant, relaxing chore to do.

He did not, however.

Each overgrown bundle of leaves, and the many flowers that bloomed within them, was a reminder of what he had lost.

Ten of the fourteen doors were covered in glistening leaves and flowers, each one in a different stage of its life, and blooming and wilting accordingly. Each one now sat as a grave to his children. Every morning he would traipse forward, doing his best to keep his attention ahead, but the many colors of the flowers always caught his eye. He learned that it was better to ignore them and to keep moving forward, lest he get caught up in memories that brought a painful nostalgia to him. The four doors that were clean always helped to bring him back to the present. Each one gave him just that little bit of extra energy needed to step forward one more time. Through this, he always reached the end of the hall before he knew it. There was a perfectly cut circle in the floor, with a bundle of thick, healthy vines leading down through it. A quick hop and a squeeze of his paws and feet, and he made his way down to the lower floor.

It was a much more open space. More windows, more light from the morning sun passing through. Most of the items in the room were covered in makeshift tarps and blankets. His wife did well to try and keep it clean and dust-free, but their home was five stories tall, and this floor was the least important to attend to. It also merely reminded him again of things he would rather not remember. He always twitched his whiskers as he passed through. He didn't know if it was due to the dust, or if it was a habitual reaction spurred on by a deeper feeling within him. Still, he continued farther down.

He felt a sense of relief as he finally reached the kitchen. It was the one place in their home that seemed to filter the morning light in a pleasing way. He remembered when he first built the home and even remembered the pure glee he saw in his wife's eyes when he promised to build their dream home far away from the city. She provided so much input on how things should be built, and he had no issue with following any of it—the placement of the front door, the specific flowers and vines she wanted to grow through the home, the direction the many windows would face. He swore that she really didn't know what she was doing, and it must have been an accident that the kitchen turned out the way it did, but regardless, he was grateful. He was always grateful for her input.

First things first—the morning ritual went along as it always did, opening the same cabinets, pulling out the same trays and the same cups, sixteen to be exact. Once everything was set up on the circular countertop in the center of the kitchen, he went over to the stove, plucking specific leaves all along the way. A flick of some spare flintstone beneath a metal rim lit the flame on a stove. More metal linked and clacked as he rummaged through a series of meticulous pots and pans he had used countless times to brew the same teas he always did. It was a special brew consisting of leaves born from the polliflowers that the tree grew constantly. When ground up and heated, and applied to boiling water, it turned into a pink, citrusy beverage whose fumes did much for the sinuses. Even the most ailed of Tarsers would feel at least a tiny sliver of relief when breathing these fumes. It was potent enough to cure nearly any sinus or lung ailment imaginable.

Almost anything... he thought.

The illymites—the small, edible insect Tarsers all over the world of Halifell were now consuming in large numbers—unfortunately proved to be the first true obstacle for the cure-all concoction. He could remember when he first saw how profitable the creatures were. He could recall nervously spending his life's savings on acquiring as many of them as he could manage. The dread he felt from the risk he took was still palpable, and the relief he felt when it paid off even more so. They had a consistent source of food, plenty of runes to pay off their home, and their children were secure. Everything seemed to be going well, until the coughing began.

His oldest child was the first to fall ill. Within the year, half of his children had become bedridden. A few years after that, three of his children perished, and the remaining survivors were bedridden. The process was the same every time—first began the coughing, then the complete drying up of their sinuses, the withering of their whiskers, acute dehydration, and eventually death. It was a long, painful process, and nothing seemed to be able to stop it. By the time he figured out which plants and teas and concoctions could at least provide some relief from the ailment, this procession of symptoms had played out ten times. And now ten flowered graves stood within his home, each adorned with the same flowers and plants he tried to use to heal them.

Ow!

A burning sensation broke him out of his stupor. One of his whiskers seemed to have drifted into one of the teas he was mindlessly brewing. It appeared his brews were ready. He tried to begin pouring in the scorching beverages, only to find himself having to constantly push his whiskers aside. Eventually, he grew frustrated enough that he merely pulled all his whiskers together and loosely tied them back. Every morning, he tried to avoid doing it, and every morning, he eventually caved. In his own words, he thought that doing so made him look "girly." His wife would always chuckle when he said that, but he swore he was being serious. Her laughter did much to ease the pain of embarrassment he felt from having to do it.

Just as he finished pouring his tea into every cup, he could hear the pitter-patter of feet a couple of stories up.

She's finally up. That's good. I'd like to head to the market early today.

He picked up the large tray, whipped his thick tail around, and perfectly balanced his plate on top of it. A Tarser's tail may as well be a fifth limb. Many considered it the best limb, and the health and condition of one's tail often denoted their etiquette. Though, there were some who argued that taking care of one's whiskers was more important. To be honest, it was not a debate he cared much for, and he left it behind as he made his way up the vines, taking great care not to spill anything. As he made his way up, he stopped to greet his loving wife, waiting patiently for him to climb by.

"Good morning, Yuto," she mumbled.

"Good morning, Jeea," he mumbled back.

Yuto pulled away a few of his long whiskers to rub noses with his beloved, and the two shared a quick kiss before he continued up. His arm and his tail were getting tired, and he wanted to hurry and settle down on stable ground. He could hear the pitter-patter of his wife gently making her way farther down. The sounds of her moving—still as spry and capable as ever—did much to comfort Yuto.

Yuto climbed up to the top floor of his home, staring down the dark hallway once again. The steam from all of the cups of tea on his plate reflected the sparse morning light that seeped in brilliantly. He moved forward and began his morning ritual.

The first door he entered was already cracked. Little Tilly didn't like being closed off from anything. Though she was bedridden like the other children, she remained very curious and open. She was still asleep, however. Yuto could hear her strained breathing from across the room. He slowly crept in and placed her cup on a small stand right next to her bed, and left just as quickly. It would have been easier to just close the door, giving it no time to creak, but he knew better. A rough, squeaking sound followed, and he left behind him a sliver of light coming in from the hallway as he continued.

A few doors down, and he entered another room. Barkov was always loud, whether he was laughing, crying, or even when he went to the bathroom. His one remaining son almost seemed proud of the noise he made when he relieved himself. Strangely, he was a relatively quiet sleeper. He was so quiet in fact that

Jeea often worried that something had happened to him when he slept, and she would check in on him a few extra times to make sure he was okay. He was also still asleep, and Yuto quietly placed down a cup for him as well before leaving.

Just across the hall was another clear door. Sween was a very sensitive sleeper. Yuto even went so far as to quietly place his tray on the floor and carry Sween's cup in only. The excess smell and vapors from the tea, while often helpful in aiding their condition, would irritate Sween's sinuses and wake her up instantly. A quick peek through the cracked door and his daughter appeared to be asleep. Yuto gave out a sigh of relief, and he did the same for her as he did the others.

He made his way to the final door, a few doors down the hall and away from the others. Her room was actually the last one Yuto had furnished, as she was the last to be born. His youngest daughter, Niora, was fortunate enough that she was born at the tail end of Yuto's obsession with the illymites. He was grateful that she had been fed so few of them. She was the healthiest of the remaining four, but being so young meant that the symptoms of whatever ailment the illymites brought hit her particularly hard. Still, he was more than grateful that she was still alive, and to him, that was all that really mattered.

The small lump huddled under a set of light purple covers indicated that Niora was still asleep. Yuto smiled, then began to tiptoe his way in. He was quite proud of how efficiently he had performed this morning's tea-serving ritual. Each step emboldened him in a way. Despite his age, he knew he still had it.

Rrrr!

A careless step caused a particularly sensitive wooden board to squeak beneath his feet. Instantly he winced, squinting his eyes and bringing his shoulders up as he looked anxiously ahead. The tiny body beneath the covers seemed unphased, and the relief was enough to cause Yuto to sigh.

"Dad?" a tiny voice whispered out from beneath the covers.

Whoops…

"Good morning, sweety," Yuto whispered back.

"Hello. Did you… Did you make—" Niora began to cough. She rolled over, revealing her face to Yuto. Yuto hurried over, set down his tray, placed down her cup, and began to caress her. As he rubbed the short fur on her head, she started to calm down. Niora took in a deep breath and slightly opened her eyes, revealing two large and normally black orbs that shone almost crystal blue in the light.

"You're so fortunate," Yuto said as he continued to comfort his daughter. "You got your mother's eyes."

Niora smiled and closed her eyes to relax. Yuto began to pick up his tray, finally noticing he had spilled a bit of tea on the tray. Fortunately, none got on the floor, so he wouldn't be leaving behind a mess of any sort.

"You made way too much again, didn't you?" Niora muttered.

Yuto's eyes grew wide as he stopped to look at his daughter. Her eyes were closed, and she seemed ready to go back to sleep.

"No, no, not really…" Yuto smiled weakly but kept his attention on his current task. He began to feel whatever confidence he had earlier leaving him as he thoughtlessly pondered over his daughter's words. How does one comfort a child who has already seen so much death? Yuto had to admit that Jeea was better at talking about these sorts of things.

Niora continued, "It's… It's alright, Dad. It's nice to know that someone remembers them. I think that would make them happy."

A strained tensing of his lips crawled across his short snout. Yuto did everything he could to not tear up, but he could already feel some wetness gathering up at the corners of his eyes. Even his rounded glasses began to fog up. He instinctively picked himself up and held his daughter once more.

"Get some sleep, Niora. Please rest." Yuto leaned over and gave her a small peck on her forehead, right in the middle of a light brown spot in her fur. Her mother had a similar spot in her fur when she was younger, and Yuto could remember the early days of their relationship when he would lean over to give it a peck.

Niora rolled over happily under her sheets. Yuto smiled, wiped away the would-be tears, and gathered the tray of extra tea before leaving his daughter to rest.

"How were the children this morning?" Jeea was quick to greet Yuto as he made his way back down into the kitchen. Despite having greeted him in such a way countless times, she always managed to show just a bit of enthusiasm each time. Yuto always noticed her exuberance and couldn't help but smile.

"They were well, as they have been for a while now," Yuto said as he began to clean up.

Jeea, who was already in the middle of preparing several other tools and pots and pans, looked over her shoulder to look at what exactly Yuto was pouring away.

"How'd you sleep?" she said.

"Hmm?" he grumbled.

"You seem a bit more tired than usual. Did you drink any tea yourself? Get yourself some energy?"

"Mm-hmm."

Jeea stopped, dried her paws, and brushed aside her whiskers to silently watch Yuto as he continued to pour out the excess tea.

"You made too much tea again, didn't you?" she said, finally softening her smile into a more concerned expression. Yuto remained quiet, continuing his task.

"You can't blame yourself for their deaths, Yuto," Jeea continued. "There was no way for you to know any more than anyone else the effects that those bugs would have."

"No, that's no excuse." Yuto sighed. He finally stopped to place his paws on the counter, his head hung low. "I fell for the gold rush, and I got greedy. I thought we would make it big. It seemed so simple, gathering as many illymites as possible, selling as many as we could, and even eating the extra ones before they died and went bad. I pushed for us to eat them, for snacks, for breakfast, lunch, and dinner. And look where it got us. Look at what it did to our poor..."

Yuto couldn't finish the sentence. He gripped the still-wet counter's edge as he seemed to be lost in his regret. It took the soft, warm grip of his wife's pink paw to break him out of his trance.

"Yuto… It's okay. Please don't blame yourself," she whispered as she went in to wrap her arms around him. "We all make mistakes. The best thing we can do is learn and move on."

Yuto smiled and turned to hug his beloved more fully. The two rubbed their wet noses together, sharing their warm breath as their whiskers loosely brushed past each other.

"You of all Tarsers should be angry at me," Yuto whispered. "All the trouble you went through giving us so many beautiful children…"

"I could never be angry with you," Jeea whispered back.

Yuto chuckled and squeezed Jeea tightly. "I don't deserve you."

"You say that every day," Jeea said.

"I know. I just want to make sure that I never forget it. It helps to keep me grateful."

"Well, I am just as undeserving of you." Jeea leaned back, though she made sure to play a bit with Yuto's whiskers before letting go. Yuto always liked the way her short, clean coat of fur shone in the morning light. The edges lit up in the light, as if she were exuding an angelic aura. However, his attention stayed mostly on her eyes—two large dark irises that reflected a slight, crystalline blue when the light hit them just right. It usually took him remembering to adjust his own rounded glasses to get him to stop staring at her.

"Will you be heading to the market today?" Jeea asked, finally letting go and turning to return to her cleaning.

"Yeah, yeah." Yuto looked out the window once again. The city was hardly visible, even from their large home in the treetops. Despite the long trek to the city, he often reminded himself that was the point—having their own secluded haven in the calm forest was always their dream. Part of him also enjoyed the voyage. It was a peaceful way to relive his days as an adventurer.

"I'll probably travel lightly today," Yuto continued. "I've heard more than a few of the other merchants pining for repairs to their carriages and booths. I want to stay mobile today."

"Uh-huh." Jeea remained playful, but she knew full well what "traveling light" meant—Yuto was planning on barging into the merchant's guild again to plead for a ban on the illymites. Yuto knew that she knew this, and Yuto knew that she had grown used to him getting into a little bit of trouble. He was grateful to be with someone so tolerant—otherwise, he may not have a proper outlet for his frustrations.

"Just try not to make too much of a fuss today," Jeea said in a playful tone.

Yuto chuffed slightly, then began to gather his things for the day ahead. The two kept warm smiles for the rest of their morning together.

CHAPTER 14

THE TRAIL THROUGH THE FOGGY forest always went by so quickly. Yuto wondered if they were too calm and too peaceful—he could hardly remember passing through it, despite doing so nearly every morning. The cool, dark soil and countless chirps of the many critters of the impossibly tall forest always gave way to the bustle of the city well before he even took his first step onto the harsh pavement.

For a people so adept at climbing, they did not like to build high. It was far more efficient to walk most of the time, and Tarsers always appreciated an opportunity to exercise their underutilized, thin, and springy legs. The bright gray pavement led the way forward as Yuto walked past many small, dark almond structures, most of which were housing supplies or more established storefronts. The pavement eventually began to split into many different paths, with plenty of room between them for Tarsers to move back and forth.

Tarsers of all shapes and sizes could be seen making their way through the city. Most wore simple clothes and robes—anything loose that allowed one to easily move their limbs, and especially their tails, with ease. As a sign of status, some Tarsers would wear clothing with long, billowing sleeves that would drag along the ground as they moved about. If one really wished to show off, they would make sure to have these robes knitted from the finest and smoothest silks, just to show that they did not care if these clothes were dirtied, as they presumably could easily afford more. Yuto, of course, was far past the age where such ostentatious displays mattered to him. He was just fine with his much more efficient and properly fitted dark brown and bluish-gray shirt and trousers. Though perhaps the more extravagant colors were meant to help distinguish them from the more homogenous shades of brown and beige that constituted the fur of most Tarsers? The question left Yuto as quickly as it came as he trudged forward.

Many more wooden dome-shaped structures lined the path farther into the city. Here were the homes and hostels travelers would often stay at. For a mere dozen runes a night, one could have a nice stack of hay in a corner to lay on for the night. Yuto wondered how he would have managed in his youth—back when a single rune would afford you the same, as well as a free meal. Sure, it was little more than lightly seasoned porridge, but a meal was a meal, and it did much to help him and Jeea on their travels when they were younger. He pondered this thought for a little longer before snapping out of it and moving on.

Finally, he made it to the center of the city, where the great bazaar stood. Every established city on Halifell was required to have a proper market. Each vendor was required by law to be licensed, specifically for what they were selling. There were regular fees associated with these licenses, and these fees varied depending on what the vendor wanted to sell—the greater the demand, and the more inquiries there were, the more expensive the fees. Yuto took advantage of this by shifting his focus to working with tools, as most Tarsers seemed averse to working with their paws. Selling food and silk was standard fare, but the most sought-after commodity was definitely the illymites. The tiny, gelatinous, cherry-red insects seemed to breed in impossible numbers. Their lifespans were short, and they withered quickly, but when ripe, they were the prime delicacy of Tarsers all over the world. They were a relatively new discovery, seemingly discovered hardly a generation ago.

A renowned explorer had apparently found them far to the north, deep within the volcanic mountains on the edge of the continent. Tarsers were not well adapted to such a harsh environment, and many of the volcanoes were still active, so few were crazy enough to venture there. Yuto remembered his early days, when he wasn't even considered an adult, and hearing stories of the great adventurer, which inspired him to become a traveler himself. If not for the inspiration, he may well have not met Jeea. In a way, the illymites were responsible for his marriage, and his children, but they also seemed to take much from him. Whatever ailments the insects caused, it seemed rare enough that it was easy for the merchant's guild—and most Tarsers for that matter—to ignore them. Yuto despised his complicated relationship with the addictive insects. It was much easier to just cut any pondering over it short. A quick shake of his head and he returned to the present.

It was unfortunate then that nearly everyone in the market seemed to be selling illymites. A massive, domed building acting as the city's merchant guildhall sat on top of a mountain of steps at the city's center. It was a monument to Tarser architecture, bearing a number of shining, curved tree trunks spread along the four "corners" of the building. The peak of the dome was covered in stitched leaves gathered from all over the world, each one displaying a slightly different shade, though when gathered together, they all blended into a sort of messy assortment of greens and yellows that waved loosely in the wind. It was by far the largest structure in the city, and the market was the busiest right underneath it. The permits required to sell right under the guildhall were notoriously expensive. Yuto wondered how much more money he could make managing and accounting for all of these different fees—if only he were heartless, he jokingly lamented. It was the perfect place to hawk wares—namely illymites.

Yuto made his way right to the guildhall's steps. Once close enough, he was presented with a wall of towering gray steps. A number of Tarser guards stood valiantly, and evenly spread on each side all the way to the top. Unlike most of the citizen Tarsers below, the guards wore tightly fitted wood and steel armor and stood at attention holding long axes and spears in alternating order. Yuto knew most of them by name, actually, and they were far less intimidating to him as a result.

"Yuto! Hey, Yuto!"

That was a name he wasn't necessarily prepared to hear so soon, though the voice was familiar. It took a moment of stopping and peering through the crowd of furry tan bodies scurrying to and fro for him to see who was calling out to him. It was a sharp-looking Tarser with a number of dark brown diamond spots dotting his exposed fur. His bleached whiskers were braided finely and his deep blue robe shined with the brilliance of the night sky.

Ah, Attl, old friend…

Yuto smiled and waved, though he needed to nearly hop up to be seen clearly through the crowd. Yuto's small, rounded spectacles nearly bounced off of his face when he did so. As Yuto snaked and wormed his way through a sea of bodies, he reminisced about many of the adventures they shared. In fact, Yuto knew Attl even before he met Jeea, but the three of them traveled together quite a bit. It was a shame, at least in his mind, that they all decided to settle down. Yuto always wanted to go on one last venture. He found it easy enough to get into trouble, but Attl had a special talent for getting him out of it.

Yuto, after pushing his way past several obnoxiously aggressive vendors shoving the iconic cherry-red insects in his face, finally made it to Attl's humble booth.

"How are you, Attl?" Yuto said.

"I'm fine, Yuto, but I should be asking how you are," Attl responded. He was casually leaning forward on the countertop of his booth, his calm demeanor in stark contrast to the chaotic energy surrounding the two.

"How is Jeea?" Attl, composed as ever, looked at Yuto sternly. Attl always was rather serious. Yuto chalked it up to him needing to be the "mature" one in the group.

"She's doing well, as positive and chipper as ever." Yuto couldn't help but shrug a little as he said so. It was a question he had answered many times, and he felt as if his response never changed enough to warrant its asking in the first place.

Attl looked over Yuto. It was a quick gesture, but it was long enough for him to notice it and to feel slightly anxious about it.

"You're still refusing to sell illymites, I see?" Attl finally said.

"Of course," Yuto responded, almost dismissively so, as he turned his head away to look on defiantly at the rest of the market, obsessing over the creatures.

"I understand your distaste for the things, but there is a lot of money to be made. You could at least, I don't know, suck it up for a year or two, earn enough to pay off those back fees on your licenses, maybe pay off some of that debt on your home, the materials and loans you borrowed to build it? Perhaps you could even earn enough to be granted a real audience with the guild and enact some change regarding the—"

"What grounds would I have to stand on if the only way I was able to get the merchant's guild to listen to me was to depend on the very creatures I wished to ban?" Yuto snapped and squinted at Attl, who seemed caught off guard by his friend's stern response. "They could so easily dismiss me as a hypocrite, perhaps even accuse me of trying to monopolize the illymite market in some way. No, no… That would never work, friend."

"I mean, I don't think it would hurt to merely sell them for a short time. I'm not asking you or Jeea or your children to consume them yourselves—"

"Attl… You know my conscience would never allow that. Knowing that I was helping to distribute the very same things that sickened my own children, knowing that I was potentially helping to hurt others, or their children… You know all of this, Attl. We have spoken of this many times before."

"I know, I know." Attl was the first to break eye contact. Yuto looked on, but Attl seemed to need to look away, even listlessly waving a light paw as he did so. "I just worry about you two, you know? You moved all the way out into the woods, and you have to walk so far every morning just to reach the city, only to make a meager wage selling a most efficient trade."

"I don't mind the walk, Attl. In fact, it helps to keep me limber and healthy, gives my arms and legs a good workout—"

"It's not just you, I worry about, Yuto. It's Jeea, and your children as well. You have to consider what they go through as well whenever you take risks or even just take extra time to travel, or when you go to bother the guild…"

"Oh! That's right!" Yuto seemed to snap out of something. In truth, he was using his feigned forgetfulness to avoid what he saw was a difficult conversation on the horizon. "We can speak more later, Attl. I need to go see the guild." Yuto was a half-step away and moving toward the towering stairs leading up to the guildhall as he spoke. He made sure to quickly (though carelessly) wave to his friend as he left.

Attl could be heard yelling a few final words through the crowd behind him, "The market demands adaptation, Yuto! You can't just keep doing the same thing again and again! Adapt! Even if just for a bit!"

Yuto pretended to not hear his friend, though the words did ring against the inner walls of his mind.

Adapt... Adapt to what? Slowly poisoning our children? No thanks...

Something caught the corner of Yuto's eye. Among the light gray steps, the many bright beige shades of the people, and the calm, earthy colors they wore, something stood out—a strangely dark and young Tarser making good use of the shade provided by a nearby building. While most Tarser fur was primarily some shade of light brown, his was nearly all black, save for a few bright spots on his face that gave the impression of a reverse-mask. Yuto looked over to see the stranger's sharp ears twitch just as the two noticed each other. Yuto squinted, adjusted his glasses, and he was gone.

He stood and stared for a moment, wondering if he had just seen a ghost.

And now I'm seeing things? Maybe I need more sleep...

Yuto shook his head and continued his way toward the guildhall.

Yuto had made this same trip countless times. He swore that he knew every grain of stone in every step by heart, and could see imprints in the steps where he had walked before.

Perhaps those were merely silly things he would tell himself to mitigate the anxiety of having barged into the guildhall so often. It also helped that he knew many of the guards stationed outside by name.

Derf and Hettle were always stationed at the bottom steps. The two were young twins, and Yuto often had fun mixing up who he would greet first, as it always prompted a reaction from the other one. Derf was the more excitable of the two, so today Yuto felt it would be fun to greet Hettle first to get a rise out of him.

"Howdy, Hettle," Yuto said, taking his first step upward and bowing his head down slightly.

"Hello, Mr. Yuto," Hettle responded solemnly.

"Hey, Mr. Yuto! Hi!" Derf said. His excitement could be heard in the frantic clinks and clanks of his armor that he was hardly large enough to fit into.

Yuto turned his head and gave Derf a smile, a nod, and a wave before continuing.

Farther up the mighty steps was another face he recognized. Karo was a diligent guard, always quite serious and straightforward. It was perhaps the reason why he was stationed above Derf and Hettle, and within earshot, no less. It made it easy for Karo to ensure the inexperienced twins stayed in line and on duty.

"Karo," Yuto said through a stern nod.

"Yuto," Karo responded, slightly tipping his head, though keeping his gaze set forward and out toward the city below.

It was always easy to tell when he was reaching Maiya's station—it was around here that his knees would finally begin to remind him of his age. Still, he was too far to quit now. This was considered the point of no return for him.

"Hello Maiya, how are you today?" Yuto said. It was then that he noticed he was still carrying the same smile he had at the bottom of the steps, as his cheeks started to ache as well.

"You're a bit late today, aren't you, Mr. Haelsker?" Maiya said. She was always so formal, even for a guard, yet she felt comfortable enough to speak so straight-forwardly with Yuto. It used to catch him off guard constantly, but he had long since grown used to it. He even enjoyed it now.

"Well, I stopped to speak with an old friend, that's all," Yuto said, still moving forward as he spoke. He caught a glimpse of her smiling from the corner of his eye before she returned to her position. He was high enough now that he could turn around and get a good look at the horizon. He was always tempted to do so, but he knew that if he stopped now, it would be incredibly difficult to begin again. Besides, he knew that he would get a good look at the scenery on the way down.

Tarsers didn't sweat, but they did exude any excess heat from their pink wrists, paws, and feet. Their bellies and the underside of their tails—areas that had very little fur compared to the rest of their bodies—would also release heat as well. As Yuto neared the top, he could feel each and every one of these parts of his own body burning up. He swore he could see the very tips of distant volcanoes from this high up, though he knew this was false. The northern volcanoes were too far away to be seen, even from there. Still, he often wondered just how anyone could go venturing there. Tarsers were not well adapted to heat of any sort.

"Halt, citizen!" A boisterous voice seemed to call down from the sky above. A quick glance upward revealed it was just another guard standing alone at the top of the mountain of steps.

"Hi Rackel," Yuto responded.

"You shall address me properly, citizen—First Sergeant Rackel, Chief Guardsmen of the Southeastern Division of the Merchant's Hall."

Yuto finally reached the final step and took a moment to rest and look at the guard accosting him.

"Hi Rackel, how are you doing today?"

The guard merely sighed, though he maintained his tight posture as he towered nearly a full head's length above Yuto.

"Hi Yuto," Rackel said, finally caving in to Yuto's casual demeanor. "I presume you are here to bother the guild masters again? If you're here to ask for another loan, you may be disappointed."

"No, no Rackel, but what do you mean? What's going on?"

"An eastern diplomat has arrived, just in time for a bit of a crisis—apparently some unknown ne'er-do-well has been posting propaganda criticizing the illy-mites in the form of crude posters all over the city."

"Any suspects? Hopefully, I am not one."

"Tch." Rackel sneered, shook his head, then looked back at Yuto. "I know it was not you. The suspect must have done it in the dark hours of the morning, and I know you have to walk a long ways just to reach the town. If I had to guess, you arrived not long ago this afternoon."

"True, but…" Yuto reached a thin, pink paw to his whiskers, stroking them curiously. "Who is this diplomat? What is going on?"

"Well, not that it's the business of a commoner to know such things, but apparently a new trade deal is being set between the western and eastern quadrants. The diplomat is specifically from the mid-western quadrant, looking to establish a proper trade route overseas with us. Illymites may soon become a world-wide commodity—"

"Ah! Perfect timing! Maybe a foreigner's perspective is precisely what's needed!"

"Wait! Yuto! I can't allow you to—"

It was too late. Yuto, despite his age, could be fleet of foot and quick of wit when motivated. The massive oak doors leading in were cracked even, allowing the slippery Tarser to worm his way in and make his way for the meeting room. A few odd looks, and even more stairs, did little to deter Yuto as he barged his way into a final room near the back of the building. A final kick against hardwood had the Tarser now facing a room full of shocked faces. The room was near the top of the domed structure, noticeable by the rounded ceiling high above. The massive leaves that covered the dome's crown wafted a constant, fresh scent of nature into the room. There were no less than eight circular windows that were evenly spread across the room's walls that did well to light the many faces sitting within the room. Yuto swore there were new people in the guildhall every time he visited, as he didn't recognize most of the faces now staring at him. Some of them had exotic, peach-colored fur. Others possessed striking dark patterns that accentuated their expressions. All of them wore complex outfits, far more elaborate than most of the Tarsers walking the streets below. Many layers of silk and shining threads and glistening gold and silver laces and jewelry gave their every movement an air of luxuriance. Foreign wealth permeated the air.

"I heard about the posters!" Yuto exclaimed. "The illymites—people are finally beginning to see how dangerous they are! Surely this is a sign we should at least consider cutting back on their distribution? Maybe more research is needed to see—"

"Yuto!" A deep voice echoed through the room, across a large, shining table, and past several dozen faces. It was a particularly tall and wide Tarser dressed complexly. Yuto always found himself staring for an extra moment at him, trying to parse the layers of cloth and buckles that covered his otherwise unimpressive body.

"Senator! Good senator! The posters, I heard—"

"I could have sworn Rackel was on duty," the senator mumbled, loudly enough to interrupt Yuto. He turned to another Tarser, who was much slimmer and wore his own assortment of layered clothing, though their design and make were clearly foreign. The leafy green sleeves and dull orange under-clothing clashed with the foreign Tarser's pink paws in an eye-catching way.

The senator continued, "I am so sorry, your lordship. I was certain our guards were not entirely incompetent. Yuto here is a regular nuisance, a recognizable face in the community that should have been easy to notice and even easier to prevent from intruding.”

“Ah, it is fine, good sir.” The foreign Tarser seemed amused more than anything, speaking in a light, hushed tone as he smiled. “Perhaps it is for the best. I could use a break from everything. If you don't mind, I would much prefer to continue this discussion tomorrow.”

“O-of course, your lordship.”

The senator and the foreigner shared a quick bow. The senator was the first to get up, even moving over to help pull out the foreigner's seat and gently guide him out of the room. As they passed, the foreigner smiled at Yuto and nodded. Yuto reflexively bowed and looked away. Quiet footsteps were soon overwhelmed by countless whispers from a number of helpers and advisors swarming him. The sharp nails of their feet clicked against the ceramic floor as they faded into the distance.

“Yuto!” The senator's deep voice seemed to echo across the room, and was powerful enough to rattle the wood making up the dome's walls. “Why? Why do you always do this?”

Yuto nervously rubbed his paws together. “I guess I interrupted something important…”

The husky senator clenched his tiny fists and stamped his slightly less tiny foot before growling his words at the intruder. “Important?! That was Ambassador Torril! Head of the entire western trades division! We are on the brink of establishing a true overseas trade route! Illymite trade will be through the roof, and our shabby little capital could very well be the first to take advantage of it!”

"That sounds horrible!" Yuto reflexively blurted out his response. Before he even finished his words, he realized his mistake. He was beginning to think Attl had a point about him—without Jeea or Attl around to bail him out or guide him, it seemed he couldn't help but act out.

"Horrible?! What do you—ugh..." The senator finally relaxed his tensed muscles and looked away to rub the bridge of his nose. All was silent as he slowly lurched his way back to his seat at the end of the large oak table. It seemed everyone else was too afraid to potentially interrupt the senator.

The senator finally plopped into his oversized, comfy seat and glared right at Yuto. "I know of your situation, Yuto. One does not go about borrowing so many risky loans without word of them spreading. I know your family is struggling, and I am truly sorry about your children, but," the senator sat himself upright in his seat, taking a deep breath but never breaking eye contact, "there is not enough evidence to say that illymites are that much of a concern to the greater populace. Most everyone else seems to be having no issues with the creatures. There is no real case to be made against them, I'm afraid. What happened to you and your children... Truly, I am sorry, but it is just unfortunate luck on your part. We cannot risk our entire economy because of that. There just haven't been that many cases of the creatures causing harm or death—"

"But there *are* other cases, no?" Yuto interrupted, once again speaking reflexively and without thought.

A sneer cut its way across the senator's snout. He clenched his fist once again and barely kept himself from slamming the table. "We don't have time for this—guards! Rackel! Where is everyone?!"

Finally, a round of heavy steps clamored their way toward the room. Rackel, as well as Derf, Hettle, and several other guards appeared.

"Arrest this nuisance," the senator continued, "and tighten up the security here. Yuto Haelsker is henceforth banished from the guildhall, and the market, until I decide otherwise."

"What?! B-but senator—"

"No, Yuto, there's no talking your way out of this one. That will be all."

A feeling of dread weighed down on Yuto in that instance. It was as if a giant stone block had been dropped on his chest, and his heart was the first thing to burst. His mind raced as he wondered about what he would do now. Other than offering trades and services at the market, there weren't many ways for a Tarser to make a living. Perhaps he could sell himself to the miner's guild, but he knew his old body was insufficient for such work. His mind went blank as he ran out of options and struggled to soak in the ramifications of his reckless outburst.

"Come on, Yuto, let's get you out of here," Rackel said. He placed a soft paw on the old Tarser's shoulder and gently began to push him away. Yuto's head remained low as he dragged himself away.

Yuto stood at the bottom of the guildhall steps. He had kept his eyes toward the ground all the way down, and only realized just then that he had forgotten to at least soak in the scenery from up high. He wasn't in a good enough mood to enjoy it anyway, but the thought of missing out on a nice sunset before heading home only added to the sting of his situation.

He could feel the guards that escorted him out still watching him. Yuto knew that they were only doing their jobs, but he still felt a tinge of betrayal from them.

I should have known... They are, in fact, little more than light acquaintances. Still... it would be nice to know that someone, anyone, other than myself felt this way. Jeea supports me no matter what I do, which I love, but... I could never expect her to come out here and risk anything speaking out against everyone. It's also not fair of me to expect anything more from Attl. He has looked out for me for years, me and Jeea... And worse yet, I'm probably going to need his help again... How shameful...

Yuto took in a deep breath, soaking in the cool dusk air, and prepared himself for a long walk home.

That was when he noticed him again—the same young, dark, and mysterious Tarser peering at him from the shadows. If not for the orange light of the late evening glistening off of his eyes, Yuto very well may have missed him. Tarsers were not particularly furtive people, yet this youth was proving to be an exception. It was strange that no one else seemed to take notice of him. Tarsers were in fact hypersensitive to their surroundings, yet Yuto once again felt alone in his awareness of something. Frustration welled up in his chest. The old Tarser decided he had finally had enough shenanigans for the day and decided to take action once again.

"Hey! You!" Yuto called out. The guards had already made their way back up the steps, and there were not many other citizens walking about near the guildhall. Yuto's voice cut clearly through the air.

The strange young Tarser seemed unphased and actually smiled. Yuto was prepared for a chase of some sort—perhaps the stalker would try to run away since he had clearly been discovered. Yuto, tired as he was, felt fully prepared to chase after him.

Yuto quickly stomped his way over, making sure to keep his heels raised and his weight on his toes, ready to spring forth. It was strange then that Yuto's speed got him nearly face-to-face with the stranger quicker than he expected. They did not seem intent on running away.

"I can call the guards, you know!" Yuto exclaimed, loudly enough to get the attention of the handful of Tarsers still nearby. "I don't know what you're after, but I—"

"There is no need for that, friend. I am not looking for trouble." The young Tarser's voice seemed to betray his appearance. It was clear, concise, and carried a certain something to it—the weight of someone much more experienced than a youth should be. There was a strange duality to his voice—it was as clear and sharp as ice, yet somehow smooth and warm, the way a loving family member might speak to someone close.

"Oh, well, at least you're friendly." Yuto expressed quick relief in a much-needed breath. He relaxed his thin arms and crossed them, nestling his paws within the folds of fur lining their upper half. "I don't think

I've seen you around the city, or the guildhall for that matter, before. What's your angle?"

"I do not really have an angle, but I am definitely looking for help." The dark Tarser, still sitting under the shade of a wide alleyway, was looking about as if lost in thought. The orange specks of the dusk light bouncing off of his eyes revealed quite a bit about his expression.

He turned his head back up and looked at Yuto before continuing, "I have been looking for someone to help me. I have been trying to convince others of the dangers of illymites. I even made some crude posters and hung them up around town, though that did not seem to do much—"

"Oh! So that was you! Splendid!" Yuto couldn't help but clasp his paws together and smile. He did so with so much force that he needed to immediately reach up and readjust his glasses before they fell to the ground. "I too have been trying to convince at least some of these fools that these little creatures are not safe to consume. But no one will listen… I must say, it is interesting to see someone so young also carry such wisdom and initiative. Actually, most youths seem to be quite hungry and ambitious, ready to pounce on selling a hot commodity. What's your name, stranger?"

The dark Tarser stepped forward into the honey-hued light of the setting sun, carrying with him a warm smile. "You can call me Linx. It is a pleasure to meet you, good sir."

CHAPTER 15

"Linx?" Yuto reached up again to scratch at the pointed, bony tip of his chin tucked neatly beneath his copious whiskers. "That is an interesting name, certainly not one I have ever heard before. Family name?"

"It is not one you would have ever heard of." Linx seemed bashful, going so far as to raise a healthy, almost tan-pink paw to his own head to scratch it. "We, um, live quite far away from any cities, and in the forest—"

"Ah! Me too! The peace and quiet of the forests and fog is like nothing else, isn't it?"

"Of course, and the view of the night sky is at its best away from all the lights and noise."

"We are two of a kind then, it seems." Yuto opened up his posture, doing his best to appear friendly. Linx remained still, and quite calm and disciplined looking. "So, what exactly are you trying to do? Do you have a means of convincing the good people of the dangers of the insects?"

"Indeed, I think I do—"

"Really?! I have to hear this." Yuto, finally becoming situationally aware, quieted himself down and moved in closer to speak more privately. "I must know. What sort of plan do you have cooking?"

Linx remained still and even adopted a stern look as he began to recall his knowledge. "I have seen precisely where the insects come from. I have seen how they are born, how they live, and how they mature. I have seen what they consume, and indeed it proves that they are a potent health hazard. Their queens—large, bulbous, and putrid red things—if people saw what they are, and how they operate, they may think twice before consuming any more of their offspring."

"Wait..." Yuto playfully squinted at Linx, a failed attempt to hide his skepticism. "You've been to the mountains up north? That is ... a lengthy journey, to say the least, and there isn't much up there save for volcanoes and lava and rocky cliffs and danger and excitement and..." Yuto stopped, catching himself smiling wider and wider as he spoke. Linx seemed a bit confused, but Yuto didn't mind. This was a feeling he had not experienced in a long time, and it was a perfect replacement for the dread he was feeling just moments earlier. "I sense an adventure coming along. Am I right?"

Linx raised a curious brow before continuing, "In truth, I expected you to be a bit more skeptical. I suppose I was right to think you would be the perfect partner—"

"Ah! So we're 'partners' now?" A mischievous smile stretched across the old Tarser's snout.

"Oh, well, I did not mean anything by it, I just—"

"Linx, it is fine! It's fine. I am merely messing with you. 'Yanking your tail,' as the youngsters like to say."

"Oh… I apologize."

"You are far too polite, perhaps too polite for your age, and your own good. But I think that's a good thing, especially for someone so young. When I was your age… well, all I'll say is that I could have been a bit more careful and thoughtful, as you are, Linx."

"Well, thank you very much, Yuto. That means a lot."

"So!" Yuto clapped his pink paws together, his smile still carrying on as it pushed his cheeks and his whiskers skyward. "If there is any way I could help you, just ask, young Linx. I am truly motivated to put an end to this current mercantile madness that these wretched bugs have caused."

"I noticed you are a craftsman." Linx pointed (politely) toward Yuto's loose belt, now mostly a series of leather loops missing their contents. If not for the odd chisel and screwdriver, and some other tool that even Yuto had forgotten about, it would have been difficult to discern the accessory as a tool belt.

"Ah, yes, I am, though such a trade makes few runes compared to selling those wretched bugs."

"Well, I believe that skill may be most useful. I wish to commission you to build a cage for one of the super queens—"

"By all in Halifell—that sounds like a grand time!" Yuto's excitement got the better of him once again, and his voice seemed to echo against the alley walls and into the street. "Whoops. Perhaps we should go somewhere more appropriate and discuss this. I'm not sure if this is the place for such talks."

"What did you have in mind?"

"Well…" Yuto stretched his back and readjusted his belt as he sucked in a heaving breath. Linx seemed to be catching on that Yuto was playful, and even expressed his slight annoyance with his raised eyebrows and half-shut eyes—the first time Linx acted his age in Yuto's eyes. "The way I see it, if you've got nowhere else to be, you could stay with me and my wife for a bit. We could discuss the payment and the parameters for what it is you need. We have plenty of wood and other materials at my place as well."

"Very well then." Linx gave a polite bow before continuing, "Lead the way, good sir."

⌘

Yuto found a new energy in his step as he led the youth forward. The sky was covered in a deep, reddish-orange and dotted with many long, overstretched clouds that reflected deep violets and grays against the dusk light. The many brighter coats of most of the Tarsers filling the streets away from the guildhall did well to reflect the twilight. Linx, being a rare, black-coated specimen, stood out then—his coat was not just dark, but appeared to be similar to the night sky, hardly reflecting any light. Yuto admitted his childish fascination with the look, even going so far as to mention that he thought Linx's coat looked "cool." Linx didn't have much to say about it, merely smiling and mumbling a quick "thanks" in response. Yuto could feel his interest in the young Tarser's ideas boiling over, yet he was disciplined enough to hold back. Wanting to save the more important discussion of Linx's commission for later, he tried to talk of other, lighter things. It proved to be quite the struggle, however, as he was not able to get the stranger to open up much.

He noticed that Linx never started any sort of discussion, instead choosing to be reserved, to sit and wait for Yuto to move the conversation forward. Yuto would ask about the youth's favorite food, and he would shyly mention some simple recipe his mother apparently used to make. Yuto would ask about his mother, only for Linx to merely mention that she was an alchemist of some sort. Yuto found this especially interesting, as alchemy was long ago considered mostly pseudoscience, yet there were a number of far-removed Tarsers in more primitive communities that still practiced it. Still, Linx was not very forthcoming. Yuto, having the social awareness to move on, decided to ask about the youth's father. Linx was not very forthcoming about that either, merely stating that he was "once an explorer, but a grave mistake led to his downfall." Yuto couldn't help but rub his chin and ponder the boy's words—a strange choice of words by all accounts. *Downfall? Really?* Yuto thought to himself. Yuto wanted to ask about the mysterious father's exploits, hoping to relate to some of his adventures, but Linx's down-turned eyes said everything he needed to know, and he decided to move on to other things.

Yuto wondered about his own children as he spoke with Linx. There was still quite a bit of a walk before they made their way out of the city, but the end was in sight. As one ventured farther away from the guild-hall, the buildings became much smaller and shorter, taking up less and less of the horizon and disappearing beneath the lines of trees and fog that took up much of the distant landscape. The rising wall of dark sage leaves and bushy tree tops was a calming enough view that Yuto's mind began to wander. None of his children had yet even reached puberty, with only a few reaching their early teenage years. Despite having a healthy number of offspring, he had no experience dealing with anyone Linx's age just yet. It was a good enough opportunity to try and experiment, to maybe learn just how to speak with a young Tarser burgeoning on true adulthood. Though, even he had to admit that he was struggling to get a flowing conversation going. He couldn't bring himself to blame any of it on Linx, as the two had just met. Part of him wished Jeea was there—she was always so good at dealing with young-sters, even during the hardest of times. He could see Linx looking at him quizzically from the corner of his eye, hardly paying attention to what was in front of them as they walked.

I suppose some things never really change. Even after all this time… What would I do without Jeea? Without Attl? I suppose I would not have lasted long in this world otherwise—

"Yeeow!"

A woman's screech pierced Yuto's large, round ear. His shoulders shot up and his head dragged down as he winced, as if trying to cover himself from the painful cry. A quick peek to his right revealed that Linx was standing oddly—he had a leg raised and his own arms and shoulders up.

"Hey!" another voice, this time a huskier male voice, barked toward them. "What did you do, you little moron?!"

"W-what happened?" Yuto called out.

"It was an accident," Linx said, calmly as ever. "I sincerely apologize, madam. I did not mean to—"

"You stepped on my wife's tail!" The male Tarser was beyond reasoning. Linx's usual polite charm was not going to be of any use here, and Yuto knew it. The angry Tarser was practically shoving his snout into Linx's eye, snarling all the while. Linx remained remarkably calm as he tried to de-escalate the situation. A crowd began to form around the group. Waves of murmurs and mumbles followed as hushed gossip swarmed them all. The wife sat huddled not far from the others and seemed to nearly blend into the sea of beige and tan bodies. As far as Yuto could tell, she seemed alright, but he knew that wouldn't be enough to calm down her more aggressive husband.

"It was an accident, sir," Yuto said, traipsing forward carefully as he lightly waved his paws, mimicking some of Linx's movements. "He's just a young Tarser from the woods. He didn't mean—"

"It don't matter where he's from," the husband snarled. "All Tarsers know how disrespectful it is t'step on someone's tail!"

Everyone settled their mumbling and formed a perfect circle around Linx and the angry Tarser.

"This is ridiculous," Yuto exclaimed. "I refuse to let this stupid, outdated ritual commence."

"One way or another, someone's gettin' beat!" The angry Tarser turned, his broad, squared shoulders now directed at Yuto. "How's about I start with you then, old man? You wanna take the boy's place?!"

"Come on, Berhl!" A familiar voice wormed its way through the crowd. Before long, Attl was quickly stepping forward, trying to get in between Yuto and his potential assailant. "It's late, everyone is tired. Just drop it and we can all go home."

"This could be fun!" Berhl smiled and held his arms out, as if ready to embrace the coming chaos. "I'll gladly kick three a'yer asses if I need ta."

Attl merely crossed his arms and chuckled, much to Berhl's dismay. "There won't be any fighting here today, Berhl. If it was anyone else, maybe… but you were always easy to deal with."

"What?!" Berhl's shoulders shot up, his fists clenched and his sharp teeth glistened in the late day's light. He was more than ready to pounce on Attl. "What're you talkin' about?! How about I just start with—"

"Here, you can have this."

Attl swiftly reached beneath a flap in his shirt and tossed out a heavy pouch that landed at Berhl's feet. A satisfying plap followed the quick brush of dirt on the stone road as little red bodies could be seen wriggling about from the pouch's half-open top.

Illymites! Yuto thought, his eyes transfixed on the insects.

"You leave us alone, and you can have 'em," Attl said. His voice seemed heavy, weighty, and confident, as if he had done this before. He even crossed his arms and

looked down his snout at Berhl, who was equally fixated on the pouch as everyone else.

Everyone was quiet, even Berhl. It seemed as if he
needed an extra moment to process the offer. Perhaps
he could have just swiped the bag and continued his
assault, anyway. If not for the crowd watching, he very
well may have done just that. Berhl snarled a final time
and quickly bent down to snatch the bag and stomp
over to his wife. Berhl put an arm around his wife
and began to lead her away, but made sure to turn his
head and spit at Linx's feet before disappearing into
the crowd. An air of disappointment seemed to weigh
heavily on everyone as they dispersed.

Attl sighed, finally releasing his arms from their
crossing to address his friend. "How do you always get
into such trouble, Yuto? And worse, you dragged this
poor boy into it."

"To be fair," Linx interjected, "it was my own fault.
I made the mistake of stepping on another's tail."

"Well, you're young, so mistakes are to be expected,"
Attl said. "Though you seem awfully polite and wise for
someone your age. What's your name?"

"I am Linx. It is nice to meet you, Attl."

"Nice to meet you! Though I don't think we've ever
met. How do you know my name?"

"I, uh, heard Yuto mention it once earlier."

"I see. Speaking of which," Attl turned to Yuto,
placing a soft paw on his shoulder, "what's going on,
Yuto? What happened at the guild? I've heard some
things from the guards. Should I be worried?"

"You know, it is actually good timing that you happened along when you did," Yuto said.

"I see that. I came just in time to help you avoid a pummeling—"

"No, no, not that! Linx here has provided me with the most interesting commission!"

"Oh, boy…" Attl released his paws, only to bring them to his own face. He, too, possessed a healthy bundle of whiskers that he had to spend a second working his arms around in order to properly rub at his temples.

"It's not as bad as you think it's going to be, Attl! Linx has information on the illymites! Their origins, their habits, and proof that they should be banned immediately!"

"What?" Attl's shock seemed enough to cause him to jump out of his own skin. "I just helped you out of one jam, and now you're looking to cause more trouble? The guards told me about your predicament. Now is not the time to be testing fate like this."

"I disagree!" Yuto said, loudly. "Now is the perfect time to *work* with fate! Lady fate has granted me, no, all of us, a perfect opportunity!"

"You seem awfully confident in this, and this boy— er, I mean, in Linx. No offense, Linx."

"None taken," Linx said through a warm smile.

Yuto turned to Attle. "Are you doing anything tonight? I would very much like to get your input on everything."

"I mean… not necessarily. I was hoping for a peaceful night, but now I'm worried about you, and Jeea, and how you're going to pay your bills, and… I'll just come along. I'd be unable to live it down if I didn't help you and Jeea through whatever this is going to inevitably turn into."

"Perfect!" Yuto jumped with joy, his fur and whiskers waving in the wind, their frayed edges diffusing the light pleasantly, casting a rounded shadow that danced along the stone ground with him. "I'll explain along the way. Come on you two."

The night had long since come, yet the fog and the forests remained. Halifell only had two moons, but that was all it took to set the grounded mist covering the forest floors ablaze with a cool, burning light. The dark, mossy green treetops reflected the silvery moonlight and could do little to stop it from reaching the ground below. Yuto always loved the walk home on such nights—the slight dew in the air and the chilled moonlight mist made for a pleasant trip.

It wasn't long before the trio were sitting on the bottom-most floor of Yuto's spacious abode. There were far too many seats and cushions, and things were in general disarray, but it didn't take Jeea and Yuto long to scurry about and organize things to make for a presentable meeting space. It was a big, square room dotted with numerous lanterns that covered everything in a pleasing, soft hue—its warm yellow shine provided a nice contrast to the silvery gray and blue of the moonlit fog outside. A circular, dark wooden table was pulled into the center of the room, and around it were several large, cushioned seats with plenty enough space for even the largest Tarser to plop down and not accidentally pinch their tail in the process. Yuto himself sat at the side closest to the counters, making up a humble little preparation corner where Jeea moved back and forth, getting everyone's drinks together. He was still quite a distance away, however, but he could at least look over his shoulder and easily speak with and direct Jeea, or spring up and offer assistance if needed. Attl sat on his favorite blue cushion to Yuto's right, nestled perfectly within a nook that had been worn into it. It seemed to be a seat that was generally untouched, save for when the sharp-eyebrowed Tarser came to visit. Linx decided to sit across from Yuto, at the end closest to a large, square window that let in plenty of reflected fog light from outside. Every so often, the young, dark Tarser would peer up and out the window, trying to look at the stars. Yuto chuckled, knowing that it must have been difficult to see anything from below the treetops. He wondered if he should offer to take the young Tarser up top after their discussion so he could stargaze more easily.

"I'm still not sure I believe it." Attl's cool tone echoed with a nice rhythm through the spacious area. It was like a soft, ethereal paw reached out to embrace the group when he spoke.

"Well, it makes enough sense if you think about it." Yuto readjusted himself in his own worn, pink cushion. The sound of fur lightly rubbing against itself and against the frayed edges of the seat as he moved made a subtle, cozy brushing sound. He couldn't help but wiggle back and forth a few extra times, making sure to get his body and his whiskers in just the right position, achieving maximum comfort. "Every swarm comes in from the north, the same general direction as the volcanic regions. These swarms also seem to move and migrate at all times of the year, regardless of the weather. The only place on Halifell that anyone knows of that has consistent enough weather, separate from everywhere else, would have to be the volcanic regions. Fresh illymites also tend to have faint traces of ash and gray dirt on them. It's one of the reasons why we have to wash them off before consumption. Even Mitus DeTrell first discovered them from up north, though he never specifically said where he discovered them, or how he apparently woke them up—"

A sharp scuffling of bristly fur on a smooth, barely used lime-green cushion caught Yuto's ear in a twitch. Linx had finally turned his attention away from the night sky to partake in the discussion. His young eyes were wide and curious looking and reflected the warm light inside brilliantly.

"Mitus DeTrell?" Linx asked.

"Yes," Yuto continued. "He was an old explorer, well known for venturing deep into places he shouldn't. If an uncharted part of the sea frightened most Tarsers, he would be the first to sail headfirst into it, and bring back news that it was merely a collection of whirlpools and storms. If legends spread about an unexplored part of a southern continent, said to be filled with gold and silver ruins and undead spirits watching over it, he would form a one-Tarser expedition and head straight into the heart of the place."

"What did he find there?" Linx asked, in an excited, almost childish way.

"Well, that time not much." Yuto smiled, and scratched at one of his ears, its twitching casting a quick shadow across the table. "Some worried he had brought back disease and ill omens with him, but he swore he saw nothing but shining vines and mud and some rather mundane insects and the like."

"When did he discover the illymites?"

"Well, that was near the end of his career. He brought a large haul of them back with him after his final voyage to the north. At first, no one believed him when he said he had accidentally awoken a swarm of the critters, but lo-and-behold, by the next summer there they were—an army of glittering red blobs weaving through the air on the outskirts of civilization."

Attl leaned forward, resting an elbow to one side on a knee that was embedded in his cushioned seat, stroking his whiskers gingerly. "He made quite a killing off of the insects, being the first in on the market after all. He swiftly retired, and no one knows where exactly he ended up. It's been several hundred years, and illymites are now sold all over the continent."

"Worse yet," Yuto said, leaning forward himself to look down at his pink paws now clasped together, "the guild is in talks with foreign ambassadors, trying to set up trade routes across the sea... before long everyone the world over will be consuming the things, dooming themselves and their children to their ill effects..."

"I still do not think we have any hope of changing anyone's minds on the creatures." Attl leaned back; a satisfying plop echoed out from the action. "The things are nearly ubiquitous with runes. They may as well be the new currency. Also, Yuto, Mitus was your inspiration—he was the sole reason you took up exploring in the first place. Do you really wish to tarnish his legacy?"

"Eh." Yuto shrugged, his large, brown eyes nearly glazing over as he performed the casual gesture. "He made so many runes and retired well, and more than likely died doing what he loved. I doubt he would have much to complain about, all things considered. And legacy doesn't matter anyway, as lives are at stake."

"Linx," Attl turned his attention toward the young Tarser, who was now paying close attention to everything going on, "what precisely is so bad about illymites? I know that Yuto and Jeea have suffered because of them, but cases are rare. Why do you wish to expose them, if such a thing is even possible?"

Linx took a moment to think. He sat his oddly dark pink paws in his lap and looked down solemnly toward the ground. Even Jeea seemed interested, as Yuto heard the sudden stop of dishes and kitchenware clacking together to listen. "I have been to the mountains up north. I have seen them—the illymites—up close. I have seen their life cycles, from birth to death. I have seen their super queens, and what they feed her, and I have seen what the creatures subsist on exclusively. Deep in the volcanoes, about as close as a living thing can get to hot magma without burning up, where the ash is hottest and least refined, they eat. The tiny males will often gorge themselves on this ash, and bring it to their queen, to eject the contents of their bright red bulbs into her. As the queen grows, she eventually becomes too big and bulbous to move on her own, and the smaller worker illymites will bury her in the volcanic ash, continuing to feed her. Needless to say, trace amounts of volcanic ash remain in their systems even after they migrate. This ash is ultimately what you all are consuming, and in large quantities it collects inside of your lungs, causing irreparable damage to one's respiratory system—"

"Irreparable?" Yuto didn't mean to interrupt, but the dejected thought seemed to slip out without him knowing. Attl looked down and away, though Linx kept his gaze forward, giving the old Tarser a forlorn look. Yuto found it strange for a Tarser so young to be capable of such a sad expression, the sort one would expect from a world-weary veteran, perhaps.

"Yes, unfortunately. I am sorry, Yuto." Linx continued, "Though there is a remedy capable of relieving at least some of the damage—"

"Truly?!" Yuto nearly flew from his seat, his own wide eyes meeting Linx's who now sat surprised at the old Tarser's outburst. "W-what is it? I'll try anything!"

"The polliflowers, when heated and mixed into an herbal tea, create particularly potent fumes that help to break down small and unrefined material, such as grains or ash."

"Polliflower? Are you sure? I have been making tea with them for ages and have been giving my children polliflower tea for a while now. I've noticed it does help a little bit, but... well, it doesn't seem terribly effective."

"The key is to use them while they're still in the bud, preferably just before they bloom."

"Can you be more specific?" Yuto couldn't help but squint and play with his whiskers, all while leaning on a bony elbow on his crossed legs.

Linx smiled, then obliged the old Tarser. "You need to watch the tips of the bud. Pluck them once they begin to turn bright in color, but before the fronds actually split. Quickly grind the entire bud and use it to make the tea. Make sure the water used is boiling hot—the more fumes, the better."

"You know," Attl's cushion pressed into the wooden floorboards as he leaned forward himself, forcing a scratching creak to echo throughout the room, "you're awfully knowledgeable for one so young. Where did you learn this?"

"Ah, well, my mother was a botanist."

"You have quite the family, young one," Attl said, rubbing his chin and sharing a curious look with Linx. "An explorer for a father, and a competent botanist for a mother. Where did she practice?"

"Well, she was, what would you call them, a naturalist? She learned the trade from her mother, and her mother from her mother's mother, and so on. Considering our family has always traveled and chosen to live far away from the hustle and bustle of civilization, I suppose there was no other way for them to learn."

Yuto scratched his chin, flared a whisker, and chimed in, "Most 'naturalist' remedies are junk, unfortunately. We have schools and licenses for a reason."

"I am inclined to agree with you," Linx said, "but I noticed you said 'most,' not all."

"Clever, young Linx, and that is true, I suppose… I must say, I wish my head was on as straight as yours back in my youth! It would have saved me a lot of trouble."

"It would have saved all of us a fair bit of trouble, and our adventures would have been incredibly boring," Jeea said playfully from the other side of the room. Attl immediately laughed, his crossed arms bobbing up and down as he expressed his amusement. Yuto merely scratched his head, but the look on his face said it all—he knew they were right, and couldn't deny it. Linx chuckled himself, shaking his head and leaning back in his seat.

A harsh clearing of his throat readied Attl to continue the conversation proper. "So, what exactly do you wish to do, Linx? We've practically talked the night away and have yet to even discuss your commission or the payment—"

"Oh!" Linx sprang up as if remembering something important. "I wanted to commission Yuto to craft a proper cage for a super queen. Super queens are generally quite fragile and would need special accommodations in order to be transported over any significant distance. I would love to bring one of these queens back to show the populace, and let them decide for themselves if they wish to continue consuming the excretions of the disgusting things."

"Hah! I'll drag this supposed 'queen' like a lowly knave straight to the guildhall myself!" Yuto said proudly.

"A knave? Really?" Jeea said, placing a discerning paw on her hip as she leaned against a spotless counter.

"Yep. A knave!" Yuto said, his pride intact as his voice boomed across the spacious room.

"Ugh, you're going to wake the kids," Jeea chided. "Why can't you be calmer, more polite, like our young friend Linx here?"

"Because that would be boring," Yuto said through a proud smirk.

"Boring would be nice for a change," Attl said. "We could use the peace and quiet. But I'm curious, Linx, what is your offer? You're asking for quite a lot here."

"Oh well, I have some runes here." Linx sat back, reaching beneath a flap in his fitted shirt. "I do not have much need for runes, so you are free to everything I have here if it is sufficient."

Linx calmly retrieved a hefty pouch from his shirt and tossed it onto the table. A satisfying clunk of stony material followed as several rows of small, finely carved rocks that reflected an odd color, caught between gray and violet—glistened as the soft lamplight bounced off of their many gold and silver etchings.

"My word!" Attl said, slowly pushing himself forward to get a better look at the runes.

"Astounding!" Yuto said, stamping an excited foot forward as he was compelled to dart ahead and examine the runes more closely.

Jeea gasped. "H-how much is all that?! How did you get a hold of so much? You're far too young to be carrying around that kind of money, Linx!"

"Is it really that much?" Linx nervously scratched his head, seeming thankful that everyone was too fixated on the contents of the sack on the table to notice his worried expression. "I was not sure how much would be enough, so I merely brought—"

"W-we could pay off, well… everything!" Yuto picked up a particularly hefty rune, spinning it around between the fingers of one paw as he adjusted his small, circular spectacles with the other. "The home, the medical bills, all of our loans, and my licensing fees… Heh, I could even pay off everything I owe you and more, Attl!"

"Indeed, you could…" Attl mumbled, barely holding himself upright as he curiously rubbed the pointed tip of a chin that was hardly long enough to poke out from his copious whiskers. "That is a lot of money—"

Clank!

The sound of a single stone falling on hardwood silenced the room.

Yuto settled himself, cleared his throat, then took the floor. "Now listen, all of you. This is about more than money. In truth, money doesn't really matter. If this works, we would be saving potentially thousands, maybe millions of future lives. No more Tarser children would have to suffer from these things. If this works, the entire world's economy could be disrupted, so maybe this money won't even matter, but… I don't care. If we can convince even one parent to stop feeding their family these wretched insects, and save even one child, I would be satisfied. All other consequences be damned."

"Oh, Yuto!" Jeea's light feet tapped swiftly along the wooden floorboards, and in an instant, she was embracing her beloved. "This is why I always loved you. You're too sweet for your own good."

Yuto smiled, Linx smiled, and Attl… well, in truth, Yuto couldn't really tell what Attl was thinking or expressing, but he assumed it was good. Attl was never one to disrupt a good mood, at least as far as Yuto knew. And Yuto had known Attl for so many years, and was never wrong about him! It was enough to nearly make the old Tarser shed a tear, and he very well may have, if not for the fear of looking unseemly in front of their new guest and staining the beautiful wood floors Jeea kept spotless.

"I knew I made a good choice when I chose you," Linx said.

"Heh, the way you say that makes you sound like some sort of divine being, coming down from on high to choose a holy warrior—or something silly and poetic like that," Yuto said.

"W-well, when you put it like that…" Linx seemed genuinely caught off guard. Yuto couldn't help but chuckle when he saw the young Tarser, who had been so calm and polite and proper, finally relax a bit.

"What sort of cage do you need built for one of these queens?" Attl said, his stern voice doing its best to get things back on track.

"Well, they can grow to be quite large. From what I saw, before they are submerged, they are about as large as a small child." Linx held out his paws just a bit wider than his chest, gesturing as if he were holding a ball in front of him. "At their apex, they can be about half the size of an average adult Tarser. Most of their bodies consist of their glowing red bulbous sacs, and they are very fragile. The males will carry them to a suitable spot to submerge them in loose ash, from which the queen will use its many silvery pinchers and legs to reach out and feed. It is actually quite difficult to spot them at a glance—the only real giveaway is the slight shifting of hard ash, moving around almost like a slow liquid as they breathe. Their dry, leathery bodies seem to have little issue dealing with the heat, but if you move them too much, such as carelessly digging them out from the ground, the contents of their bulbs slosh around and break open their sacs. Their bodies seem to wither and break apart very quickly once they pass. Oh! Also, sometimes you can see them give birth. It almost looks like a small geyser shooting out little specks of wet tar from their rear ends—"

"Ugh! No more, please." Jeea finally released Yuto, excusing herself back to her chores.

Yuto kept his smile, and his eyes down-turned and toward the runes on the table, lost in thought. Attl seemed to take special attention of Jeea as she scuttled away, though his expression also seemed vacant, as if lost in his own mind as well. Yuto worried that Attl was worried about something—probably trying to think of more questions to ask about the potentially dangerous commission. As much as Yuto wished to no longer cause anyone any trouble or worry, the thought of another adventure—with a glorious payout, and a righteous cause to boot—was too great to ignore. He could feel a certain giddiness nearly overtaking his body, his thin paws nearly trembling from the excitement of it all.

"Aside from the obvious environmental dangers," Attl said, breaking the silence, "are the queens dangerous?"

"Not normally," Linx said, "but when they burst, depending on how large they are, they can explode. It is sort of like a small gas explosion, with matter and ash and tiny rocks spewing everywhere."

"Ah, like a grenade," Attl said.

"Yeah, like that…"

"It'll be easy!" Yuto said, waving a confident paw in the air as his smile and perked ears nearly reached the ceiling.

"And how, pray tell, do you plan on making this voyage, Yuto?" Attl said, stern as ever.

"Well, you have quite the sturdy carriage, no?" Yuto said. "And even a small herd of beautiful, sturdy, healthy, luxurious nequines that can pull said carriage. The ones you breed are always such nice specimens, great to show off, and—"

Attl chuckled and waved his own paw dismissively. "Yuto, friend, you don't need to slather me with flattery. I will gladly offer transport."

"What is a nequine?" Linx asked.

"You've never seen one?" Yuto asked.

Linx shook his head, in an innocent, disarming way that reminded Yuto of his own children. The old Tarser couldn't help but smile and stare for a moment.

"They are nice steeds," Yuto continued, "big and brawny, with tough, short coats of fur that come in all sorts of shiny, dark colors—they're even hypoallergenic! Normally, the market has at least a few of them, carrying materials and carts back and forth. I suppose it's a bit strange that we didn't get to see one earlier. If Attl had brought one of his purebreds, he would have had the whole city staring in awe—"

"Ugh, Yuto…" Attl sighed. He shook his head, but a slight smirk was enough to show that he appreciated the compliments.

"I am curious about one thing, however," Linx added, and all eyes were instantly on him. "Jeea, you seem awfully at peace with Yuto potentially going into danger. I do not wish for anyone to put themselves at risk—"

"Nonsense!" Jeea's good mood from earlier seemed to carry over into a current wave of glee as she interrupted the young Tarser. "I know Yuto—he gets a whiff of adventure, of some excuse to do something interesting, and nothing will stop him. I've more or less come to accept that it is just the way it is."

"Well, if all goes well, I would be more than ready to retire fully, and live out the rest of my days peacefully," Yuto said. He twiddled his thumbs thoughtfully as he spoke.

"You say that, but I know something will come up eventually and you'll be getting involved in something else you probably shouldn't," Jeea said.

"I will make sure he stays safe, Mrs. Haelsker," Linx said.

"'Mrs. Haelsker?' How formal! You can just call me Jeea, as you have before. But also, I will hold you to that, little mister. Not a single hair better be missing on Yuto! I will personally and meticulously count each and every whisker on his face upon your return."

"I promise, ma'am, Yuto will return safely, no matter what."

Yuto swore he could feel the warmth of the smiles being shared that night. Even Attl seemed unable to resist as he was fully relaxed in his seat. Attl, of all Tarsers, was relaxed! Yuto was so used to his friend being "mature" and, in a less kind word, uptight. Yuto often worried that his own antics were the cause of his friend's rigid demeanor, and despite his best efforts, he was often unable to get Attl to loosen up. He hadn't even known this strange young Tarser for a full day, and yet Yuto couldn't help but hope that Linx would remain a close friend for many years to come, no matter what came of their risky venture. He could use another source of positivity in his life.

"As nice as this all is," Attl said, finally shuffling himself upward to address the room more formally, "the night is young, and we should perhaps make good use of this time to begin working out the details of this commission."

"I agree!" Yuto said. "I'll go gather some parchment, and we can begin."

CHAPTER 16

THE COMING DAYS CAME AND WENT quickly, even for Yuto's liking. However, he didn't mind, as his excitement as he worked with Linx seemed to consume all of his other thoughts. It had been a long time since he had lost himself in his craft, and it was yet one more thing he had to thank Linx for. Yuto hoped that their working together would give him ample opportunity to learn more about the mysterious young Tarser, and his wish had more or less been granted.

For one thing, Linx was incredibly patient. He had no issue merely sitting and waiting and watching as Yuto rummaged through his tools, went back and forth to gather materials, and even mumbled to himself in frustration for minutes on end when dealing with a particularly troublesome aspect of the device's design. Every time, without fail, Linx would merely sit and watch, waiting for Yuto to come back to his senses, and the young Tarser would continue their conversation as if not a single beat had been missed.

He also had an eye for detail. Despite claiming to not be a craftsman himself, Linx was very specific about what he wanted from the commission. The image of the young Tarser's dark paw and nails were practically burned into Yuto's peripherals, as Linx was regularly guiding him along. Linx admitted he underestimated the size of the super queens initially, and asked Yuto to make the cage itself at least a foot larger in dimensions to accommodate. The extra space turned the cushioned interior into a notable shock absorber. Extra material, consisting of dark red velvet carpeting, was used to round out the harsh creases caused by the connecting edges of the cube's interior. The centers of each wall of the cage were hollowed out, allowing for even more shock absorption, and a number of small, smooth, and fibrous ropes were tied to the outer layers of the cushioned interior. This was to keep the interior from potentially falling out of any of the cage wall's large and hollow openings, and also allowed whatever was being carried to move around independently as its carrier moved around. A final detail—one that Yuto particularly liked—was the addition of countless tiny holes poked into the cushions near the cage's top end. Linx said that they could put tiny traces of cooled ash into these holes, and the queen would naturally be drawn to sticking her prickly appendages into them. The queen would use the holes to hold on and stabilize itself, and the spare ash could even be used as food that the creature would use to keep itself fed during the trip home. Yuto mentioned that, by carriage, the trip to the volcanic region up north would take just over two months. Linx decided it would be best to bring along a spare sack and a long pair of tongs. The sack could be used to carry extra ash, and the tongs could be used to feed the queen safely. Yuto couldn't help but laugh at the thought—they may as well be carrying a newborn around.

Yuto's mind wandered, which only made the days go by faster. He was almost caught off guard when Linx finally expressed some glee at the construction's completion.

"This will be perfect," Linx said.

"Huh?" Yuto said, half-dazed from stubbornly refusing to sleep for the several days it took to finish the construction.

"This will work," Linx continued. "This should suffice."

"Splendid! Splendid. Attl mentioned he would be here early this morning with the carriage." Yuto gave the cage another look. It was quite large, almost too large for a single Tarser to lift on their own. "Are you sure this is fine? This is going to be difficult to carry."

"It will be fine," Linx said, as cool and confident as ever. "I could hold this up, no problem."

"Even with a queen inside of it? How heavy are they?"

"Not that heavy, I assure you."

"Well, I suppose me and Attl will be there to help out anyway. Teamwork, you know?"

"Of course."

Rustling leaves and tapping vines signaled Jeea's descent into the room. The pleasing way they fluttered in the traces of morning light seeping in through the cracks of the wooden walls and floors seemed to force the old Tarser to stare. "Good morning, Linx."

Uh oh… Yuto immediately tensed up. Jeea normally greeted Yuto first thing every morning. If she ever delayed that greeting, it meant she was angry about something.

"Yuto!" Jeea's voice was sharp, and as crisp as the fresh, dew-covered leaves surrounding their home. "You forgot to make tea for the children again, didn't you? It's already late morning."

"Ah, I'm sorry, dear." Yuto held his head low, though whether it was from exhaustion or shame, not even he knew. He looked over to see Linx smiling from beneath a short bushel of burgeoning, youthful whiskers. An immediate thought entered his mind.

How is he still so upbeat and fresh? He's been up for as long as I have. Actually, I haven't seen Linx sleep a single time… I know he's young, but… Eh, maybe I really am just getting old…

"Yuto!" Jeea's exclamation maintained its piercing quality, cutting right through the early morning mist.

"Huh?"

"Ugh, Yuto, it's fine. I'll get things ready for the children. You just keep doing what you need to." Jeea's usual light, deft taps turned to heavy stomps as she made her way to the kitchen a floor above. A quick rustle of vines and leaves marked her exit.

"She'll be fine," Yuto quickly muttered. He gestured the utterance toward Linx, but was saying it more for his own assurance than anything else.

Another sharp sound echoed through the room, this time from the entrance hatch behind the two—a slow, methodical knock at the door. Linx remained calm, though Yuto perked up and nearly tripped over his own whiskers as he scurried over to greet their guest.

"Attl!" Yuto said. "Glad you made it."

"Good morning, Yuto," Attl said.

"Please, please, come in, friend. Can't have you hanging around outside like some lowly door-to-door salesman."

"Of course. I figured you'd be done with the cage by now, so I came with a carriage and—oh! Good morning, Linx." Attl gave a swift wave to the young Tarser, who returned the gesture with a mild bow. Yuto quickly shut the hatch behind Attl, and scurried forward to address both of his guests.

"This is so exciting! Another adventure!" Yuto's scurrying nearly turned to dancing as he moved between Linx and Attl. "I could have sworn our adventuring days were behind us, yet here we are!"

"Well, I'm not surprised," Attl said. "You always were adept at dragging us all into trou—into 'interesting' predicaments."

"No need to be so polite, Attl," Yuto said, waving his pink paw dismissively toward his friend. "You can always be honest with me, or any of us, for that matter."

"No, no, I don't mean any harm by my words..." Attl seemed occupied with something, as if a thought at the back of his mind was dragging him down.

"You seem more stern than usual," Yuto said. "I could get Jeea to make you some citrusy tea, if you'd like?"

"Jeea..." Attl almost ignored Yuto, his head still looking curiously about as he scratched his pointed chin.

"Hmm?" Yuto began to reach out to his friend. "Attl, are you alri—"

"Is that Attl I hear? Welcome again!" Jeea's piercing voice cut through the air once more from the floor above. All eyes were wide and looked up to follow the sound of pitter-patters trailing across the floorboards above. Not a moment later was Jeea's lithe, furry form descending the vines above.

"Attl, thank goodness," Jeea said, quickly making her way over to their newest guest. "With you around, Yuto always perks up and pays more attention. How have you been?" Jeea quickly wrapped her arms around Attl for a friendly hug. Attl himself still seemed concerned with something, but he returned the gesture with a light pat on her back.

"I'm fine, Jeea. How are the kids this morning?"

"Oh, they're fine. I'm still making their usual morning tea, abiding by Linx's suggestions, of course."

"I see… That's good, that's good."

What would have been an awkward silence was immediately interrupted by Yuto's enthusiasm—complete with several excited steps forward and a loud clasping of paws.

"Well! If we're all ready, I'll gather my things, and Linx and I will carry the cage down and—"

"Mom? Dad?"

All eyes shot open wide and turned to the vines leading up to the second floor. A small, beige body was stumbling to make its way down the shining, dark green vines, yet she kept her attention forward, staring back with her large black eyes that reflected a crystalline blue in the morning light.

"Niora!" Jeea yelled, hurrying to her youngest daughter. She practically pulled her daughter down and onto the ground, and caressed Niora as she began coughing. "What are you doing out of bed so early?! You know you have to rest. You can't just—"

"I-I've been feeling a little better, Mom. Please don't be mad. Also," the little one looked over her mother's shoulder and to the others, who were still staring in surprise, "I was wondering where Dad was. He always brings us tea, and I hadn't seen him in… seen in him in—"

Another harsh, wet cough shot out from Niora's tiny chest, and then another, and another, before a series of coughs began to come out in such numbers that they were nearly interrupting one another. Jeea held her tight, and rocked back and forth slightly, trying to calm the child down. Yuto quickly made his way over and held them both. It took a long, grueling minute of constant coughing and wheezing before she finally began to calm down. A heavy breath of relief followed, and the exhausted child nearly fell over in her mother's arms, giving herself up completely. Jeea whispered several shushes and other sweet encouragements as she carried the tiny Tarser back up the vines. Yuto stood and watched with a worried smile, then turned his attention back to his guests.

"I'm sorry you had to see all that," Yuto said.

"It is quite alright, Yuto," Linx said, raising a dark paw and a smile. "It is for young ones such as her that we are doing this."

"Indeed." Yuto struggled to look Linx in the eye, having to adjust his glasses as he hung his head shamefully low. "I guess I got carried away again. Here I am getting all giddy at some selfish sense of adventure when I should really be more concerned about how well this is all going to work out. I can't stand the thought of other children potentially suffering because of the illymites."

Attl rubbed his arm and nodded in quiet agreement as he looked about. Linx smiled wide, and even held his paws together and close to his chest. Yuto wondered where this strange Tarser came from—how one could be so kind-hearted and seemingly pure in his intentions. Yuto could feel it—everything was primed to go beautifully, and Linx seemed to know it, which only filled him with further confidence.

"Alright then, let's hurry up and get this underway," Yuto said proudly.

❦

The bottoms of the forests were surprisingly easy to navigate. As Tarsers were nomadic, mercantile people, most were traveling constantly. Even far out in the woods, miles away from civilization, the ground was well worn from countless years of Tarsers and carriages traveling by. There was even a path of worn dirt that tracked Yuto's trail to and from the capital city. The trio very well may have seen a number of his footsteps from the other day if they were not heading in the exact opposite direction. The distant northern mountains, barely visible above the treetops from Yuto's home, marked their destination.

A simple, dark brown carriage made its way along the foggy forest floor. The regular creaks and squeaks of the wooden vessel dragging its large wheels along the hard soil blended with the chirps and squawks that echoed smoothly from the forest, well beyond the fog and out of sight. The steeds pulling the vessel forward seemed at peace, entirely unperturbed by the thick, smooth mist hiding anything farther than a stone's throw away. The nequines themselves were just as Yuto had described them—large, brawny packets of muscle with sturdy, short, and shining coats. Their colors were dark, yet still expressed interesting shades. The one on the left shined an odd hue that sat somewhere between a watery blue and dewy green. The other was an earthy violet color. Their long, stringy manes were each pitch-black bundles of thin and oily vines. Their tails were especially unique—each one splitting into two long bundles that swayed back and forth, adding a rhythmic, bristling sound to the symphony of wet and lively forest ambiance. Attl had only brought two of them, but they appeared nearly too large for the cart they were pulling.

Attl himself guided the carriage, sitting on the front perch, managing the reins. Yuto and Linx sat in the back end, taking special care of the cage that left little room for the two Tarsers to sit themselves. Yuto seemed to struggle the most. He regularly needed to clean his glasses from the fog, but then he would immediately worry about the cage, which would take his paws away from his spectacles, allowing them to fog up once more. Linx, polite as he was, was unable to not at least chuckle at the old Tarser's plight. Yuto himself at least wasn't bothered too much by it. Making youngsters laugh was always a good time for him, even if it came ever so slightly at his expense. He often wished his children were able to laugh more.

"I could have sworn we packed relatively light," Attl mumbled, twirling the thick rope between his paws. "I figured we weren't nearly heavy enough to cause my nequines any strain, but they appear to be pushing themselves quite a bit."

"Well, maybe it's my fault," Yuto said. "Try as I might, I very well may have gained some weight ever since settling down."

"I do not blame you," Linx added. "Jeea makes wonderful food. I could not help but eat as much as I could manage while staying with you."

"Well, I have to agree! Though, don't tell anyone but," Yuto leaned in, going so far as to put a paw up to his snout to whisper something, "Jeea learned most of her recipes from Attl. She thinks I don't know, but I know. Before we got married, she was, um, well…"

"She was quite the amateur chef," Attl said.

"We all must start somewhere, I suppose," Linx said, shrugging his sharp shoulders.

"She is a quick learner, however," Attl continued. "She makes for a lovely student."

"Indeed," Yuto said. "It seemed as if all three of us were great learners back in our traveling days. Though I always feared you two surpassed me relatively quickly."

"What were your early travels like?" Linx asked. "I would love to hear more of your early adventures."

"Well! Our time as young adventurers was certainly exciting," Yuto said. "Part of it was a foolish ambition we all shared—that of making a name for ourselves, much like Mitus DeTrell. Perhaps it was foolish for all of us, but especially me."

"You are far too humble, Mr. Haelsker," Linx said, waving a dismissive paw as he spoke.

Yuto, for once, couldn't help but let his glasses fog up as he felt compelled to lower his head and scratch an ear. "I mean… I can't help but be humble—all three of us met through the merchant's guild, but Attl joined due to coming from a long line of merchants and explorers, and Jeea was actually the heir to a small trading company. I came with nothing more than the rags on my back and the handful of rusty tools and compasses in my knapsack. Would you believe me if I said that I used to be horribly indecisive? I considered taking up other occupations, such as botany, or entomology, and even went through a fierce archeology phase for a while. Yet mercantilism won out, as the promise of travel was too much to resist. I chose it on a bit of a whim, and I am glad, as I met my beloved and best friend."

"Attl is the beloved, right?" Linx said jokingly.

Yuto couldn't help but guffaw, his pink palm slapping his bony knee. Linx shared a wide smile of his own. Yuto looked over, ready to jab a playful elbow into Attl, but was surprised to see their coachman remained stoic, focused on the path ahead. Yuto merely turned back to Linx and allowed his cavorting to finish. He wiped away a tear and let loose a final chuckle before relaxing.

"Attl, you're too serious," Yuto said through a smile. "I thought it was funny, at least."

Attl merely turned his head a little and gave a weak smile before looking back ahead.

"I think it is fine, Yuto," Linx continued. "Coming from nothing is, well, nothing to be ashamed of. We all must start somewhere, and you have built up a loving family and a good friendship from it. And who knows? Maybe stories of your adventures will go on to inspire others, just as Mitus DeTrell inspired you? Your own children could go on to follow in your footsteps, and their children as well. You could very well have begun a great, long-lasting legacy, and all 'from nothing.'"

Yuto looked on at the young Tarser, wide-eyed and silent. He would have been completely still, if not for their carriage rocking them back and forth slightly as they pulled ahead. His fogged spectacles did little to hide the teary traces that began to form beneath his eyes. The thought of his children, and others just like them, being inspired by his acts, was perhaps the greatest thing he could ever ask for. In fact, in his mind, it was too great, and too much to ask for. He knew he was often little more than a troublemaker, whether it be bothering the merchant's hall, or needing Attl or Jeea to pull him out of some unsavory situation. He was always making things more complicated. He never meant to do such things, but he knew himself well—his personality never allowed him to sit still, and thus he always ended up "rocking the boat" in some way. Who was he to think that he was worth inspiring anyone? And who was Linx to think so highly of him? Perhaps it was selfish, but more and more he wished that his own remaining children could grow up to look at him the way Linx did. The thought was enough to finally send a heavy, wet bead trailing down the side of his face. A quick turn and a quicker wipe at his eye with his pink paw broke him out of his trance.

"I-I suppose so," Yuto said, now looking away from the youngster. "I would appreciate that more than anything."

Another warm smile from Linx marked a tranquil moment. It didn't last long, however, as Attl soon interrupted the silence, ready to change the subject.

"So, Linx," Attl said over his shoulder, "did you have anything specific in mind? Any mountains in particular that you believe we should go to?"

"We merely need to go as far north as we can possibly go," Linx said. "The smaller males can travel far, but their queens cannot travel much at all, and tend to cluster in the hottest and most northern regions."

"Unfortunately, we may not be able to ride more than 50 or so miles beyond the volcanic perimeter," Attl said. "The farther north you go, the hotter it gets, and the worse the terrain gets. Our carriage will only be able to handle so much."

"I will walk barefoot into a volcano myself if I have to. I'll do anything if it means we can change things for the better," Yuto added.

"Well, I saw plenty of long, decent trails leading into the mountains when I went there, tip-toeing my way across the many charred grounds and winding paths formed by cooled magma," Linx said. "Perhaps that will not be necessary, Yuto."

"You're a brave one, Linx," Yuto said. "We Tarsers are not built to withstand heat at all. And in truth, if anyone from the guild found out you were venturing

into these regions on your own, without their say-so…
well, at least you'd be able to pay off the fines, but as
for the jail time—"

"Are you certain that you know what you are looking
for, young one?" Attl said. "You are confident that you
will be able to find one of these super queens, and will
be able to get it out in one piece?"

"Yes." A single word and a curt response came from
the young Tarser. A heavy, stern sense of confidence
seemed to echo from him in a way that both Yuto and
Attl could feel. Attl went silent once again, ceasing
his question and diligently focusing on pulling them
forward through the silvery gray fog and dark, sage
green forest.

"Let's lighten the mood a bit," Yuto said. He
pointed toward some of the sacks of food they had
brought for their trip, motioning for Linx to grab them.
"It wouldn't hurt to share a few of Jeea's treats and talk
of more fun things. Linx, hand me a biscuit, if you
would be so kind?"

CHAPTER 17

IT WASN'T LONG BEFORE THE SHROUDED, foggy forests began to disperse into new lands. The cozy grays and greens of the woods, within less than a week of traveling, opened up into much wider fields. Much of the fog remained, though it was closer to the ground, and one could at least look up and see the sky more easily. Yuto noticed that Linx in particular seemed more at ease in the more expansive landscape, and spent many of the coming nights quietly looking up at the stars. Yuto was not necessarily a stargazer, but he noticed that the young Tarser's eyes lit up whenever he pointed out a few of the constellations he knew of. Even Attl joined in and would share his knowledge of the night sky, oftentimes playfully one-upping what little bits of knowledge Yuto had to share on the subject. Yuto knew it was all in good fun, and the many nights they spent camping out in the soft grassy fields and rolling hills of the plains beyond the forest were pleasant ones. It was not unlike the time he and Attl and Jeea spent together in their youth.

The different setting also brought with it different wildlife and new fauna. At least it seemed new to Linx. Yuto delighted in explaining the new creatures and elements to the young Tarser, the way he envisioned sharing knowledge with his own children one day if their health ever improved and allowed them to travel. Seeing the young Tarser's large, dark eyes light up whenever a new bird flew above, or an odd critter or insect would crawl into the carriage, Yuto couldn't help but smile. Each fresh bit of nature that introduced itself was a new opportunity to share some knowledge with Linx. In fact, he ended up having to explain so much that Yuto began to wonder if he should have been a teacher or instructor of some sort. He also began to wonder just what the young Tarser's education consisted of. Linx seemed rather wise and patient for someone so young, and yet, most common knowledge escaped him.

A common, tri-tailed featherling would fly above and Linx would stare cautiously, fearing its large, tri-clawed feet, and even likening its trailing tails to a dark, shimmering tendril cutting across the sky. Yuto had to explain the creatures were actually common house pets and were both docile and herbivorous. A glowing green beetle crawled into the carriage, and Yuto swore that Linx nearly jumped out of his fur. Yuto laughed, and merely picked the creature up, letting the palm-sized critter crawl up and down his arm, its little chitinous legs tickling him as it moved. Yuto even offered to let the creature crawl on him a bit, just to get used to it. Linx politely declined, and Yuto released it back into the air. Linx almost jumped when he saw the thing split its shell open to reveal a dozen clear wings that buzzed against each other as it flew away. At least Linx seemed comfortable when watching the occasional wild herd of nequines dashing about in the distance. Attl even took the opportunity to share some other common facts about the beasts—such as how if a mother nequine had multiple offspring, she would have them hold on to the multiple tips of her tails as they ran, to ensure they didn't lose them. The slight curve of the front hooves the males possessed made them slower runners, but exceptionally dangerous fighters. During mating season, the otherwise calm beasts would nearly go mad, trespassing into other nequine's territories to fight over potential mates. Attl lamented how difficult it was to tame feral male nequines, and how one would need to file down their curved, sharp hooves every other day, not just to make them quicker steeds, but to make them at least somewhat safe to approach. Linx seemed to enjoy learning as much as he did. He absorbed so much information so readily that Yuto even joked that if he wasn't careful, his young brain would burst like a sponge under a waterfall.

The herds of nequines soon became rare, and the soft grassy plains began to give way to hard and grainy soil. The once clear blue and teal skies were becoming more and more gray by the day. As much as Yuto enjoyed a cozy, gray, and cloudy day, he knew that these skies were the result of far-off volcanic activity. They were officially in no-man's-land. The chance of the rare Tarser patrol was now no longer of any concern, as none were normally allowed to go out that far. Attl had been driving the entire journey, and Yuto offered many times to take the reins and give his friend a chance to rest, but he refused every time. Attl's mind always seemed preoccupied, though about what Yuto couldn't figure out. He had learned that it was best to not push Attl, and let him have his alone time when need be.

Another form of discomfort came from the increasingly warm winds surrounding them. The clouds far off in the distance looked perpetually stormy, and the landscape itself was becoming more arid. The wildlife became more scarce, and what few examples of living nature there only reminded Yuto of the harsh environment to come. There were no more birds, now instead only the occasional flightless and featherless raptor scavenging for scraps between hard and dry cracks in the ground. Rather than the pleasing, tickling glowing beetles there were now an assortment of dark corroaches and burning red and orange snails with caustic-looking shells. Everyone knew that the illymites came from much farther north, and the farther north one went, the nastier life became. Why were Tarsers so easily tempted into just accepting and consuming such things? It was only natural to think that anything from such regions would be dangerous to eat, and yet even Yuto himself fell victim to them for a short time. Yuto worried about how Tarsers could so unquestioningly accept something, just because some legendary explorer of old brought them. Yuto remembered Linx's kind words about him leaving a legacy of his own, but if it ended up having an effect at all similar to what the late and great Mitus DeTrell's legacy had, perhaps he was fine with remaining humble and unknown.

The hard soil only became darker, and wild lines and formations from unknown tectonic activity began to become more noticeable. The gray skies soon began to show more colors—ominous deep violets mixed with washed-out yellows and burnt oranges that moved and swirled around. It was an unpleasant display, but it signaled that volcanoes were close. As if that were not enough, bits of ash and other burned material could be seen occasionally fluttering about the air, downwind of the menacing mountains to come. Mixed in with the debris were the occasional swarms of illymites. Little cherry-red bulbs buzzed around constantly in search of food. These were clearly younger and fresher than most of the specimens preserved for the markets. It was currently the off season for illymites, so it would be a while before any large swarms would make their way south for harvesting. If so inclined, Yuto could perhaps make quite a bit of money catching and selling them. He refused the thought, knowing the damage they caused. Linx seemed to share Yuto's own disdain for the creatures, observing each swarm with a stern look similar to his own. Attl seemed more curious than anything, watching each bundle that flew nearby or in the distance intently. Yuto never blamed Attl for continuing to sell them—he had his own bills and debts to pay off—but it still made him feel uneasy seeing his friend constantly tempted by the things.

Great, dark clouds covered much of the horizon, which would have appeared as a flat line of charcoal and soil if not for a series of peculiar, bumpy forms poking into the skyline.

"Volcanoes!" Yuto's excitement got the better of him. He nearly fell out of the wooden carriage. He immediately noticed his mistake, as he whipped his head around to make sure he didn't let go of the delicate cage he and Linx had been holding on to for the entire trip. He looked over to see Linx, patient as ever, taking care of it.

Attl casually looked over his shoulder once again to address his passengers. "I would wager we have another four, maybe five miles before the nequines will refuse to go any farther. I hope you two have no problem carrying that thing the rest of the way."

"Of course not!" Yuto exclaimed.

"If need be, I can carry it myself," Linx said.

"Nonsense, young one," Yuto said, gesturing dismissively toward Linx. "Attl and I will do everything we can to help. Plus, it's not good for your back to carry such a load for so long! Trust me, you'll regret it when you get older if you're not careful now."

"I'll never understand how you can get excited at the sight of such things," Attl said. He squirmed in his seat and rolled his shoulders. He seemed to be trying to ring out his anxiety any way he could. He even shifted his tail from his left side to his right—a rare tail-based expression from the otherwise cool and stoic Tarser.

"Well, I find them fascinating," Yuto added.

"Fascinating, and deadly…These things could erupt at any moment," Attl said.

"Bah!" Yuto scoffed. "This continent has not experienced an eruption in over a hundred years! Not even Mitus ever witnessed an erupting volcano in his life. What are the odds one would choose now of all times to—"

Rrrr-rrrr-rrrr...

The ground itself seemed to be grumbling, as distant rumbles slightly shifted beneath them. The silence sitting between the three was heavy, seemingly bearing down on the hopes and fears of all unfortunate enough to be within earshot.

"Heh, well," Yuto said, smiling meekly, and tugging playfully at his collar, "is it getting hot out here, or is it just—"

Attl swiftly raised a paw of his own and glared over his shoulder. "Yuto, please, just once, could you be serious?"

"Fine, fine," Yuto said, "but it truly is getting quite warm."

"It is only going to get warmer, unfortunately," Linx said.

"How did you manage the heat?" Yuto asked.

"Honestly? I never thought much of it. I just ignored it."

"What a reassuring plan..." Attl tried mumbling, though his exasperation came out louder than even he expected. Linx shrugged, Yuto smiled, and the three continued their journey.

It wasn't long before their cart began to struggle to evenly traverse the terrain. Back and forth the carriage went, tipping ever so slightly to each side as the large wheels bumped and ground across the dark ground. A strange mixture of hardened soil and strains of cooled magma swirled together to form a rocky ground. Some of the terrain began to reveal tiny geysers that shot out spurts of hot gas above. Most of them made little sound, but every so often a larger one would whistle its excesses out, startling the steeds that pulled them forward. Attl struggled to keep them in line as the beasts became more agitated.

"Alright, that's far enough for the steeds," Attl said. "Let's set up a resting area for them. We'll have to walk the rest of the way."

"Well, here comes the hard part," Yuto said jokingly toward Linx.

"I can carry the cage on my own, Yuto, please," Linx said, even going so far as to hop out of the carriage on his own, his grip still on the large cage and effortlessly lifting it with him.

"I mean… You certainly seem to have a good handle on the contraption," Yuto said. "If at any point you need a break, let us know, and Attl and I will take over."

Linx nodded as he shifted a few ropes attached to the cage around his shoulders, carrying the construct like a bulky backpack.

"Yuto, you can help me set things up then," Attl said, thumbing through a bag of tools that clinked messily as he pulled out materials from within. "You can set up a few of the troughs and get their food and water ready. I'll hammer in the stakes and tie them up."

Yuto nodded and began. Linx stood and watched curiously as the two set everything up. Normally, Yuto would have loved to take the opportunity to explain the entire process, such as setting down a few grassy blankets on the ground for the nequines to rest on, but made of a certain species of grass that they will not eat.

Then there was folding out a few wooden, rectangular boxes that would act as troughs for the beast's actual food to keep them satisfied while they were away. There was also an interesting fact regarding the spiky, metal stakes Attl hammered into the ground; they were actually not strong enough to hold the beasts in place—instead, the visual of seeing their reins wrapped around them was enough to convince the beasts that they were being held and would remain compliant. Unless startled—whether by surprising natural phenomena or a predator, neither of which seemed possible far out in the middle of nowhere—they would remain calm and merely munch on their feed. The straps also needed to be long enough to allow the creatures to venture a fair distance away to relieve themselves. They were beasts, but even they valued keeping their sleeping and feeding grounds sanitary. Yuto always liked that about the creatures.

All of this information went through his mind, and in the blink of an eye, he was already done. Yuto again wondered about his age—he used to be so attentive to every little detail, which always made things drag, and yet now it was easy for his mind to wander on interesting bits of trivia, and time would fly. He looked over to Attl to see that he had already measured the rope, set the stakes, and even pushed the now empty carriage to the perfect spot, allowing it to act as a sort of "wall" that the nequines could use to rest against. Or sleep under. Attl only did that specifically if he wasn't sure how long he would be gone. Attl always was the most forward-thinking and practical Tarser of their troupe, back when they were all young, brash, ambitious, and thirsty for adventure. It was strange then, that even as Yuto sat out in the midst of a volcanic field, embarking on another journey with friends, he couldn't help but still miss the old days. Yuto, lost in thought once again, couldn't help but ponder.

Is this not enough adventure for me? Will this be enough? I don't think anything I do will be enough to make up for the trouble I've caused, to Attl, to Jeea, or even to our children who still struggle. I miss being young and carefree, back when we could just put on a backpack and head off, with nothing more than a few rations and tools to weigh us down. Those were much lighter than whatever is bothering me now...

"Yuto!" Attl called out.

Yuto jumped up, his small round spectacles nearly falling off of his snout as he looked ahead to see Linx and Attl looking back at him.

"Linx will be guiding us farther in, as he has the most experience with the landscape," Attl added. Yuto smiled, picked up his own sack of tools—and some snacks—and pushed forward.

The three furry figures pushed along, in single file and, at least to Yuto's amusement, in order of youngest to oldest. Linx carried himself both cautiously and adeptly, as he was the first to crawl or tiptoe over any obstacles. He showed an uncanny knowledge of how precisely to move along the growing number of cooled magma formations creating large, loosely linked bridges between open caverns and past moderately spaced cliffsides. Countless pieces of dark ash were floating all around them like unholy snow, being constantly pushed around by whatever wind the rocky region would allow. The burnt orange glow of distant magma lined the many winding and spiraling black formations with a hellish hue. The sounds of shifting rock and crawling magmatic ooze filled the air with oddly soothing rumbles. They reminded Yuto of distant thunder clouds that often signaled the coming of a soothing, rainy evening. Such peaceful thoughts were often interrupted by the ever-growing and oppressive haze of heat weighing down the air like a hot blanket around him. Once again, Yuto was reminded of how Tarsers were not built for heat, as the pink, unfurred skin around his paws and feet, and his underbelly, were now wet and slick with sweat. He could feel his body working overtime to keep him cool. It was working for now, but he knew it would only get more difficult. Seeing Linx at the head of the pack pushing on effortlessly helped to motivate the old Tarser.

Attl also seemed unphased, though not in the same way as Linx. Yuto knew when something was bothering his longtime friend. Attl's face remained flat and stern, but his shoulders could be seen constantly shrugging and his clawed feet digging deeper than necessary into the ground. He was sweating just as much as Yuto, but Attl was the type to clench his teeth and keep quiet. Yuto admired many things about Attl, and his resolve and discipline were among the top of the list of traits. What he didn't understand, however, was Attl's insistence on wearing heavy, dark clothing regardless of the situation. Attl wore his usual dark blue tunic and hood, and even his belt was a near black-oak brown leather that shined in the heated light as if it were sweating as well. Still, Attl remained vigilant and kept his eyes locked on their guide as they all ventured deeper into the harsh territory.

"So, remind me what specifically we should be looking out for?" Attl asked.

"The queens, when fully grown and mature, prefer to remain fully submerged," Linx said. "They do not seem particular about what they are submerged under, but of course, they seem to prosper when embedded in rock or soil, near or within a volcano, where they have access to the most ash."

"There's quite a bit of ash just floating around us," Yuto said with an exasperated breath. "You'd think they would just hang out in the open and feast."

"Well, they also do it for protection," Linx added.

"They're already practically living in magma," Attl said. "What more do they need protection from?"

"Well, I am sure the odd bird or rival illymite swarm, for one," Linx said.

"Or perhaps a few foolish Tarsers looking to dig them up?" Yuto said, smiling playfully against a thin wall of sweat that had built up on the less furry parts of his snout and face.

"Perhaps," Linx said through a half-chuckle. Yuto looked to Attl, who seemed to remain unphased by Yuto's light jesting. It was expected, but Yuto always looked for an opportunity to lighten the mood and cheer up his friend.

"You seem to be moving forward confidently," Attl said. "Any idea of where specifically you are taking us? Or where to look?"

"Yes, actually," Linx said. "I recognize some of these formations and know for a fact that a particular volcano up ahead will have what we need."

"Really?" Yuto said. "What's so special about it?"

"A number of queens live within it. Usually, the queens prefer to settle far away from one another, giving each one ample space to grow their brood and their swarm. They form loose territories, and unless a rival swarm is looking to invade and take over, they do not intermingle. Because of this, there can be a lot of space between each queen, and it would take us perhaps far too much time to find one. For some reason, however, particularly dangerous volcanoes are treated as miniature colonies, housing multiple super queens all existing within close proximity. You can see them shifting and pulsating within the walls lining the inner caverns, and their brood will intermingle and sometimes even assist each other in gathering food for their queens."

"That sounds fascinating!" Yuto exclaimed. "You have seen all of this firsthand?"

"That I have," Linx said.

"I will believe it when I see it," Attl said.

"Linx does not seem like the type of Tarser to lie," Yuto said.

"No, but I know how easy it is to exaggerate things when you're young and inexperienced," Attl said, shifting a stern look downward.

"Attl! There's no reason to be so skeptical of Linx. He has been nothing but a pleasant guest and forthright commissioner—"

"I still find it odd he would bother commissioning anyone for anything when he has access to this sort of burgeoning wealth."

"Some people value things other than money, Attl."

"I suppose…"

Linx only listened and kept going. He didn't seem too bothered by any of Attl's skepticism, allowing his words to roll off of him. As much as it seemed to frustrate Attl, Yuto found that the young Tarser's mature handling of it all was a sign that he was confident and earnest. If nothing else, Yuto figured his presence helped to prevent any discussion from getting too heated.

Hehe, heated… Yuto couldn't help but chuckle at the irony of his words.

Linx had already led them to a particularly frightening-looking volcano. From a fair distance away, it appeared little more than another spiked pile of cooled magma and dark soil that cut into the sky. There were few clouds above it, but clearly, there was life brewing within. Hot, slow-moving winds carried sweltering heat from its innards. Linx barged ahead fearlessly into the first cave on the mountain's side he could find. Yuto and Attl had to look at one another before going in. Both Tarsers pulled at small flasks on their belts and dowsed themselves in water. Unfortunately, the insulated flasks were not entirely successful at keeping their liquids cool, but lukewarm water was preferred to dry, arid heat. It was then that the two noticed Linx had gone in without a light!

That young fool, Yuto thought. *He's probably bumbling in the dark right now. I was brash, too, when I was young, but this may be a bit much, even for me!*

"Linx! Wait!" Attl called out.

A slow rumble of the mountain followed a crackling of the walls. All went silent before a friendly voice echoed from inside.

"My apologies," Linx called out, his voice echoing from a fair distance within.

"Hold on, Linx, we'll bring torches!" Yuto said.

Attl lit his first—a swift strike against the end of a small club whose end was covered in volatile powder and cloth lit the way. Yuto did the same and followed suit.

Not a minute later were the two greeted with the back of a young Tarser, still pushing ahead as he carried the large, square contraption on his back as if it were nothing.

"You need to be careful, Linx," Attl said.

"Thank you for the concern, but I will be fine," Linx responded. "I am more than used to the dark."

"Confidence is a swift killer," Attl responded. He waved his torch in Linx's direction, causing the many shadows cast upon the black, rocky walls to dance.

"Perhaps," Linx responded, "but what if I am swifter?"

"That is exactly what I am talking about," Attl said. "I know you are young, but to think you are quicker than death… Well, let me just say I have seen more than a few adventurers fall victim to such thoughts."

"You are probably right, Attl," Linx said. "I merely jest."

"I swear, if your 'jesting' is not the end of me, an eruption most certainly will be," Attl grumbled.

"Nonsense!" Yuto said. "Besides, you aren't fooling me—when you were young, you would have loved to see something as rare and grand as a volcanic eruption!"

"That was when I was young and dumb," Attl said. "Nowadays, I do value my safety."

"Why not take more risks, Attl?" Yuto asked. "It's not as if you have a family at home worrying about you."

Yuto jolted up for a moment, realizing how insensitive his remark might have been. He could feel his face and snout being stretched in all directions—his eyes wide and his mouth flattened and wider—as he looked on worriedly at his friend.

Attl was quiet for a time, before finally speaking. "I suppose you're right, Yuto."

Yuto felt at least a tinge of relief, even letting out a small sigh, hearing his mostly serious friend take his unintended slight with stride.

Linx kept up the pace, as if he knew exactly where he was going. Attl at least had his torch and the young Tarser in front of him. Yuto felt as if he could barely keep up. Several times he almost tripped over an unseen rock and struggled to differentiate between the conflicting shadows cast by his torch and Attl's and the many formations dotting the cavern's floor. It didn't help that the heat was getting to him once again, and worst of all, he couldn't spare a paw to properly wipe the fog and sweat off of his glasses.

Fortunately, it was not long before a new light presented itself—a hellish red dot peering from far beyond. Finally, the occasional illymite began to reveal itself—more of the smaller males, probably scouts of some sort, looking to see who had intruded upon their territory. One of the best things about illymites, when consumed, was that initial gush of filling dashing across your tongue. Though it would be immediately followed by a grainy, warm, and even salty aftertaste. Yuto was getting tired and hungry, but not enough to have to deal with such unpleasant sensations. He may as well just take a bite out of the volcano's side, as far as he was concerned.

"There," Linx said, shrugging his shoulders and pointing ahead. "If we are to find any queens, it will be there."

"Thank goodness," Yuto heaved. "I'd like to just get this over with and start the pleasant journey home."

It took a moment for Yuto's eyes to begin adjusting to the new light. At first, he couldn't see much beyond the burning orange light, but he could make out Linx's boxy silhouette quickly moving ahead and darting to the side. Attl followed suit, though Yuto felt far more hesitant.

Something is wrong, and I can't quite put my paw on it... Strangely, it doesn't even seem to have anything to do with the mountain... Why does this place, of all places, give me the chills?

Yuto finally stepped forward and looked on. He could finally take a moment to set down his torch and wipe his glasses. Between the smudges of sweat and fog, he could see a great ring of precarious ledges jutting out like half-made stairs from the walls of the volcano's center. There was enough steam to put any sauna on Halifell to shame, but at least the magma itself was far down enough to not be a huge concern. Yuto peered over the first edge he could and needed to squint to look into the slushy pool of neon crimson, burnt oranges, and near-white yellows all mixing together into a sizzling ooze. It was quite the sight, and he would have looked on for longer, if the brightness were not akin to staring at the sun. It was then that he noticed that the sweat on his snout had made for a slick surface, nearly causing his glasses to slide off. His heart jumped as he immediately flung his paws up and his head back to catch them. Another sigh of relief followed as he looked over to the side where Linx and Attl had crept.

Linx was pointing at something on a far-off wall, and Attl was staring at it intently. Yuto made his way over to see what it was and was shocked at the realization—it was a horde of illymites! Countless small black shells and bright cherry-red sacs covered a portion of the wall that seemed to gyrate beneath. Linx pointed over to several more spots, with Attl turning a sharp eye to each point of interest. Yuto, following their lead, was the last to notice another swarm each time. The way the small illymites covered and moved across each spot made it look as if the walls had fresh scabs that were sizzling and bubbling just beneath a fire. It was as fascinating as it was revolting, and Yuto could not bring himself to look away.

"Yuto, here." Attl's calm voice reached out, snapping Yuto out of his trance.

"Huh?"

"Have some berries and water, Yuto. This next part is going to be quite demanding."

"What do you mean?"

Linx stepped in, lightly snacking on a small pawful of sweating, purple berries. "You and I will make our way across this ledge here. See that spot on the wall? That, I believe, is the easiest queen to reach. Attl has agreed to be the anchor. He will put down the anchor stakes and hold on to our harnesses as we make our way across the ledge."

"You seem to be the strongest among us though," Yuto said. "Shouldn't you be the anchor, Linx?"

"Linx may very well be the only one who can fully hold the cage up, especially when the super queen is dropped into it," Attl said, already hammering several metal stakes into the ground.

"Ah, that makes sense, I suppose," Yuto added.

Things were oddly quiet and tense as everyone prepared. Linx seemed unphased, as usual, even going so far as to whip around the cage as if it were nothing to grab at his ropes and harnesses. Yuto had only shown Linx once how to properly tie harnesses, both around himself and around the cage, but the young Tarser seemed to rake in the knowledge well and needed no further instruction. It was actually impressive—at least to Yuto—how good of a learner Linx was.

Attl continued as before, hammering no less than eight metal stakes into the ground and weaving the ends of their ropes through the opening loops at the top of each one. Yuto wanted to break the silence, maybe tell a joke, anything to lighten the mood, but he couldn't. Nothing came to mind, forcing him to focus fully on the task at hand. Yuto always hated harnesses. Tarsers were already great climbers, so having to admit to needing extra tools was always at least a little humbling. Still, even Yuto recognized the dangers, and didn't want to take any chances.

The quiet moment at least offered a good opportunity to listen to the sounds of the volcano. For something so dangerous and potentially destructive, it created an oddly calming ambiance. The dark gray clouds above made for a pleasantly cozy, if ominous, sky. It was indeed far too hot, but Yuto could imagine subjecting himself to similar heat in a nice hot spring or sauna, perhaps on a vacation that he previously could never afford. With little life around, and what life that did exist was mostly slow-moving and uninterested in bothering him, it was a good opportunity to get away from everything. The slow rumbling of shifting magma and the regular trickling of crumbling rock were similar to the white noise provided by the rain. As a final stroke, the regular plumes of smoke—displaying different colors and textures and thickness—always gave the observer something interesting to look out for. The more Yuto thought about it, the more he came to appreciate the wild environment.

And then he chuckled to himself as he realized that he was perhaps merely coping with his current predicament. He was about to perform something dangerous, life-threatening even, and yet his mind went to saunas and cozy rainy days.

What's the difference between coping and delusion, anyway? Yuto thought. *Maybe I'll ask Attl or Jeea what their thoughts are later.*

"Everything's ready." Once again, Attl's stern voice snapped Yuto out of his trance. The old Tarser's wandering mind seemed to be getting the better of him.

"I am also ready," Linx said. He shrugged his shoulders, and was already a half step ahead, nearly holding the cage up with a single arm. His harness was attached to Yuto, who was at the end of the entire rope. Seeing that he had both Linx, who was deceptively strong, and Attl holding on, Yuto felt the surge of much-needed confidence in going forward.

"Alright, then," Yuto said, shrugging his own shoulders and slightly tightening his own harness, "follow my lead, Linx."

Before beginning his trek, Yuto remembered a final bit of preparation needed—to tie back his whiskers. A quick tug and pull around the back of his head allowed him to tie the bundles of long, fibrous fur into a loose braid behind him. He looked on at Linx, who, due to his age, had whiskers that were nowhere near long enough to require such a thing. It was the one and only time he was envious of someone with short whiskers.

Yuto went first, pressing himself against the wall of warm rock and traipsing along the thin ledge. It was at least wide enough for his feet to shift around, but keeping them pointed forward and slowly shuffling to the side was the best way forward. As his chest and whiskers pressed against the wall of stone, and his back felt the occasional gusts of quick steam, he couldn't help but imagine himself as a piece of meat in a sandwich being cooked. It was silly, at least in his mind, but it was perhaps just another attempt to get his mind off of the danger.

It was then that he realized he was barely helping to carry the cage. He looked over to his right to see Linx still holding up the cage with his left paw, and his right paw firmly on the ropes leading back to Attl, who had woven them between the handful of stakes he had set. Linx looked back and smiled, untroubled by the situation, and his grip and balance as firm and stable as one could hope. Yuto smiled worriedly back, extended a limp arm to the cage's wooden underside to at least help carry it a little, and turned back to his left to keep moving forward.

Yuto glanced up and above his now entirely fogged and sweaty spectacles to see the lump in the wall that was their destination. He had almost forgotten about what exactly they were aiming for. The suspicious lump in the wall almost seemed to breathe—like a grainy boil with forsaken liquids flowing and bubbling just beneath a thin, uppermost membrane. The burning reddish-orange rocks on the wall all nearly blended together, and it was mostly the shifting shadows cast by the wall's bumpy texture that gave the queen's position away. The closer they crept to their destination, the more the creatures seemed to notice—at first only a scant few illymites could be seen scurrying in and out of crevices in the wall, but it was not long before there were no less than twenty or so of the creatures diving in and out of their precipitous burrow. Their trademark cherry-red bulbs blended in with the orange light, and it was mostly their glistening, almost wet-looking shine that gave them away.

Whoosh!

A great burst of colorless smoke shot up from the volcano's depths, behind the two Tarsers, and up into the air. Linx remained unphased, though Yuto nearly jumped. Once again, his wandering mind was interrupted, though this time in a way he thoroughly did not appreciate. Linx, and his grip on the large cage, acted as an anchor of sorts for the old Tarser. Even when he jolted from shock, Linx's hold of the cage remained completely stable. It very well may have been the one thing keeping Yuto safe.

Clack!

Another harsh sound interrupted Yuto's thoughts. He whipped his head up and around, and looked to the top of the cage to see the source. Fortunately, it was merely a few loose rocks that bounced off of the topmost rim of the contraption. Yuto gave a sigh of relief. Linx feigned a similar motion, but Yuto knew full well that the young Tarser was faking it. The two shared a brief chuckle before Yuto looked back to check on Attl. He was quite a ways away and had remained oddly silent the entire time. His focus was almost menacing. Yuto was glad his companions were both so composed.

Yuto picked up the pace, and it only took another minute of crawling along the ledge that they were finally at their destination. The shifting bulb of stone in the wall was between Linx and Yuto, and within arm's reach above them.

This is it, Yuto thought. *So close, so close!*

First things first—hammering in a couple of hooked stakes for the two corners of the cage facing the cavern wall. These would be used for support. The ledge Yuto and Linx stood on would be used to help support the bottom of the cage, and the two, along with Attl, were holding on to the ropes wrapping around the back of the cage. This would form the "base," making use of an excessive number of points of contact—the two hooked corners, the ledge, Yuto and Linx's grip, the ropes on the back, and finally Attl's anchor.

Next, Yuto and Linx began to slowly—painfully slowly—excavate around the perimeter of the lump. The open-concept design of the cage, which made it look more like a piece of scaffolding than anything, would allow most of the stones dug out to merely fall through and out of the way. The suspended harness in the cage's center would catch some stray rocks, but Linx assured them that it would merely offer some extra cushioning for the queen's eventual descent. The male illymites were constantly breaking up and shifting the rock inside the lump, making it refined and soft, which was what allowed the queen to move about and breathe beneath the surface. Carving out a thin, deep perimeter around the queen prompted the queen to begin kicking its many silvery pinchers and legs around as the creature desperately tried to cover itself back up. As more orange stones crumbled and fell away from their claws and metal picks, slivers of something large, glistening, and neon red began to poke through.

"That's it!" Yuto called out, beads of sweat hammering his face and weighing down his eyes. "We're almost there! Just dig a little more!"

Linx increased his pace, chucking large clumps of sand and rock behind him with each swing. Attl merely looked on. Yuto felt a bit awkward, speaking with no response. It always made him feel as if he were talking to himself. Still, their goal was within reach. The more they dug into the wall, the softer the grain became, and the easier the task grew. The heavy brush and creaks of the queen's bulbous, gyrating form as it slowly began to fall out of the burrow prompted Linx and Yuto to stop. The two put away their picks and braced themselves. Yuto's heart raced, nearly beating its way out of his chest. He was tired and hungry, his arms were weak, and his back was starting to ache. The only thing that kept him going was the confident, still unaffected look on Linx's face on the opposite side of the cage. The young fool had both paws on the cage, and Yuto thought this might be the end for his friend. Every moment the loosening sand grew in number, and the queen's massive, bulbous sac inched out from the wall, seemed to go on for an eternity. Yuto was forced to sit and watch and wait for the final descent. He took note of some of the queen's features, most notably its mandibles—they were long and wiry, not particularly adept at biting anything but acting more as slimy sifters that did well to dig into and latch on to any loose bits of ash and sand. It too possessed a dry, chitinous outer shell, with a contrasting bulbous body filled with a bright cherry-red fluid. A mere squint was enough to allow Yuto to see countless bits of ash swimming around inside of it.

It makes a lot more sense now, Yuto thought. *I doubt the smaller male illymites are much different. All this time*

*we have been eating chunks of… of volcanic ash and sand
and who knows what else… Disgusting… I can't believe
I ever fed these things to my family…*

Unable to bear the tense waiting any longer, Yuto
had to say something, anything, to ease his nerves. He
looked at Attl and called out, "Attl! Tighten the slack
on the rope! She's about ready to drop!"

Strangely, Attl didn't move, or respond in any way
for that matter. Yuto furrowed his brow, wondering
what was wrong. At least Attl had both paws on the
rope, and his stance was wide, as if ready to catch the
oncoming weight.

Fwump!

To Yuto's shock, the queen fell into the cage and
landed neatly in the suspended red seat! Dozens of tiny
illymites fell out, mixed in with countless bits of stone
and sand that all fell to the wayside and between the
wooden scaffolding of the cage. The cage itself didn't
even budge. Linx looked stable as ever, as if the creature's weight wasn't even a factor. Still, the young Tarser
smiled wide, the orange light from the magma deep
below bouncing off of his large, dark eyes and into
Yuto's. Yuto couldn't help but smile back, as he let loose
a sigh of relief. More than a sigh, he nearly began to
heave as he let out his joy.

"Heh, hehe! Ha! We did it! Excellent work, young
man!" Yuto cried out. He didn't even care that his
glasses had slid to the tip of his nose, about to join
the waterfall of sweat coming off of him in the heated
abyss below. Yuto collected himself and turned to Attl,
who had remained still during the whole affair. "Attl!
We're ready! Tighten the slack and help guide us back!"

Again, Attl stood, staring silently. Linx finally seemed to notice, and he turned his head around to look at the darkly dressed and dour Tarser as well.

"Attl? Attl! What's wrong? Are you alright?" Yuto yelled. The constant grumbling of the volcano only seemed to get louder. Yuto was tired of yelling, but he was more worried about his friend than anything.

Yuto looked down and noticed something frightening—the rope had too much slack! There was little support on the back of the cage! The whole thing was slowly tipping backward now. Linx was still staring at Attl, probably as puzzled as Yuto was. Still, Yuto was too weak to hold the cage by himself—he had to get Linx back on track.

"Linx!" Yuto screamed. "Linx! The cage! It's gonna fall! Help!"

Linx whipped his head back and noticed the cage creeping backward toward the abyss. He whipped his arm around, swirling thick rope with it, and tightening it into a lumpy bundle around his limb. With a heaving pull, Linx was able to hold the cage in place, its back end now hanging at a steep angle off the small ledge. The suspended seat swung around, but kept the bulbous creature within it held. The two stared for a moment and caught their breath. Yuto looked back up to see that his young companion had one paw on the cage, and had dug the claws on the other into a deep crevice in the wall. Yuto grit his teeth and stared back at Attl, before calling out to him again.

"Attl! What on Halifell is wrong with you?! What's wrong—"

"Nothing is wrong, Yuto, at least not with me," Attl said. He was doing his best to remain composed, but the growing sounds of the volcano forced him to nearly yell.

"What? What do you mean—"

"I am tired, Yuto. I am tired of this thankless existence, having to be responsible for you, and assisting you during your wild ventures, and getting you out of trouble. All the while *you* get to have a family, *you* get to do as you please, *you* get to ignore the market and bother the guild and still find, by pure happenstance, the most profitable commission seen this side of the country! Here we have an opportunity, and yet you are too dumb to see it! You would instead cause trouble, rather than make use of this venture to achieve fathomless wealth! The sort of wealth that would finally allow you to take proper care of poor Jeea and your children."

"Attl, where is this all coming from?"

"You know exactly where this is all coming from. I am tired of being a third wheel. I knew Jeea long before you did. I even knew her father and assisted with his trading company before he died and it went under. We both decided to begin traveling, and I figured it would help us bond and we could forge a path together. But then *you* came along and did what you do best! Disrupting what should have been an easy course!"

"Attl, I thought you and Jeea broke up amicably! We have talked about this before! I thought—"

"You thought wrong!" Attl pulled hard on the rope, angling his entire body to make use of each pivot created by the hooked stakes he had put in the ground.

Linx felt it first, his body being tugged slightly outward, though his iron grip remained. Every movement could be seen affecting the cage, however. The wooden edges creaked under the weight of the suspended cushion and the swaying of the illymite queen inside of it. The sounds of loose rock falling off the edge faded into nothing, and for a time there was little else but the grumbling volcano filling the air.

Attl continued, "Jeea and I argued quite a bit whenever you weren't around, before finally putting it to rest. Or, at least, *she* put it to rest. To be honest, I could never truly let it go. I could never let her go."

"Attl… we have remained friends for decades. We have all continued to spend time together, to talk, and laugh and reminisce… Don't tell me that all this time you were merely holding on to an old grudge? Even the children loved to come over and play on your ranch, back when they were still healthy enough to do so."

"Ah, yes, your children… Having to sit by and watch you continue to make trouble for your family, for Jeea and your children…" Attl stared blankly for a moment, his mind pacing through unknown thoughts. He fiddled anxiously with the rope in his paws, the thick and yellowed twine barely making its way through and across his fingers. His nails occasionally picked at bits of frayed and burned pieces of the rope. It seemed as if he was struggling to cope with his uncharacteristically emotional outburst. Attl clearly wasn't comfortable expressing himself in such a way, but whatever emotions were spurring him forth seemed to be winning out.

"You're not the only one who has suffered, Attl!" Yuto leaned forward, bracing his feet and his claws on the wall. He even leaned on the cage that Linx was still holding, hoping desperately that the young Tarser could handle it all. At least Linx was remaining calm—it was once again the only thing giving Yuto any sense of stability. "I was there, Attl! I had to watch each and every single one of them die off slowly! Every day I regret ever feeding them these wretched things, these disgusting bugs! I… I know I can be a troublesome friend. I've been, at times, a less-than-ideal husband—unable to provide a proper home and money without loans. I've certainly been a less-than-ideal father, and each closed door on the floor of my children's bedrooms is a testament to that. That is why I am here, and that is why we need to get this creature back for everyone to see! They need to know the truth! I know *you* can see that!"

Attl shifted his weight down, pulling hard on the rope connecting them all. A stiff wave snapped through the rope, hitting everything in order—through Linx, who merely tensed himself and bore the brunt of the motion, leading to a snap of yellow twine against the back end of the wooden cage, and finally ending with Yuto, whose entire body nearly flew up and then off the ledge. Yuto had completely given up on holding the cage and had to leave his physical safety in Linx's capable paws. He hated that he was once again burdening someone else with his own troubles—especially a new and recent friend—but the current circumstances demanded he do so.

Yuto widened his stance and stabilized himself on the ledge. Another great burst of hot smoke from the magma-filled abyss below gave him a chance to catch his breath. It was perhaps the least satisfactory breath he had ever taken—he may as well have inhaled a bag of steam for what it was worth—but it was enough.

"Whatever it is you want," Yuto continued, "we can work something out! You don't want to kill us! You are better than that, Attl! You've always been better than that! Better than me!"

"Indeed, I suppose I am better," Attl said, his body still low, and his weight still pulling tightly on the rope, "and yet *you* seem to always get what you really want, while I'm stuck with the cleanup. I suppose I am better, because I have never been able to rely on anyone else to bail me out. Yet… I suppose it has made me bitter. You get to completely ignore the market, and play around with loans while I toil day and night selling these things, these illymites, competing with everyone else, all the while having to manage a nequine ranch on the side. All of this, just to get dragged into more of your troubles, because I know how much Jeea, and your children, have needed you in the past."

"S-so you will stop this? You will calm down, and allow us to carefully return from this ledge and we can take the queen to—"

"No!" Attl shifted his weight again. This time in the opposite direction, and the pull was enough to nearly loosen the stakes holding everything together. Another wave snapped through the rope, even greater than the last. The sinewy, dark muscles in Linx's arms tensed as he tried to take the oncoming force, but the snap was enough to make him flinch. A crack in the rope whipped against the wooden cage, enough to cause its nearest wall to snap! A sickening screech echoed out from the splintering scaffold as it slid right off the ledge, with its now disconnected side stretching open like the jaw of an injured beast. Yuto, who still had a paw on the cage, felt its weight nearly carry him down. If not for his harness, and the rope wrapped around his left arm, he very well may have been fed to the volcano at that moment. It took a solid minute of crying and heavy breathing before Yuto realized he had stopped falling. He slowly opened an eye to see Linx kneeling down, now using both of his paws and arms to hold the cage and a bundle of the rope leading to Yuto. Streams of sweat were getting caught in the many crevices and wrinkles of the young, dark Tarser's face, more than a few droplets were pelting Yuto. A drop hit Yuto's nose and he realized that his glasses were now long gone, though he no longer cared. Habits built up over a lifetime still nearly caused him to reach for his glasses to try to readjust them. He would have laughed, if not for the sizzling heat against the pads of his feet, reminding him of his predicament.

The clinking of metal being pulled from soil, and the brush of loosening twine to the side caught Yuto's attention. Through a few plumes of steam, he could see glimpses of Attl's body slowly and methodically removing each stake and pulling out the rope. Attl finished his endeavor and made his way over to the far side of the ledge.

"You have no idea how much of our economy depends on the illymites now," Attl said, staring down his snout at his old friend. "The thing is… the merchant's guild already knows about the queens. They used to post far more guards along the forest perimeter, but so few Tarsers were foolish enough to ever tempt this region, and the few who were, well… they never returned. Even the so-called legendary Mitus DeTrell never bothered with these godforsaken lands. I'm sorry, Yuto, but I've settled this in my mind—this is for the greater good. I'm sorry about your children, I truly am. Trust me, I wish every day that Jeea would have ended up with me—things may have turned out different… But what's done is done, and we all must move forward. The market demands adaptation, Yuto. You either adapt or get left behind. That is how life works."

"Attl! Attl please!" Yuto cried. "It's not too late! I don't hold anything against you! Just please, please, my friend, don't do this!"

"I am sorry it has come to this, old friend." Attl took in a deep breath—a final contemplation, perhaps his way of quelling whatever emotions may still be holding him back—before looking to Linx. "I also have to apologize to you, Linx. At least this will be the last time Yuto drags anyone else into trouble."

"Attl!" Yuto let loose a final cry but to no avail. Attl began to pull and ready the rope, and the twine tightened all along the backs and harnesses of the two Tarsers and the cage. Yuto looked desperately at Linx, who remained calm. In fact, Linx was expressing a new emotion—a sort of quiet, stirring anger had forced his face into a dense mask of stone-like features, his breath still and his eyes set on Attl. Yuto swore he could see a slight grimace on the boy's face. He couldn't help but wonder what was going through Linx's mind at that moment.

Attl slowly shifted his weight back up and readied himself for a final pull. "I'm sorry, you two."

"No need to apologize!" Linx snapped.

The moment his grip on the rope tightened a final time, Linx sprang into action, tightening his own grip and whipping the rope down with such force that it cracked the wind. Attl, not anticipating such a maneuver, and his grip still firm on the rope, face-planted into the volcanic soil and found himself sliding forward several feet and clear off of the ledge! A guttural, phlegmy grunt followed the brush of a body being dragged over the soil and soon Attl found himself swinging through the air. Linx shifted his arms around to work with the momentum and tensed his shoulders. It took both paws and all his strength to keep everyone suspended. Yuto, still hanging on by the tight rope wrapped around his arm, instinctively reached out to grab his friend. Attl immediately reached out and caught Yuto's paw, and their movement settled after a few moments of swaying.

"Attl!" Yuto cried out once more. "I've got you! It's okay, we can work this out! I don't—"

Ptoo!

A steaming, wet slime hit Yuto straight in his eye. Attl's spit shocked Yuto, and instinctively he released his grip as he recoiled. He frantically rubbed his face and tried to get another look at his friend, but he was gone. He only caught a glimpse of burning fur and a dark blue tunic disappearing silently into the sea of orange liquid and hot gray steam below. Yuto couldn't help but sit and stare into the volcanic abyss. He swore his arm was broken. He couldn't tell the difference between the spit and the copious amount of sweat sitting on his face like a burning mask. Yet this didn't stop him. He stared into the bright and burning lava for so long that his eyes began to hurt. The occasional gust of steam and gas bursting up and against them did not deter him either. His mind was blank, and no matter how long he stared, he couldn't believe that his once best friend was dead.

Was it all a lie? All of the good times we shared? The years of traveling and settling down? All this time... He held on to such anger... Because of me...

The rope began to sway once more. It felt as if Yuto had to use all of his strength to turn his attention away from the magma below to look up. Linx, his grip still tight on all of the ropes keeping Yuto and the cage suspended, was slowly inching his way along the wall, back toward safer ground.

Yuto should have felt relieved, but in truth, at least in that moment, he felt nothing. He decided to let Linx carry him forward for just a little bit longer.

CHAPTER 18

THE TRIP BACK TO THE CAPITAL WAS long. Every moment seemed to drag in Yuto's mind. He remembered the instant relief he felt when Linx pulled him up onto stable land. The sting in his dislocated—but at least not broken—arm as he finally let it loose from the bundle of tight ropes wrapped around it. He also remembered the look on Linx's face when he remarked that they somehow got the queen out of there in one piece—it was a look caught between turmoil and satisfaction. Linx smiled, but not with his whole face—his eyes remained down-turned, and his brow sat furrowed into a dense packing of muscle and wrinkles. Yuto remembered the guilt he felt, knowing that no one so young should have to go through something like that. Yuto couldn't help but hug Linx, as if he were one of his own. He remembered apologizing and thanking the young Tarser profusely, so much so that both his words of gratitude and pleas for forgiveness began to trip over each other until the old Tarser was little more than a bumbling mess.

Most of all, he remembered Linx's soft paw patting his back, before merely saying, "It is alright, Yuto."

Yuto cried for what felt like the longest minute of his life. He could remember settling himself down, and from there, the rest was honestly a blur.

Though he did remember Linx offering to drive the carriage home. Yuto declined and said that Linx had done more than enough. The young Tarser had little trouble carrying the mangled cage to the carriage, at least. Yuto offered to help carry it, but Linx of course declined, though he appreciated the gesture.

Yuto was so used to keeping the conversation going that the consistent quiet that sat between them was difficult to adjust to. Linx tried regularly to get a conversation going, but he clearly wasn't comfortable with that either. Yuto found it charming, in a way. Every other youngster he had ever met loved to talk and could hardly hold their attention on anything for more than a minute. Linx eventually found that they were both at ease with merely sharing each other's company in peace. Yuto needed the time to think over their next move.

The queen was still intact. Despite the complications, they could continue with the commission. It was difficult to notice when surrounded by sweltering, smothering heat and rumbling volcanoes, but the smell was nigh unbearable. It was caught somewhere between rotting eggs, fish intestines, and wet flatulence. In the fresh air of the open fields on the way back home, there was little else to conceal the odor. Its physical appearance was equally detestable. In the bright, clear light of the day, away from the steamy, cloudy air of the volcanic region, more of its features became apparent. Its silvery pinchers were in fact a grainy brown, and it was mostly the light of the magma and the constant stream of wet steam creating its luster. Fortunately, it appeared to be calm enough in its suspended harness, and Linx took great care to feed it bits and pieces of ash he had gathered before they ventured off.

A number of small, male illymites followed them for miles before giving up. They would buzz around constantly as if trying to attack the poachers who dared to kidnap their queen. They were easy enough to swat away, but their persistence was commendable. The fact that they eventually decided to abandon their queen was humorous to Yuto, however.

How should I go about this?

Yuto kept asking himself this, and every time his mind would settle on a blank.

Was Attl telling the truth? If the guild already knows about the queens and their diet, and what we have all been eating this whole time...

His first thought was to take the queen straight to the merchant's guild, but Attl's words stuck in his mind. If they were already in on it, then that would do no good. He couldn't just leave the queen somewhere and hope it would get attention, obviously. There was no one else Yuto knew who could help. He caught himself just before thinking of asking Attl for help. The emptiness he felt made it all the clearer that Attl perhaps spoke more than a few uncomfortable truths in the volcano. Attl had no reason to lie about that, so why would he lie about the guild?

Yuto knew he had to decide quickly. They would only be able to keep the queen alive for so long. For the time being, it would occasionally spit out new illymites. It was the perfect condition to show the monstrosity off, but how should they go about it? Perhaps he could take it into the center of town, make a big scene, and expose the truth to everyone? And then what? They get arrested? Everyone calls them nutters and ignores them? Maybe they actually do rile up the common folk enough and a riot begins? Yuto wasn't interested in playing a revolutionary. Round and round his thoughts swirled, as day turned into night, and back into day again. The black soil of the magma fields had long since given way to the lush plains beyond the forest. The fog of the wet woods had since overtaken Yuto's senses, though he hardly noticed as he continued to constantly ruminate over his next move.

How am I going to break the news to Jeea? She went to so much trouble to keep Attl around as a close friend. She perhaps thought just as much as I did that he had come to terms with how things turned out. I hope she doesn't hate me too much for losing a dear friend…

"Looks like we are almost there," Linx said.

"Huh?" Yuto snapped out of his trance and whipped his head to the side to peer over his shoulder at his patient passenger.

"We are nearly back at the city," Linx said, pointing a dark claw ahead.

Yuto looked forward and could see a number of familiar domes and beige-robed Tarsers shuffling back and forth. The early morning sun was already peeking over the horizon formed of wooden structures and buildings.

"Oh, boy…" Yuto didn't necessarily mean to let out his anxiety, but the words slipped out before he could even think to stop it. He only grew more anxious as he realized he had completely missed a most important stop—his home. It would have to wait, as any moment wasted was a moment that the queen may perish, and whatever effect it may have on whoever they decide to show it to would be diminished.

Yuto looked over his shoulder once again to bark an order to Linx. "Hey, gather up some blankets or something, and cover the cage."

"Sure, but… do you still plan to take the queen to the guild?" Linx asked. He spoke as he shuffled around to gather what pieces of cloth remained—little more than a few musty pink and violet sheets that they had been using to sleep on. It wasn't much, but it would do for the time being.

"Yes," Yuto replied, turning his head back to look ahead. "I can't think of any better way to go about this. Maybe if they discover that I know the truth, they'll consider working something out or listening. Maybe I could even threaten to let the word out."

"I thought you were planning on doing that, anyway?"

"I am. But if I can get the guild talking, and get some proof of their duplicity… I don't know, maybe it will help. At the very least, we could work on weeding out the rats among our guild leaders."

Since they were traveling by carriage, they had to take the largest and most open paths through the city.

They would be striding right through the heart of the capital and through the market. Normally such visibility was great—letting the eyes of hundreds of potential customers catch a glimpse of your wares on the way to set up was more than enough to get business going. Though the last thing Yuto wanted was immediate suspicion. He also wondered if he was still banned from the market, or the guildhall—he had been gone for months on his misadventure. Perhaps they had lightened up during the relative peace his absence surely provided?"

"You two! Halt! Stop right there!"

A great, husky voice called out, booming directly at the duo of weary travelers. Yuto nearly jumped out of his seat, and let go of his reins. Fortunately, the nequines remained calm, as did Linx. A guard strapped in well-fitted wood and steel armor, brandishing a long and shining silver spear, made his way over to the side of their carriage.

"Oh, uh, hi again, Rackel," Yuto said, almost shrugging as his meek tone barely allowed the words to pass through his snout.

"That's First Sergeant Rackel, Chief Guardsmen of the Southeastern Divison of the Merchant's Hall, to you, citizen," Rackel said, as loud as ever. He was loud enough that he actually began to draw the attention of a number of Tarser passersby. "What is this you have here? You *do* realize you're *still* banned from both the market *and* the guildhall, Yuto?"

"But I've been gone for so long!" Yuto shouted. "I've been quiet, and surely things have been peaceful? I haven't caused any trouble—"

"You are an adult, are you not Yuto?" Rackel lightly lifted his weapon and gave the ground a heavy tap with its blunt end. "You know full well that is not how this works? Besides, you finally return with what looks like one of Attl's carriages, yet I see Attl is nowhere to be found? And what on Halifell do you have there? The smell is enough to get you banned from the capital wholesale for life. And you! In the back there? Who are you?"

Yuto looked over to see Linx with the most bewildered expression he had ever seen. Normally Linx was so calm and collected—it was a bit strange to see him so stunned. The young Tarser merely stared at the guard, almost as if he knew him.

"What is wrong with you?" Rackel sneered. "Are you on some sort of drug? Is that what you're carting around, Yuto? Couldn't hack it in the legal market, so you've taken to sneaking in contraband? Let me see what you have—"

"No! Rackel, wait!"

It was too late. Rackel quickly swiped his free paw at the haphazard collection of musty blankets covering the cage. He whipped the covers off with such speed that the splintered cage nearly tore apart from the motion. The queen, now languid and barely hanging on to its life, bobbed back and forth in its suspended seat as its pointed pinchers slowly creaked back and forth. Its great, bulbous red body sac was still bright red, and countless bits of ash and something else seemed to be swimming inside of it.

"My word! What is that?!" Rackel recoiled, throwing a paw up to his face to cover his snout. All eyes were suddenly on the pulsating monstrosity sitting in the back of the carriage. A crowd began to gather, and countless hushed murmurs surrounded the scene.

"Hey! You guardsmen over there!" Rackel shouted. "Hurry up and get over here! Help me confiscate this… this… whatever it is, so we can dispose of it. And one of you apprehend these two—"

"No! Wait! You don't understand!" Yuto cried. He nearly leaped from his seat to grab Rackel's paw. The two began to struggle, and the whole carriage began to wobble. It seemed to have taken on quite a bit of wear and tear over the course of their journey, and the wooden planks making up the carriage's sides began to show it by stretching loose as the two pushed and pulled at one another. Linx stood up, ready to assist Yuto, but this only seemed to worsen the carriage's condition. Before Linx could take another step, the nequines began to show agitation, and both of the creatures began to pull and thrash about in opposing directions. The guards Rackel beckoned—about three more armor-clad Tarsers—rushed in to try to calm the beasts, to no avail. Yuto and Rackel's voices were rapidly growing in volume, and the crowd that had formed around them followed suit, their hushed murmurs and whispers turning into loud proclamations, and even some members of the audience were shouting obscenities, though at what or who, Yuto couldn't tell.

At the peak of the commotion, Rackel tried to get a hold of Yuto, nearly locking his arms in an iron grip. Yuto thrashed, not realizing that the reins to the nequines had gotten wrapped around one of his legs. He kicked as hard as he could, not only knocking back

Rackel a foot or so onto the pavement but also whipping the reins with a painful snap that cracked the air. A shrill neighing rolled out from each nequine, and both huddled together before sprinting forward. The crowd dispersed, a wave of beige and brown and fur and whiskers parting like water in all directions to give the runaway vehicle space to speed ahead. A chaotic cacophony took the wind—the frantic galloping of hooves against pavement, the fracturing of weathered wood splitting apart, Yuto's scurrying pitter-patters as he desperately tried to regain control of the vessel, and the many gasps and screams of wandering Tarsers unfortunate enough to nearly get run over. The only thing that remained quiet was Linx, who merely held on, both to the carriage and the queen in its cushioned seat.

Everything came to a violent end when the carriage crashed directly into the wall of stairs leading right to the guildhall. Everything, save for the brawny nequines, flew in all directions. Wood and cloth and bits of ash now dotted the otherwise pristine steps. Yuto fell back first on a few steps higher up, forcing out a loud shriek and a trailing whimper after landing. Linx landed right on the bottom step, seemingly unnerved by the pain and his arms outstretched as he had tried his best to maintain the queen's condition. Unfortunately, the queen had partially fallen out of the velvet red cushion, and its bulbous sac was now split open, painting a shocking amount of the once clean steps with grainy fluid. Its coloring was an indistinct mixture of pale red and black-brown grains. Many smaller cherry red bulbs could be seen swimming in the fluid, and a number of even smaller insects were still inside the queen, desperately attempting to stay within her abdomen. The two nequines had long since split apart and, now free from their reins, ran off in opposite directions and past the quickly oncoming crowd of Tarsers curious to see the result of the commotion.

It was a fortunate moment of calm, as everyone slowly gathered around to witness the barely living, pulsating insectoid mass desperately grasping for life. The peace was soon interrupted by several silent spasms, with thick guts alternating between dripping and bursting out of the split sac. Several gasps echoed out from the group, and Yuto swore he could hear at least one Tarser throwing up in the back. The queen then caught everyone's breath as it sucked in, then let loose a gurgling spurt that prematurely birthed a handful of illymites from some orifice that had been covered and caked in the creature's own quickly drying guts. A few were just strong enough to buzz their wings and fly away, though most merely struggled to move in the mucousy liquid staging the steps.

It's now or never, I suppose, Yuto thought. He picked himself up, leaning on one side as he held what may have been a broken rib, and he finally addressed the crowd.

"This… This is where your precious illymites are coming from! These things, they subsist on harmful volcanic ash. How do you think you are digesting this? Where do you think all of that goes?! You see it, don't you?"

Yuto pointed a sharp claw at the creature, its form still gestating on the steps. A sea of confused and worried faces watched, unsure of what to make of the display. Yuto, growing frustrated, kneeled down and scooped up a pawful of the queen's innards, a writhing mass of stillborn insects and muck and ash.

"I see a few of you are still holding on to parcels of preserved illymites. Here, have some more, free of charge!"

Yuto reeled his arm back, and chucked the glob forward, a satisfying plop echoing out from its impact with the pavement at the feet of a few unfortunate onlookers. They immediately needed to pinch their noses and cover their snouts.

"How many of you have been subsisting on these things alone? How many of you have been feeding this—*this!* This disgusting goo to your children?! Where do you think that ash goes?! If you are not fortunate enough to have it pass through your stomachs, it goes straight to your lungs! And once it's there, the damage is done! There is no getting rid of it! Can you sleep easy knowing that your children may forever need to breathe hard?! Is the money, and the occasional snack, worth it?!"

The sounds of armored feet clinking against the pavement cut through the crowd. A few open helmets and waving spears followed a small group of guards pushed through.

"What have you done?!" Rackel barked. "Why do you insist on causing trouble, Yuto?! Now I have to apprehend you—"

"Apprehend me for what, Rackel?" Yuto snapped back, whipping his frail arm in front of him, accentuating every word as best as he could. "Finally telling everyone the truth? Letting everyone see what the guild masters have known for years?!"

More whispers and confused murmurs echoed from the crowd.

"The guild?"

"What is he talking about?"

"This can't be where illymites actually come from… right?"

"Why would the guild know anything about this?"

"No more of this nonsense! Yuto!" Rackel turned a fierce snarl and a sharp glare at the old Tarser standing on the steps above him. "Normally you just barge in and get in the way, but now you resort to blasphemy? You do realize you are effectively tarnishing Mitus DeTrell's name, correct? When word gets out about this, his estate is going to be looking for blood—they'll sue you for all your worth! And then some!"

"Why does that matter?" Yuto snapped back. "Why are you so simple-minded, 'oh, great first sergeant?'"

"And now you openly mock a high-ranking officer?! That's it, you are coming with me—"

"Not if I can help it!" Linx stamped forward, ready to place himself between Rackel and Yuto. The young Tarser's footsteps were surprisingly heavy, clapping the ground with perhaps greater force than the guards in all their armor could ever manage.

"Ah, I nearly forgot about you," Rackel said, turning his attention to the dark Tarser. "You may as well be an accomplice in all this. I'll have you both imprisoned."

"For what?! Trying to inform everyone that they are being slowly poisoned?!" Yuto couldn't help but stare in shock. Linx was always so quiet, and mild-mannered, yet here he was screaming. He was also very loud, as his voice somehow carried off into the distance, as if echoing in a great canyon.

"You two are clearly a threat, not just to this city, but perhaps to our very economy!" Rackel shouted back.

"The only threat I see is the guard trying to silence an innocent man attempting to warn everyone! You all are being poisoned! And you are paying for the privilege!"

"Guards!" Rackel snapped, whipping a quick paw behind him to gesture for assistance. "Come on! Help me round these two up!"

Voices began to ring out from the crowd, their tone energized with malcontent.

"What?! No! Let them speak!"

"Why are we not allowed to hear more about this creature?"

"What is the guild hiding from us?!"

"I want to speak with the guild masters! Let us in the hall!"

"Everyone stand back!" Rackel turned his spear sideways and began to push against the restless bodies surrounding them. "This is official guild business! Any actions you take to disrupt our procedures can and will—*Argh!* I said *stand back!*"

Rackel pushed at least a half dozen bodies back, and the gesture was merely returned with a full dozen angered Tarsers stomping back. More guards could be heard clamoring their way down the steps. Demands for an audience with the guild could be heard echoing out from the crowd. Demands from the guards now piling down upon them to settle and step back were only met with more angry responses, and before long, everything turned to noise as the first blows were exchanged. Two guards had already placed their paws on Yuto and began to drag him up the steps.

"Hettle? Derf? Is that you?" Yuto said as he was lifted up by his arms.

"Sorry, Mr. Yuto." Derf could hardly look Yuto in the eye.

"It's nothing personal, but we have to do our jobs," Hettle said.

"You two boys shouldn't be getting caught up in this," Yuto said.

"Yuto!" Linx's shouting rang out from below. Yuto looked over his shoulder to see Linx pushing away guard after guard as if they were nothing. A few seemed to get the hint, and merely circled around him, but didn't approach him, or at least get close enough for Linx to get a hold of them. The guards were hesitant to point their weapons at them. In truth, Tarser guards were more for show than anything. Riots were so rare, and often so uncalled for, yet here Yuto found himself in the midst of one.

"Everyone! This way!" Linx shouted. "Do not let them take Yuto!"

Hettle and Derf picked up the pace, tugging harshly at Yuto's aching arms as they pulled him into the merchant's hall at the peak of the mountain of steps. They sped through the same doorways and hallways that Yuto often barged through to address the guild masters directly. The rumbling of countless feet storming behind quickly grew, and in a flash, the three were overtaken and forced into the meeting hall. A small group of finely dressed and noble-looking Tarsers—no more than four or five, as far as Yuto could tell—stared back at them in shock.

Yuto immediately locked eyes with the senator, the same finely dressed, husky Tarser who banished him from the market. An awkward, tense moment sat between them as they looked at one another before the husky Tarser turned his attention toward the crowd bulging through his door.

How do I always end up here? Yuto thought.

"What is this?!" the senator bellowed. "What is going on—"

The noble was unable to finish his statement, as the crowd immediately answered with a chorus of complaints, questions, exasperations, grievances, and every other sort of response that would turn up the nose of any Tarser who had ever worked in management. Hettle and Derf had to release Yuto to hold back the crowd. In truth, he felt just as trapped as the nobles, caught between both sides and unable to worm his way out through the sea of raucous Tarsers pushing back against the growing line of guards. Eventually, the crowd began to settle down as something seemed to be worming its way from the back. The sea of furry bodies eventually split in two, allowing a couple of particularly stubborn Tarsers to shuffle ahead, all the while carrying a messy pile of dried muck and insect parts. Everyone went quiet as countless wide, dark eyes fixated on the creature as it was unceremoniously thrown onto the otherwise pristine hardwood table in the room's center. All eyes looked down, and then turned upward to the senator, who couldn't seem to take his eyes off of the monstrosity.

The senator finally took in a breath and nearly whimpered as he cleared his throat.

"O-oh, look," the senator whimpered. "How interesting! I think I can see a few illymites in there—"

It was no use. The people were not interested in hearing the senator's defense, detecting the insincerity in his attempted deflection when presented bluntly with the truth. There must have been no less than a hundred Tarsers caught up in the fervor at that time, and every one of them seemed to work in unison. A coarse wave of screams followed a heaving wall of bodies as they descended into the room. The guards, try as they might, were seemingly consumed by the horde. Hettle was the first to draw blood, using his spear for the first time. It was an awkward cut, but the blood-curdling shriek was enough to grab the attention of the masses, and the beatings began. Derf desperately tried to reach his friend, and his own weapon carelessly cut several other Tarsers along the way. Blood and stripped fur followed as he, too, was forcefully assimilated. The senator and his compatriots, who had until then remained silent, were screaming in the corner. They, too, were taken by the horde. It was akin to watching a flame slowly overtake a land that had never experienced such a catastrophe.

More bodies began to flood in. Yuto found himself pressed against the walls of the meeting hall. He too was taken by the undiscerning wave of fury. Everything melded into one—the screams, the shared body heat, the strips of fur and streaks of blood—he couldn't even tell one Tarser from another as he found himself caught beneath the weight of countless rioters all constantly moving, swimming back and forth over each other to express their anger.

The mob was, somehow, more suffocating, more oppressive, and more threatening than the volcano Yuto was dangling from a ledge in only a few months prior. He found his body being pushed and pulled in every direction, as if the ocean had taken him, and its waves had wrenched all control from him. At least he had proper company in the volcano. There, suppressed beneath the weight of countless strangers lashing out, he felt alone. He was still struggling to determine how he should feel about Attl. He did not feel animosity toward him. In truth, Yuto missed his old friend, wishing to return to simpler times. He reminded himself that he had yet to give Jeea the bad news, though he wondered if it was for the best—should her view of their relationship be tainted with the truth?

Yes… The thought cut into the old Tarser's mind immediately. If he was willing to risk so much to share the truth with total strangers, the good Tarsers of his city, then why not his wife as well? The weight of another failure pulled mightily, and painfully, at his heart. It felt more as if his heart had turned to stone and dropped into his gut. Despite this, he held on to his conviction. Jeea always said that it was his earnestness that she appreciated most of all. It never mattered what he did—she was willing to support him regardless of his mistakes, and never blamed him for any of them. He always thought that he didn't deserve her. Even now he wondered if Attl was in fact more deserving of her, but the same thought cut into his mind immediately.

She would just smile, and say that I shouldn't blame myself, knowing full well that I do anyways...

The heavy darkness of the mob began to push down on him. It was enough to suffocate him. Yuto felt strangely calm, as if he had accepted his fate and had achieved peace. It was a feeling he had not fully experienced since all of his children were alive. It had only been a few years since one of his children died, but a startling realization jumped his heart—he struggled to remember the faces of the ones who had passed. It felt as if it were only yesterday that they had been born, and only yesterday that they had died.

What kind of father struggles to remember their own children—regardless of where they were? Tilly, Barkov, Sween, Niora... Would I forget them, too?

Despair took hold as Yuto worked himself into a fit. The fact that he could not even physically express these thoughts, as the swarm of paws and bodies and screams had long since consumed him and made it nigh impossible for him to move or do anything of his own volition. Though it pained him, he at least found some solace in that his final thoughts may be that of his family.

Another sharp sensation cut into his mind, though it wasn't a thought, but something gripping his arm. The feeling was deliberate enough that it caused Yuto to muster enough strength to look down and parse what was happening. It was a dark Tarser paw that seemed to effortlessly break through the sea of bodies.

There was only one Tarser Yuto knew who was capable of such a thing.

Linx! Yuto's mind called out since he physically could not. The muscly limb pulled Yuto through the chaotic mass with ease. The force was such that Yuto worried about his arm getting dislocated once again, or even getting ripped off. It was preferable to slowly smothering under the mob, so he was happy to go along. It was only for a few moments, but he could hardly see much of anything as his body was whipped through a sea of fur and anger and blood and something else—something that took Yuto an extra second of thought and sniffing to determine.

Smoke? In the midst of the ever-growing madness, he could see gusts of smoke! Colorless puffs of air that signaled an oncoming fire. It took a while for the smell to catch up to the sight, which piqued Yuto's curiosity to no end. It was enough of an oddity that he nearly forgot he was being pulled by the arm through a violent mob.

Finally, he felt his back hitting the pavement. He was dizzy from moving so quickly, and he swore the grip on his arm was tight enough that it cut off at least some of his blood supply. Even after stopping, he could feel his insides swirling and his mind racing. Though a few deep breaths were all it took for the old Tarser to recollect himself. With one paw on his head, he instinctively reached for his glasses with the other, only to chuckle once he realized his folly.

"Thank you, Linx," Yuto finally said, "if not for you, I... Linx?"

Yuto looked up to notice that he was sitting on the edge of town. Between the smoke and the increasing orange haze of light burning through the city, it was difficult for Yuto to tell precisely what time of day it was. It almost looked as if dusk had come early to the humble Tarser capital. He could hear screaming and fighting echoing past the many wooden domes and the stomps of armor-clad feet chasing after who knows what. From afar, the chaos settled onto something almost bearable—everything save for the smell. The burning heat filling the air reminded Yuto of the volcano. He wanted to go look for Linx, but a deeper urge compelled him to turn back toward the forest, where a much cooler fog and his family still waited.

Yuto gave a final look to the city and then turned around to scurry home. He figured it would be best to not tempt fate and wanted nothing more than to see his family once again.

CHAPTER 19

THE DAY BEGAN WITH AN UNUSUALLY bright morning. What many would consider a beautiful sight did well to fill a certain soul with a light and airy exuberance.

What a lovely morning!

The furred being quickly jumped down from his bed, showing little care for whether or not it awoke his wife, whose head was still buried deep in a fluffed pillow. He could hear several feet pittering around on the floor below.

Ah, they woke up before me again, Yuto thought. *I wish I weren't so old. It'd be nice if I could wake them up with a simple "good morning" first, like I used to.*

Yuto fluffed his whiskers, brushed his tail aside, and quickly put on a simple beige robe before nearly jumping through the door to his bedroom. Hardly a moment passed before he was sliding down the vines leading to the bottom floor of his home, where all of the cushions were, and the floor that offered the most spacious area for his children to play in. Before he could even look up from his vines, he could hear several squeaky voices already calling out to him.

"Good morning, Daddy!" Niora said first, her large shining eyes revealing their almost crystalline blue sheen as they shifted in the early day's light.

"Hey, Daddy!" Tilly called out, in a hurried manner, as if trying to catch up with Niora.

"Hey, Dad," Barkov said, doing his best to make his young voice sound deep and authoritative.

"Dad! Hi! Is Mom awake yet?" Sween said, her smooth voice like silk flowing in the morning breeze.

Yuto merely smiled, settled himself down on the floor, and reached out. All four of the little bodies of fur and energy hurried forth and gave the old Tarser a hug. It was a new custom in the Haelsker household to start each day with a hug. Yuto always worried about his children, even as their health started to improve, and he would hold on to them and check their breathing. Ever since Jeea made sure to give them the specific brew of polliflower tea—courtesy of Linx's suggestion—it didn't take long for the children's health to begin improving. It had only been a few months since the riots, and a couple months since illymites were entirely banned from the capital city, and a month or so since Yuto had felt it was safe enough to begin going back into town again. Yet in that short time, his children began to breathe much easier. Yuto could remember the first time he woke up one morning to the sound of feet scattering about on the lower floors of his home. He had thought there was an intruder, but was only met with the wide, expectant eyes of his youngest child. He nearly fell to the floor into a puddle of his own tears as he ran forth to embrace her. It wasn't long before the others followed suit. They still needed plenty of rest, and they weren't able to stay up for an entire day without needing sleep, and it was also a lot of work to continue cultivating the plants necessary for their brews, which they needed more of now that the children were moving on their own, but it was a start. Yuto couldn't have been more grateful for the improvement.

Every day, he wanted to show his appreciation to Linx but was only met with the one bit of disappointment in his current life when he remembered the strange Tarser's absence.

It did eat away at Yuto's heart when his children eventually stopped asking about Linx. He felt as if he owed the dark Tarser so much, and yet he had no way of repaying him. The least he could have done was remember him, but he had stayed around for such a short time that it was difficult to imprint any memory of him on his children. Even Niora, who had gotten a glimpse of Linx on his first night staying at their home, couldn't remember anything about the stranger. Yuto had begun to make the rounds back into town to help clean up the mess and rebuild. His middling crafting skill was more valuable than ever, though they hardly needed the money, considering how much Linx left behind. Attl had left behind his nequine ranch, and since he had no other close kin, Yuto and Jeea took it upon themselves to buy the property and begin taking care of it. Jeea hoped that one day when their children were older and healthier, they'd get to learn how to ride and care for the creatures.

Yuto constantly felt as if others had left behind blessings for him. Despite his mistakes, things somehow worked out for them. Though with Attl and Linx gone, he knew he had to take it upon himself to begin acting more carefully. He had hoped for a final moment with Linx, to at least say something cool, maybe something along the lines of:

Heh, no more adventures for me, I suppose…

"Dad? Can we go now?"

"H-huh?" Yuto looked down to see four bright and fuzzy faces staring at him curiously. It was then that Yuto realized he had been holding onto his children for the entire length of his ponderings. He quickly released them and cleared his throat.

"Is Mom up yet?" Niora spoke up again. Yuto never felt ready for her—she was so talkative now. He knew that it would take some time to adjust, but it wasn't his first time having to carry a conversation with young Tarsers—Linx was prone to spacing out and staying quiet as well.

A soft thump could be heard from the upper floor, followed by a series of feet slowly pittering across the wooden floor.

"Looks like she's up now," Yuto said. "Be sure to give her a big hug too, okay?"

CHAPTER 20

THE BRIGHT VOID GREETED THE jester. Above the great white expanse of the inverse universe, a boisterous star cheered out from below.

"Cynkz! You did it! And so efficiently too!" Jio-Mol said. "Overseas trading of the illymites is now off the table! The queen's body has been passed around like candy, grossing out the populace! Word of mouth spreads quickly among Tarsers, as I'm sure you could tell. I must say, you are plenty fun to have around. If you're looking for a new world to stay at permanently…"

"I believe Cynkz's talents could be of much use elsewhere, Jio-Mol," Helon said, sparkling high above and center of the jester's vision.

"Ah yes, of course." Jio-Mol mimicked the clearing of his throat as he spoke. His disappointment was palpable, clear for all to see despite his best attempt to hide it.

"Cynkz! Cynkz, please, if I may have your attention." Anim called out from the void, appearing as a twinkling black speck just beside Helon.

"Greetings, Anim," Cynkz said, instinctively bowing once again. "How are you faring, friend?"

"All is well," Anim continued, "actually, more than well! Lend me your mind's eye, just for a moment."

Cynkz looked on, and closed his eyes, though a vision remained. His mind was taken through a familiar landscape, though one that had been undeniably changed. The barren, gray and brown wastes were now dotted with countless pockets of trees, their many limbs and lavender-tinted leaves reaching up toward the sky like fingers on long hands. The pale figures populating the forests before were now taller, leaner, almost streamlined in their appearance. A few of them were even wearing clothing! Or armor—it was difficult to tell, from the way they were being worn and how they were being used specifically to cover more vulnerable parts of the body. The vision pulled in farther, revealing a number of shabby looking huts built into the trees themselves—each one sticking out of the sides of the grainy trunks like beehives. The pale figures even used a number of crude tools to mark their territory, and to climb and build.

Impressive! It was the first thought that cut into Cynkz's mind. He had trouble discerning anything in specific, but he was given more than enough of a view to see that serious progress had been made.

"Indeed! Isn't it amazing?" Anim responded. His voice was enough to pull Cynkz from his trance, placing his consciousness back into the pale void.

"How much time has passed since I was last there?" Cynkz asked. Part of him dreaded the answer, but his curiosity compelled him to ask regardless.

"Well, if you must know… only around a couple hundred years," Anim said.

"And how much time would have passed in Potarium, then?" The heavy dread remained, and only seemed to be intensifying, yet once again curiosity spurred Cynkz forward. Cynkz wondered how easy it was for Anim to read his expression—he could feel the press of his worried brow straining his face.

"Are you sure you want to know?" Anim said, his restrained tone signaling that he could sense the jester's apprehension.

"Actually, it does not matter," Cynkz said. "I am sure everyone is doing fine back in Potarium."

"You realize you may go home at any point?" A sharp voice cut through the void, and a third speck twinkled into view, on the opposite side of Anim. Siar'C made his presence known the same way he always did. Cynkz found it almost comforting.

"It would not feel right," Cynkz said. "I have yet to achieve anything truly of note."

Helon's fierce twinkling interrupted the jester, her rays cutting into Cynkz's vision from above: "You have technically saved two worlds? And you assisted Anim with cultivating his world as well? All of this, right after saving Potarium—and potentially the rest of the universe—from Eshra'Tel's wrath? This, after deciding, of your own volition, to travel through Munderworld, assisting stray po souls and helping them find salvation, as well as energizing the Sisters of Elm, spurring them on to save even more souls? Do you even understand the implications of your actions? The consequences your decisions and accomplishments may have as they echo into eternity?"

Cynkz shrugged, then politely responded: "To be quite honest, Helon, at the end of the day, I am still just a po. I can only comprehend so much of 'eternity.' If I spent my time trying to parse the infinite consequences of every action I took... Well, I believe I would have been paralyzed from the beginning. If I had known what precisely I was getting into, or what effects it may have, or worried about every possible consequence of my actions, I very well may have never embarked on this adventure to begin with. I know full well that I am small minded when compared to you, to the Omun, to Paithos, and even the Munder King, regardless of what his current position may be. The thing about having an eternity to look forward to, is that you learn to appreciate the present more than anything. The past and future are like a miasma that spreads forth forever in all directions—but the present? It is the one thing that is concrete, palpable, and it is from this center that all else either originates or refers to. I can only look ahead so far, and I can only spend so much time pondering the past—so why not relish the moment? Why not merely move ahead, and do the best that I can? Is that so wrong?"

"I can agree with you on one thing," Siar'C said, "you are small minded. You sound akin to a child that fears looking ahead or thinking their actions through."

"Or," Anim interrupted, "he is merely one po, who is willingly taking on far more responsibility than a mere single mortal soul should ever bear, and is doing his best to come to terms with his position?"

"I quite admire his perspective," Sihl said, his own twinkling speck fading into view above the other stars. "Such a concrete view of existence would do us all well, I believe."

Cynkz couldn't help but notice Sihl's tone. He was more serious than before, and more confident, even going out of his way to compliment Cynkz, without any worry of how Siar'C would respond. Perhaps he, a mere po, a lowly jester, was beginning to rub off on these celestial entities? If he could bring about such change among the Omun, then who is to say that Paithos, the Creator of all things, was any different? Just moments ago he spoke so well of living in the present, yet a small part of Cynkz began to worry about the future—just how would his actions affect the Creator? What larger impact could his conduct have on the cosmos? Could he inadvertently influence all of creation?

New rays began to cut into the void. Cynkz looked up from beneath the brim of his pointed hat to notice that more stars were coming into view. In fact, there were so many pouring in that they nearly turned the pale realm black as they bunched together, crowding each other out to get into view.

"Are these Omun as well?" Cynkz asked.

"Yes," Helon said, "your actions are beginning to get the attention of more Omun. Most are merely curious, though a fair number of them come seeking aid—Muspelios, Xilthim, the twin Omun Norai and Delai, Wel-Dahime, Fr'Oll, Yotheimhe—"

"Entropy will claim us all before you are able to finish your introductions, Helon," Siar'C interrupted.

"I suppose you are right," Helon said, "I apologize if I was not able to introduce you by name to our friend."

Cynkz glanced around, flared his cloak to its side and gave a polite bow to the speckled void: "It is a pleasure to meet you all, regardless."

"Have you noticed anything with the thread?" Anim said. "You have gone through Omundisia multiple times now, perhaps our Lord and Creator has given us a subtle hint of his thoughts on everything?"

"Well, let us see then," Cynkz reached into his cloak once again, and pressed between a sharp forefinger and thumb, he held it out for all to see. The void went silent as the dark sliver took hold of Omundisia's light, and all stared in awe. It was difficult to see the usual specks of ethereal dust emanating from the thread against the backdrop of countless Omun filling the void, but beyond that, it did nothing notable.

Just as Cynkz pulled the thread back into his cloak, Siar'C's sharp voice cut in: "I am beginning to believe this is all merely a waste of time. If the Creator cared, he would have done or said something by now."

"I would gladly assist you and your world next, Siar'C," Cynkz said. "Surely that would get His attention?"

"Pah. Never. This childish game you play is getting tiring. If nothing else, my world will forever be beyond you, mortal."

"All in due time, then."

A new voice, one refined and clear, spoke up: "Well, if he doesn't want your help, I, Muspelios, would love to have you."

Another voice, lighter, almost childlike in its tone, interrupted: "No! We should be next, help us instead!"

"I agree—Norai and I, Delai, would love to have you come with us."

"Technically, Sihl has the greater claim here," Helon said.

"No, it is fine," Sihl said. "My world is fine for the time being. There are others with more pressing concerns. He can come to my world later."

"Splendid!" Muspelios spoke once again. Or at least Cynkz thought it was Muspelios. He could hear growing murmurs and whispers among the thousands of stars littering the void before him. All seemed interested in what he, the strange newcomer, would do. Cynkz tugged his capped and smiled wide, ready to take on his next challenge.

Chapter 21

Time flew by in Omundisia.

Time flew by out of Omundisia as well.

Cynkz could hardly keep track of it all, try as he might. Though the poem always seemed to ground him, in a way:

> *Every star*
> *Near and far*
> *Waits for us*
> *To just*
> *Reach out*
> *And accept them…*

In a selfish way, Cynkz hoped above all else to discover the meaning of that verse. The thread, Paithos, the fate of Peara—these mysteries stood at the front of his mind, but only when he was afforded time to think of them. The poem always sat at the back of his mind, regardless of the circumstances. Why have those words stayed with him for so long? He had long since attempted to parse its meaning, though he never thought of taking its words literally.

Yet here he was—a child of the cosmos, lost to time, and serving the stars themselves. Time flew by, and he struggled to think back and remember just how much he had accomplished thus far:

Muspelios' world—a red hot planet, from afar that looked akin to a cherry marble called Calarin… It only possessed a single moon—a tiny orange pebble in the sky that did little to help illuminate the night. Still, it was quite pretty, as it sat still in the night sky. It was a fun game of the local populations to look up and try to find the moon hidden among the countless stars on clear nights.

I must admit, I was initially disappointed when presented with the prospect of having to spend more time in any sort of volcanic environment. This, especially after having previously witnessed Yuto's dilemma play out in the volcanic region on Halifell…

It was refreshing then to witness simpler people—tall and stony people who consisted of tight knit communities— making full use of their adaptations to the environment. In fact, their tribes were so tight knit that they hardly ever willingly worked together, with anyone outside of their immediate social circles. When they weren't fighting, they were traveling across fields of igneous rock and sparse woodlands. What vegetation that did exist was charred, with near-black leaves and tree bark that crackled in the heated winds.

It was quite easy to impersonate a traveling seer, who could 'foresee' oncoming calamities. In truth, all I did was relay information directly from Muspelios, under the guise of their creator—the all-consuming life rock Skyma, they called him—in order to lead the larger tribes away from natural disasters.

I cannot remember precisely how many tribes I assisted in this way, but it must have been no less than twelve different settlements across two continents. The people of Calarin began to notice the patterns of the volcanoes themselves, and seemed to not need me anymore after a mere half year. This was good timing, as word began to spread of the 'strange seer whose premonitions equaled that of Skyma himself.' I took that as my cue to leave, lest my meddling begin to impose upon their view of the Creator.

The twin stars Norai and Delai watched over a single world—named Istwell. This was a curious oddity, considering the practice of Omun directly assisting one another had long since been discontinued, thanks to the actions of his father Krull, and Eshra-Tel. Their union was apparently a hold over from that bygone time, and as such their people had long since adapted to a second sun, and thus the two stars were allowed to remain in one another's embrace. He wondered if there was something special about the union, as his memories of their world were vivid:

I still remember my first night on Istwell. I remember the heavy sense of dread as I was presented with another desert, and the joy of eventually discovering a more varied landscape.

The days were arid, sure, but the nights were cool as ice. A relaxing chill washed over fields of bleached white sands that almost appeared as snow in the silvery light of Istwell's many moons. Istwell possessed seven moons, and on any given night no fewer than four could be seen at any time. As such, they reflected much of Norai and Delai's light, igniting the world with an enchanting pale illumination.

If I had to describe the world succinctly, I would use the term 'pale crystal.' The burning orange sands of the day more resembled white snow at night. The many creatures—whom were nearly all nocturnal due to Istwell's unusually long nights—also reflected light hues. Flying critters often shone with iridescent lavenders and layered pastel blues and greens that, when the moon hit their shells just right, looked more like emerald and turquoise. Otherwise clear wings looked like paper thin icicles when exposed to the moonlight. The many birds and beasts of the land and air possessed feathers and fur of lily pinks, washed out violets and minty off-whites often speckled with dots of other colors that were often difficult to discern in the night's light.

Nearly everything was reflective in one way or another. It was as if a thin crystalline layer had been spread over everything. That wet layer that caused the eye to look sparkling and reflective in the light seemed to be affecting everything—the ground, the trees, even the bottoms of clouds as they flew overhead. Even the mountaintops in the distance, countless miles away, poked into the dark night sky like twinkling stalagmites. During the day, the intense brightness of the two stars nearly burned out all colors, and most life chose to stay hidden and sleep in the many shadows of the world. It was one of my favorite worlds to merely fly around in, taking in the scenery and watching the world completely transform as Norai and Delai rose and set.

Many of the people of Istwell—smaller, rounder beings that lived primarily underground in complex collections of caverns and tunnels—had begun to hunt during the day. Just as many found the practice unholy, and too risky. Terms such as 'day walker' and 'night strider' became slurs that they would throw at one another during an argument.

They had begun to fight over the practice, even going so far as to begin attacking one another during their opposing time of day. Day walkers would attack night striders in the day when they were vulnerable and asleep, and night striders would attack day walkers during the night. It appeared as if they were all at each other's throats.

It was simple enough to fix the issue—I merely warmed up to the largest colonies of each faction, and began to plant the seeds of affection between the sons and daughters of each group's leaders. Secret letters and spoken testimonials were easy enough to forge, given my talents. One particular union took hold, and after much argumentation and fighting, a settlement was agreed upon.

I only meant to stay for an extra night, which quickly turned into another year of night flying and stargazing. It was quite funny, then, to see the people of Istwell taking the path of least resistance, and slowly integrate back into their naturally nocturnal schedules. I took this as my cue to leave and continue on.

Cynkz struggled to think back on the worlds that came after. Time was moving so fast, and so much was happening, that his mind struggled to remember it all. He could feel that he had experienced things, but he could not specifically remember them. The present

itself was becoming a blur in his mind, leaving the past like a dense fog in his mind.

Though he could remember some things, such as Xilthim's world, with its many small continents dotting a vast plane of strangely shallow waters. Fortunately its people, being an avian species, allowed him to take to the skies more often than not:

Veros—a world of endless skies and countless roosts poking up from below to perch upon—that was how the bird-like people of the planet often described it. It at least had a somewhat normal day and night cycle, which was refreshing. The mornings were a bit longer than I was used to, and dusk was a prolonged time of deep green skies of moody clouds that appeared like rows of virid plums from below that melted into dark violet nights, appearing as if a thick grape wine had covered the world.

It was a far more populous world than most others, which admittedly made shapeshifting in secret a fair bit more challenging than usual. I found that I adored the challenge, which… I am not sure what precisely that says about me. It forced me to focus, and be in the moment, so I suppose it was good.

The people of Veros—verets, they called themselves— were a wonderfully colorful and diverse race of people. It appeared as though anything with wings in this universe bred a bewildering variety. The only thing the many different verets shared were their avian qualities—such as possessing beaks and feathers and long limbs and puffed chests filled with strong muscles that carried them great distances across the sky—and their love of music.

The many regions and clans of verets were often at odds with one another. They were obsessively territorial and constantly looking to expand their reach. There was more than enough land on Veros to accommodate the population tenfold, yet they struggled to keep everyone sequestered in their chosen territories. They did not fight often, but when they did, it was a bloody affair. I despise fighting, and bloodshed of any kind... I decided to play into an old role of mine and took on the appearance of a traveling bard.

It was some of the most fun I ever had. I got to travel around many continents and learn so much about their music. Bards were highly respected, and given free rein to move about as they pleased, so long as they provided good songs. They had many roles for their music making. Chirpers, for those gifted in singing. Tweeters, for those who commanded a talent for more niche ambient sounds and effects. Ringers, for those good with a combination of singing and ringed instruments. Oh! The rings! Somehow they made these collections of interlocking rings that one would hold on to their ends with each wing, and as you waved it through the air, the motions flowing from your limbs would cause the many rings to collide in different ways, producing different sounds. These rings could be adorned with a number of accessories, each one adding a different effect to the ring it was attached to—shells, for example, would provide more tinny and high pitched sounds. Some insects could give certain rings a pleasing vibrato, or an elegant chitter, or even a deep, guttural buzzing. A room full of experienced ringers with a single, master chirper leading them on was a sight to behold.

Patient as I am, I eventually commanded some mastery over every instrument they possessed. It was here that I first noticed my powers beginning to expand beyond me. Fortunately I was alone on the night this first happened, but to say I was spooked would be an understatement. While practicing, I decided to try creating an illusion of another veret, to work on synchronization. Before I could even finish the thought, a burst of ashen smoke plumed before me, and an exact copy of myself stood, playing a series of crude rings in horrible fashion. At first, I was shocked, but I still had some control over the illusion. I took in a breath, and the illusion vanished.

I did not have complete control. I was scared—was I losing myself, in some way? Was I losing control of my own abilities?

Curiosity spurred me on, and I attempted the illusion again. And it was successful! An illusion of myself, even more meticulous than the last, played a series of rings in a (mostly) melodious manner. I was thrilled.

Not content with that, I created more illusions, and before long I was sitting on a treetop with a crowd of verets, a chorus of illusioned musicians each bearing different fashions and instruments. We sang and played random nothings well into the night.

I say we, but... It was just me... All alone... I was playing with myself? But those illusions felt separate in a way, as if each and every one could have lived a life of its own before I unceremoniously puffed them out of existence... Was I alone or not? I was so very far away from the po, from Fiddle, from everything I knew and the world and afterlife I was most familiar with. And yet... I never felt as if I belonged with them. I knew for a fact that I did not belong there or anywhere really. Was I merely some cosmic vagabond? What was my place in this universe? Even my mother and father werere things that seemed beyond me. If I had known that the Munder King, Krull, was my father all along... I would have asked him about my mother...

Not wanting to get too lost in my own head, I decided to put all of that behind me. I wanted to bring everyone together with a most magnificent concerto! One that all the people of Veros could enjoy. But I needed something more, something that could really get everyone's attention if I wanted to garner the sort of pull needed to bring the world together.

That was when I made an interesting discovery—blood feathering.

Veret musicians of old would often practice so much that the feathers on the tips of their wings would regularly fracture, breaking the hollow bones holding them in place and causing them to bleed slightly. What was one to do when they had the music bug, and wished to practice all night long, but their feathers were already bleeding?

Well, you played lighter!

It was best when used on a percussive instrument, but the technique could be used for anything—stringed, ringed or otherwise. By using the thin blood held in the loose and hollow bone, purposefully letting it loose like liquid from a needle, you could use it to dampen the impact of your feathers on whatever instrument you were using. Also, rather than applying direct pressure on your instrument of choice, you pressed at an angle. The sound you were looking for was a sort of multi-layered trailing of frequencies following a single beat. If you could do all of this, while also not making a mess, you were considered a master musician.

Not many verets even attempedt the technique anymore, seeing it as unnecessary, and taking far too much time— and pain—to learn. I suppose the technique was meant for me, considering I had nothing but time, and I could simulate the effects without any personal pain. Sometimes I felt as though my abilities were too convenient, but I could never bring myself to complain about them.

It was not long before I could not help myself from bringing a horde of illusioned musicians to follow me and play and sing in harmony. I had initially planned to organize a serious concert, but one just sort of happened as I was lost in my play. Many other verets took notice and began to follow. For fifty days and nights it seemed as though I had swooped up verets from every region, before we settled on a great mountain peak to the north. The back and forth between my illusions and their songs and dances—all entirely improvised, by the way—seemed to bring nothing but joy. Not a drop of blood made its way to the snow-covered ground, amazingly. Even more amazing was how well the other verets went along with the improvisation, considering the somewhat unseemly technique being used. There was truly nothing capable of ruining everyone's good time. Veret faces were not particularly expressive, due to their limited facial muscles and their beaks, but I swore I could see every single one of them smiling during the festivities.

I eventually exhausted myself, and had to let my disguise and the illusions go. It happened again without my say, though fortunately the usual pale smoke blended in with the light snow everyone was kicking up on the great mountain top. I managed to slip away unnoticed, and even noticed the party was still ongoing when Xilthim himself beckoned me, joyously calling to me and letting me know I had done well enough.

I wondered if he noticed that by that point I had completely forgotten what specifically I was meant to do. I suppose bringing everyone together in harmony was enough to solve most problems? It was certainly enough for me.

Much of what happened after Cynkz's time on Veros was a blur, though he did remember Sihl's world, for how different it was. Cynkz didn't even know what a gas giant was, but apparently Sihl's world was one such planet, and it took some getting used to:

Sihl's world... Sihl's world... Cyndrihelios-Acar... It was one of the largest planets I had ever been to, and also one of the least stable. The Omun referred to it as a 'gas giant.' They are ancient planets that, for one reason or another, were able to gather the necessary elements to form the base for a new Omun but could not fully do so. Most merely sat as large graves—grim reminders that even the Omun were not immune to chance. Sihl's world was a special case, then, in that it was capable of harnessing a unique form of life.

They were more akin to collected bundles of gas, talking clouds and expressive smoke. They blended in with the world itself, which was little more than a chaotic mass of turbulent clouds and grainy fumes that whipped past and through one another effortlessly. Imagine handfuls of sand being thrown and filtered through one another. The people of Cyndrihelios-Acar—who referred to themselves as sporehim—had unknowingly ingested a viral disease from a passing meteorite. At least… it was a disease to them. Something about the rock making up the meteorite was poisonous to the sporehim. Sihl explained that, as it passed over the planet, it was mostly burned up, but a scant few grains remained, and infected with a group of compounds that when filtered together and given enough time could…

I could not remember the entire story. I must admit, Sihl, for as polite as he is and well spoken he has become, did not know how to relay information in a compelling way. None of it mattered, anyway. All that I needed to do was introduce a new gaseous compound that could counteract the slow-growing disease. Following Sihl's instruction, I transformed into a sporehim, and only had to fly through the planet's many gases for a few minutes. One other sporehim caught wind of me, and as a final coup de grâce, I coughed in his face, mixing the new gas with his. He closed his eyes and recoiled, or at least I think he closed his eyes, and I believe he recoiled, which gave me the opportunity to disappear. Sihl was happy with the result, saying that he could already see the benevolent effects of the new gas strengthening the infected. It spread quickly, and all was well.

It took every ounce of discipline I had to not laugh over the whole endeavor. I believe Sihl could sense my reaction, but he remained polite and courteous regardless. I was grateful, as the last thing I would ever want to do is laugh at an Omun's expense, especially regarding his troubles.

"Cynkz, are you there?" A sharp voice cut into the jester's wandering mind as he sat in the pale void.

"Huh?" Cynkz whipped his head up, somehow instinctively knowing precisely where to look to greet the star speaking to him.

"Cynkz, I would like to speak with you next." It was Siar'C, though his tone was far more accommodating than normal. The usual bitter twang in his voice was purposefully reigned in.

"Of course, Siar'C, what do you need?" Cynkz asked.

"I am surprised you are still so polite with me," Siar'C said, "considering how… difficult I have been with you, and the fact that I brought you back to Omundisia without warning."

"Oh? Oh, I suppose you did…" Cynkz furrowed his brow and looked about the void. He had not even noticed that someone had brought him back. For a moment he worried about his perception of the present once again. Why was it becoming so difficult to keep track of what was happening at any given moment?

The jester shook his head and steeled himself, getting back to the conversation at hand, lest he become lost in his rememberings and ponderings once again.

"I would like to apologize for my previous conduct," Siar'C continued. "After having witnessed you assist so many other Omun, I see that you are certainly capable and well intentioned, if nothing else. Also, I can see a burning question at the forefront of your mind."

"Ah, yes. Exactly how many Omun have I assisted so far? I am struggling a bit to remember them all."

"That is understandable, considering you have assisted no fewer than 300 Omun—"

"What?! How?! I… How much time has passed since I first came to Omundisia?"

"Well, time does not pass at all points equally, but if you are speaking of Potarium… It has been approximately 750,000 years—"

"What?!" As shocked as Cynkz was, his mind only formed a blank as he struggled to comprehend his predicament. The present was only growing more difficult to perceive. The past was difficult for him to remember, resulting in mere fragments of experiences and happenings that only seemed to be drifting farther and farther away into the nothingness of his mind. As for the future, he still had little idea of what precisely he was moving toward. Curiosity often grounded him, if nothing else, as his thoughts went back to something he had been told near the beginning of his current ventures.

"How is Guronimhal doing?" Cynkz asked.

"Ah, old Guro…" Siar'C slowly twinkled, as if needing a moment to think the question over. "He is still around, though his time is quickly dwindling. He possesses maybe a few hundred thousand years left, give or take. These things are never precise."

"I suppose I only have myself to blame…" Cynkz said. "I should not be losing track of so much time. I would like to find the Creator as soon as possible, and maybe prevent Guro and his world turning to dust, the way mine did…"

Siar'C shifted, his star turning over and dragging with it several sharp rays of black light. "Yes, I too feel your frustration, and Guro's life could be seen as a timer of sorts. It is never a good thing to watch an Omun pass."

Cynkz perked up, lifting a curious finger to his chin as he raised his shoulders. "What happens when an Omun passes?"

"That depends on the Omun," Siar'C said. "Some change hue, others expand. Most merely fade away, and others violently collapse in on themselves, supplying much of the universe with new material that will form the basis of new worlds, and possibly even new life, mortal, Omun, or otherwise."

"If an Omun's death can create new life… Should we even be attempting to save him?" Cynkz asked. "How much future life would we prevent from ever existing if we did so?"

"It is difficult to say." Siar'C paused for a moment, then continued. "Guro is certainly large enough for the process to occur—the violent implosion leading to material for life to scatter, but as with all things, we do not know. There is also the world he currently watches over, housing life of its own. They already exist, and have done so for eons. Is it fair to them that they should merely move aside to make way for a slim chance of new life to come into being? Why should that be their responsibility? Why should they be forced to carry such a burden?"

"If I possessed such answers, then I would perhaps be more than a mere servant of the Creator," Siar'C said. It was the first time Cynkz had ever heard trepidation in the otherwise sharp Omun's voice. If there was ever a time to dig into the star's woes, this was it, as far as the jester figured.

"Your world is war-torn, is it not?" Cynkz asked. "Considering the high value of life, it must be difficult to watch such atrocities unfold."

"Indeed, Cynkz. It is without a doubt the most challenging aspect of being an Omun. We witness everything that occurs in our worlds, both good and bad. For every virtuous exchange, there is often an equally, if not more, heinous act that occurs. As Omun, we must have a broader view of things, but it is far too easy to get caught up in every moment. It is far too easy to fall to the temptation of diving in to intervene, to prevent every injustice, every atrocity, every meaningless waste of life and goodwill. Yet, we must remain stern and disciplined. Every moment represents an infinitesimally small component of existence, yet their consequences each echo on into eternity. We Omun are farseeing, but we cannot see into eternity. Only the Creator—or Paithos, as you po call Him—possesses such wisdom."

"My father, Krull… I have wondered about something—the lower layers of Munderworld are believed to have not existed before the end of Peara. If they are machinations of the Munder King, then are all Omun capable of creating worlds or realms? Surely even an Omun does not possess the foresight to manage such a task?"

Siar'C took in a deep breath before responding, as if ready to get something off of his chest: "Indeed. If I had to posit a theory—Krull, being rid of his station as an Omun, may have found a new sort of freedom, as he retains much of his power, but few of the responsibilities. He may have attempted to create worlds of his own, only to find that the task was beyond him. And, with the risk of snuffing out any sort of life or material from existence, decided to leave things be."

Cynkz found himself speechless. To think that so many things—lives, creatures, entire worlds and realms—could result from mere fancy and whim, the result of a greater being testing out their capabilities, was a revealing notion. Krull was indeed his father. Using whimsy and curiosity as inspiration seemed to run in the family.

"Cynkz!" Another clear voice called out from the void, and before long Anim's star drifted into view above Cynkz, next to Siar'C.

"Hello again, Anim. How have you been?" Cynkz said.

"Cynkz! I have something wonderful to show you!" Anim was uncharacteristically impatient. Between his restlessness and Siar'C's politeness, it felt as if everyone was taking the opportunity to express themselves differently than usual.

Before Cynkz could even respond, his mind opened, and visions took his thoughts. It was Anim's world once again, its people standing taller and straighter than before, and even bearing comparatively sophisticated clothes. The forests now appeared almost designed, showing that Anim's people had learned how to cultivate the land itself to their needs. In fact many of the trees were of a larger breed, and their cores had been hollowed out, giving room to living spaces within. Intricate markings and finely woven flags stood out in bright colors against the even, dull bark of the many trees. One symbol in particular stood out, always sitting prominently at or near the top of any given structure—a neat swirling circle with tapering lines extending around the center, both outward and upward. Unlike most of the other markings, these were filled with glittering sap, making their shapes glisten in Anim's light.

"That! Right there!" Anim said excitedly. It was enough to knock Cynkz out of his vision.

"Your people seem to be doing very well, Anim," Cynkz said as he took a moment to rub his temples, gathering his senses.

"They are doing more than well," Anim continued, "they have begun to form religions! That symbol, for example, is what they use to represent the Creator himself! And guess what they call Him?"

Cynkz stood and waited patiently for a moment before asking: "What do they call Him?"

"They call Him," Anim paused for dramatic effect, "the Anmirosen! It is an ancient term of theirs, translating to 'The One Risen Hand of Light.' It is fascinating, isn't it?!"

"Indeed, but…" Cynkz looked back down, trying to look over the images of his vision in his mind again, "the hand symbolism, that is more than a coincidence, isn't it?"

"I believe so," Anim said, finally calming down and regulating his tone. "They may never know it, but my people seem to remember your actions in some way."

"I… do not know how to feel about that, to be honest." Cynkz revealed his hands from his cloak to look down at them. He stared at the many lines and creases that formed along his pale palms, shadowed etchings that had been imprinted upon his hands from countless years of use. He wondered if his actions had a similar effect on those he interacted with. He couldn'tpossibly comprehend how each one would affect the greater cosmos, just as he couldn't comprehend how each wrinkle formed on his hands. So many things seemed beyond him, and no matter how much experience he gained, he never felt completely sure of his actions. There were just too many lines to keep track of, too many wrinkles to comprehend.

"You have done wonders, Cynkz," Anim said. The subtle tenderness in his voice gave away that he could sense the jester's uncertainty. "What other way do you need to feel about your deeds? You have, and will continue, to be a good force in the universe."

"I suppose so," Cynkz said, resting his hands to look back up to the stars, "but I never meant to take on the role of something larger, and I have never believed myself to be worthy of deciding the fate of so many. Then again, I never asked to be born, I never asked for my mere existence to be such a burden, to be such a great disruptor that an entire world—my world— would need to perish as a result."

"You still feel regret..." Anim continued: "You blame yourself for things that are ultimately beyond your control. Cynkz… We all have our place in the universe, 'our station in life,' as some would say. Learning to be grateful for, and to make the most of, what life, the universe, existence itself has gifted us—this is one of His greatest lessons. We merely do the best with what we have—it is all we can do, and more often than not, that is enough."

"Thank you, Anim." Cynkz smiled warmly, so warmly in fact that he could feel it over his entire body. He finally noticed that the abyss' unrelenting chill no longer bothered him. Omundisia had become quite warm and comforting. He wondered if the Omun were subtly making his stay in their realm more inviting. He would have given thanks, but chose not to spoil the moment with something that didn't need to be said. They more than likely already knew of his gratitude for all that they had done.

Siar'C allowed just enough time for the quiet moment to rest before speaking up once more: "If you are ready, Cynkz, we may go to my world, and you can continue your work."

"I am more than ready, Siar'C. Let us move, then."

PART 4
OZAIROS

CHAPTER 22

THROUGH THE LIGHT HE COULD SEE hills of green. Fluffy, viridescent mounds appeared to roll over one other and endlessly into an olive hued horizon. It took a moment for him to realize that he was in actuality viewing cloud tops rather than grassy plains, and that the olive sky was a new world's interpretation of twilight's onset.

"Welcome to Ozairos," Siar'C said.

Cynkz could hear the voice behind him, weighing down from the heavens, as he kept his eyes focused down. His curiosity was festering, growing into something nigh unbearable as he wondered what lay below. It shouldn't have been any different from any of the other hundreds of worlds he had visited before, but it was the fact that he had been secretly looking forward to this one in particular for so long that gave its inevitable introduction so much more weight. His curiosity seemed different this time, as if tainted ever so slightly by the nibbling bite of anxiety. It was easy to speak through confidence, but living up to those expectations was an entirely different matter. Still, all it took was a deep breath and a quick brush of his cloak to steel himself and clear his mind, as it usually did.

I am ready…

"I know you are, you have proven that many times over," Siar'C said.

Cynkz didn't even react. He was certain it was not the first time he had grown so used to the act that he felt no emotion or expressed any reaction to it, but it was the first time he truly noticed it. He struggled for a moment, trying desperately to remember the first time, but it was a futile effort. It was just one more lost memory to push to the back of his mind.

Siar'C continued: "I understand you may struggle a fair bit coming to terms with all of the information I gave you. It is perhaps more than you are used to digesting, considering the divided races."

"Well, it is only two major races," Cynkz replied, finally turning to look up at the sky, bathing his face in Siar'C's light. Its pale orange somehow blended well with the lime colored world around him.

"True, but most worlds have a single dominant species, and the few that had more were much simpler," Siar'C said. "We can review a few things while we wait."

"Wait for what?" Cynkz asked. His brow perked up, pushing the tip of his pointed cap just a bit out of his vision.

"My people are constantly at war. Just below the clouds another pointless battle is taking place."

"I would like to see this battle. I would rather not sit by and allow such violence to—"

"Cynkz, please wait. You know how we Omun operate. We must work carefully and be patient. You can't just—"

It was too late. As if not of his own will, Cynkz felt himself being pulled to the clouds below. The green mist of the clouds quickly brushed aside as he flew down, ready to see the lands of Ozairos for the first time. What he thought was merely the sound of wind and cloud swiftly brushing past him was in fact the sounds of battle echoing into the distance. A sea of bodies flew back and forth, overtaking one another like waves in a storm. Screams followed swift strikes, cries followed fierce cuts and sliced limbs. The weight of the world crashing down followed as heaving masses of bodies would clump together and fly in formation in preparation for an assault. The resulting dissipation of living mass would leave a crater of dead and injured forms, a mangled and tangled mess of ripped flesh and glistening yellow blood pooled beneath a discolored soup of splayed innards. He had hoped to see the lands of Ozairos, yet it was entirely covered in carnage.

The two opposing forces became easier to discern upon further viewing. One side possessed beings who were taller and leaner—the storns—and immediately caught the eye with their angular features, bony and gaunt bodies, and multitude of spiked stingers protruding from their bodies like extra limbs. Their colors were slightly warmer, consisting of yellowed chitinous skin and reddish-orange complexions. Thin manes of dark fur around select areas was the perfect complement to their streamlined forms. Their musculature was exquisitely defined, and their wings were large, meaty membranes, their appearance not dissimilar to dragonfly wings that had somehow grown to an unnatural size. They put these bodies to great use as they effortlessly cut paths through the air, cutting down their foes with a physical prowess only known to the greatest of hunters. The physical world proved to be of little obstacle—it may as well have been their playground.

Their opponents—called the ptomera—were equally striking, though in the exact opposite way. Rather than immediately imposing physical dominance, their forms struck the eye with an enchanting, even mesmerizing and otherworldly aura that wrenched the mind into captivation. Soft pale teals and lavenders and cloudy purples and blues reflected off of their textured skin. Their eyes were larger, but revealed no sclera, adding to their insectoid appearance. Neither faction, despite being overall humanoid, both hinted at having bug-like ancestors. Instead of spikes and stingers they possessed luxurious bundles of fur that covered much of their bodies like clothing, as well as a number of antennae. These antennae seemed to come in every imaginable form, from bundles of thin frills to rows of prickly appendages that stood out like long grass from their heads and bodies, as well as those who merely possessed only two or three antennae with fuzzy bits on their ends. All of them appeared deadly, as their movement would affect things beyond them, as if telekinetically disrupting things at a distance. Their wings were larger, and most only consisted of a single layer of large, rounded membranes that, when fully extended, dazzled the eye with confusing, asymmetrical patterns. They were reminiscent of monstrous butterfly wings, and were bewitching from a distance, capturing the mind's eye with a spellbinding effect.

Back and forth the two factions went—for every broken stinger, a severed antennae flew ahead. For every triumphant battle cry, a screeching sonar attack would follow. The gnashing of sharp teeth let loose spittles of toxic green and yellow blood. Shredded wings covered the floor with a combination of thin, sliced and ice-like membranes and torn butterfly wings that looked more like colorful tapestry that had been haphazardly thrown to the floor. Everything one's senses picked up, overwhelmed with the sheer amount of chaos going on, merged together into a cacophony of madness and death that ravaged the land and air below.

"I can sense that you desperately want to barge in and intervene," Siar'C said.

Cynkz remained unresponsive, entirely transfixed on the happenings below.

"I am afraid we must let this play out," Siar'C continued, "we must wait for a better opportunity for you to disguise yourself and blend in—"

Cynkz completely ignored the Omun and dashed back into the clouds, disappearing before the mounds of green mist.

"Cynkz! Wait!" Siar'C called out, though this too was ignored completely.

The sky began to darken as the olive sky slowly covered with a gloomy green overcast. The combatants below hardly noticed, and continued their battle. The clouded shadow only grew darker, and the wind began to pick up. Still the battle raged on, completely oblivious to the happenings above. The wind soon turned to violent gales and gusts that were so forceful the world below almost appeared to move at its whim. This was finally enough to force the attention of the people of Ozairos fighting below to stop and look up. The image of a swirling mass descending from the clouds themselves cutting its way down and toward them reflected off of their many large, black eyes. The dark green tornado finally touched the ground, and whipped its surroundings into a frenzy. Everyone instinctually dispersed, and flew away in a panic to get away form the calamity. Strangely, no actual people were pulled into the twister, which merely seemed to kick up mountains of dirt and soil and even much of the trees on the edge of the battlefield. Fortunately no one seemed keen on testing the limits of the tornado, and it was not long before the land was clear of life.

The wind began to slow and settle, though the dark green overcast remained. Soon a familiarly cloaked jester stood alone high above a sea of torn soil and what remained of the deceased.

"Phew, I am surprised that worked," Cynkz muttered to himself. He gathered himself and turned to the sky: "Sorry, Siar'C, I did not mean to act against your wishes, but I could not just sit by and watch such bloodshed. I… Siar'C?"

All was quiet. It was the first time he could remember the Omun being unresponsive. At least, it was the first time that he could recall. The air was tense, and Siar'C's light hid well behind the overcast. He looked around to see not a single living soul in sight. He was relieved, as he was not in any sort of disguise, but this was soon replaced with dread when he looked down to see the many large, dark and reflective eyes of those he had failed to save. This was a type of solitude he detested, but for the time being, it was one that he figured he must bear.

"Siar'C?" He looked back up to the sky, awaiting a response that he knew wouldn't come. He turned his attention back to the world below, and reluctantly began to drift forward.

CHAPTER 23

NGRY FOOTSTEPS ECHOED throughout a near empty hall. Each stomp clanging against the wide stretch of cool marbled flooring and bouncing off of ivory walls whose shine was suppressed beneath the strange overcast just outside. The only thing louder were the rantings of an angry storn man releasing his fury upon an unfortunate subordinate.

"Why do you have to make things so difficult, Zzira?!" the man yelled. He would stop talking for just long enough for another step to be heard clearly as he paced back and forth.

"I speak the truth, Father," Zzira said, her large eyes turned down as she kneeled.

"Do not call me 'father,' you brat!" The tall storn man took another step, before stopping to face his daughter, leering down her past his short nose. "Think of all the work I put into training you? The responsibility placed upon your shoulders as you lead our platoons? And yet you come back from a battle with *nothing* to show for it! And worse yet—you come with excuses! Empty handed and a mouth full of excuses! What a waste!"

"Fa—… Emperor, I assure you I am not trying to make excuses. You can ask any of my soldiers. We were fighting, and doing quite well, and the overcast, much of which still remains even here, began to whip up a great tornado. Everyone was forced to leave. We had no choice but to—"

"You had a choice, Zzira, and you chose to flee, rather than take advantage of the opportunity to wipe the rest of those damned ptomera freaks out!"

The room fell silent. There was no refuge from his wrath—not even a gust of wind or the sounds of voices in the distance to give the mind something to settle on. Zzira, as a child, once thought the great, expansive halls of the storn palace were wondrous, and a way of exemplifying grandeur. Now she sees their true purpose—to establish dominance, to easily isolate any and all who are beckoned by the emperor. Storns can fly, but such disturbances are forbidden within such places, and the wide, empty rooms and halls would force the buzzing of one's wings throughout the entire palace. Anyone attempting to sneak in, anyone wishing to whisper heresy or insults, anyone who was unfortunate enough to drop or break one of the many relics within—all would be instantly revealed, and would quickly be apprehended and forced to face his wrath, the same wrath that Zzira was currently bearing. She much preferred the open air, and to be in battle.

Zzira's mind wandered, as her father's ravings continued. Storns were born and bred for battle. All storns were meant to fight, and to sacrifice for the greater good. All were conscripted to lifelong service. Beyond early childhood, the battlefield was the one place a storn was truly free, the one place where you did not have a superior breathing down your neck. She was grateful that she was more than a mere broodling, a storn female whose life constantly oscillated between birthing new storns and the battlefield. Being the emperor's one and only child had its perks, though she wondered even about that as she was forced to kneel before him and endure his wrath. His echoed screams disappeared behind her thoughts as her attention wavered.

"Zzira!"

"Huh?" Zzira whipped her head upward, looking at her father for the first time since her return. She saw a thin, unimpressive man garbed in ornate, white robes, and bearing a spiked crown lined with violet fur plucked from countless ptomera victims. He sat upon his tall, spiked throne loosely, as if the mere act of having to exist in a lesser's presence was causing him annoyance. His gaunt features made the shadows that formed on his face harsh, as if accentuating his constant anger and disdain for those beneath him. Zzira couldn't think of a single time the man smiled, and her own mother, when she was alive, never smiled when looking at him.

"Are you even paying attention?" the emperor said, waving a thin, clawed hand against the air.

"I am," Zzira muttered.

"Then you are aware of the punishment I just laid out for you, then?"

"I… A punishment?"

The emperor sighed, and pulled his hand back to rub at his temples: "Yes. You are being demoted. You are clearly not yet ready to lead an army. You can rough it with the other pawns in the scouting groups."

"What?!" Zzira's response was nearly a shriek, and it was the first time she herself echoed throughout the many halls of their grand palace. She even stood up as she spoke, completely dropping any sort of respectful stance toward her father.

"Do not raise your voice at me, child," the emperor said. "I, as your lord and emperor Anzinius Kul, assign you to the scouts. You may choose your squad, and you are tasked with taking them immediately back to the battlefield you most recently abandoned to search for any survivors. Bring back any storn soldiers, and finish off any lingering ptomeras."

"I know what scouts do, 'my lord and emperor Anzinius.'"

"Good. Off you go, then." Anzinius waved a dismissive hand away, and even refused to hold eye contact with Zzira as he slumped back in his seat, rubbing his temples once more.

Zzira could feel her nails digging into her palm, and her own temples pulsing from the pressure caused by her clenched teeth. Yet this anger simmered as she held herself back, remembering her place and turning to leave. Since she was not allowed to fly in the palace, she chose to stomp, leaving an echoing path of disdain trailing off behind her. She knew her father would just

ignore it, but any relief for her growing frustration was appreciated.

The frustrated princess found herself at a nearby camp. Storns were taken in at a very young age—no fewer than a few years old, and just as adolescence began— in order to begin training them for combat. Most new recruits were sent out to their first battle only a year into their training, and any who survived would be instantly promoted, and their training increased ten- fold. It was because of this that most camps and out- posts were populated by the young. Zzira hated going to any such camp, as she hated seeing so many young storns that she knew would soon be dead. She looked down to see mostly adolescent male storns being carted around, and performing a wide variety of drills in large, immaculate formations.

Female recruits at least had the opportunity to become brood storns after merely two years of service. This was to ensure that only the best genes were allowed to propagate, or at least that was what her father always told her. Her mother always doubted this, and said it was merely to hide the fact that they were desperate for as many warriors on the field as possible. Anzinius always hated that it was ultimately better to not have their females on the battlefield for too long, lest they potentially lose too many and doom their entire race to extinction. Her mother was horrified when Zzira first mentioned her distaste for ever becoming a brood storn, though her father was delighted. Thinking about it now, Zzira remembered that it was in fact the only time her father ever smiled, and it just so happened to occur at a time when her mother was the most disappointed in her.

Zzira looked down from her perch, several stories up in some shambly barracks, and finally noticed a handful of female storns in the mix of formations below. She noticed how much softer and brighter they appeared. Zzira thought of a time when she too must have looked the same way. Though her time spent on the battlefield, exposed to the elements and straining her body in skirmish after skirmish had hardened her. She now stood as a muscular woman, and her once smooth and pale yellow chitinous skin had nearly become a tanned orange, complete with more than a few scars to decorate her. The one thing that truly got to her was her hair. Storns did not possess much in the way of hair, but they had just enough to cover vital areas of their body—the groin, the lower abdomen, parts of the chest, and so on. Most of any storn's hair—or fur, to be more precise—was located on their head as it wrapped around the skull, covered the sides of their heads, and draped down past their necks and naturally pooled into a fine point on the chest. Males would often have more of this particular fur reaching out toward their shoulders and onto their backs, and the females would have more draping down their chests, usually doing well enough to cover their bosoms. Zzira, due to the stresses of prolonged battle, was finding her hair growing ever shorter and thinner. This was normal, and most females would find the hair on and around their heads and bosoms slowly growing back after settling into a life of breeding. Zzira never allowed herself such comfort, instead finding solace and freedom in battle. Though she would be lying to herself if she never thought about giving up her duty, just to get some of her hair back.

"General!" A young voice called from down the walkway. Zzira looked over to see a rather inexperienced looking storn cadet hurrying toward her.

"General Zzira," he said once again after getting close enough to speak normally. The cadet stood and assumed a proper greeting stance one gave to a superior—hands at his sides, the stingers on the back of his forearms pulled in and pointed upward, chin up and eyes slightly looking up farther to avoid direct eye contact. "I have orders to report to you in regards to forming a scouting party."

"Yes, well, I have been demoted recently," Zzira said. She was still partly facing toward the balcony, and kept her eyes on the recruits training below. "I am no longer a general. You can just call me lieutenant."

"My apologies gener—lieutenant Zzira…" he said, nearly tripping over his words as he corrected himself, "Commander Riul sent me directly to you for orders. He wishes to ensure that whoever you choose for the next scouting party is up to the task, as they will be mostly first years—"

"Ugh," Zzira scoffed.

"Is… Is something wrong, lieutenant?"

Why did it have to be Riul, of all storns? That bastard has his nose in everything the emperor does, and by proxy nearly everything I do. His bloodthirst and single minded approach is… more than likely exactly what my father prefers. I swear to Buuziliel that he wanted a son instead, and that he sees that brown-noser Riul as the closest thing to a son he'll ever have... If father didn't have so much trouble conceiving, he probably would have had so many more children, and easily gotten rid of me...

"General? I-I mean, lieutenant—"

"Just go and tell Commander Riul he may choose my squad for me, and that they should meet me up front," Zzira said.

The cadet stayed silent, straightened his back and whipped up a hand into a salute before flying away. Zzira turned her attention back down to the recruits training below. A few of them seemed to have tripped over themselves, or each other, she wasn't sure. Seeing a swarm of sergeants descend upon them, screaming insults, gesturing so aggressively that from certain angles it would look like an attack toward them, was funny in a way. Zzira remembered stumbling similarly to them. She also remembered how when she was very young her mother would zoom over, doting on her daughter if she sneezed or dropped something. The great empty halls of their palace home were quite noisy from her mother's buzzing as she constantly flew about, tending to her precious daughter. Anzinius would often respond to any of Zzira's mistakes with anger, chastising her for any mistakes or stumbles. Anzinius would constantly fill her head with stories of what tortures the ptomeras would inflict upon her if she did such a thing on the battlefield. A single moment spent crying or stumbling or hesitating and "Pop!" Your head was gone. At least, that was the way the "great lord and emperor" would always describe it.

Zzira's ponderings were interrupted once again as a particularly loud and highly decorated storn forced his way through the crowds below. He wore a number of medals on his burly, tanned and scarred arms. Rows of violet and burgundy strands—slivers of ptomera fur—were wrapped around his burly arms, and from their ends were countless medals. He had sparse fur that hardly covered his head, with a noticeable widow's peak giving the two antennae on his head plenty of room to move as he bobbed around, shouting orders and getting people into position. The once neat formations of storn scattered messily to make way for him.

There he is… Commander Riul, proactive as ever I see… He is probably taking the news of my demotion well… Looks as though he is quickly getting my squad ready. I suppose I too should get ready.

Zzira looked on for a moment too long, her mind empty, and she took in a much needed breath. With a squat and a flap of her wings, she flew off from the balcony and toward the front gates of the camp.

CHAPTER 24

BUZZING WINGS SLOWLY DRIFTED IN from over the horizon. Six figures flew in from above, their many wings moving so quickly they blurred together in the late day's light. They were fast approaching an open wasteland, a place where the forest trees stopped and there was nothing to obstruct the distant mountains. Much of the soil below was covered in layers of dead and mangled bodies, a sea of the damned filling up the otherwise empty plain.

"Looks as if we're almost there, general—I mean… lieutenant…" the cadet said.

Zzira ignored him, deciding to not waste anymore energy on the boy's stumbling. She flew ahead a fair distance from the rest of the group—five storns who were about as inexperienced as one could manage. Zzira scoffed internally at the thought of having to deal with such green storns. The one recruit among them who had any sort of experience, possessing only a single scar to show for it, was the same cadet that first approached her at the camp. She sneered as she thought about Riul—he had to be doing this on purpose, as far as she thought. She was not in the mood to babysit anyone, but orders were orders.

"What was your name, anyway?" Zzira said over her shoulder to the cadet.

"Oh, um, I am Katarmin, lieutenant," he said. His stuttering was beginning to annoy Zzira, but she could understand his anxiety. She was much the same when she first started venturing the battlefield.

"Just relax, Katarmin," Zzira said, turning her attention back ahead, "it will all be alright. Just focus on the task at hand. No matter how overwhelming things may seem, if you just relax, and take things one step at a time, you can handle anything."

"Y-yes, lieutenant."

The landscape had been overtaken by the deceased. It felt as if only moments ago every single one of them were alive. Whatever hopes and dreams or aspirations they held, whatever relationships they had back home, whatever potential they possessed—it was all gone, reduced to the same grainy and slick layer of death. It was dangerous to think too far ahead when in the midst of battle. Every battle could be your last, and it was best to treat each one as such. One battle at a time, and if you are strong, one will turn into two, and then three, and before long you have experienced enough to gain some respect. It was funny to Zzira, as at that point the mental scars began to show more than the physical ones, and that was when most storns finally got the respect they so desperately wanted. She almost wondered if it was all worth it in the end, but stopped herself as she noticed that she was breaking her own rule of looking too far ahead.

Just one battle at a time... One scouting mission at a time...

Perhaps it would not be long before she was back in the good graces of her father, and she could return to her proper position in what remained of the storn empire.

Despite being later in the day, it was surprisingly bright. The pale orange light from above blended well with the deep olive sky, illuminating the death and decay below with a sickening hue. There were few clouds in the sky as well, which only made what happened earlier that day all the more strange.

Where did that tornado come from? Zzira thought. *Tornadoes are so rare on Ozairos... They are typically thought of as bad omens—a sign that Buuziliel himself is intervening, looking to change something he is displeased with... It was just another battle. There should not have been anything remarkable about the skirmish. I figured it would have been an easy victory—we lose a few handfuls of storn, we wipe out the ptomeras, and I take a few of their heads and manes back to my father to have their fur added to his collection. It should have been so simple, and yet here I am... There is nothing of value here. This is worse than a waste of time. I'll be forced to return home empty handed again, and who knows what my father will—*

"Lieutenant! Over there!" One of the cadets had caught up to Zzira, and was pointing his thin and wiry arm to a peculiar pile of bodies not far off. Something was moving ever so slightly beneath the bodies!

Stranger still were the odd puffs of gray smoke dissipating just above.

Zzira rushed over without a word. She stopped just above the pile, and without needing to give a single order, two of her scouts descended and began to push aside the mangled bodies. It wasn't long before a hand rose up from below, and a new storn face greeted them, one that Zzira didn't recognize. He appeared to be in good health, and also unharmed.

"You there!" Zzira barked. "Who are you? What platoon are you from? I don't remember leading you into this battle."

"Ah, thank you, all of you!" the stranger said as he dragged himself out from the remaining bodies covering him. The two cadets quickly backed away, and assumed defensive stances in the air.

The stranger rose up, brushed himself off, and continued: "There is no need to be alarmed. I am merely a traveler and merchant. My name is Zinx, and—"

"I have never heard that name before," Zzira snapped. "I remember the faces of every storn in my army, every one that I lead into battle. And you call yourself a traveler? No storn is a mere 'traveler.' You're a cowardly deserter, aren't you?"

"What? No ma'am! I would say I am more cautious than cowardly. In truth, I am just—"

"I am no mere 'ma'am.' I am Zzira Kul, daughter of our great storn lord and emperor Anzinius Kul! You will address me appropriately as… lieutenant."

"Ah, my apologies, lieutenant Zzira Kul," Zinx said with a bow.

"What are you doing?" Zzira said.

"E-excuse me?"

"Are you bowing? Why? You are supposed to salute a superior officer." Zzira stopped for a moment to look the stranger up and down. "Bowing, of all things… What a soft gesture… Have you been hanging out with ptomeras? Are you colluding with ptomera deserters? You would not even be worth court-martialing. It would be straight to execution for you, deserter."

"Oh, a salute! Well of course ma'am—uh, I mean, lieutenant, ma'am, sir—"

"Ugh, just… at least show me you know how to salute?"

"Of course, of course, um…"

The stranger looked on awkwardly. All eyes were on him, and it clearly affected him. He took in a breath, straightened his back, clicked his heels, and raised a limp hand to his brow. A round of light snickering could be heard under the constant buzzing of everyone's wings. Zzira herself remained stern, keeping her eyes right on Zinx's. She peered into him like daggers, and Zinx himself anxiously looked a bit up and to the side, unsure of what to do. Zzira couldn't help but notice the stranger's features. He was tall, and long-limbed, with a good physique—more or less the perfect storn specimen to be a soldier, and yet he had not a single scar. He carried himself with a fair bit more gravitas than the average young recruit. In truth, Zzira couldn't quite tell how old he was. If she had to guess, he may be right around her age, though he was unfortunate enough to not possess any signs of true combat experience. His skin was a single, pale layer of off-white that mostly took on the color of the olive dusk light. His eyes were sharp, but he held a constant wide-eyed expression that rounded them out, the way a child might look. The stingers on the back of his fore-arms and calves were immaculate—clearly they had never been used. His hair caught Zzira's eye, as it was too luscious and bountiful for any normal male storn. It dropped down from his crown and cradled his neck and shoulders, almost as if it were a thick hood and cloak. It reached down to his shoulders, and covered much of his upper chest. It was also pitch black, and reflected no light. An intense jealousy stirred within her, causing her to sneer as she immediately dampened the emotions, not wanting to appear weak in front of her men.

"You have no idea what you're doing, do you?" Zzira said.

Zinx looked back at the lieutenant, relaxing his hand before answering: "I do not understand—"

"Never mind. I am tired of all this." Zzira raised a hand and looked over her shoulder at a couple of her scouts. "Apprehend him. At least I won't have to return to my father empty handed."

The same two scouts that dug the stranger out began to drift in toward him, ready to follow orders. The stranger seemed hardly phased by it, and Zzira swore she could see the slightest smile beginning to form on his face.

Just who is this guy? What a perplexing individual—
"Lieutenant!"

The cadet's scream snapped Zzira out of her ponderings. She didn't even need to look at her subordinate to see what was wrong. A distant fluttering of

fast approaching wings began to drown out the wasteland's ambience.

Ptomeras!

"Ptomera scouts! There appear to be at least fourteen." The scout whipped his head around to look at
his superior. Zzira kept her eyes on the oncoming
enemy, but she could see the glint of the cadet's worried eyes from the corner of her own. "W-what do we
do, lieutenant?"

Zzira sat silent for a moment, thinking over her
options as quickly as her mind could manage.

*They can see us, and are heading straight for us. Storns
are fast, but we are already in their view. We cannot
outrun sonar attacks, especially from such a large group.
They appear to be far more experienced than our group as
well... Was this a trap? That bastard, Riul... How could
I have been so naive? I should have known better than to
take such a weak group to scout a fresh battlefield...*

"I can help," Zinx said.

"What?" Zzira snapped.

"Maybe I can just go talk to them? I doubt they
would want to just throw their lives away for some
pointless scouting, or whatever it is you all are doing
out here."

"You are a fool," Zzira hissed. The constant annoy-
ances were starting to get to her. "Just help us fight
them, and if you survive, I will see about lightening
whatever sentence my father gives you."

"That sounds like a nice deal, but..."

"But what?!"

"I am not really much of a fighter—"

"What?! Where is your storn pride?!" Zzira swung her arms and clenched her fists. A quick breath helped her gather herself, and she pointed a fierce claw toward the stranger. "We storns are born and bred for combat! It is the greatest glory! Why do you think we—"

"Lieutenant! They are almost here," another scout cried out from behind.

Zzira leered at the stranger, then turned to her men. "Assume a v-formation, behind me. And you, stranger, stick close to me and follow my lead, and you may survive this. Don't allow the mind warpers to get a hold of you. Do not hesitate."

Zinx playfully shrugged and hovered close by. It took every ounce of discipline from Zzira to refrain from spitting at him out of disgust. She looked ahead to see a horde of dazzling wings and shining rainbowed fur covering the center of the horizon. The many asymmetrical patterns in their large, rounded wings made it difficult to focus on any one ptomera in particular. Their soft forms and smooth bodies lacked any harsh contrast. Even their colors were soft and easy on the eyes, consisting of many pastel hues and shades, though they shared one thing in common—every single one possessed lime-green skin and fur, causing them to nearly blend in with the olive sky. The group was coming in from the west, with what remained of the soon setting sun lighting them from behind, and burning straight into her eyes. The ptomeras had put just that extra bit of thought and planning into their excursion. Zzira could not have felt more unprepared. She could easily take out a few ptomeras on her own— she was quick enough to keep four or five ptomeras from focusing on her, but fourteen? It didn't help that her only added assistance was some buffoon whose training, if he had any, Zzira was entirely unaware of.

I may have to sacrifice a few of my scouts... Zzira dreaded the thought, but she feared death, or whatever her father may do if she returned empty handed, even more.

A flash of shimmering light filtered through a wide row of decorated wings in front. The ptomeras spread themselves, their movements synchronized—the battle had begun.

Zzira moved first, taking advantage of her great speed. She flew forward, baiting the ptomeras into a front-facing formation. As they separated, Zzira twisted her wings and burst upward, forcing the ptomeras themselves to now look up and into what light remained. She was not aware of ptomera ranks, and most ptomeras looked the same to her, but she easily spotted her first target—a ptomera had assumed the topmost position of their formation, and the rest of their squad appeared to be following his movements. They were a slow moving breed, relying more on their situational awareness and telekinetic and sonar abilities. All Zzira had to do was curve her flight inward, taking an awkward angle for the enemy to see, and she could slice her opponent. She moved through pure instinct, and had already completed the action before her thoughts could finish. The cool wet slick of murky green blood could be felt dripping from her right stinger. A quick glance behind her and she could see the remnants of shredded wings falling below, like a beautifully woven tapestry whose threads had come loose and fell to the wind.

One down…

The heavy gust of wind bellowed from the sides, and she noticed six of the ptomeras had spread out, their wings reaching out and bowling upward.

Sonar incoming!

It was too late. A world-shattering screech shot out from the enemy formation, their ear-splitting effect amplified by their cupped wings. Zzira was fast, but she could not outrun the sound. A defensive position was needed.

Arms up—palms to ears—eyes closed, breath halted— wings and legs in.

Zzira reflexively curled her body, pulling her wings around her front and forming a loose cocoon. Much of the attack could be felt deflecting from her wings, but it was enough to push and shake her. For a moment everything went silent, but she had felt this before. She gathered herself immediately, and looked down to see her scouts had taken advantage of the situation to begin an assault of their own. Two storn scouts had taken the flanks, stingers extended, and ripped into the outermost ptomeras that had attacked Zzira.

Two more down, three total, eleven remaining—

A scream paused the battle, and couldn't even finish before a grisly tearing of bone and chitin released in a shattering pop. One unfortunate storn recruit farther below had hesitated, and gotten caught under a ptomera spell.

One casualty, four scouts remaining, as well as the stranger…

Curiosity took hold as she attempted to look around for the stranger, only to be met with the frightening visage of outstretched wings dotted with bright, rounded patterns. Two ptomeras had taken it upon themselves to try and sneak in a telekinetic attack of their own, the light itself focusing their gaze into fierce glints peering directly into her mind. Zzira gritted her teeth, and wrenched her body away and down, breaking her opponent's focus. It was only then that she realized her mistake—she had flown downward, giving the ptomeras pursuing her the height advantage. This allowed the ptomeras to make full use of the light above, spreading their wings to block out much of the light, and their shade creating a harsh contrast the way an eclipse would. Colored light filtered through their patterned wings and would momentarily stall the viewer, giving them ample time to prepare another psychic attack. This was a common tactic, and one Zzira was prepared for.

Squint, broaden focus, look to the ground and find a flight line—

"Zzira!" A familiar young voice called out, and could be heard dashing in from the side. Zzira looked from the corner of her eye to see Katarmin flying in.

That fool! I'm fine… He's going to get himself killed!

Katarmin's thin form dashed through the air, piercing the wind like a needle. He positioned himself between Zzira and the ptomeras above. Katarmin stumbled, but kept himself moving forward and up, and his left arm stinger cracked as he extended the sharp cartilage and it found its mark, piercing the squishy, pasty green abdomen that spurt out reams of muddy fluids. Here the new recruit learned a most important and final lesson—the moment of victory is often the moment of greatest vulnerability. Katarmin sat for a moment too long to relish in his kill. The second ptomera, being far more experienced, never relinquished their focus, and merely shifted their wings and their attack to Katarmin.

Zzira was fast, but not fast enough, and a stomach churning pop followed as the young storm recruit's innards and brain matter rained down, lightly splattering Zzira's legs on its way down. Zzira, through pure instinct, took advantage of the opening to dash in and slice the killer's abdomen, quickly inserting and then sheathing her stinger in a single swift motion.

Another slain, ten remaining. Another scout lost…

A glance below revealed a most curious sight—her remaining three scouts were still alive, and their formation, while remaining tight and disciplined as they continuously hovered around and past one another to cover any potential opening, they were following someone's lead—the stranger! Zinx would burst between the ptomera's at lightning speed, with enough force to break the wind itself and knock the ptomera's off balance just enough to make them stumble. Zzira's scouts would rush in and make quick work of the enemy. This process repeated itself several times, as the ptomeras seemed entirely unprepared for the strategy. Zzira even struggled to keep count of everyone as she watched.

Three scouts, the stranger… Two, three, no… Four ptomeras slain! Zzira whipped her eyes back and forth as she tried to keep track of the stranger's movements. *Why doesn't the stranger merely kill the enemy himself?*

Every moment he spends merely incapacitating the round-wings is moment one of my scouts could—

Another pop of bone and flesh shattered the air, and the formation was broken. One of the scouts found himself the unfortunate focus of the remaining six ptomeras. Her two remaining scouts, as well as Zinx, appeared to be shocked by the sight. This was the trouble with leading the inexperienced into battle—any small development is enough to make them stumble. The remaining ptomeras made a fatal mistake of their own, however—they seemed to have forgotten about Zzira. The round-winged ptomeras gathered and shifted their position upward to focus a final assault. All this did was bring them closer to Zzira, who took the opportunity to fly in herself. A single swift motion, flowing like a stream of water, stingers extended, slicing through foe after foe.

One down… Two… Three…

Another pop, and another scout fell, their remains adding to the mass grave constituting the wasteland below. Zzira now sat not far above the ground, staring down two ptomeras as they finally took notice of her. She expected another telekinetic attack of some sort, and readied herself to dash in and cut down her opponents. Here she realized another mistake, one that even the most experienced combatants face from time to time—conditioning. Instead, the two ptomeras quickly curled their wings inward, shading much of their bodies within curtains of colorful membranes, and amplified a swift sonar attack. Zzira hurried to ready her defense.

Arms up—palms to ears—eyes closed, breath—

She was not quick enough, and in that moment she could feel a terrifying warmth building up within every orifice. Her vision blurred, her hearing muffled, her teeth rattled, and her wings may as well have been liquid. Her chest rattled, her shoulders tensed and her neck strained, as if she were choking on the air itself. Finally, a heaving, unnatural pressure seemed to be banging at the walls of her skull. It was as if a hurricane had come for her, and its world shattering winds were looking to crush her.

Strangely, the thoughts of wind cracking the air continued, though her pain slowly ceased. The sound grew more distant, and she found herself regaining her senses—the pain in her head, the ringing in her ears, the pounding in her chest—everything went to the wayside, and she was finally able to breathe again. The last thing to return to her was her vision. As the blurred image before her sharpened, she struggled to make clear what exactly she was seeing. She noticed a stream of blood following the descent of her final scout, his head turned to paste and their innards lagging behind as the body fell. She looked farther up and above the horizon to see the stranger whipping past ptomeras at lightning speed. With each dash strong enough to crack the wind and leave behind faint plumes of smoke that burst before dissipating. The remaining ptomeras did their best to keep the stranger away from them, and within a three-point formation—a classic tactic of using one body to distract while the other two snuck behind to focus an attack, though it did little to help. Zinx was too quick, and took advantage of the formation's angling to send the ptomera at the bottom of the formation—the "tip" of the aerial triangle—hurtling toward the ground. The ptomera's wings nearly flew apart from the force of the maneuver, and every bone in their body must have been broken as they finally landed onto a pile of bodies below, but they were still alive.

Why is he not killing them?! We storns do not take hostages, we can't afford to. What an imbecile.

Something pale shot up above past both Zinx and Zzira, its form blurring before suddenly stopping, and the light itself began to dim. The remaining two ptomeras were reading a final attack! Though they seemed to be ignoring Zzira, and instead focused the light filtering through their colorful, rounded wings right toward the stranger below. Their wings, acting as prisms, began to reveal each subtle movement as bright and colorful shapes shone on the world below. Brilliant streaks of pink followed vivid blocks of near white greens, cerulean shapes shifted as a spotlight would across a dark marble floor. It was akin to watching a rainbow splinter into a million pieces, only to have its colored fragments strewn about carelessly across the world.

The sea of dead bodies revealed much through the light shining on them, as the many eyes and exposed teeth and blood glistened, and countless expressions reflected back up, each one a still and unique form of anguish. Getting lost in such details was exactly how the ptomera operated, and Zzira resorted to shaking her head and gritting her teeth in order to bring herself back to the present. She looked over beneath the colorful shade the ptomeras were providing to see the stranger, his once shineless hair now perfectly reflecting each streak of color provided by the enemy. He was dead center of the ptomera assault, and too far away for Zzira to do anything about it. It seemed that the stranger's foolishness had finally caught up to him, and she awaited the end of his final moments alive on Ozairos.

Except her growing dread was soon met with confusion. The ominous ptomeras continued their mental assault, and it appeared to have no effect. They may as well have been performing a mere light show for the stranger, who only sat in the air and watched the many colors and shades provided by their wings fly by and over him. Though they all only sat for a few moments, it was the most uncomfortable, and tense, moments of silence Zzira ever endured. She was ready to see the naive stranger's head explode, the same as what happened to her scouts. Instead, the only thing that shook her out of her stupor was seeing the stranger fly up at supersonic speeds, the windfall behind him dragging his foes up with him. The colorful shade instantly dissipated as the ptomeras were knocked around like leaves in a hurricane, only to be violently dragged back to the ground as Zinx flew back, faster than before. A final crash of bodies echoed, signaling the end of the battle.

How anticlimactic…

She noticed the stranger staring at something below. His pained expression and stillness was enough to put her on edge. Then her ears caught something faint in the distance—several of the ptomeras Zinx had disposed of were still alive and breathing. Without a moment's thought, Zzira focused her sharp vision below, and picked out their positions among the piles of dead bodies. She tensed the muscles in her back, whipped her wings up, forward, and then backward with enough force to send her flying to her prey within seconds. In a single swift motion, she tensed the muscles in her forearm, forcing her stinger out, and sliced through several bodies.

One... Two... Three... All enemies slain. It's only me and the stranger now...

"Wait! Why did you—" Zinx stopped himself, then merely huffed at the realization that he was far too late to do anything.

The fact that he showed any sympathy for the enemy at all annoyed Zzira to no end. She couldn't even find the bodies of her lost scouts among the wastes, each one a soldier through and through, and each one who had fallen unceremoniously in battle. They each followed their duty to the end, no matter how short their service was, and each one merely a victim of chance and inexperience. Yet here the stranger stood, flinging himself around carelessly, hesitating, and showing weakness—sympathy, of all things, for ptomeras, of all creatures. It sickened her.

She looked above and into the eyes of her remaining ally. To her, he was a living bundle of contradictions. He was cowardly, yet "cautious," as he called himself, yet he flung himself recklessly into battle. He appeared to be a healthy specimen, which was odd if what the stranger said about himself was true—Zzira had seen a number of deserters, and heard of every excuse imaginable, and they were always in poor shape, having spent their lives subsisting off of what little the land could afford them. He was fit with all of the usual adaptations storns prized for killing, yet he merely incapacitated his enemies, ptomeras who just now showed no such hesitation toward taking his own life. Speaking of which, his strangest trait of all—his seeming immunity to the ptomera's psychic attacks. Zzira had never seen a proper psychic assault from a ptomera fail. It was the sole reason why storns needed to be fast to kill swiftly, so as to not give their opponents time to use this ability.

Zzira grew tired of sitting about, and grew even more tired of this wretched battlefield, a land of waste that was little more than a glorified graveyard to her. She quickly hovered upward and approached the stranger, ready to question him.

"Just what are you, stranger?" Zzira asked.

"What?" Zinx appeared caught off guard, as if he too had been lost in thought.

"What is your deal?" Zzira continued. "You are strange, unlike any storn I have met."

"I am a storn like any other, lieutenant."

"Hmph, at least you can remember my rank. But no, you are not. How are you not dead? You were caught right in the center of several ptomeras as they assaulted you with their telekinetics."

"Telekinetics?" Zinx looked puzzled, his eyes shifting around as he thought once more. He looked to the ground and at the bodies below, before looking back at Zzira. "Is that what they were doing? I was a bit confused. I thought they were merely giving me a light show—"

"This is not a joke, you idiot," Zzira snapped, "this is a battlefield. All of my scouts are dead, having fallen victim to the ptomeras, and yet here you stand, as if completely immune to them. How?"

"Perhaps I merely possess a stronger than normal mental fortitude?" Zinx shrugged, almost playfully.

"I doubt that."

"Well, perhaps I merely got lucky?"

"No one gets 'lucky' on the battlefield." Zzira looked the stranger up and down, thinking over her options, and what her father may think upon her return.

"I will admit, lieutenant, I find it a bit uncomfortable to be stared at—"

"You're coming with me," Zzira interrupted.

"Huh?"

"My father will want to know about this. I would rather not return empty handed, and you may possess some trait that helps you against the ptomeras. This will work out for both of us—I will have something to show for all of this, and you may very well earn a proper place back within our empire, deserter."

"I told you, I am not... Hmm..." Yet again the stranger seemed lost in thought. He scratched his pointed, pale chin with a sharp knuckle as his eyes looked past Zzira, scanning over nothing in particular.

"I'm not giving you a choice," Zzira continued. "Either you come with me willingly, or I drag you back—"

"Okay."

"What?"

"I said okay! I will accompany you—"

"You idiot," Zzira huffed. "You are not 'accompanying me.' You are my prisoner."

"It would not be the first time I held that title."

Zzira merely sighed, then gestured for the stranger to come. Zinx drifted forward, following closely behind Zzira as she led them away and into the dim olive horizon.

CHAPTER 25

BACK IN THE GREAT AND EMPTY HALLS of her father's palace, a sense of unease rolled over her. She wasn't sure what it was, but something was off. She could sense something foreboding, some great change in the still quiet of the empty and reverberant halls, where all things seemed to lead back to that dreadful throne room.

Zzira noted the strange look on her father's face when she walked back into his throne room, with nothing in hand and merely a stranger, loosely bound and following close behind. She also noticed Commander Riul was already there, discussing far more important matters without her. She was after all merely a lieutenant now—what reason was there for them to care what she thought about anything now?

Riul went so far as to pretend he didn't notice her arrival. He kept his attention on the emperor, mumbling who knows what to him. Riul did this often, and she hated him for it. Even when she was a general, and higher ranking than Riul, he would act this way, even in front of the emperor. It wasn't so much the direct disrespect that bothered her, but the fact that Riul only did so because he knew he could get away from it. The two may as well have been made for each other, as far as Zzira was concerned. At least when she held the rank of general, she could force respect from the commander, but as it stood now, she had to defer to him. She grit her teeth as she approached the two storns at the throne, using every ounce of discipline to refrain from bursting forth and snapping Riul's neck.

"I have returned, Lord Anzinius," Zzira muttered, letting the vast room's echo do most of the work.

The emperor, whose attention had been on the woman storn and her prisoner since their arrival, looked down his nose at them. Commander Riul finally stopped and turned, the weight of his broad shoulders and heavy figure making itself known with each movement. Zzira was already kneeling, her head turned down toward the dark marble floor, but she could feel her father's gaze bearing down on her. The specks of glittering stone and bleached granite in the floor's makeup reminded her of the dim light reflected off of the many faces of the dead on the battlefield. Somehow that was more comforting than her current location.

"I can see that," the emperor said. "What do you have to report? Where are your scouts?"

"We were ambushed by an opposing ptomera scouting party," Zzira said, her head still downturned, and her voice still soft enough to force the room's echo to carry it. "We were heavily outnumbered, and—"

"And you ran?" Commander Riul interrupted. His voice boomed, a robust air that had little trouble filling the room. "I imagine that is the only reason why you are still alive?"

Zzira grit her teeth, and could feel her knuckles tensing against the hard floor, the smooth and polished surface pulling at her skin. It would have been so easy to leap forward and deal with the impudent storn commander, and perhaps even her father, but discipline stayed her hand.

"Riul, hush," Anzinius said. "Don't interrupt us again, and let me speak."

Riul quickly stepped back and bowed, his hands behind his back, and his gaze now set to nothing in particular in the distance.

Anzinius continued: "You know better than to return empty handed. You said you were outnumbered? How many were there?"

"Fourteen," Zzira said.

"Your scouts?"

"They did not survive."

"The ptomera scouts?"

"They too were slain. Some of their blood still stains my stingers."

"I see… Against fourteen ptomeras, those odds are impossible for a party as small as yours was. And who is this?"

All went silent, and all eyes and ears turned toward the stranger. Zinx was so quiet that Zzira nearly forgot that he was even there. She wondered if he was even reacting to anything that was happening.

"We found this deserter hiding amongst the bodies, and—"

"You may stand, Zzira, I'd rather not look at the top of your head for the entire conversation."

Zzira stood up, and continued: "This stranger, clearly a deserter, was hiding amongst the bodies. He calls himself Zinx, and after we found him the ptomeras attacked. Our scouts were taken out one by one, and yet…" Zzira turned to look at Zinx, who seemed oddly calm and at peace, despite his arms and stingers being tied up, and being presented to his emperor like cattle. "Zinx expressed an immunity to the ptomera's psychic attacks. He is also quite strong, and fast, his speed alone enough to whip around the ptomera's soft bodies like rags in the air. I would have not survived if not for his intervention."

"Really?" Anzinius perked up, for the first time showing a glimmer of interest in his eyes. The soft brush of his robes pulling against his throne blew through the air as he leaned forward. The emperor even raised a curious hand to his chin, scratching at its pointed tip.

"Your lord, if I may?" Riul said, tilting his head slightly as he spoke.

"You may," Anzinius said, never taking his eyes off of the newcomer.

Riul continued: "This… Zinx, was it? He appears suspicious. He is obviously not trained, he is obviously not accustomed to battle, what with that doe-eyed expression of his, and how pristine his stingers are. For all we know, Zzira may well have fled, left her precious scouts to die, and came up with this elaborate excuse for her obvious failure to do anything productive?"

All went quiet again. Not a single sound was present to give Zzira reprieve. At least when she was kneeled down she could partially hide her grimace, but now, as she stood at attention, she was forced to restrain herself—even the slightest expression could be seen as disrespect, or some form of impudence. If she still held her previous rank, then perhaps she could express herself more freely. Her only solace was that this terrible day would eventually end, at some point.

"I'm afraid you do not know my daughter as well as I do, or as well as you'd hope to," Anzinus said, grinning wickedly as he leaned back in his cushioned throne. "Zzira knows better than to ever lie to me, or to truly come back empty handed. I must say, if this is all true… If this strapping, healthy young storn truly possesses an immunity… This is it… This is it!"

The emperor's voice rang through the massive halls, bouncing violently off of every smooth surface. Riul was the first to turn and look confused to his superior, sharing a similar expression with his guests as everyone looked curiously at the mad emperor sitting above them.

"My lord?" Riul muttered.

"This is perhaps the first time I have ever been truly grateful to have a daughter," Anzinius said, chortling behind a limp hand held up to his face.

"What?" Zzira said, for the first time raising her voice enough to carry its own weight.

The emperor continued: "You two, Zzira and Zinx, will begin reproducing immediately."

"What?!" Zzira shouted, going so far as to step forward, her clenched fists and sharp, gritted teeth on full display.

"M-my lord," Riul stammered, his broad shoulders slumped, and his palms open as he leaned forward to address his emperor, "what exactly are you planning? That seems to be an odd—"

"I would think that you of all storns would see the utility, Riul," Anzinius said, still grinning as he dismissively talked down to his commander, all while keeping a gleaming eye on the stranger. "If this is true, if Zinx has an immunity, then he should be passing his genetics on as soon as possible. Before long we could have entire legions of storn soldiers that are entirely immune to the ptomera's tricks! We would finally have a true advantage! We could wipe them out once and for all, and finally begin to rebuild Ozairos. The world will be ours once again, as is our birthright!"

As the emperor's words trailed off into the distance, a tense air remained. All were stunned, and none knew quite how to react to the news. Zzira figured that Riul would relish such a humiliating proposition for her. Instead his expression seemed pained, with harsh lines digging into his brow, and his usual cutting and pretentious glare rounded into worry. She couldn't help but look back at her prisoner, wondering what he thought of the situation—not that it mattered, as the emperor's word was law. Zinx appeared strangely calm, and almost amused by the drama unfolding before him.

Hmph… The sick bastard… He is probably getting a lot of enjoyment out of this, imagining what fetishes he will soon get to indulge in…

She looked over the stranger once more—his luxurious, pitch black mane, his refined features, his conditioned body and tall stature, even the thin membranes that constituted his wings reflected the throne room's light brilliantly. He was obviously coddled, protected from the elements, the stresses of battle, and was allowed to look prettier than she perhaps ever could. Her disdain turned into resentment as she tried to come to terms with her father's plan.

I hate every single storn in this room.

"Ah, but I suppose I should express at least some manners," Anzinius straightened his back, attempting to appear noble and proper, "Zinx, you may step forward. Let us know your thoughts on the matter. What do you think of all this? My daughter is a fine specimen, wouldn't you say?"

Zinx quiet expression turned to surprise, his eyes widening as he looked up at the emperor. He was like a child that had been caught disobeying a parent. Zzira chortled, letting out a quick huff beneath a thin smile.

The stranger straightened his back, and let out a soft breath before speaking: "Well, her highness is certainly an attractive storn, befitting a princess."

Princess?! Not even my father, nor even my mother, ever referred to me as such. How embarrassing…

Zinx continued: "I know I do not truly have a say in the matter, but when you say 'immediately,' I hope you do not mean that literally, your lordship? It would be quite awkward to begin birthing your future legion right here and now, in your impeccably kept throne room?"

Is he joking?! Jokes, now, of all times? Perhaps he was a jester in a previous life, and not a particularly good one—

"Hah!" The emperor's outburst, complete with a whipping snap of his callous palm hitting a sharp, scaly knee, filled the room with an echoing pop that caught everyone off guard. Zzira most of all, as she hardly ever saw her own father smiling—let alone laughing—at anything. At most he would express some dark glee at the news of a won battle, or after seeing a decapitated ptomera head being presented to him. Zzira never dared to waste his time with simple jokes.

Anzinius spoke once more: "I do appreciate the good humor, young storn. And no, I didn't mean it literally. You may settle in the finest cell we have to offer for the night. Who knows? Mayhaps you and Zzira can chat with one another? Get to know each other, and learn to make the most of this arrangement? If everything works out, all of our futures will be bright indeed."

"Father!" Zzira snapped, finally stepping forward with a satisfying snap of her foot against the hard marble floor. "Don't I get a say in this? This is absurd—"

"Hush child," Anzinius said, refusing to even look his daughter in the eye. He did turn his attention up and toward the giant wooden doors on the opposite end of the room, and looked expectantly into the darkened hall beyond. "Guards! Hurry up and show our newest guest his new living quarters. Bind his wings, and give him a cell with a nice window, if you don't mind."

A harsh buzzing began to seep in from the dark. It was not long before six storn guards had descended into the room and surrounded the newcomer. Zzira couldn't help but note how calm Zinx looked, even as his wings were clamped together and he was forcefully lifted into the air and carried off. Normally whenever a prisoner was whisked away the many halls were filled with cries and screams. She was not sure how to feel about the newcomer's reaction.

"You are dismissed, Zzira," Anzinius said, still refusing to look at his own daughter, "Riul and I have much to discuss—we will need a new, advanced training regimen. Also, appoint your finest guardsmen to watch over the new legion to be. I want every camp to make room for the new arrivals."

Commander Riul snapped to attention, his wings flaring up and his posturing whipping into a straight line: "Yes, my lord!"

The commander quickly turned and flew off himself. Zzira watched as he too eventually disappeared into the dark hall. It was now just her and her father.

"You may leave now, Zzira," Anzinius said.

Zzira turned, only to see her father had finally considered it appropriate to look at her. The deep olive light seeping in from above lined the emperor's dark eyes with a satisfied glint. He may as well have been salivating at the thought of what his new army would accomplish—an army that she herself would be forced to bring to life.

"Am I just a mere brood storn now?" Zzira muttered.

"Your mother would be proud," Anzinius said, relaxing his posture as he sat comfortably in the cushions of his lofty throne.

"What in the hell would you know?" Zzira snapped. "As if you ever cared about what mother wanted, or ever knew what would make her proud or happy? Perhaps she is the fortunate one—she is no longer here, and no longer has to put up with you."

Anzinius huffed, then smiled. "If I were not in such a good mood, and if I were not so keen on my lineage being at the forefront of the new world, I would have you imprisoned. But you are still my daughter, and I want you to be healthy and… satisfied enough to birth equally healthy stornlings. Enjoy the night, Zzira. We will have much to do moving forward. Just know that I am proud of you."

Zzira stared at the emperor, a crooked smile still plastered on his face. A wet warmth began to swell beneath her eyes, and nothing more than her anger held back the tears.

As expected, words are wasted on you, father…

After staring for a moment too long, she finally turned her back to the man on his throne, and disappeared into the dark hall herself.

CHAPTER 26

THE LIGHT OF A PALE GREEN MOON washed over Ozairos. The dark of night was imbued with a slight olive tint, allowing even the most maladapted creatures to see the world's hidden secrets. It was one of those nights where the storns tending to the palace didn't even need to light any torches or lamps—the moon alone was enough.

Zzira crept her way up the many winding, expansive halls and stairs of the palace. She knew exactly where Zinx was being held—it was a special cell, one that her father reserved for prisoners he was especially keen on torturing. It was a surprisingly well furnished cell, with a comfortable bed, plenty of room for an average storn to stand and stretch, and even a barred window high above and positioned just right to watch the moon for most of the night. The comfort was the whole point—it was to lull said prisoner into a false sense of security, to raise their hopes, only to dash them when they least expected it. It always bothered Zzira just how much her father seemed to enjoy utilizing the environment and their architecture against his opponents. Physical warfare was easy for her, but psychological warfare felt wrong—messy and complicated, unlike the battlefield.

She happened upon a room isolated in a far corner of an upper floor in the palace, one with a shabby wooden surface and whose seems hardly kept out the night light seeping in from beyond. She could see something casting frantic shadows against what little light did poke through the cracks, as if something were moving back and forth across the room.

Maybe he's pacing back and forth across his cell? I guess he couldn't keep up the act forever—his circumstances must finally be setting in. Though... I could say the same thing for myself. I just want someone I can open up to, about anything...

Something strange caught her ear as she approached the door—something small and lively scurrying about, and laughter! Tiny giggles and irreverent taps of small feet against the floor could be heard faintly on the other side. Her surprise soon settled into an intense curiosity that weighed her down, stopping her for but a moment from opening the door. There was no possible way the prisoner could have escaped—his wings were clamped together, and even if he did make it out, the noise would have echoed through the palace's empty halls, alerting every guard in the fortress.

Eventually she clasped the door handle and pushed her way inside, only to see several faint gusts of colorless smoke fading into the rays of moonlight reaching in from outside. She looked to the other side of the room to see the stranger sitting calmly on the carpeted floor, wide awake though staring at nothing in particular. He seemed quite alert and aware. He was looking at his hand, its palm open as his arm rested on his knee. He looked at it as if it belonged to someone else, and he didn't recognize it.

What was that? Did he know I was there? I could have sworn I was quiet. I couldn't even hear myself moving through the halls below. Hmm...

Zinx slightly turned his head, just enough to get a decent look at his visitor. He smiled warmly. For a moment she felt disarmed by the genuine gesture, only to have her thoughts come crashing down as she reminded herself of her predicament. She finally stepped inside, and slowly shut the door behind her.

"It is a pleasure to have your company tonight, princess," Zinx said, smiling all the while.

Princess? Again?

Zzira could feel something warm brewing in her face. Her cheeks tightened, and her brow furrowed.

Am I... blushing? No... What a preposterous thought...

Zzira lightly shook her head, then spoke: "I am no princess. I am a general. Or... I was, at least..."

"What is in a title anyway?" Zinx said. "I always find the person behind the title far more interesting."

"Hmph," Zzira crossed her arms, relaxed her wings, and leaned on one leg. She almost sneered at the prisoner daring to speak to a supposed princess so casually. "You appear quite calm. Even, dare I say, pleased? Are you so looking forward to getting to mate with royalty that not even imprisonment worries you?"

Zinx laughed, and heartily so. It was loud enough that Zzira even began to worry about the rest of the palace hearing him. More than that was the sudden shock of seeing the otherwise composed storn express himself in such a way. Something about the way his sharp features effortlessly molded into soft expressions was soothing.

"Ugh, this was exactly what I was trying to avoid," Zzira muttered, going so far as to place her head in a listless hand.

"Excuse me?" Zinx said, his head tilted in a way that Zzira couldn't tell if it was to just get a better look at her, or to charm her further. "In truth, I am not in favor of this current arrangement either. Love cannot be forced, I would never want to force—"

"Never mind," Zzira drew a quick breath, and recollected herself before looking back at the calm prisoner. "It's fine. I can tell that you don't have any ulterior motive."

"How so?"

"We storns are not good at hiding our emotions, our true thoughts. Our feelings and wants tend to be extreme, and we express them thoughtlessly. You, however, are quite calm, as if your mind is elsewhere. Also, you don't seem like the lustful type."

Zinx drew in a deep breath, leaning against the wall in his cell and stretching his arms up. "Well, my mind may be gone, but my ears are still here, more than willing to listen to whatever you need to say. Care for a chat?"

"It's that obvious huh? I could use someone to talk to. There is no one else I can open up to, and you seem nice enough."

"It is nice to see the appearance of kindness being seen as something other than weakness."

"It is the storn way—we have to be strong. We have to be quick and direct and vicious. There is no other way. Kindness may seem noble on the surface, but such surface level niceties can be a breeding ground for all sorts of deception."

"What a way to look at the world," Zinx sighed.

"But it *is* the way of the world," Zzira said.

"I would not say that," Zinx said, "it is merely *one* way that the world can be. Genuine kindness can exist for its own sake, without any ulterior motives or deception or as a cover for weakness."

Zzira perked up, staring wide-eyed at Zinx. "You sound just like my mother."

Zinx chuckled before leaning forward to rest his arm on a bent knee. "Your mother must have been a sweet, kind and wise storn then."

She was... Zzira thought. She couldn't help but turn her eyes away from the Zinx as she looked to the ground, her mind elsewhere and focused on other things.

Her mother was the only other person she truly trusted. Her mother was the only one who remained genuine and loving, despite her father's constant power games and manipulations. Something within her always pulled at her heart whenever she realized that she never trusted her father, even now. With her mother gone, what did she really have left? Her father,

her empire, the battlefield—all of it was merely a distraction, something to allow her to focus on something other than her own sadness. It was easy to lose herself in the midst of a fight, to forget her demanding position and beyond the leering eye of her father. Perhaps that was why she ultimately decided to become a soldier, rather than a mere brood storn. It was just a means of giving herself some reprieve from her responsibilities, and from her father. Though now even that seemed to be slipping away from her. She looked back up to see the stranger looking warmly at her, the pale green moonlight accentuating the edges of his sharp lips like a knife's edge that somehow curved softly into a gentle smile. His pale complexion reflected the moonlight well, nearly taking on its hue entirely. The slight glitters of reflected light bouncing off of his large dark eyes may as well have been the stars themselves smiling at her.

"Oh, wait, that might have come across as conceited," Zinx said, breaking eye contact first to rub the back of his head. Zzira kept her eyes on the prisoner, watching his clawed fingers glide effortlessly through the sea of pitch black locks. Zzira chuckled, then moved forward to sit down and back against the silver bars containing Zinx.

The two sat in silence for a while, merely taking in the other's company. It was only then that Zzira noted how difficult it was to actually engage in conversation without some form of pressing need or duty to force it. Nearly every conversation she had with others up to this point in her life, and after her mother's death, was work related. Without this, she struggled to think of anything to say. The moon's light against her back cast her shadow across the rest of the room. It was difficult for her to not focus on the shadow's top, revealing the coarse and pointed hair on her head that stretched forth like a spiked nail into the dark end of the room. Her attention eventually shifted over to Zinx's shadow, his silhouette much softer in comparison, and eerily still. She was grateful for Zinx's patience. A tingling sensation began to grow within her, and before long anxiety began to set in. The night was wasting away, and she wanted to make the most of what little free time she was permitted. Eventually she decided to force something out, and that merely being honest with her feelings was as good a place as any to start.

"My father is quite the handful," Zzira muttered.

"I can imagine," Zinx said.

"He's always been so singularly focused on himself, his wants and his needs," Zzira said.

"Let me guess—he conflates his own desires with that of his empire?" Zinx said.

"Heh, yeah," Zzira said through a soft chuckle and sigh.

"I have dealt with kings and queens and royalty before," Zinx said, "they are often unable to separate themselves from their duty. In their view, they essentially *are* their kingdom, or empire, or whatever they wish to call it."

"How shrewd," Zzira said, turning her head to peer over her shoulder.

"What about your mother, if I may be so bold as to ask?"

"She is…" Zzira sighed, then turned her attention back forward, looking at nothing in particular toward the ground, feeling the weight of her brow and her heart pulling down on her. "I miss her…"

"I am sorry, you do not have to talk about it if you do not want to," Zinx said.

"No, it's fine," Zzira said. "Father has always been so selfish. He never cared about what my mother wanted, or what she was capable of. Father wanted many children, 'a small and elite army fueled by his own blood.' Unfortunately, for one reason or another, they struggled to have any children. Mother always said it was a small miracle that I was even born. If I had at least been born a boy, then father would have had a proper heir and successor to the throne. As it stands now, it's a bit complicated—more complicated than my father would like."

"It seems harsh to have his only daughter become a general, and allowed to fight on the front lines," Zinx said. Zzira could hear the storn shuffling around, and his shadow moving forward and closer to hers. His back rested against the opposite side of the silver bars, and she could practically feel the warmth of his body, despite him being at least half a foot away and to the side.

"Well, it was my decision to become a soldier instead," Zzira said, her words laced with a bitter tinge.

"I suppose the alternative was not particularly attractive?" Zinx asked.

"It was either that, or become a brood storn. I guess I merely wanted an excuse to leave home, to get away from my father's strict rule. The battlefield is at least a place of freedom, where you do not have to worry about someone above you looking down and judging and directing everything you do.”

“That sounds horrible,” Zinx said. “That does not sound like true freedom to me. You have this great, beautiful world, and the only way you get to experience it is through battle?”

“Yes, I suppose,” Zzira muttered, leaning forward to rest her head in her crossed arms. “I suppose I also wanted to prove myself in some way, to prove that it was okay that I was born. Maybe if I could prove myself in battle, then my father wouldn’t be so upset that he had been given just a daughter. Maybe then my father could relax, and begin to get along with my mother, and things would get better.”

“A child should never have to bear such a burden,” Zinx said.

“I couldn’t help it. It seemed as if the more my mother comforted me, the angrier my father became. Even after I decided to become a soldier, and after my mother’s anguish and protests to the decision, she ultimately supported me. She tried to be a source of comfort, while my father saw it as inviting weakness. ‘Such softness should be reserved for the weak and vile ptomeras,’ as he would often say. They argued a lot, and eventually mother became sick, though the disagreements never ceased.”

“I am noticing that there seems to be very little focus on what *you* want,” Zinx said.

“What I want…” Zzira paused, as if struggling to think of an answer, which only seemed to embolden

Zinx's accusation, "is what's good for the empire, my father and our people."

Zinx laughed, thankfully quietly, so as to not fill the empty halls beyond the prison door. Zzira's brow furrowed, and a fierce sneer pressed hard lines into her face. She shifted herself around to face the petulant storn laughing at her.

"What's so funny?" Zzira hissed.

"I am sorry, truly, I am," Zinx said. "It is just that, well…"

"What is it? Spit it out."

"I mean no offense, but you now sound more like your father, putting the needs of the empire before your own, even when asked specifically about *your* wants and needs."

"I…I mean…" Zzira stewed in an indiscernible mix of emotions. There was some anger at being compared to her father, some dread at the realization that Zinx was right, and some confusion over how she should respond. For a moment, she couldn't even look Zinx in the eye, and instead rested her eyes on the ground.

Zzira eventually turned herself back around, and rested against the silver bars once more. "I suppose it doesn't matter what I want, in the end. All that matters is winning this war, and ensuring that our people are not wiped out."

"I do not think you will need to worry about that happening," Zinx said, a confident air underlying his smooth tone, as if he had seen the future and was certain of something the rest of the world couldn't see.

"You are so strange," Zzira said, "and paradoxically confident, despite your circumstances…"

Zinx chuckled once again, and shrugged, seemingly with little regard to the metal clamp on his wings as it clanged against the silver bars: "Like I said, I have been in much worse situations."

Zzira sighed, but through a smile she couldn't restrain: "I'm almost afraid to ask what you mean by that."

"Be careful, princess—if you learn too much about me, you just might fall for me."

"Tch," Zzira huffed, but her smile remained. Try as she might, she couldn't help but revel in the good mood. "I hope you aren't offended when I say this—"

"Oh boy."

"—but I'm not necessarily attracted to you, not in that way."

"Honestly, that is probably for the best." Zinx, still bearing a smile himself that Zzira could see from the corner of her eye, leaned back and drew in a deep breath. "In fact, I might still have someone waiting for me back home, if she even remembers me still…"

"Home?" Zzira perked up yet again, enough to cause her antenna to shuffle around the way a child's ponytail might. "Where is 'home?' Where exactly are you from, stranger? Some ravaged wasteland of a continent on the opposite side of Ozairos? Actually, you are so strange that I could believe you were from one of the moons."

"Ah, yeah," Zinx looked out the open window high above and on the far wall. He seemed to stare for a moment too long toward the opening, but Zzira didn't want to interrupt him, no matter how much she desperately wanted to keep the conversation going. "Your moons are beautiful," Zinx said.

"Right, 'my' moons…"

"In a way, your assessment of me is more accurate than you know."

A subtle sneer made its way onto Zzira's face. Such vagaries, and blatant esotericism, was beginning to annoy her. It was time to change the subject to something more concrete, something she was more familiar with.

"Where did you learn to fight like that?" Zzira asked.

"Hmm?"

"You know what I mean. Don't be coy. I have never seen a storn—soldier or otherwise—fight in such an… odd, yet effective way."

"I just, well," Zinx paused, though he kept his attention to the stars and moon outside, "I just did what was natural. In truth I do not care for fighting. I have never liked it, and I am not particularly good at it myself."

"Nonsense," Zzira snapped, "all storns are raised for combat. We are bred for combat. We live and die for the glory of battle. Why do you think you have those stingers on your arms and legs? Those sharp teeth? Those slim, efficient, sinewy muscles and that hardened chitin covering your body like armor? Countless generations of fighters and warriors make us who we are today."

"That sounds horrible," Zinx muttered.

"If you don't mind me asking, then, where does your zuthra lie, then?"

"My what?!" Zinx's head whipped around so fast that Zzira thought his head might leave his body. His quizzical brow and wide eyes were so funny to her. Fortunately she was able to withhold any laughter.

"You must know what a zuthra is," Zzira continued. "It is an old saying, one taught to all young storns as soon as they are able to speak and begin to comprehend language."

"Pretend I am such a young storn then," Zinx said, "explain it to me—how do you view and use the term?"

"It means 'your heart.' In essence, it is meant to represent where your heart lies, what values you possess, where you find your purpose and inspiration. If not combat, then what is it that drives you, stranger?"

"I… hmm…" Zinx looked back out the window, the silver bars lined at their edges with pale green moonlight and starlight seeping through in soft rays from the cosmos. Zzira kept her attention on him, curious as to what his answer would be. For her, and most other storns, the answer was immediate—most found their purpose in battle, and it was as simple as that.

Zinx finally drew another deep breath, and gave his answer: "I suppose I find it in helping others."

"In helping others? Like a servant of some kind?"

"Well, not necessarily in that way," Zinx said, "but… in life I have seen so many different people, all of them with problems unique to them. Life is a tough, weighty thing, and it brings me great joy to take some of that burden off of the shoulders of those who need it most. Life is precious, and every moment spent enjoying it, away from struggle and hardship—as necessary as those things may be—is priceless. Such are the seeds of fond memories, which is all we have to look back on in the end."

A silent air sat between them. The moonlight gave the room a sweet flair, and the starlight twinkling above danced. The silver bars separating them may as well have not existed as Zzira looked right at Zinx, unsure of how to take his words. Her gut reaction normally would have been—and perhaps should have been, as she knew herself to be a true storn—to rebuke such sentiments as signs of weakness. She knew she should have but she couldn't. Something about his words wormed their way warmly into her heart. It reminded her of a time when she was young, and she was still able to appreciate beauty in the world, something beyond combat. She knew how her father would react to hearing such things, the same way he reacted to her mother trying to express anything softer to her as a child, yet such thoughts were, for once, easy to push aside. For what must have been minutes, she was able to fully indulge in something sappy, something mushy and schmaltzy, and she loved every moment of it.

"You speak as if Buuziliel himself were channeling wisdom through you."

"Who?" Zinx asked, as if completely unaware of her silent fixation on him for the past minute.

"Now I know you're messing with me," Zzira said, shuffling herself back to her initial position, on the ground and back against the bars, her knees bent, arms forward and crossed, a perfect cradle for her chin to rest on. "I'll play along, I suppose. I speak of Buuziliel, the one creator of all life on Ozairos, whose beating, buzzing wings continue to provide wind and air for us to fly upon, to breathe in and live."

"He sounds like a swell guy," Zinx said.

"Hmph. You should be careful when speaking of Him. His is a name that all on Ozairos respect, both storn and ptomera alike."

"I suppose it is nice that you all have something in common, at least."

"More than that, it is said that Buuziliel is the source of all life, and the basis for our common ancestor."

"Storns and ptomeras have a common ancestor?" Zinx said, scratching his head with a sharp claw that had to dig deep through a thick volume of pitch black strands. "That is honestly a bit difficult to believe. Storns and ptomeras seem so different."

"Indeed, but…" Zzira paused, as if lost in thought, then continued, keeping her chin resting on her crossed arms, "it's not something most like to admit. If our histories were not so intertwined we would probably merely regard each other as monsters, maybe even demons that need to be purged."

"What happened?" Zinx asked. "How did storns and ptomeras grow to hate each other? How did they grow to be so different?"

"Well, I am no scholar, or historian,' Zzira said, "but I have learned a few things in my education. Our ancestors ruled over the world as one, but somewhere along the line, thousands and thousands of years ago, newborns began to exhibit deviations. The most notable deviations were things like the stingers we storns now have exclusively, and the odd wing patterns and layered antenna the ptomera often have. No one knew how to handle the abrupt changes. It is said that some were ready to embrace the changes, but many more argued over them. Some wanted segregation, others wanted to… 'purge' them, seeing them as defects, merely allowing weak genes into their blood. Decades went by as conflict grew, and everything came to a head when that night happened…"

"What night? What happened?"

"The Night of Red Stings…"

"That sounds ominous…"

"It was the night that cemented this never ending war of ours, the night where everyone was forced to take a stand. The exact date is lost to time, but it is believed to have occurred just over a thousand and one years ago as of now. A group of precursor storns snuck into the palace of a queen harboring children—children who exhibited a combination of storn and ptomera traits. The invaders slaughtered hundreds of innocents that night—men, women, children, it didn't matter. A few escaped, and quickly rallied whoever they could. The invaders were all caught and slain by the morning."

"Precursor storns?" Zinx asked. "Do the storns bear any guilt for essentially starting the conflict?"

"Some do," Zzira said, "others take pride in it. Most don't have the time to ponder such things, and I don't blame them for taking the easy route and merely focusing on their jobs and on the battlefield. It's what I often do."

"Perhaps conflict was inevitable, in some form or another. Perhaps they merely wished to get in a pre-emptive strike?"

"Ah! Now you're beginning to sound like a true storn!"

"Is that a good thing?"

"I mean... I should say yes, but I don't know anymore..."

"That sort of doubt seems odd for you," Zinx said, a warm breath further softening his already calm and inviting tone.

"It's just that... Whenever I stop and begin thinking, I begin to doubt everything. All I have ever done has been for others—my father, my mother, our empire—and what has it gotten me? My mother is gone, I'm apparently never good enough for my father, and the best thing I can seemingly do for the empire is lead others into battle, and to their deaths..."

Zzira lowered her head, weighed down by thoughts of death, by the voices of those that fought beneath her. She couldn't think of the screams and cries of the fallen without the sounds of flesh ripping, of bones snapping, of wings tearing and blood spilling. Normally she would merely push such thoughts to a dark corner of her mind, dismissing the agony as being expected, as her soldiers merely fulfilling their duty to the empire.

What else would we do, anyway? We find our zuthra in battle. It is what makes us strong and driven. To claim glory, and rise up in rank. But... How many storns have I watched die? How many storns could have been like Zinx? How many innocent souls and capable minds have I steered to a premature death? How much wasted potential is now just gone? How many children that would have been, and should have been, now will never be... because of me?

The sharp ting of chitin casually tapping against a metal bar shook Zzira out of her trance. She looked over to see Zinx reaching up and stretching, only to rest his hands behind his head.

"What was that one young storn's name?" Zinx asked. "The one that called out to you earlier today?"

"You mean… I think it was, um… Katarmin!" Zzira snapped her fingers, her long, dark nails striking against one another and filling the room with a quick, echoing snap. "I remember him, a young fresh scout. He needed more training. He should have known better than to dash into the sights of a group of ptomeras readying their psychic blasts."

"Katarmin, huh… Nice name."

"What's it matter, anyway?" Zzira hissed. "He's dead now, just like the rest of them."

"I always try to remember people's names," Zinx said. "I do not like the idea of people being forgotten."

"Well, what difference does it make remembering those who are long gone?" Zzira said. "Especially those who died young and foolishly, before they could accomplish anything of note?"

"We all have a place in this life," Zinx said, "we all do our part and add to this big, crazy thing we call existence."

"I suppose some people's existence is merely to be fodder, to add fuel and weight to conflict," Zzira said, a callous tone weighing down her words.

"Conflict is inevitable, it is just as much a part of life as death," Zinx said. "The tricky part is realizing that we have a choice in the matter—a choice in how that conflict manifests or plays out. Killing and death only leads to more of it. But we can each choose something different, that much at least is within our power. No single storn or ptomera or whoever can bear all of the responsibility, but we must also realize that no single one of us is entirely free from what happens, from the part we all play in things."

"So we should all just huddle together, sing and stop fighting? Pft." Zzira glared from the corner of her eye, then back to the ground. "You'll have to go to the ptomeras if you want that kind of therapy. We storns do not allow such softness."

"Hmm… Alright then," Zinx shrugged.

"Huh?" Zzira raised her brow, and with it her arm to rest on as she leaned toward the source of her sudden befuddlement.

"Let us go to the ptomeras and speak with them," Zinx said. "If they are indeed more open to 'softness' then perhaps a simple conversation could lead to great things."

"What are you babbling about now?" Zzira said, squinting her large, dark eyes at the stranger confined in his cell.

Zinx stretched, then pushed himself up to his feet. He wiped himself down as if preparing for something. "I am getting tired of hiding everything about myself. If I could let loose, just a little bit, I think I could help out so much more."

Zzira stood as well, in contrast to Zinx her movements were quick and alert. She even flexed her wings—just a bit—as if ready to move at a moment's notice. "Just what are you planning? What odd scheme have you skittering around in that pretty little head of yours?"

"Excuse me princess," Zinx said, waving ahead just enough so as to not seem as a presumptuous or forceful demand, "if you would be so kind as to step back a few feet."

Zzira squinted, a fierce glare meeting Zinx's large, open eyes. A tense moment passed, but curiosity pushed her to obey the prisoner's wishes. She stepped back, nearly disappearing into the heavy shadow cast on the opposite side of the room.

Zinx smiled, then stepped forward, seemingly with no regard to the bars containing him. Before his foot could touch the first silver bar, a burst of colorless smoke filled the prisoner's cell, and nearly covered the entire row of bars! Zzira stepped back, raising her arms to cover her mouth and eyes. Strangely, the smoke was smooth and near odorless, prompting no response from her. It was as easy on the lungs as air, and Zzira was able to keep her attention focused ahead. The smoke began to fade quickly, and Zinx now stood on the same side of the room as her, though he remained fully in the moonlight. He appeared as calm and non-threatening as usual, though Zzira couldn't help but maintain her guard.

"W-what was that? Some kind of trick?!" Zzira snarled. "Are you working for the ptomeras? Try anything, and I'll cut you down, and every guard in this palace will be witness to your funeral—"

"Princess, please," Zinx kept his cool, and merely raised his own clawed hands to gesture for her to calm down. "I am not trying to 'trick' you. I only wish to help."

"Wait," Zzira said, lowering her guard to stare with wide eyes as a niggling thought caught up with her, "that was the same smoke we saw when we first found you... And the same smoke I saw faint traces of when I entered... Just what are you?"

"I... well, I am a storn, just like you."

"Why does it sound as if you don't even believe that?" Zzira rested her stance, but kept a harsh squint on the now-freed prisoner. "Could you have escaped at any time?"

"Yes."

"Then why didn't you?"

"I wanted to meet some of you, and maybe learn a thing or two about the storn empire, in order to better think of a plan to address your conflict."

"What do you plan to do? Why shouldn't I just cut you down now? Or call the guards to come and apprehend you?"

"I suppose that is well within your right, but," Zinx paused, took in a deep breath and looked to the ground. He was considering his next words carefully—perhaps too carefully, "that all depends on what you want, Zzira."

"What?"

"You seem to be unhappy with your situation. You seem rather powerless, operating under the current regime, under your father's rule, and the greater conflict dictating all of it. I will not force you to do anything, and I will not trouble you further if you do not want me to. If you refuse me, I will merely leave you and go about my way."

"Just spit it out, stranger. What do you want?" Zzira's words came out in an uncontrollable hiss, though it was not the result of anger, but of uncertainty. All she wanted was a peaceful conversation before an end to this strangest of days. She wanted nothing more than for everything to be over. It would be nice to at least get a good night's sleep before having to explain all of this to her father in the morning.

Zinx smiled warmly, then held out a soft hand to her: "Would you like to accompany me? Escape with me to the ptomera empire? I think an understanding storn such as yourself would be a great ally, and help me in beginning to establish some sort of peace."

Zzira stood, shocked and speechless. Her thoughts raced, her mind dizzying from the frantic patterns whirling around inside. It was difficult for her to even keep her eyes focused on the stranger in front of her, despite his calm, almost motionless stance as he waited patiently with a soft, self-assured smile.

What on Ozairos does he plan to do?! How did he do that?! What is he? Is this a trap? What does he hope to accomplish? What makes him think he can just waltz up to me—me! Of all storns! Zzira Kul and empress to be—and make me any sort of offer! How presumptuous! How preposterous! As if I would just up and leave all of… As if I would leave… All of…

Something warm welled up from below, and her eyes became wet and her vision clouded. Through a wall of barely contained tears she could see the stranger still smiling, still waiting patiently, still giving her the world's attention—something that even her father refused to do. The last time she could remember someone—anyone—giving her such attention was her mother.

"I am sorry," Zinx said, finally bringing back his hand and turning his attention away, "I suppose I cannot ask you to leave so much behind. Your remaining family, your empire, it is not fair of me to—"

"No!" Zzira shrieked.

Zinx whipped his head up and about, enough so that it nearly tossed his luxuriously kept hair into a mess. He stared with wide, dark eyes at the girl, clearly startled, but still sat quietly and waited patiently for her to gather herself and continue speaking.

"No, please," Zzira said, bringing up a clenched fist to wipe away the excesses of her sniveling, "I don't know why it took me this long to realize this, but... I have no reason to stay here anymore. What has this empire, this war, my father, any of it... What has any of it given me? We constantly fight, and lead swarms to their deaths, and when we're not fighting we are at each other's throats, vying for rank and status and training just so we can fight again. Even my father... He never cared about me. Even now he wishes to merely use me to bring more poor souls into the world, bore wasted lives and wasted potential, all so he can have his supposed 'elite army.' And yet, I went along with it, because I thought he was all I had, especially after my mother... After she..."

"Zzira," Zinx said, "it is alright, you do not have to—"

Zzira dashed in and hugged Zinx tightly. It was easier to let loose a few tears with her face hidden. She took special care to make sure her sharp claws avoided the wings on his back. She also took full advantage of his greater height, nuzzling her head into a bushel of soft black hair that reached down from his head and neck and was nestled on his chest. She couldn't help but sob, forcing her wings to flex and expand and contract ever so slightly as she released her emotions into the stranger's chest. Zzira never dared to hug anyone, not even her father, for fear of a swift claw digging into her back for showing such weakness. She was ill-prepared for the soft, warm hand that eventually greeted her back, and gave several gentle pats on the raised, hard muscles located at the base of each of her wings. The new sensation forced them to twitch rapidly before settling down.

"I don't know what you're planning, or what makes you so sure of what you're doing," Zzira whispered, "but I don't care anymore. Just take me away from here. I could use a vacation."

Zinx chuckled, then smiled. "As you wish, princess."

CHAPTER 27

SEEING THE WORLD THROUGH NEW eyes was surreal for her. Zzira was so conditioned for combat, to the constant cries and screams and sounds of battle. She could not remember a time where she had been allowed to leave her palace, or a storn camp or barracks, without it leading into a fight of some sort. Some of her earliest missions as a new scout came to mind, but such memories were drowned out by the countless battles that constituted her daily business.

Tornadoes were rare on Ozairos, primarily due to the fact that extreme weather of any kind was rare. The many olive lands and skies of the world were so calm, and so temperate, that if one were to sit still and watch silently, they would be forgiven for thinking that time did not move on Ozairos. Puffed sleeves of pale greens and warm yellows cast soft shadows against the smooth, sand lands and even mountains below. Countless forests filled the spaces in between with rows upon rows of fluffy leaves that glittered calmly during the day, and danced sweetly in the night. Wherever an open plain revealed itself, some of the continent's harsher features revealed themselves—spiky plants and thorny bark showed weedy, brown roots dotted with prickly bushes that seemed completely unable to hold the few berries they were capable of producing. Theirs was a land that seemed as if it couldn't decide if it wanted to provide sustenance or challenge. The winds never rose to particularly high speeds, caressing the world like the arm of a beloved parent reaching up and from below to carry their child. A few creatures could be heard or seen going about their business below, but they too were calm, and merely blended in with the surrounding peace. The occasional leathery serpent or sprinting herbivore would leave as quickly as they showed themselves, disappearing into the tranquil woods.

Far beyond the storn capital, two little dragonflies made their way toward an ocean on the horizon. The ocean too was calm and peaceful, at ease with itself as it presented a seemingly never ending flat plane of lime green that reflected near rosy pink colors as it glittered in the day's light. It was an enchanting view of placidity that invited the heart to rest as the eye glazed over serenity in its most literal form.

Zzira felt completely at peace with the absurdity of her current situation. Zinx did his best to explain that he had other abilities, and that he could sneak them through anything. Zinx warned her of the feeling of a great weight bearing down on her as he transformed her into something he could control and hide. In all honesty, the weight was more than tolerable. It was a strange, compressing feeling that was almost cozy in how it enveloped her entire being. What truly caught her off guard was the lack of control. She could still sense herself, and perceive things on her own, but her mind and view were one with the stranger's. Her mind was her own, but Zinx was in full control of everything they did. It was as if the weight of the world, the weight of having to exist, had been temporarily taken off of her shoulders. Flying was a strenuous activity for storns. One needed to be healthy and strong to maintain flight, and it was tiring having to constantly manage and flex the muscles on her back to keep her wings buzzing. For once she could just relax, and let someone else take care of the stress, allowing her to enjoy an unseen side of her world.

The only interruptions along the way were the occasional skirmishes that cropped up from time to time. Zinx was quick to take note of any battle, and would fly them both up and above into the clouds to look down upon the carnage. She would feel her form changing once again, beyond her will, as the world began to shift. The pale, cushy pillows of clouds swirled and hardened into darkened plumes, focusing their shadow into an intense cast on the battles below. The temperate, salty sea air rose into something heavy and menacing, bearing down with an ever increasing intensity that filled the ear with a long, drawn out howl. The once flat and glassy ocean surface began to ripple, tearing itself apart as dagger-like waves shot out in all directions as the water tried and failed to follow the wind's direction. Zzira fully expected the combatants to remain locked in combat, to completely ignore the growing calamity surrounding them like a viper slowly strangling its prey without its notice. She full expected this, yet it still somehow perplexed her to see it unfold—to see living, breathing people, storn and ptomera alike, completely disregarding their safety and situational awareness to blindly continue their skirmish. Zinx had full control of the growing hurricane, and would only push as far as needed to stop the fighting. Normally this meant having to drag a few unknowing bodies into the water itself, which forced their attention to the oncoming hazardous weather, and with their wings heavy and wet, would need to call out for their allies to carry them away. Both sides had to resort to this, which usually was signal enough to end the conflict. Once the scene was clear, Zinx would bring them both down below, back in some transformed state, and they would continue forward.

What stood out to Zzira was just how determined Zinx was to end any skirmish as soon as he noticed them. Not a single battle across the great ocean went unimpeded. Wherever there was a battle, an inexplicable storm would soon follow. Zzira couldn't help but wonder how many lives Zinx saved during their trip, and how fruitless the endeavor may be, considering that the same storns and ptomeras he spared would be right back on the battlefield by the next day. Perhaps Zinx didn't think that far ahead, or perhaps that didn't matter to him. Perhaps another day of life was worth the trouble. The several days and nights it took for the duo to make their way across the great ocean gave Zzira more than enough time to ponder

these things—thoughts that, under normal circumstances would have had no time or place in between
her daily duties and battles. Zinx's calm and introspec-
tive demeanor was beginning to make sense.

A new land began to poke through the distant
horizon. It was a new continent, one Zzira herself had
never been to, and one few storns dared to approach
willingly. In fact, rather than exile, storns who had
committed some slight against the empire, or merely
annoyed the emperor, were forcefully tasked with
scouting out the ptomera continent, with the expec-
tation that it would be their last mission. The storns
never bothered with specific names for their homes
or lands, with everything merely considered property
of the storn empire. The ptomeras, on the other hand,
were much more fanciful. They were approaching the
Land of Lanu.

Both empires took great pride in their current
rulers, but the ptomeras took even that a step further
by naming their land after whoever was currently in
rule. Rumors of an exceptionally powerful ptomera
empress—a mysterious woman who rarely, if ever,
showed herself to anyone beyond her grand palace.
Zzira couldn't help but be skeptical, thinking that if
this ptomera woman was so powerful, then why not
join the frontlines? Why not try to gain an advantage
for herself and her people? Zzira wasn't particularly
special, but she was more than capable enough to add
positively to any skirmish she was a part of, and all she
could do was move fast and cut quicker. Perhaps this
empress was merely a coward, and spoiled due to her
station as royalty. Even Zinx was not afraid of hurling

himself head first into an engagement. He had special abilities, and seemed unafraid to utilize them, to be productive, so what was the empress' excuse?

As the two dragonflies approached the Land of Lanu, new senses began to fill Zzira's mind. Sweet, fruity scents followed colorful plumage as softer, rounder trees and bushes covered the land in lush foliage. While storn lands were often covered in desaturated browns and greens, the ptomera landscape immediately hit the eye with intense blues and violets. Flowers of dizzying variety dotted the intensely colored forests with a rainbow of petals. Countless small insects and other critters—furred and scaled alike—scurried about, adding a lively flair to the forests below. Rather than the occasional sandy wind and harsh buzzing of insect wings or sharp scraping or serpentine claws on bark, everything sounded much softer, more harmonious, as if nature itself were dancing to a smooth rhythm. Zinx was the first to take notice of this, and lowered them both beneath the treetops to transform them in the shade. A quick puff of colorless smoke revealed two butterflies which emerged and continued their path farther inland.

Zzira had never seen or heard of butterflies before. She didn't even know Ozairos had such creatures. They were eerily similar to ptomeras in their appearance, particularly when it came to their rounded wings and the wild patterns that covered them. She had seen dragonflies, however, though most storns referred to them as drakewings. It seemed redundant to her to call things that could clearly fly 'flies,' but she found Zinx's naming conventions interesting nonetheless.

Settlements began to come into view, signaled by the growing number of ptomeras flying above and around them. Storn architecture was incredibly utilitarian—mostly consisting of large, spacious rooms and simple open blocks of brown wood and dull stone. The only buildings that were allowed to be made of more extravagant material was any place the emperor might be expected to visit personally. Even the emperor's palace, despite being made of sparkling marbles and refined granite, mostly consisted of large, empty spaces that gave the average storn plenty of room to flex their wings—if they are so permitted. Everything was sharp, simple, droll, and angular. Ptomeras seemed to almost relish in excess artistry. Rounded domes, curved walls, useless bridges, streams of hanging fruits decorating any sharp corners or hard angles. They even painted most of their buildings! Storns hardly ever painted anything, let alone would they allow themselves to waste so much time coloring everything. Even the emperor's palace mostly stuck to the original hues of the materials used in its construction. As Zzira flew over the many settlements, her eyes could hardly keep track of all the different and unnecessary details that formed their whole. From high above their cities looked more akin to flower forests than anything else. Thinking back to her own homeland, storn cities looked more like stony thorn bushes. It was rather shameful to think of how unappealing her lands were in comparison.

As they progressed inland, the structures became taller, the forests thicker, and the more intertwined the trees themselves became with the architecture. From afar it merely looked as if many small insects were going between flowers, but upon closer inspection it was revealed to be ptomeras going in and out of buildings—homes and barracks and camps embedded within massive trunks. The ptomeras themselves moved so casually, slowly fluttering their many colored wings and expressing their vibrant and wild patterns as if showing off their individuality to the world. Everything had a tendency to blend together on the battlefield, but in a calmer setting it was easy to see how and why the ptomeras would take pride in such a thing, in such artistic expression. The only flourish storns possessed naturally was their hair, and even that suffered under enough stress, as her own coarse mane revealed about her.

Something stood out to her in the distance—a particularly tall tree that poked through the horizon, and whose multicolored plumage sat amongst the clouds. Tiny rainbowed specks in the distance revealed themselves to be petals and leaves of every imaginable color, and some even beyond that. Every possible type of flower seemed to be growing somewhere on its surface, leaving little room for the tree's dark and shiny bark to show itself. Countless creatures of all kinds skittered and crawled along the tree's surface. Even the insects themselves shone and glittered in the sunlight, adding to the already overwhelming display of life. Every sound came together in a sort of chaotic harmony—the skittering of tiny feet, the fluttering of many wings, the soothing wind gently blowing beneath it all—nothing was out of place. The only thing that stood out in an almost unpleasant way was the smell—a constant, sweet scent followed the duo wherever they went. It was enough to make her sick, at least at first, but she eventually began to adjust and could focus on the path Zinx was taking them on.

If the supposed Land of Lanu did in fact possess a reclusive, mysterious empress, this tree would be the place to find her.

Finally an opening presented itself as groups of ptomeras moved in and out of a suspicious tree hollow. Zinx, showing no fear, went straight for it, and the two butterflies were now lost among a sea of vibrant, rounded wings fluttering about. It took a moment for her eyes to adjust from the light outside to the shade inside the tree, but soon its inner splendor became apparent. The tree was appropriately massive inside as well, and there was plenty of open space for the ptomeras to fly around. On every wall and at every corner were furnishings and decor! Actual art hung along the bark-coated walls, and bushels of glittering fruit and berries could be found growing at specific locations throughout, as if the inside of the tree palace were a designed garden.

Father would hate it here, Zzira thought. *I could only imagine how irritating he would find all of these "distractions" taking up "his" valuable air space... And everyone gets to fly so freely! Even in royal air space.*

Zinx seemed to notice something farther up, though it took Zzira a moment to figure out what it was. One ptomera in particular, hidden amongst the crowd, was moving slowly, and regally, as if with no concern to the constant energy surrounding them. Her body was a bit smaller than average, though her wings were slightly larger than average. Two great plumes of fur stood out from her crown and swerved back, each an antenna resting on top of her meticulously kept lavender hair. Her hair wrapped around her head and neck, and covered her entire bosom as well. Zzira thought the peculiar ptomera's hair would give even Zinx's hair a run for its money. Her near black wings stood out against her bright, icy blue skin, and whenever they flexed, the light itself seemed to surrender to the material, filtering out as it passed through the rounded membranes and leaving patterns in its cast shadow that looked almost like art. She seemed to move against everyone else, who were forced to move out of her way. Many ptomeras tended to her, going to and fro to speak with her, often with a lowered head. She kept her head held high, and looked as if she was practically ignoring them as she went about her way. She disappeared into another opening that led farther into the tree. Zzira could feel curiosity welling within Zinx like an uncontrollable wildfire, and the two flew after her.

In a flash, the deeper shade revealed another large and empty space. It was as decorated as any other part of the tree palace, but there were no other ptomeras, save for the mysterious woman trying to be alone. Not a word needed to be said, yet the command was obvious. The new space seemed to lead upward, and the regal ptomera continued her unhurried pace along this path. The hard part for Zinx was to remain inconspicuous, to not make their stalking too obvious among the now quiet area all three of them now flew through.

The mysterious woman eventually happened upon a large, open area near the tree's top. She settled on the ground and began to walk along, taking note of the many branches and vines seeping in from the outside, walking between the beams of light peeking through the many openings between the bountiful bushels of leaves above that lined the center of the room like spotlights. The ptomera's eyes flashed subtly whenever in the dark, her great luminous eyes revealing that she had little trouble seeing in the shade. Even the insects hiding in the dark, flowered corners of the room chittered with a quiet respect as the ptomera made her way through. The only sounds present were that of the ptomera's footsteps, along with the flaps of her wings whenever she felt the need to flex them. Though if one listened carefully, they could hear the passing of wind rustling the leaves above.

The mysterious ptomera disappeared into a particularly dark area of the shade ahead. For the first time since their travels, Zzira could sense hesitation with Zinx. The two butterflies sat and hovered for a moment as they looked on, a sheet of pitch black shadow hiding the world in front of them. Curiosity welled up within Zinx again, and the two began to flutter forward. Before they could cross the shadowy barrier, two golden orbs pierced the dark, and flashed a new thought into Zzira's mind:

I can see you.

Zzira's heart jumped. Zinx as well seemed caught off guard as well, nearly twisting the both of them into a spin as he shifted their wings to stop. The golden orbs flashed a terrifying sheen of crystalline blue, like ice forming over something solid. The voice rose once again from the depths of Zzira's mind, a voice that was felt, rather than heard:

You cannot hide from me. Come here.

Zzira could feel a great weight on her chest. A massive burst of colorless smoke took her vision, and she soon felt her body hitting the floor with a weighty thump. The shift in perspective was enough to nearly make her nauseous, and her head continued to spin. Getting to feel solid ground as she stretched her long arms and legs, as well as getting her first real breath of air in what felt like too long, was enough to allow her to get her bearings. She looked to her side to see Zinx doing the same, though he was holding on to his head for dear life. Otherwise her companion seemed fine.

As if she had forgotten, only to realize at the last moment, Zzira remembered the ptomera woman. She whipped her head up only to lock eyes with the ptomera, her golden orbs still peering into her. The ptomera was eerily still and calm, as if possessing full control of the situation. Her black wings nearly disappeared into the shade behind her. In contrast to Zzira, and most storns, the ptomera was short, bore slim shoulders and wide hips, and little in the way of notable muscle definition. She bore a few pieces of cloth that wrapped around her like a loose robe. Clothing was something most storns did not bother with, and to wear them in such a fashion as to show off was unheard of. If the emperor, or anyone beneath him, caught wind of such impudence, they would be made into an example and a warning. Looking over the majestic ptomera, Zzira couldn't help but finally notice how much she compared their lands and their culture to her own. Pride prevented her from admitting jealousy, but the thought niggled fiercely at the back of her mind—a mind that seemed totally vulnerable to the mysterious being staring her down.

"How interesting," the mysterious ptomera whispered, never letting up her gaze, and in the same voice that pierced Zzira's thoughts. "I can sense that at least one of you is a storn, but the other…" The woman slightly shifted her sight to Zinx, looking on more curiously than anything.

Zinx and the ptomera stared at one another for what felt like an eternity to Zzira. The way their eyes and expressions shifted slightly suggested that the two were perhaps communicating. The frustration of feeling left out, while at the same time in danger, ate away at Zzira, enough to cause her to grimace.

"You two may stand," the lady ptomera said. "Let us address one another appropriately."

Zzira looked at the woman, her grimace now stretched into a wide shock. She looked over to Zinx, who seemed more composed. He gave a stern nod, and was the first to stand up. Zzira quickly followed suit, and the two were now towering over the ptomera. Even when looked down upon, the ptomera kept her regal air, as if looking down her own nose at them. It was the same pompous look Zzira's father held constantly.

"It is a pleasure to finally meet your majesty and empress, Lady Lanu," Zinx said with a bow.

Ugh, Zzira thought, *Zinx and his weak gestures—*

"Ah, so what I saw in you was not wrong," the empress said, her plump, violet lips stretching into a smile. "You are quite familiar with royalty of all kinds, no?"

Zinx stood himself back up before replying. "Yes, your highness."

"Does the girl know?" Lady Lanu asked.

"Know what?" Zzira said, butting her way into the conversation.

"I apologize," Lanu said, "but I have seen much of your thoughts already. You harbor growing feelings for this young storn man, which is… quite tragic."

"What?!" Zzira hissed. "Wait, we just met, and yet here you are—"

"I'm sorry, again," Lanu said, "due to my powers, I have a bit of trouble distinguishing between normal conversation and the thoughts of those around me. We have yet to properly greet one another."

"You could start by looking me in the eye, 'Lady Lanu,'" Zzira said, crossing her arms defiantly as she raised her head to look down her nose at the ptomera.

Lady Lanu chuckled, enough to press her cheeks up and into her eyes.

"What's so funny?" Zzira hissed once more.

"I am blind," Lanu said, calming her expression and resting her hands together as they hung in front of her.

"Oh, um, I'm sorry," Zzira said, loosening her stance to scratch her head.

"It is fine," Lanu said, "the eyes lie all the time. That I am blessed with the ability to see deeper, well, I am grateful. There is no need to apologize, and no need to pity me. Please, tell me your names."

"I am Zzira Kul, the one and only child and daughter of his highness Emperor Anzinius Kul."

"And you?" Lanu said, shifting her gaze to the Zinx, with a look of self assurance, as if she already knew the answer.

"I am Zinx."

"Zinx… Only Zinx? No family name? No title? Something along the lines of… Zinx the jester? Zinx the world traveler? Zinx, the Buuzine Herald?"

"Buuzine?" Zinx said, now curiously scratching his own head.

"Ah, that is right, you're not from around here," Lanu said, a wry grin covering her otherwise smooth and placid face, "buuzine are what we call great servants of Buuziliel, our great lord and the creator of the very winds that give the people of Ozairos the means to fly."

"Yes, Buuziliel," Zzira said, feeling the need to force her way into the conversation once more, "the greatest and mightiest of storns, from whom we all descend, whose stingers reach the sky, and whose transparent wings shift and color the clouds themselves."

"Stingers? Heh." Lanu raised a thin hand to her face, as if trying, and failing, to cover her chuckling. "We ptomeras view the great Buuziliel a fair bit differently. His rounded wings helped to form the mountains themselves, and whose furred antennae gave thought and sentience to his chosen children."

"As expected, your interpretation is entirely wrong," Zzira said.

"I am jesting, if just a bit," Lanu said. "I always suspected that our interpretations may both be wrong, though not quite as wrong as I expected…"

"What do you mean?" Zzira said, raising a bony brow to the short ptomera.

"I believe Zinx has a much better idea of what either of us could possibly know," Lanu said.

"You speak as if Zinx were some sort of alien, some… thing… from the outer space."

"Hah! If only you knew, child."

"Child? You dare to call me a child? The daughter of an emperor? The same emperor whose forces continue to whittle away at your ranks and people?"

"I am sorry," Lanu said, "but neither side is gaining any true ground in this conflict."

"What makes you say that?"

"Think about it—this war has been going on for centuries, literally thousands of years. What are we doing now that is any different than our predecessors? We live in the same lands as our ancestors, performing the same rituals as them, and we die the same way they did. All of this fighting and killing is for nothing. We struggle and die, ultimately for nothing, just as many of our ancestors did, and just as many of our children might."

Zzira wanted to say something—anything—to try and rebuke the ptomera, but nothing came to mind. It angered her that she felt so powerless, and worse still, speechless even, as if she were being denied any sort of expression. She hated being called a "child," but she knew that lashing out would only prove Lanu's point. She merely tightened her fists, bit her tongue and looked away. Zinx seemed to take notice, showing worry for his companion as he furrowed his brow and reached over for Zzira, though he couldn't bring himself to actually touch her.

Lady Lanu continued: "You show an awful lot of compassion for those you barely know, Zinx. Stranger still that you show such feelings for those you know you must abandon."

Zzira whipped her head back to look at Lanu. "What do you mean? What is so special about Zinx? I know he has certain abilities, but—"

Lady Lanu threw up a defiant hand, hushing Zzira, though the ptomera kept her reflective eyes on Zinx. "I think you should just show her your true form. You may as well, Zinx."

Zinx looked on, his dark eyes nearly falling out of their sockets as he stared dumbfounded at Lanu.

"I refuse to operate through any sort of trickery," Lanu said, "I am willing to help you, Zinx, and I will be as open and honest as you wish, but I first demand that you are honest with me. You do not need to worry about anyone else knowing—I can sense every living being around for miles, and I can instantly deter any who would intrude upon our private meeting."

"I… I do not think that would be wise," Zinx said, "it also seems unnecessary, you seem to already know much about me. Is that not good enough?"

"No," Lanu said, her voice stern, her conviction clear. "You and I both have an idea for what we could do to end all of this. But in order for anything to work, we will need Zzira's assistance, and she will need to be on the same page as us. I would rather not force images and memories into her mind."

"I still do not think that is a good idea, your highness," Zinx said.

"Hmm, very well then."

Lady Lanu whipped her head back, only to stop her gaze immediately on Zzira. Lanu's golden orbs shot a reflective flash right into Zzira, and her mind was rendered blank and heavy, forcing her to her knees. Zinx gasped, then rushed over to try and help Zzira, but it was no use—Zzira shook and groaned, requiring every ounce of strength within her to not entirely collapse onto the moss and dew covered floor.

"Stop!' Zinx cried. "Please! Do not hurt her! You said we need her!"

"I will stop as soon as you comply," Lanu said, her tone frighteningly calm as her gaze remained fixed on Zzira.

Zinx looked on for a moment, first at Zzira, then back up to Lanu. He grit his teeth, and allowed his frustration out in a single, pained huff. He quickly stood, and burst into smoke, revealing the form of a cloaked jester—pale skin, sharp eyes, a pointed hat and an impossibly long ponytail that nearly touched the floor as he stood.

"Good, now we can speak candidly," Lanu said. She relaxed her gaze and took in a soft, deep breath.

Zzira could feel that a great weight had been lifted from her mind. She felt as if she could breathe again, and felt light as air. She shot herself up to her feet, anger nearly spurring her forward to attack the ptomera empress. Yet curiosity held her back as she looked on to her companion, now in a form that was nearly incomprehensible to her.

"What… are you supposed to be?" Zzira asked. "It's true, isn't it? You really are from…"

"The cosmos," Lady Lanu said, through a wry grin she could not hold back. "Or, even better, he is from a place beyond the mere 'cosmos,' from someplace greater, where mortal souls are not supposed to tread. Yet here you are, going about as if for a stroll through realms. How remarkable."

"I don't understand any of this," Zzira said. "Just what are you trying to do, Zinx? If that's even your real name?"

"It's not," Lanu said. "What is your real name, stranger?"

"I am Cynkz, Cynkz Alabaster Krullowski II."

"What a mouthful," Zzira muttered.

"Names and titles are a bit more involved back where he comes from," Lanu said, keeping her eyes on the strange being in front of her.

"What are you?" Zzira asked.

"I… I am a po, though one who was born under strange circumstances."

"More vagueness," Zzira hissed.

"He means no harm," Lanu said, "he was not trying to deceive you, or lie to you, or take advantage of you—"

"Then what *is* he doing?" Zzira snapped. "Without your telekinetic hold, I could dash in and cut you both down in a flash!"

Lady Lanu smiled, then chuckled, doing her best to maintain her regal appearance.

"What's so funny?" Zzira said, her grip tightening well enough to dig her nails deep into her calloused palms.

"You storns are all the same," Lanu said. "You put such emphasis on physical prowess and speed, yet you fail to realize just how slow bodily movement is to thought—our weapon of choice, and my specialty. Besides, our friend here wouldn't allow it. He is remarkably resistant to my abilities, it seems, and he is desperate to prevent any more bloodshed."

"So what are you here to do, anyway?" Zzira said, turning her attention back to the cloaked jester, who now stood nearly a foot below her in height.

"I have been tasked with ending this pointless war," Cynkz said, keeping his gaze out of sight below the brim of his pointed cap. "This conflict will only ruin all of you in the end, and that is an unacceptable outcome."

"'Tasked?'" Zzira said. "By whom?"

"By the buuzine," Lanu said, "by the stars themselves, angels who work for the one we call Buuziliel."

"Y-you… You know Buuziliel directly?" Zzira asked, her disbelief softening her otherwise harsh tone.

"I know of Him, but…" Cynkz paused, and looked to the ground as he considered his next words carefully.

"The Creator," Lanu interrupted, "or Paithos, as his people, the po, call Him. It seems that there are many interpretations of this godlike being. Ours does not seem to be necessarily wrong, just… personalized."

"This is too much to take in," Zzira said. "If this is all true… How would the other storns—or the other ptomeras, for that matter—take this? That our source of worship is so different… This could cause so much disorder, and chaos."

"You seem to be taking it well," Lady Lanu said, going so far as to extend a gentle hand toward Zzira.

"I suppose… I am not sure, I would need more time to think it all over," Zzira said. "Our purpose and being is directly tied to Buuziliel, and the image of his wings giving us our strength to fly and fight. That Buuziliel is the one and only, and is *ours*."

"It is no different for us Ptomeras," Lanu said, bringing her hands back together to rest in front of her, "I do not plan on ever letting this knowledge get out. In fact, the idea I have in mind for forcing peace between us hinges on that notion."

"You seem awfully quick to accept peace," Zzira said, squinting her own dark eyes and even tilting her head toward the ptomera as she scrutinized the empress. "What is in it for you? What do you want? If there is one thing that I know of royalty, it is that they understand that incentives drive us better than anyone, and often have their own wants and needs clearly defined."

All went quiet. Even the distant birds and insects that were able to sneak into the tree palace seemed to respect the empress's solemnity. Her golden eyes shifted to a crystalline blue, and her expression softened as she looked to the ground, lost in thought. It was a pained expression, the same sort of look Zzira's mother gave the few times she disappointed her.

"I can understand some of your familial woes," Lanu said, her head still tilted downward, "I can sense that you loved your mother dearly—"

"And what would you know of my mother?!" Zzira snapped. "What would you know of my troubles, my family, or familial burdens?"

"All that I have left of any real family will soon be cursed to live in this world soon," Lanu said. She kept her head held low, and reached lovingly for her abdomen to rub it gently, as if caressing it.

Zzira nearly stepped back in shock. She instinctively turned to Cynkz, who returned a pair of wide eyes of his own, before the two turned their attention back to Lanu.

"Wait… So you are… expecting?" Zzira stuttered.

Lanu remained quiet, focusing on her womb.

"Who is the father, if I may be so bold as to ask?" Cynkz said.

"That… is the troublesome part," Lanu whispered, in an almost shameful way, her hesitation breaking away the air of confidence she had held onto for their entire conversation.

"Why does everything need to be so cryptic?" Zzira sighed, leaning back to rub her hand along the side of her head.

"I'm sorry," Lanu said, "I made such a fuss about being honest, and here I am being coy…" Lanu took in a deep breath, and lifted her head to look at Zzira and Cynkz. "The father was a storn."

"What?!" Zzira nearly fell back, and her voice nearly carried to the ends of the massive space, echoing into the distant wooded shade. "H-how?! Such a birth has not been seen in eons! Storns and ptomeras are so different that many have thought it was impossible."

"It is not impossible," Lanu said, "but you must think, young Zzira—any mixed born would be unable to survive long with things the way they are. They would be incredibly rare, and detested, especially if born to anyone of a lesser station and without the means to hide them."

"I know we used to share a common ancestor, but… it has been so long, we do not even remember what they were called."

"Is the father anyone we would know?" Cynkz asked.

"No… They died not long after our final tryst. Such is the way of life on Ozairos, apparently," Lanu said.

"Where did you even escape to in order to have a 'tryst?'" Zzira asked.

"To the great Gnorel Basin, far in the eastern sea," Lanu said.

"That is quite a long flight, even for us," Zzira said.

"What is the Gnorel Basin?" Cynkz asked.

Lanu took another breath before looking up to Cynkz to respond: "On Ozairos, there are in fact a few grounds which are considered sacred, where storns and ptomeras keep a sort of quiet agreement to not invade, and to not shed blood there. In the sea, there are a number of large plateaus that look something close to elevated island platforms. Most are small, and very isolated, meaning there are no nearby areas for a storn or ptomera to rest their wings during the trip. It is a taxing trip, and a true test of one's endurance. In truth, even we royalty are not supposed to go to these places, and flaunting such a transgression would have everyone—storn and ptomera alike—turning on you. But we didn't care. We would venture to this basin, and many others, in order to indulge in one another in peace. The Gnorel Basin is a rather large plateau, though it is also rather desolate."

"The fact that you would dare to go that far out, just for a tryst, is… daring," Zzira said.

"Well, just how far have you gone out of your way to travel with your companion here?" Lanu said. Cynkz perked up, looking surprised once again at the wry ptomera. "If you would do all of that with Cynkz, then imagine how far you would be willing to go for a lover."

Zzira sneered. *Having the words "Cynkz" and "lover" in the same sentence makes me unbelievably uncomfortable.*

Lanu smiled warmly at Zzira. It took Zzira a moment to understand why, and instantly quieted her thoughts, though she could not hide her blushing. Fortunately, Cynkz did not seem to notice.

Zzira, desperate to change the topic of the conversation, quickly cut: "So what do you two plan to do, then? What could we possibly do to help Cynkz achieve his goal and finally bring peace?"

Cynkz stepped forward, chest out, as cool and confident as he often was in his storn form. Despite his entirely alien appearance, Zzira instantly recognized his luxurious braid of pitch black hair trailing behind him. She hated that of all things, her jealousy of his hair would remain.

"If I have learned anything, it is that merely getting people to sit down and talk things out does wonders," Cynkz said.

"You have met my father yourself," Zzira said, "and you still believe that merely setting up a chat will do anything?"

"You would be surprised, princess," Cynkz said.

There he goes again…

"I believe the stranger has a good plan, though it lacks a certain and much needed edge," Lanu said.

"Edge?" Cynkz said, raising a thin hand to rub his chin curiously.

"Yes," Lanu continued, "I believe we need to make this a grand event, one that must be remembered."

"And how do you plan to do that?" Zzira asked.

"We will host a grand summit, right on top of the Gnorel Basin."

"I suppose gathering the most important figures in this world on holy, forbidden grounds would do just that," Cynkz said.

"So what? We'll all just sit down around a campfire and have a leisurely conversation? Do you think it will be that easy?" Zzira said, leaning more into an accusatory tone that Lanu began to take notice of.

"My people will set everything up," Lanu continued, "we will organize a great feast. The necessary precautions will be taken, and most of all, we will have you as a mediator."

"What?! Me? Why me?" Zzira said.

"Why not? Considering that, for now, the storn emperor's daughter, and his supposed 'secret weapon' are both under my tutelage, it would only make sense that he will abide by our rules. If he will listen to anyone during a discussion, it will be you, Zzira."

Zzira scoffed and crossed her arms, turning her attention to a few critters casting quick shadows beneath a beam of light in the far corner of the room.

"My father never listens to me. If anything, that bastard Riul has more say than I do."

"I believe your father cares more than he lets on," Cynkz said, "he merely struggles to express it in a productive or healthy way."

"I guess 'Zinx the jester' is an apt title for you. That is quite an understatement," Zzira said.

Cynkz shrugged playfully, though Zzira remained stern, and unamused. She focused her attention on Lanu: "Why would anyone accept me as a mediator anyway? What is to stop one of your ptomera soldiers from exploding my skull the moment I try to fly out of here?"

"I am the empress, Lanu Il Yoritz, the supreme ruler of all ptomeras, whose name defines this land and whose rule commands all here. My word is final, and if I say that you are an honorary guest, and are not to be messed with, then that is what will happen."

"I suppose I will just have to take your word for it," Zzira muttered. "But what of Cynkz? What will his role be in all of this?"

"I believe it would be best for Cynkz to maintain his previous storn disguise. The storn emperor can continue to believe that 'Zinx' is his secret weapon, while acting as our own little wild card."

"Wild card?" Cynkz asked.

"Yes, you see," Lanu continued, "I believe we may need something more than a mere chat, and I want to ensure that my child is accepted. In order to ensure this, I must ask you to do something you may not agree with."

"I do not like where this is going…" Cynkz said.

"I want you to appear as Buuziliel himself, and designate my child's birth as a holy one."

"What?! Are you mad?!" Zzira could hardly contain herself. It took every ounce of discipline within her to not dash forward and attempt to shake some sense into the little ptomera.

"I am perfectly sane and sober, Zzira," Lanu said calmly.

"That is a tall order, your highness," Cynkz said, equally calmly, and surprising enough to catch Zzira off guard.

"I know, and I am sorry to ask such a thing of you."

"That seems a bit extreme, doesn't it?" Zzira asked.

"Yes, but it would ensure a positive outcome for all involved."

"It seems wrong to deceive the people of Ozairos in such a way," Cynkz said.

"I don't care," Lanu snapped back, "my child has just as much right to exist in this world as any storn or ptomera. Is it not wrong that a newborn should be doomed before even being allowed to set foot or wing into this world?"

"The consequences of such a thing would be far reaching, and could potentially be devastating. I dare not break a core tenet of the universe, of His creation."

"If nothing else, at least consider it as a final resort, if all else fails."

"I pray that I am not pushed to such an extreme."

All stood in silence for a final time. The soft rustling of colorful leaves above filtered many dotted shadows through the beams of sunlight peering into the room. Cynkz looked worried, fearing the consequences of what may transpire. Zzira could not imagine what sort of burden he was forcing himself to endure. He was so calm and collected in his disguise, as if his resolve merely resided behind a mask. Zzira couldn't help but look over his odd form and doubt him. Even now he stood with his head downturned, a dark shadow cast upon his pale face from the light above hitting his pointed cap, though the glint of an upturned eye peered from beneath its rim.

Lanu looked on as well, right back as Cynkz. Despite being a fair bit shorter than him, and needing to look up to meet eyes with him, she stood confidently, so sure of herself and her wants and needs. She outwardly appeared to agree to a disagreement with the stranger, but Zzira knew royalty—one way or another, Lanu would try to find a way to get what she wanted. Zzira's father worked in much the same way, often acting in a way that at first seemed accommodating, extending an open palm with one hand while keeping a tight fist and at the ready behind his back. She hated to admit it, but the ptomera empress frightened Zzira, and she did not want to risk giving such feelings away by thinking too much about it.

Zzira couldn't help but feel a bit detached from the situation, despite being just as involved as the other two. The way Cynkz and Lanu looked at one another in silence seemed to suggest that the conversation had continued without her. For the first time in her life, the storn princess wished she possessed the same mental abilities as the ptomeras. If only she could listen in on what they were saying. What secrets was Cynkz keeping? What secrets about the world, the universe, and even Buuziliel—if it was even appropriate to call their lord that anymore—could she learn? Would she even want to learn such things? She already felt as if her world had been dashed to pieces when she first decided to run away from home, and forfeit her duties to her empire. Now, once again she stood in the face of exposed secrets and possible truths that forced her to rethink everything once again. It was enough to make her feel sick.

"Well then," Lanu said, smiling wide and bringing her tiny hands together, "I am tired of standing in this dark room. I say we introduce you two to some of the others. The summit, if it is to happen, will take some time to get underway. The Land of Lanu would love to have two understanding young storns as honorary guests in the meantime."

CHAPTER 28

IT WAS DIFFICULT AT FIRST. OF ALL THE things Zzira has been forced to do in her life, nothing quite compared to the anxiety she felt upon first emerging out of the tree palace's great hall with Lady Lanu and Cynkz. She remembers her eyes first adjusting to the shift in light, only to be met with hundreds of glistening wide orbs for eyes all peering into her soul. Not once did Lady Lanu seem worried, however, and just as she said, they all obeyed her orders without question, and without complaint, to not lay a hand on her or Cynkz. In a way it reminded Zzira of her father, and how he too ruled without question. Perhaps the two were more similar than she previously thought.

Zzira struggled at first when trying to keep track of who or what Cynkz was. Though it was not long before she fell back to calling him Zinx. She found it odd that she was so at ease around the shapeshifter. She now had an idea of his origins, and could still clearly remember his odd, true form, and yet seeing him in his storn guise made it easy to forget all of that and treat him like any other storn. Or at least to treat him like any other friendly storn. Storns were not often particularly friendly with one another, so even that took some adjusting. It was just another uncomfortable thing that Zzira had to adapt to. The battlefield was so easy compared to such things. So little thought and worry was involved when all one needed to do was move fast and cut flesh.

It was not long before she and Zinx were standing on top of a large, wooden balcony overlooking a huge swath of ptomeras sitting and hovering amongst a sea of colorful and flowery structures and trees. Lanu, despite being a small and delicate looking thing, had no trouble projecting her voice to the crowd, her soft voice seemingly echoing for miles. Zzira wondered if it was the ptomera's mind tricks at play, allowing her voice to carry forth into the minds of all within sight and merely mimicking a grand, loud speech. Anzinius never bothered with such things, and merely laid out his demands for those under him to carry out, which they often did, without question. Lady Lanu had several ptomeras of high command begin to organize a scouting party that would relay the message to Anzinius himself. Despite being such a dangerous mission, where all those involved faced a staggering high risk of dying, they came and went without a word of complaint or hesitation. Despite the softer methods, Lady Lanu commanded the same sort of respect as her father. Seeing Lady Lanu achieve similar results without the hostility forced Zzira to once again question everything she thought she knew or understood about her empire, their teachings and their ways.

The only thing that seemed to hold up the image of her people in her mind was pride, yet even that barrier began to erode as the coming weeks came and went.

Zzira began to notice something that ate away at her constantly—she only felt truly comfortable whenever Zinx was nearby. Lady Lanu herself was always uptight and well kept, and carried herself with a heavy air no matter the situation. It reminded her too much of her father. Otherwise Zzira often found herself alone with groups of ptomeras, ordered to cater to her every need and whim. Zzira had never been pampered before, and in truth she despised it. It made her feel like a child. It didn't help that she was spending most of her time under ptomera tutorship, being taught the ways of their people and how to handle mediation. It took some prodding, but Zzira finally agreed to help mediate the summit. Still, she hated having to be taught anything. Her school days were long behind her, and she had hoped to keep it that way, yet here she was, being coddled and spoken down to by numerous tutors and scholars and professionals alike.

She often wondered what Zinx was doing. It was a pointless thing to wonder, as she knew the answer—he was spending much of his time with Lady Lanu. Lady Lanu believed that having Zinx at her side would help to soften up the ptomeras to the presence of a storn in a non-combative scenario. Zinx was definitely better suited to the role, being as well spoken, and cool, and calm, and collected as he was.

Zzira hated being so different from everyone else. She was so tall, and bony, and muscular. Ptomera architecture was clearly not suited to storns, as she was forced many times to bend over a great deal just to fit beneath the many hallways and doorways in some of the smaller buildings. Fortunately she was able to spend most of her time being tutored in the great tree palace itself, or the many large halls and auditoriums surrounding the palace. Even ptomeras needed room to stretch their wings, something Zzira could relate to.

She often wondered about what Lady Lanu and Zinx thought of everything. Lanu herself would bear a child soon enough, and one who was not safe. She was not yet showing any signs of pregnancy, but eventually she would have to show the world a great vulnerability. Furthermore, she was potentially risking her own people, many of whom could die at this very summit. If things went poorly enough, it was difficult to say how that could shatter her people's view of her. As powerful as Lady Lanu was, she was ultimately at the mercy of her empire. She needed to set a good example.

Zinx was an entirely different case. She could not even begin to comprehend what sort of responsibility he had to bear. Lady Lanu talked of the cosmos, and celestial beings, and Buuziliel himself, in a form unrecognizable to them—and Zinx ultimately had to deal with it all. If he were to make any great mistakes, Ozairos itself could suffer. Zinx spoke of "greater consequences," most likely referring to his duty to the cosmos, but Zzira had no idea what that truly meant. A certain morbid curiosity welled up within her whenever she saw Zinx, and she would be desperate to ask him. Then dread would set in, and weigh down her heart and mind, and she would refrain from inquiring any further into Zinx's past.

Over time, Zzira did come to know and even like many of the ptomeras she often conversed with. Her primary tutor, Fera, an older ptomera female who liked to arrange bouquets, and managed many of the decorations and furnishings in Lanu's tree palace. There was Pote, a much older ptomera male who handled most of Lady Lanu's meals, as well as Zzira's. Ptomeras loved their honey and sweets. It was sickening on its own, but having a bitter drink and some sour breads nearby usually helped to balance everything out. There was Olius, a distant cousin of Pote's who handled communications between Lady Lanu and many of those working under her. He was often in a hurry, fluttering back and forth to relay messages and prepare future meetings and gatherings. He would often show up to a place well before Lanu even knew she had to set either foot or wing in it to ensure everything was up to standard. When he actually calmed down, and could take a breath and settle his usually messy dark blue hair and rattled nerves, he was actually quite funny, charming even, Zzira would say.

The many youth helpers stood out as well. Zzira never dealt with children much, and in truth she often felt nervous around such small and fragile things. Even storn children were very vulnerable before puberty. Ptomera children were no different, and in fact seemed to hold on to basic physical vulnerabilities and weaknesses of childhood for far longer than storns did. Still, they each carried themselves well as they took orders and politely spoke with their superiors. There were quite a few of them, and Zzira regularly fumbled their names, or completely forgot them at awkward times. She remembered a few in specific—Orr, Cii, and Kan—as they were in a specialized and private program due to their enhanced psychic abilities. It seemed as if, thanks to their focus on mental capabilities, their upbringing brought with it lots of reading and studying, and even meditation. The children even had time for things such as making art! Or playing games. A favorite among them was "guess what I'm thinking." One participant would go quiet and close their eyes, and the other would try and peer into their thoughts. The quiet one would seemingly try to distract the one invading their mind with strange and funny thoughts to lead their opponent astray. It was bizarre, but even Zzira had to admit it was sort of cute, if not a bit creepy at first.

Storn children were merely physically conditioned, and this would make up the bulk of their childhoods, until they hit puberty wherein nearly every waking moment would be spent training, exercising, and performing drills. Zzira was rather fortunate, as being the emperor's daughter afforded her more time to enjoy her youth, and even do a little reading herself. Her mother wanted nothing more than for her to read and learn, but Zzira instead chose to become a soldier. It was a decision that Zzira was coming to regret evermore as time passed.

Zzira would sometimes think about what it would be like to have children of her own. She had nearly become a brood storn, and would have been forced to birth many children, and more than likely would not have gotten to know any of them. She wondered what lesson she would like to teach any potential children of hers, and how she would raise and train them. Sometimes she would even think of Zinx for some reason, and this always caught her off guard. The worst of it occurred one late evening when Orr and Cii were playing, and this very thing happened. They seemed to catch wind of the intrusive thoughts, and came over and expressed interest in what she was thinking. This only caused Zzira to become more anxious. Apparently it was enough to get Kan's attention, despite him being several rooms over. She remembered seeing his little bright pink head popping through a well lit doorway, his short and fluffy antenna bobbing up and down as he nearly flung himself inside, asking what all the commotion was about. Zzira merely ran away for the evening, and retired early that night.

❧

Early one morning, while standing on a branch near the top of the tree palace, she noticed a small swarm of ptomeras flying in from the horizon. It was the same scouting party Lady Lanu had sent! Every single one of them had survived—a small miracle on its own—and they hurried directly to Lady Lanu herself. Soon word spread throughout the entire palace that the relay was a success, and that the summit was indeed happening.

The whiplash was jarring. Time had dragged for Zzira during the weeks prior. Despite the deluge of overwhelming new details and experiences, Zzira felt as if she could afford many moments of peace, many moments where she could merely sit and enjoy the world, and watch its many people and wonders. Once the messengers returned, life resumed the usual quick pace she had grown accustomed to. It was then that she finally realized that she had changed—she wanted nothing more than to return to the new slow pace of life the ptomeras had given her. But she had a responsibility, and she would do everything she could to perform it well.

Apparently her father, Anzinius himself, wrote and signed the letter the ptomera messengers brought back with them. Lady Lanu seemed more interested in the letter than Zzira herself. When Lady Lanu finally presented the letter to Zzira, she was not the least bit surprised to see no mention of her anywhere in it. It was a mere, quick and decisive acceptance of the terms of the summit. Zzira expected as much, and cared little about her father's seeming disregard for his own daughter. The mildly stunned look on Lady Lanu's face was the most memorable part of the conversation. At least it was humorous, and brought out some emotion within Zzira.

It was determined that a large ptomera squad would leave the next morning, to ensure the proper precautions and preparations would take place. It would take them a few days just to reach the Gnorel Basin, and it would take an entire day's worth of work just to set everything up. Lady Lanu would be escorted to the site soon after, along with Zzira and Zinx. Zzira could hardly keep up with the whirlwind of movement surrounding her. With so many ptomeras hurrying back and forth through every corner of the tree palace, it was as if her vision was being constantly filled with tree petals of all colors and hues caught in the wind. Every ptomera possessed a unique pattern on their wings, and filtered light in equally distinct ways. Bright shapes swirled over dark bark, and vibrant wings flared a spotlight on the world below. It was always a show whenever large groups of them moved about, and Zzira would always take at least a moment to sit and watch.

A few small hands gripped her arm, and Zzira quickly found herself being escorted away to begin preparing personally for the day to come.

Zzira was always relieved when the night came. It was a time of relative peace, as most ptomeras went to sleep rather early if able. Zzira, on the other hand, preferred to stay up late. Normally she would spend her nights training, or practicing drills, or planning her missions and battles for the next day. In the Land of Lanu there was no such need for her to do any of that. She wasn't entirely sure of what to do with the free time, but eventually she adjusted and learned to appreciate time spent doing nothing.

She knew that she had to get some sleep for the next day. The flight to the Gnorel Basin would be a rather long one. Lady Lanu would be carried there on a flying chariot, but everyone else had to fly. Zzira wasn't surprised that not every comfort could be afforded to the empress's honorary guests, and she would have felt bad making anyone carry her over such a long distance anyway. Zzira decided to fly to the highest point in the tree palace to try and find a secluded spot to merely relax and watch the stars. The sky was unusually clear that night, and the moon was reflecting a weak blue hue that hardly colored the world below. It was a perfect night for stargazing. All she had to do was follow the handful of beams of pale blue light seeping through the palace's treetop. The subtle moonlight still homogenized all of the different colors of the tree's leaves, though the bark still stood out plenty. It was easy enough to find a suitably large and twisted branch that poked through the countless leaves above.

It wasn't until she had fully emerged into the chill night air that she realized someone else beat her to the punch. A familiarly pale storm with pitch black hair was already sitting far along the branch and completely transfixed on the night sky. Zzira's heart skipped a beat, and was immediately overcome with joy at the thought of finally getting some more alone time with her most interesting companion.

"Hello, princess," Zinx said over his bony shoulder. "Would you care to join me?"

Zzira blushed yet again. Part of her hated that she had gotten used to the act. She hated the feeling of her face and cheeks warming up, as if boiling water were slowly rising up and through her body. She hated that she had no control over the feeling. Though she had at least gotten used to the feeling, and could keep herself composed.

"Of course," Zzira said. She slowly buzzed her way over to Zinx's side and settled down next to him. She accidentally sat herself uncomfortably close to him, but changing her position right after the fact seemed to be too embarrassing for her, as if admitting some sort of mistake. She decided to merely roll with it, crossing her arms and legs and looking up to the sparkling night sky.

"Are you feeling alright?" Zinx asked. "Are you worried about meeting your father again?"

"No, I mean, yes, sort of…" Zzira blushed again. Despite her efforts, she could feel the tinge of embarrassment rattling away at her insides. She had to forcefully stop herself and take in a deep breath.

Zinx turned his head and stared at her, and kept a warm smile that stretched and rounded his otherwise sharp features. Zzira could hardly maintain eye contact, instead regularly shifting her focus away, yet somehow always found it being pulled back.

"What is it?" Zzira asked meekly.

"You hair has been looking very nice lately," Zinx said. "It has this otherworldly, almost enchanting emerald hue to it."

"R-really?!" Zzira finally looked away completely, now lightly running her sharp nails through her braids. "My mother had bright green hair, with these little orange streaks that would run through it. Some of my earliest memories are of me reaching up to grab at these orange streaks, and listening to my mother giggle when I finally caught one."

"At least you will be reuniting with another family member again," Zinx said, remaining still and calm, his head now turned upward, allowing the stars to reflect soft glints in his large dark eyes.

"I guess," Zzira muttered. "A small part of me wondered if my father really cared that much, that I had left. But I doubt it."

"I think he does care," Zinx said, finally turning his attention toward Zzira. "Despite everything, you two are family. It is impossible to not care, at least a little bit, when family is involved."

"Maybe…"

"You seem to be getting along well with the ptomeras," Zinx said. "It must be quite the shift in perspective."

"Yes… I can't help but feel regret for having killed so many of them. I know that it is perhaps only because their empress is forcing them to accept me, but… it still feels nice to have such a warm welcome."

"I do not think it is merely that. I think the ptomeras have learned to appreciate your company. You may be influencing a shift in their perspective as much as they have yours."

"I… I suppose, but… I don't know…"

"Hmm?"

Zinx kept his focus on Zzira, but she looked ahead at nothing in particular. Her eyes half closed, and she rested her chin on her arms, which rested on her knees. Her thoughts were somewhere entirely different, as her blank mind provided the perfect arena to wrestle with her conflicted feelings.

Zzira finally found the energy to speak up: "It's just that… I am a storn, and I will always be loyal to them. They are my people. It is my empire. But I don't think I could willingly give this up. The ptomeras have such a nice way of doing things. I think we could learn a lot from them. This only hurts me, as I don't think we storns could teach them much of anything in return. Though, now that I think about it… You have your own people, don't you? What were they called again?"

Zinx smiled, and closed his eyes as he leaned back, as if relishing a memory. "Po. We are called po, and our world was called Peara."

"'Was?'"

"Yes… Peara was destroyed long ago."

"Destroyed?!" Zzira nearly fell over. She very well may have if not for the fact that the only place she could fall too was either off of the branch and into the dark opening below, or on top of Zinx. "Who destroyed it? How is such a thing even manageable?!"

"It was Paithos. Or, Buuziliel, as you would call Him. Or the Creator, as others would refer to Him."

"But why?"

"I do not know, unfortunately. It may have had something to do with my birth, and my father, and perhaps even my mother."

"I suppose I forgot to ask about that before." Zzira sat herself back up, though remained entirely focused on the storn sitting next to her. "Who were your parents? What were they like?"

Zinx sat still, his eyes remaining closed but his smile slowly disappeared. "My mother… I hardly remember her. She was a normal po woman, as far as I know, but she was sick, I think, perhaps bedridden."

"That sounds horrible," Zzira said. "I don't know what I would do if I didn't at least have memories of my mother. What about your father?"

"He is… You would know him as a buuzine. Though he rebelled against the Creator, or Buuziliel, and was banished, and stripped of his rank—"

"Wait!" Zzira stood up, the force of her legs pushing her up and rocking the large and sturdy branch beneath them. Even Zinx seemed effected, and needed to move and readjust so as to not fall off. He looked up into Zzira's wide, confused eyes for a moment. "Your father is a buuzine?! How is that even possible? How does that work?"

Zinx stared for a moment longer, raised a curious finger to his chin, and pushed a curious brow into his forehead. Another moment passed, and he merely smiled and shrugged. Zzira let out a frustrated sigh and shook her head before sitting back down.

"You are something, that's for sure," Zzira said. "If it weren't for your weird abilities, I probably wouldn't believe it."

"It's not all bad," Zinx said. "The po have a rather nice afterlife to look forward to—"

"An afterlife?!" Zzira said, nearly falling off the branch again. "W-what is it like? There is a true afterlife? I mean, we have our own teachings, but nothing to go on but faith. To have real evidence of an afterlife is amazing."

"Every race has an afterlife tailored specifically for their people," Zinx said. He casually leaned back once more and looked to the stars. "We po, for instance, have two separate realms—Munderworld, and Potarium."

"Why two?" Zzira asked.

"Munderworld is sort of like… a place for lost souls to journey through. Potarium is the destination."

"It seems rather pointless to me," Zzira shrugged. "Why not just have Potarium? Why force souls to go through a whole different realm? It seems like a waste of time."

"Well," Zinx scratched his chin, his eyes looking for answers in the dark of his mind, shifting through countless, fractured memories, "I suppose the journey is there to make the destination worth it."

"I think that life is enough of a journey all on its own," Zzira said.

"I have come to learn that as well," Zinx said through a wide smile.

"Will you tell me more about it? This Munderworld and Potarium?"

"Certainly. I mean, what else is there to do on a night like this?"

"I can think of a few things we could do…"

"Huh? Like what?"

Zzira looked from the corner of her eye. She couldn't help but smile seeing the naive storn's face staring back at her. She knew he was technically not a storn, but in truth, she did not care. Discipline was the only thing that kept her from lunging at the handsome storn, and her own worries about the coming day.

"Never mind," Zzira said dismissively, "I'd rather hear more about your afterlives."

"Of course, princess."

CHAPTER 29

UGH, WHY IS IT SO BRIGHT...
Zzira wondered if she had stayed up too late the night before. She even wondered why she wondered such a thing, as she knew the answer. It was worth it to her however, as she got more than her fill of conversation from Zinx. She even joked about being able to "die happy" before the two separated. Though Zinx did not seem amused by the quip. Still, the previous night had gone well, and she was able to get some sleep, enough to keep her going for the next day if nothing else.

The flight to the Gnorel Basin was rather dull. Her wings needed a good stretch, but there were a few times that she worried about her back cramping from the expenditure. No one said much of anything along the way, instead focusing entirely on the trip across the vast, flat ocean. Lady Lanu was still sitting in her chariot throne even as it sat on the raised plateau's floor.

The small ptomera empress almost looked comical as she sat against the massive crimson carpeted seat that was tall enough even Zzira needed to crane her head back to look up at.

Zinx seemed to be entirely unphased by the flight. Zzira was jealous of his seemingly endless endurance and patience. Not a single braid of hair, or golden chain or loose silk cloak now adorning the handsome storn seemed out of place. Zzira, on the other hand, very much felt the need to strain herself to maintain her composure. It didn't help that she too was adorned in a variety of shining violet cloth and golden jewelry. It was comforting at least to set her feet on the floor of the Gnorel Basin and rest while they all waited.

They had been accompanied by a fleet of no less than 500 ptomeras, mostly soldiers and scouts, as well as a handful of advisors and other assistants to tend to Lady Lanu. Zzira and Zinx were more or less free to operate on their own, and they didn't need to be constantly bothered. This mostly led to them merely waiting and watching as the ptomeras scurried back and forth making sure everything was ready. A large round table had been set up, lined on its edge with the darkest, shiniest oak Zzira had ever seen, and at its center sat a circular pattern of stained glass that reflected a deluge of colors in the temperate, olive green sunlight. From Zzira's perspective she struggled to make out much of the images constituting the table art, but she could see some simple approximations of storm and ptomera people alike, along many flowers and thorns and other patterns. There were plenty of other shapes, but Zzira would have needed to fly above to make the most sense of them.

There were only a handful of seats at the table, enough for Lady Lanu, Zinx, and Zzira, as well as five seats on the other side, presumably for Anzinius and whomever he decided was worthy enough to have a seat at the table. A handful of scouts—each bearing dull turquoise wings that blended in well with the ocean and sky—constantly hovered around keeping watch. Zzira remembered Zinx saying that he hated how everyone needed to be constantly on guard. He wanted a meeting that would be as open as possible, but ultimately he understood why the ptomeras held on to such precautions. He wanted something more idealist, while accepting the harsh reality, and somehow balanced his view between the two. It was something Zzira admired in him, and it was just the sort of perspective that helped her maintain any sort of hope that this meeting would be productive.

"You seem worried," Lady Lanu said. She kept a cool, calm air about her, even smiling slightly as she turned to Zzira.

"I'd be lying if I said I wasn't," Zzira said.

"Well, no matter what, you always have a place among my people," Lanu said, "both you and Zinx."

"Thank you, empress," Zzira said.

"Please, you can just call me Lanu. Just by agreeing to all of this, and putting so much on the line, you have earned that much at least."

"Wait, that was something we needed to earn?" Zinx said. "I have been calling you merely Lanu by accident on and off for weeks now."

"To be honest, I thought it was sort of funny," Lanu said, "seeing all the perplexed faces of my beloved ptomera looking quizzically at you as you so carelessly addressed their empress. I thought it was hilarious! The fact you never noticed was rather cute."

Zzira, without a second thought, allowed a piercing sneer to make its way onto her face. Lanu couldn't see it, but she could definitely sense her feelings.

"I'm sorry, Zzira," Lanu said. "I won't tease your companion any further."

I'm never going to get used to that... Having my thoughts exposed to someone else...

❧

Several hours passed. The sun hung high above and nearly at the sky's center. Zzira could feel every moment. The weather was just as temperate and nondescript as it normally was on Ozairos, but something about merely standing out in the sun for so long began to eat away at Zzira. More than anything, it was mere boredom that seemed to bother her more than anything. Everyone else seemed rather undisturbed by the waiting, which motivated Zzira to keep up an equally dignified appearance, but she could at least express her anguish in secret, and in her mind. Knowing that Lady Lanu was catching wind of it gave her some relief— as if she was mentally venting to an old friend about some trouble of hers.

A quick brush of wind descended down from above, and a scout landed and was already leaning over to whisper something to their empress.

"Ah, they're finally here," Lanu said, as calm as ever, as if she had not just waited hours in the evening sun.

Zzira's heart dropped, her gut now feeling akin to a pond that someone had callously thrown a stone into. She had been trained and tempered to handle conversation, to restrain her emotions, and to remain composed, yet in that moment she could feel it all melting away as her mind drew a blank. She had been told to let Lady Lanu do most of the talking. For some reason, that seemed as if it would all be for naught, as if something would happen that would force her to act. It would do no good to obsess over possible disasters, and she continued to stay calm, and to follow Lady Lanu's lead.

A fierce buzzing hum soon echoed from the horizon. The melded, hazy line blurring the olive sea and sky revealed a harsh, dark line slowly formed at its center. The humming grew, and countless bodies revealed themselves flying across the sky. The many sharp and spooky silhouettes were instantly recognizable—it was a small army of storns, all centered around the tip of a spear formation, headed by Emperor Anzinius. Anzinius was not a fighter, and never took to the battlefield himself, but he took great pride in powerful displays whenever possible. He was too far away for her to know it, but Zzira knew her father must be grinning like a madman as he sat at the front of a powerful horde, leading it forward and toward a hated enemy.

The storns were quick, and it was not long before the sky ahead was filled with them. Their numbers may well have outnumbered the ptomeras. Normally this would be worrying, but the ptomeras were used to being outnumbered, and their psychic abilities were often enough to level the playing field. What truly put Zzira's mind at ease was Zinx's presence. Having such a potent wild card hiding beneath the empress's sleeve was enough to fill both Zzira and Lady Lanu with confidence.

Perhaps this can work... Perhaps we can make something happen here... Maybe Zinx is right, and a simple chat can pave the way for an amendment of relations between us all... He has clearly achieved similar feats before—why should this be any different?

A heavy blow of wind through horns blasted all around. A line of colorful ptomera soldiers signaled the arrival of their guests with a simple, air-rending song that could practically be felt in one's chest. Zzira jokingly wondered about "that stone thrown into the pit of her stomach" and if this would shake it around. She wondered what sort of effect that would have—mostly likely just an embarrassing bit of puking. She was beginning to wonder if such childish thoughts were merely a method of coping with the stress, or if Zinx, Lanu and the ptomera really did have that much of an impact on her. Either way, the storm horde was nearly upon them, and the summit was finally about to begin.

Anzinius was the first to arrive, bearing his usual toothy, sick grin as he flew himself, his glorious purple robes shimmering in the olive light like sheets of crystal, and his path followed by an impossibly long and silvery coattail that was constantly tended to by several storn servants. Behind him was a throne, and it must have been a sick joke of his, forcing his soldiers to carry the large, bronze structure while he himself still flew ahead. Zzira never paid much attention to such displays, perhaps because of her focus on her own duties as a general, or because she merely saw such positions as a natural part of storn duty. From a new perspective, she couldn't help but find her father's ways disgusting. Storns relied on slaves heavily to get anything productive done outside of combat. At least the ptomeras utilized simple contracts, designating such responsibilities as if they were mere jobs. A part of her would not allow Zzira to truly despise her culture and her people, but the more she pondered the possibility of having to return home, the more she hated it.

Right behind the emperor was his most trusted storn, his right hand—Commander Riul. The broad shouldered storn had seemingly let his hair grow out just for the occasion, now sporting short braids placed meticulously around his head, mimicking a sort of crown. It seemed that in Zzira's absence, Anzinius' reliance on him had grown, as well as his status.

Another deep sound blasted out from above, and a long line of storns revealed themselves with simple horns in their own hands, making their own song. Each side continued a single long note, well past the rest of the storns landing on the plateau's floor. It almost seemed as if the two sides were locked in an implied contest, to see who would give out first. It went on for so long that Zzira actually began to find the whole ceremony irritating. A quick peek to her side revealed that Lady Lanu was also getting frustrated. Another peek forward showed her father, Anzinius, expressing much the same. Zzira noticed her father refused to look her in the eye, instead locked in a contest of his own as he stared down the ptomera empress. She wasn't surprised, but her curiosity prompted her to keep her eyes on Anzinius, to see if he would slip. She knew he wouldn't, but it was at least something else to keep her attention focused on something other than the many horns blaring around them all.

Eventually the great song began to simmer. The powerful chests and enduring lungs of Ozairos' greatest fliers had their limits, and everything finally faded into silence. All was quiet, save for the footsteps of a single storn servant, dressed in strangely extravagant garb, even bearing a black hood that reflected much of the olive sun's light. He stepped forward, holding a large scroll in hand, and stood at attention at the table's ledge. The silence was immediately broken by the sound of rough paper being stretched as the storn opened the scroll, took in a deep breath, and spoke:

"By her royal highness' decree, the storn lord has respected thy summons! Hear ye, hear ye, any and all who may buzz and beat and soar and sting, his great wings now bless the very air around you. The great stinger lord, the most distinguished of all who fly, the master of dignity, future ruler of Ozairos, and heir to the one true Buuziliel himself, I present to thee—"

Thump!

The heaving throne was set upon the ground, the many servants carrying the massive structure having to quickly scatter so as to not be crushed by the structure. The impact was enough to send a quick wave across the basin floor. The hooded storn continued:

"Emperor Anzinius Kul!"

Anzinius lowered himself slowly onto the cush-ioned seat of his throne. He completely ignored the seats the ptomeras had set out for him at the table, instead choosing to sit on high. Commander Riul was forced to sit in one of the comparatively pedestrian seats at the table itself, though he at least was allowed a single servant who scurried ahead of the broad shouldered storn to pull the chair out for him. Lanu motioned her hand, and several ptomeras hurried forth to prepare seats for Zinx and Zzira. Zzira still hated being catered to, but Zinx didn't seem to mind, as he moved forward and sat down with a regal flare. Zzira followed suit, and finally everyone was seated. The tense quiet remained for a while longer. Zzira couldn't help but ignore Commander Riul, who had his eyes locked on her, to instead focus on her father. Anzinius completely ignored her, however, and sat grinning, staring intently at Lady Lanu, who returned the favor with a much calmer expression of her own.

A final thought ran through Zzira's mind. *I hope more than anything that Buuziliel himself graces us this day. Please, let Zinx be right, and let something worth-while come from this summit.*

Lady Lanu wasted no time, and decided to begin the summit herself:

"It is a pleasure to finally meet you, Emperor Anzinius. I have heard much about you, and to see that you too are capable of indulging in a thoughtful and intelligent conversation says much more."

Anzinius casually leaned back in his throne, looking down his nose at everyone across the large and decorated table from him, grinning all the while.

"A pleasure to meet you too, Empress Lanu. I must say, I do like the touch—having your lands named after their current leader. Perhaps it is a practice we storns should adopt."

"Ah, the summit has just begun, and we are already learning from one another. This is going to be a very productive discussion, no doubt," Lanu said. She kept her upright, uptight position in her own seat, but raised a small hand to her dainty chin as she shared her thoughts. Zzira didn't want to make her observations obvious, and it was difficult for her to make out every subtle movement made by the empress from the corner of her eye.

Zzira turned her full attention instead back to her father, and was caught off guard to see that Anzinius had finally decided to acknowledge her—his sharp, gloomy eyes looking right back into hers. His smile slowly faded, and he seemed to look at her with a stern disgust.

I can only imagine what he is thinking, Zzira thought. *What does he think of me now? A traitor? A runaway? A deserter? A weakling? What do you really think of me, father?*

Anzinius leaned on an arm, and casually turned his attention back to Lanu.

"You have been taking good care of my beloved daughter, it seems," Anzinius said. His voice was soft, and almost strained, as if he was being forced to finally acknowledge his own flesh and blood.

"Of course!" Lanu said, her enthusiasm forcing a high pitch in her tone. "Zzira has been a lovely guest, and has gotten along so well with my lovely ptomeras.

In fact, I would go so far as to say I have learned much from her."

"What of your *other* 'guest?'" Anzinius raised his head from his hand, and peered right at Zinx. All eyes immediately shifted to the strange storn. Lanu seemed to be the only one disciplined enough to keep her attention forward, and on Anzinius.

"He too has been a wonderful guest," Lanu said. "I never would have thought that not one, but two storns would get along so well with myself and my people. It makes me wonder just what it is we are fighting over anymore."

Anzinius scoffed, going so far as to grip the arm-rests on his throne. "You know *precisely* why we fight."

"And why is that?"

"Hmph…" Anzinius turned his head and looked down at Riul, a disdainful sneer plastered across his face. "Commander, why do we fight?"

Commander Riul, as stiff and upright as he could manage in his seat, and without hesitation barked out the storn creed: "For glory. For honor. For power. To watch our enemies cower. To defend our lands. To strike down the ptomera, wherever one stands. To fly free and without worry. To hold the sky and the sea, to watch the enemy scurry. By Buuziliel's wind, we fight to the end. For glory. For honor. For power."

The lines of storn soldiers standing behind Anzinius all clapped and cheered. A raucous sea of palms colliding and wings flexing filled the air with noise. This celebration was cut short, as the storn emperor quickly raised a hand, signaling a demand for silence.

A tense moment of quiet followed, the emperor and the empress keeping their eyes locked on one another.

"Well said, Commander," Anzinius said.

"A rousing screed, indeed," Lanu said.

It's more than a screed, Zzira thought. *They are the words we live—words that define all storns. These words are the orders we follow above all else. A storn soldier is even allowed to disobey their commander if it means staying true to this screed. I used to live blindly by these very words. I used to repeat this screed every morning and every night. It was so easy, and it became second nature to define myself and my life by these words. And yet… seeing this screed from a new perspective… It seems so silly. How many lives have been thoughtlessly thrown away, all while reciting this very creed? I suppose it was easier than going through the mental turmoil of questioning it all…*

"Zzira, you remember that creed, don't you?" Anzinius said, his leering finally becoming noticeable to the young storn.

Zzira took a moment, pausing to look her father over. He was only right across a simple table from her, yet she had never felt so distanced from him. He may as well have still been sitting in his comfy throne room on the other side of the ocean.

"How could I forget?" Zzira scoffed. "I haven't been gone for *that* long."

"I suppose not," Anzinius said through a sneer. It was a subtle change of expression, but Zzira knew that her father was seething beneath the surface. She was grateful that she no longer needed to look forward to a mighty lashing for her "impudence" after such displays.

Anzinius continued, turning his attention back to Lanu: "I see you have been filling my daughter's head with ways. She even decided to come here wearing some of your people's garb. And now she talks to me with disrespect? A lifetime of service and obedience and reverence practically undone. I must say that I admire your efficiency, if nothing else."

"I would take that as a compliment," Lanu said, slightly readjusting in her seat, flexing her black wings and taking in a soft breath, "but I have done very little to your daughter. We came to an agreement, and she now lives as she wishes among my people."

"As she wishes…" Anzinius rubbed the end of his bony, pointed chin, his large eyes looking about ever so slightly, as if searching for answers in the dark of his mind. "I am to believe that you merely let her, a storn, do as she pleases in ptomera lands? In *your* lands? And among *your* people? People who, I know for a fact, would have, and very well should have, slaughtered her the moment she revealed herself? I am to believe that there is no use of force in all of this?"

"Yes," Lanu said. Her response was so quick and clear, as if the answer should have been evident, and the storn emperor's questioning had been pointless.

"I see… Fascinating." Anzinius lowered his hand and rested himself in his throne, and slowly turned his attention to Zinx. "And what of him? How does he fit into any of this? I can only imagine that he is still alive because of Zzira? I wonder why, as I always believed my one and only dearest would have preferred a more… virile storn. Perhaps one such as my truly loyal commander here?"

"Tch." Zzira didn't mean to, but she nearly spit out her vexation onto the table itself. Such disgust for Commander Riul had always been difficult to rein in. If nothing else, she was grateful for the freedom of expression her new position among the ptomeras allowed her. Riul was clearly displeased, sharing a disdainful look that could have cut the stained glass making up the tabletop like a nail through a wet leaf.

"That 'stranger' has a name. Do you remember it, by chance?" Lanu said, remaining still as a statue and as composed as one.

"Not really," Anzinius said. "I deal with so many storns everyday, and we housed him for such a short time—"

"You mean imprisoned?" Zzira interrupted, squinting hard at her father.

"—And yet," Anzinius said, seemingly having no trouble ignoring his daughter, "he seems to have made *some* sort of impact. Clearly he is important, as you have decided to keep him alive."

"Ha!" Lanu's unwavering composure finally broke. It was only a single outburst, but it was enough to catch everyone off guard. "If only you knew, emperor."

"Oh, I know very well," Anzinius said, leaning forward in his seat, going so far as to rest an elbow on his leg and his chin on his hand. "I remember hearing quite a bit about his... peculiarities."

"Yes, I remember hearing quite a bit about your efforts to breed him like cattle." Lanu rested herself in her seat, and looked over at Zzira. "You know, we ptomeras have never had to force anyone to breed. We all do so willingly. All of us."

"How lovely. But you do know we are at war? Even you must realize that merely letting everyone do as they please is not enough to live up to the demands of an empire? The demands of a war?"

"The demands of an empire are merely the demands of a people. There are many ways to meet said demands, with force perhaps being the least effective means."

"But it *is* effective, is it not?"

"I suppose it depends on what your definition of 'effective' is." Lanu's soft smile was slowly fading. Zzira could see from the corner of her eye that the empress was putting less effort into trying to physically meet eyes with her opponent, and more into her words and thoughts and how she expressed them. It appeared that she was finally getting serious about the discussion.

"I will tell you this, empress," Anzinius said, plopping himself back into his cushy throne, "we storns prefer to be direct. We are not ones to split hairs, and we say what we mean."

"Of course, I expected no less. So I suppose I will get straight to the point of this little meeting of ours." Lanu leaned forward herself, enough to rest her short arms on the table, keeping her pale, reflective eyes focused forward. "What is it that you want, Anzinius? What would it take to cease this pointless fighting? To spare the lives of all our people and begin working toward a more productive future?"

"Hmm… Productive…" Anzinius scratched his chin again, seemingly lost in thought. "In truth, I did not expect to be so directly asked what I wanted. I figured this whole thing was primarily for show…"

"Surely there is something we can do?" Lanu asked. "We ptomeras are quite resourceful, and more than capable of higher reasoning and diplomacy. Buuziliel gifts us ptomeras with such cognition, just the same as you."

"Yes… Buuziliel…" Anzinius took in a deep breath, and finally stopped rubbing and scratching his chin, a habit Zzira found more frustrating the more she noticed it. "What precisely is your interpretation of the great Buuziliel? If you do not mind me asking, dear empress?"

"My interpretation of Buuziliel is the same as my people's interpretation. I feel as though this question is rhetorical? Something tells me you are less interested in my answer as you are making a point."

"The fact that you skirt around the question like a coward, instead of giving a direct answer, marks my point exactly. I know your answer, and you know mine—we each interpret Buuziliel in accordance with our own histories, right down to our genetic origins. On this issue, we will forever be at odds. The very core of what it means to even exist on Ozairos, to be a storn or a ptomera, what it means to live and breathe, and what rights come with such a privilege—our views are entirely different, and cannot be reconciled."

"But perhaps we are both wrong?" Lanu took but a brief moment to pause, but the rustling of countless heads turning—storn and ptomera alike—to look at the empress in bewilderment filled the air. "What if Buuziliel is something beyond what we can comprehend? What if Buuziliel's origin, and thus our own, is so massive, and so great, that to even try to depict Him so simply is an act so arrogant it borders on insulting, even sinful?"

Another silent moment weighed heavy between all. Even Anzinius himself, his eyes normally thin and piercing, now sat wide eyed and stunned. Zzira couldn't tell if her father was angry, or impressed, or something indescribable, caught flailing helplessly between a number of emotions that refused to coalesce into something decipherable. A quick glance to her side revealed that even Zinx looked puzzled. Zzira's pondering as to the contents of her storm companion's mind were interrupted by the sound of her father grumbling on the other side of the table:

"Your speech borders on heresy, Lanu. You speak as if you have had a first-hand account of our lord's presence. As if, despite being something so great and incomprehensible, you are somehow capable of parsing His presence and come to us yourself to relay His prophecies?"

"I do not claim to be a prophet. I merely wish to provide an avenue for thought, and thus pave a way to further, deeper discussion," Lanu said.

"That is all you ptomera's do," Anzinius said, leaning back once again as he dismissively waved a bony hand forward. "You sit around, 'pondering' and 'thinking.' You all have spent so much time in your own heads that you have turned its expulsions into a form of combat. It would be impressive, if it weren't so craven and cowardly."

"It baffles me that you are sensitive to such questions," Lanu said, remaining still and composed. "You know very well that we all share a common ancestor, and that said ancestor had their own, unique view of Buuziliel. Is it so preposterous to think that neither of us know precisely what Buuziliel actually represents?"

"Hmph, I know for a fact that our interpretation is correct."

"How so?"

"Buuziliel is the source of all life on Ozairos. As part of His grand plan, life has been given the means to not merely survive, but to adapt. We storns have grown a number of adaptations that bring us closer to His likeness with every death, every battle, and every birth. Give our people another thousand years of honing our claws and stingers in battle and we will each be the spitting image of Buuziliel himself."

"We don't have another thousand years, great emperor," Lanu said.

"And how would you know that, 'great empress?' Have you consulted with Buuziliel? Did he tell you himself over a cup of tea and dinner?"

Anzinius chuckled, and the rest of his horde followed suit. The only storn who remained composed was Commander Riul, who had seemed strangely unmoved by everything thus far. He too refused to look Zzira in the eye, something she took advantage of to establish what dominance she could at the table. The laughter simmered, giving the floor back to Anzinius.

"Just what are you getting at, empress? What is the point of all of this?"

Lanu took a deep breath, closing her eyes noticeably for the first time since the beginning of the summit: "The point is to elaborate on something fundamental, something that separates us from mere beasts, and elevates us to a level that can truly appreciate life, and what lies beyond, so as to make Buuziliel's wonder purposeful—our ability to choose. You *chose* to come here, emperor. You *chose* to partake in a peaceable, amiable summit. Our people ultimately *chose* to follow our orders, and *choose* to pursue a greater good, on both sides of this conflict. We can choose to continue this pointless fighting, or we can choose to make history, here and now, and move forward. Why wait a thousand years for something that could potentially be accomplished in a fraction of the time? Why choose to waste so much more time, and so many more lives, on all of this? Adaptation does not require bloodshed."

"Pah!" Anzinius huffed. "Adaptation requires conflict, and what greater conflict is there beyond battle? Balancing life and death on the honed edge of a stinger makes the hand that wields it dexterous indeed."

"Beautiful choice of words, emperor," Lanu said, finally smiling once again. "Such eloquence is something one must choose to practice and hone. A honing of the mind that one can easily do beyond physical conflict.

"I suppose so," Anzinius said, scratching his bony chin once more. Zzira had told Lanu many times that stroking her father's ego was often the only way to make him consider the words of another. It was vain, but it was at least a method of opening the stubborn old man's mind to something new.

Anzinius stopped, and rested his arms on his seat before turning his head down to look at his commander: "Riul, what do you think of all this? You have been quiet. I'd like to hear from your perspective."

"I remain quiet to give you the world's attention unchallenged, emperor," Riul said.

Ugh… That brown-noser… He's only gotten worse in my absence…

"Thank you, commander, but please—share your thoughts," Anzinius said.

"Everything must come from within, first and foremost," Riul said. "Strength and vitality are the very things that allow us to even function in life. These very attributes must be cultivated, first and foremost, and above all, in order for anything else to be possible."

Anzinius grinned, in a greedy sort of way, as if he were hearing his own words being validated.

"I find it only appropriate that I consult my own advisor on this as well," Lanu said. She turned her head to Zzira's side. "What do you think, my dear?"

Zzira, for a moment, was stunned. She had hoped that Lanu and Anzinius could carry the entire conversation. She never cared much for conversation, but the ptomera's helped to shift her perspective, to make such scenarios at least a bit easier. The ptomeras viewed discussion itself as a sort of battlefield all its own—each scroll read beforehand like the sharpening of one's stingers, and each word spoken like a decisive blow against the opponent. If there was one thing Zzira knew, it was battle, and a key facet of any fight was to recognize openings. Whenever you attack, you by necessity leave yourself open, and even the smallest openings can lead to a killing blow, all the while relishing in the fact that you used your opponent's own force against them. Lanu seemed to enjoy this sort of verbal jousting, so why not her as well?

Zzira straightened her back, took in a weighty breath, and spoke: "Riul, you say that all comes from within, yet you fail to dig deeper than your physical form? How do you become strong? By choosing to train, and by choosing to hone your skills and how to refine them. You add grit to your soul by choosing to fight. Many creatures in this world do just as well by fleeing, but that is not the storn way. We choose to be strong, and to fight. Ultimately, we must think before we do anything. Perhaps this is the true source of our strength, and the ability to physically follow through and execute on such ideas is, while equally valuable and necessary, secondary to that?"

Riul rested a heavy arm on the table, mindlessly tapping a long, dark nail against the glassy top. Zzira never found it satisfying to stump the brute, but that was because she normally did so with her rank alone. Being able to garner the same effect with wit and word alone was quite surreal—even intoxicating. She truly had changed. It used to be so easy, and so simple, finding her sole enjoyment in battle. Now she yearned for something more.

"You all speak of choice, as if it is an inherent good," Riul said, readjusting himself in his seat, matching his straight-backed stature to Zzira's, and finally looking at her directly. "Choices can be good or bad. Poor choices can lead to poorer choices, their failures having effects on countless lives. Anyone of note must be careful with their choices, and I must say, Zzira, that many of your choices recently have been… questionable, if nothing else."

"Tch, as if I ever needed to concern myself with *your* questioning, Riul." Zzira's regret was immediate, but she couldn't help herself. As much as she wanted to have a controlled, intelligent discussion, to flex her new perspective, some things were just inevitable, as was her emotional retort.

"That anger, right there, is my point," Riul said, placing both hands together on the table, as if looking down at Zzira like a parent would their child. "For all of your talk of choice, you still let anger and emotion control you. You never were particularly good at holding back such feelings. I am sure you would love to *choose* to be retrained, but you lack the inner strength to do so. I was certain your father and mother raised you to have better manners—"

"Don't you *dare* speak of my mother!" Zzira hissed. The rattling echo of her clenched fists slamming against the thick, glass table echoed far beyond the plateau itself, as if rippling through the great, calm olive toned sea just beyond.

"Why not?" Riul shrugged. "I meant no offense. I am just trying to get to the heart of the situation and your current temperament."

"I know precisely what it is you're trying to do. You're trying to get under my skin, and I must say, I expected better of you, commander."

"How so?"

"You're putting all of this effort into causing me vexation, when your mere presence would suffice."

A round of murmurs and snickers ran through the crowd of soldiers on both sides—storn and ptomera alike. The hordes were disciplined enough to hardly let such an outburst last any longer than a few moments, and all that remained was a tense, weighty silence as everyone at the table parsed the situation in their own particular way. Zinx looked at Zzira, and then Lanu, a wide-eyed expression flashing before both of them. Lanu kept her head forward, but could be seen giving a conniving, scheming glare from the corner of her pale eyes. Zzira herself was staring daggers into Riul, who appeared quite relaxed and pleased with himself, mimicking his master who sat above—all without even having to look at him. Commander Riul had mastered the art of appeasing his master, and it sickened Zzira to no end.

"It appears there is quite a bit more bubbling beneath the surface here," Anzinius said. "I have a proposal, Lanu. What I ultimately want is absolute dominion over Ozairos. You seem to want compromise, so how about I offer a compromise we can both benefit from? Let us have our most trusted advisors battle—a common storn rite. Whoever wins shall be allowed to go into the other's court—with a small army in tow to occupy the other's lands and enforce said advisor's will—and they can be allowed to begin slowly enacting changes? Perhaps such an indirect and long-term approach would do much to teach us both? And this would allow the winner to provide a means to see which culture is truly superior? Whose ideas have true staying power?"

"What?!' Zinx shouted, finally making his presence known—an act which caught the entire summit off guard. "The last thing I wanted was for a resolution to be reached through battle of all things. The entire point of all of this is to pave the way for less blood-shed, not more!"

Lanu looked at Zinx, then shifted her eyes toward Zzira. "I supposed that would be up to her. If Zzira is up for it…"

Without a second thought, or an ounce of hesitation, Zzira smacked her palms against the table and pushed herself up. "Of course. All of this talking, this double-speak, it is not my forte. Fighting, on the other hand, is something I am more than comfortable with."

Zinx's brow furrowed. It may have been the first time Zzira had ever seen anger on his face. For a brief moment, Zzira was reminded of the expression her mother held when she first decided to become a soldier.

"It is settled then," Lanu said through a satisfied grin. "I will allow it."

Anzinius smiled wide, with every sharp feature and wrinkle and tooth filling his face with an angular malice. Zzira didn't care, however, and was only happy to finally have an excuse to personally destroy a rival that had persisted for far too long.

"This is ridiculous! Lanu!" Zinx turned to the empress, nearly falling out of his seat. "This was precisely what you said you would try to avoid! So much time preparing, and you were so willing to talk with me, and hear my side of things! Why are you now—"

Lanu quickly raised a small, dainty hand, signaling for Zinx to stop. Zinx stared for a moment, perhaps wondering if he should bother to obey. He ultimately did, and defiantly plopped himself back in his seat, but not before letting out a frightening gruff and slamming a clenched fist onto the tabletop. The force was enough to shatter a large portion of the stained glass. Zzira even noticed a few ptomera guards behind him getting startled, though they retained their position.

"Ah, so true storn blood does in fact run through his veins," Anzinius mumbled.

"I suppose you don't even need to ask your advisor his thoughts on the deal?" Lanu said.

"I'm not giving him a choice, anyway," Zzira said. She stood up and onto the table, and quickly tore off the few ptomera garbs and jewels, callously throwing them behind herself.

"It is settled then," Anzinius said. "Make it quick, Riul. There is little time to waste, and I grow tired of this supposed summit."

"Yes, my lord." Riul stood up himself, going as far as to flex his great, thin and clear wings to accent a hefty stomp onto the tabletop. Even on the far side of the table it was easy to see that he was proud of his physique. Unlike most storns, even Zzira, he was bulky, fleshed out and had a body filled with carved and protruding muscle. His stingers, which on a normal, thin storn would naturally lean inward and toward the body, instead naturally pushed out, as if his muscle gave them little room to even sit and rest. He was obviously strong, but Zzira was not intimidated—she knew that his physique was mostly for show. She knew that most of his time was spent at the storn palace, sucking up to her father and playing politics. Hers was a body forged by countless battles and invaluable experience. In her mind, there was nothing to be afraid of, and it was foolish of her father to even make such a rash deal. The implications of the arrangement meant little to her, as the immediate satisfaction of letting loose, and taking down the one storn that has caused her ire comparable to her father, was too great to resist.

Zzira took in a quick breath, flexed her own wings, and spoke: "Let's do this."

CHAPTER 30

EVERYONE STEPPED BACK. COUNTLESS feet in a single motion brushing against the oddly smooth floor of the rocky plateau in the middle of the ocean. There was no ceremony, there was no great celebration, it was merely the arena setting itself in place for the two combatants that were anxious to begin. It was encoded into storn blood to fight, and to find glory in fighting. It was as if being a storn could not be separated from this very truth, an integral piece of the soul propelling the body forward to enact things that were inevitable. Fate itself had imprinted upon storn blood, and violence was the final, decipherable message it left.

Zzira and Riul had quickly locked onto one another in the air above. All eyes were on them, yet none of that mattered. All that mattered were the two pairs of eyes currently locked onto one another in the midst of a violent ritual, the one stable element in a storm of emotions boiling to the surface for a final, furious release.

Wind swooshed and puffed against the speedy flails of claws and stingers flying past one another. A dance of fatal movements exchanged between the two participants as they spoke to one another through the one universal language. This was a language Zzira understood perfectly.

Storns were simple, straightforward opponents. Every strike and swipe and blow could be easily understood. It was to the point where she could almost turn her thoughts to other things, where she could easily let her mind wander, and think of her next moves well ahead of time. Riul would throw a punch, a shift in the shoulder carrying energy down through his arm and exerting past his fist, and she would merely duck out of the way. Riul would shift himself upward, carrying with him a motion that begged to be brought downward into a pommel strike onto her, and she would merely shift to her side. Riul even tried to get in a stealthy cut with his stinger, feinting a normal blow only to shift at the last moment, exposing the sharpened cartilage on his forearm as his hand twisted aside, and all Zzira had to do was pull back, causing the short ranged attack to whiff against open air. Zzira would pretend to go in for a simple punch, leaving herself exposed and making Riul think he had an opening to grab her, only to remind the large storn of his legs that he carelessly let hang about as he moved through the air with a nasty cut of her own stingers. Storns were simple and straightforward, and this was perhaps their greatest weakness in battle. Zzira began to wonder how and why the storns survived as long as they did in this never ending war.

Her blank and focused mind was interrupted with a piercing yet feminine voice forcing its way into her thoughts:

I have an idea, Zzira.

It was Lanu! The shock was enough to startle her, causing Zzira for just a moment, which was all Riul needed to get in his first strike against her. Riul was not a particularly clever fighter, but she felt the full weight of the muscled storn sending a ripple through her body with a bitter blow to her ribs. She filled her mind with an instinctual thought, remembering her training—she flew back, gathering herself with a quick breath as she tensed her body, stopping the rippling sensation and gathering her senses, and halting the pain.

You know your father is lying, do you not?

On second thought, Zzira found it so obvious that her father was lying. Why would he ever make good on such a deal? If she lost, Anzinius would do nothing but guilt trip the ptomeras to uphold their end of the bargain. If they allowed it, then Riul's influence—which is in truth nothing more than Anzinius's will—would be destructive. If they didn't uphold their end, he would use it as an excuse to ignore this entire summit, and perhaps start a bloody battle on this very plateau. If Zzira won—an outcome that was inevitable, in her mind—and the ptomeras decided to send her back with her father, he would merely capture her and try to use her to bargain with. Or she would merely be subjugated once again, perhaps forced to become a mere brood storn. She dreaded the thought. She hated how pointless this supposed summit had become.

This summit does not have to be a waste, Zzira. We can force a positive outcome. But we would need to force Zinx's hand.

"What?!" Zzira was startled once more, giving Riul his second opening. This time he attempted a fatal cut with the stinger on his left arm against a vital artery in her right leg. She caught wind of the motion at the last moment, but still took a hit. She recoiled back again, pushing the painful sensation out of her mind to remain focused. She had come to like Zinx. Perhaps she even adored him. She knew that he was not really a storn, but she had learned to not care. She appreciated him for something more, something deeper, for giving her a new perspective on life, a perspective that she was currently ignoring as her impulses and anger had brought her right back to fighting. She wondered how disappointed he may be in her at that moment, and she hated herself for it.

Zinx wants peace, as do I, and even you. You have done well to see things differently. We need to kill your father, and to force this new perspective onto your people. This can only work if you usurp your father's throne, and if Zinx makes full use of his abilities. He will hate having to expose more of his abilities than necessary, but there is no other way.

What was the point of all of this? Zzira thought. She was beginning to see the futility in enacting this fight, this summit, in everything. Even as she began to increase her aggression, getting in cut after cut against Riul, her mind was focused on other things.

> *I want nothing more than for some amount of peace to be attained. I want my child to be accepted into this world. As things are currently, a mixed-race child will not be accepted, neither by my people or yours. We have to force Zinx's hand. He will stop the fighting, force everyone to kneel, and he will assist me in mimicking a holy birth. Our perspective will be accepted, or else Zinx will fail his mission, and we all die.*

Zzira hated it. She hated the thought of using Zinx like a tool. Yet she could not think of another way, of any sort of alternate compromise. It made sense that Zinx should be used and sacrificed, essentially—she knew that Zinx would have to leave Ozairos once his duty was done, and thus his feelings in the long term were not as important. Still, she hated the thought of merely using him, and then throwing him away. Lanu's thoughts were obviously singularly focused on the future well-being of her child. Zzira, on the other hand, had nothing else to look forward to, nothing other than Zinx.

We will have a future, Zzira. We must. It is the only way.

You would deceive the world if it meant sparing your child? Zzira thought. It was almost fun as she thoughtlessly dodged Riul's strikes. The commander was clearly getting frustrated, and more manic and desperate in his attacks, which only made him easier to read, and easier to avoid and counter. This only intensified his anger, and the loop continued. Zzira had nearly forgotten how much fun a good battle was.

Of course. And you would too. You will understand one day when you have children of your own.

Lanu seemed to speak with such confidence about everything. She spoke as if she could see the future, and she knew precisely what was to come. Zzira wished she could possess such certainty. She always spoke as if her will were reality, and could not be denied. Such was the way of royalty.

Zzira's mind went quiet. She effortlessly dodged and counter strike after strike. A quick glance down at the empress revealed just how high above the two combatants had slowly flown over the course of their engagement. Countless shining eyes glittered against the midday olive sun as an audience watched on with bated breath. Zzira could still see Lanu, looking as cool and calm as ever, as if she knew what needed to be done, and that it *would* be done, one way or another. Zzira's attention turned over to Zinx, who bore the most pained expression on his face. To possess such power, and to be forced to sit back and watch violence unfold must have hurt him. Despite Zzira's best efforts, she was merely hurting another person she cared about, the same way she must have hurt her mother on the day she decided to become a soldier. She couldn't help but look over to her father as well, a simple, toothy grin peering up from a bundle of extravagant purple robes. She wondered about what her father truly thought of her, and how different things may have been had she merely been born a boy. Zzira was tired of disappointing those she cared about.

What do I need to do? Zzira thought.

Goad Riul into sending an attack toward me. Make it look like an accident. One of my servants will take the blow, first blood will be drawn, and a battle will ensue between our armies. Use the opportunity to take out your father, as well. Zinx, being the sensitive soul that he is, will eventually be forced to use his powers to stop the fighting. He knows full well the lengths he would need to go to in order to force everyone to bend the knee. He will not like it, but I don't care. This is what must be done.

That is horrible, Zzira thought

So? His feelings are not worth the death of countless storns and ptomeras, or the forsaken futures of whatever children we bear. He will be fine.

Zzira paused for a moment, casually exchanging more feint blows with her opponent. *Will he? What makes you so certain of any of this?*

If you would like to know a secret—I am not sure. I never truly am. Failure is always a possibility. But you should never let that stop you from at least attempting to do what you need to. Better to fail doing everything you possibly can, than to merely persist, and be doomed to always look back with regret at what could have been.

Zzira's mind drew a blank. She could think of no argument, no retort, against the ptomera's words. It was easy for her to come up with ideas in the midst of battle. Physical strategy was reactive, often only requiring a quick glance at the battlefield to come to a proper conclusion. This predicament was something beyond anything Zzira could think through on her own, and she knew it. She finally accepted Lanu's proposal, though she gave no thanks or further words to the empress. She knew that Lanu would sense her silent agreement, and that would have to be enough. Zzira was getting tired of this whole affair. It was time to put the plan into action.

"You seem to be enjoying yourself, Riul," Zzira said, just after blocking a heavy strike with her forearm.

"I am a true storn," Riul said, stopping to throw another punch, only to miss and back off to take a breath. "As such, a good, prolonged fight only galvanizes me."

"So this is the sort of stuff you're into, huh?"

"Yes, I suppose. Like any true storn would be."

"Exactly, this is pretty basic. I guess I was right to reject you all those years ago, if this is all you have to offer."

"You are of poor judgment, just like a spoiled child," Riul huffed. "Lord Anzinius should have merely forced a union between us. Imagine how much more productive you would be right now if he had done so."

"Hah!" Zzira shrugged, and even shook her head as she laughed. "Even my father knows that some things can't be forced. I merely would have run away sooner!"

"Again, you merely prove my point regarding your poor judgment. You refused me, and chose to elope with a weak, spineless coward of a storn who would rather hide behind enemy wings than serve his own kind."

"You have no idea…" Zzira couldn't help but look down at Zinx. The two locked eyes, and his worried gaze immediately forced her to furrow her own bony brow. She looked farther in front of Zinx to see where he had hit the table. The many dark cracks in the glass top blended in well with the image; it was a simple depiction of Buuziliel himself, surrounded by countless flying figures that lined the edges of the piece. Every figure in the artwork seemed to be looking up at the sun, illustrated with a simple, olive green circle representing the sun, whose rays spread out to cover the background of the image. This sun, and many of the rays of light extending from it, were now splintered, thanks to the cracks brought on by Zinx's outburst. The impact of something large and weighty flew into her face, nearly knocking the wind out of her. She was quick to recover, though it took everything in her to not scream out in anger at the cheap shot her opponent had taken. Though she knew she could only blame herself for being careless.

Riul backed away, grinning, satisfied with himself for getting in such a well placed strike. "You are a good fighter, Zzira, but you were always so easy to rile up, and so easily distracted. Always the unfocused child."

Zzira grumbled, then heard a familiar tapping sound. It was her father, who appeared bored and rested his head on one hand while tapping a dark nail on top of the bronze armrest of his throne with the other. The cadence was distinct, consisting of a single tap, followed by a slow pause, then another tap, again and again. The storn soldiers behind Anzinius took notice, and slowly began to chant in step with their emperor's tapping rhythm. As they chanted, they brought in their arms across their chests, and swung them out, clicking their stingers against one another. All occurred in step with Anzinius's rhythm.

"Hroh! Hroh! Hroh! Hroh!" the soldiers chanted. Each intonation was louder than the last, and before long the entire, massive plateau was caught in a raucous sound.

"It appears as if Lord Anzinius is getting bored," Riul said. "We need to end this, now—"

Zzira interrupted Riul by flinging her right arm, and finally releasing the stinger within it. The bony missile flew hard and fast, whistling sharply through the air and just past Riul's face. Enraged, Riul assumed an offensive position of his own, bringing back his thick arm to launch his own stinger. Storn stingers were valuable weapons, and it was often a waste to shoot them so recklessly. Not only was the act painful, but it took weeks for them to grow back. To casually shoot a stinger at another storn was considered the greatest of insults, and thus was the perfect way to bait Riul.

Zzira, seeing her opportunity, pretended to fly back and away toward the ground, as if trying to avoid the oncoming attack. She waited for just the right moment to begin flying in front of Lanu, setting herself between her and Riul who remained farther up in the air. Just as she turned her head, she heard the same crackling whistle of sharp cartilage cutting the wind. The attack was fast, but Zzira knew she was faster. She ducked out of the way at the last moment, and Lanu was exposed. Wide eyes shot all around as several ptomeras hurled themselves in front of their empress, though it only took one soldier to successfully block the attack. An ear-splitting crunch of flesh and bone being ripped apart echoed throughout. The chanting stopped, and a great, weighty thud slammed against the table as the now lifeless body fell. The table cracked again, and these cracks were quickly filled with slimy green and yellow blood that flowed forth like a river through a canal.

"He attacked the empress!" One soldier cried out.

"First blood! First blood has been drawn!" Another shouted.

"Sound the horns! Reinforcements!" a third barked.

Reinforcements? Zzira thought.

Riul turned to his own troops, barking orders at them as well. "Sound your horns too, you idiots! Call our back up horde! Now!"

Brass booms filled the air. Hundreds of horns rang against one another, their discordant chorus causing even the water surrounding the plateau to ripple. It was loud enough that Zzira needed to cover her own ears to save her hearing. She looked up to see lines of wings swarming in from the far reaches of the ocean, a circle of soldiers flying in as their mass shadowed both the sea and sky.

Zzira looked down to see the many soldiers on the plateau breaking formation to run ahead of Lanu, meeting an equal force of storns who had done the same for Anzinius. Stingers and claws met, and a greater fight had begun.

Riul turned to meet Zzira, but she was already a step ahead, and brought the sharpened edge of her left stinger across his throat. A thin stream of yellow fluid shot out, and before Riul could even lift his hands to grab at the wound, his body fell, mixing in with the chaos below. Zzira looked around to try and find Zinx and Lanu. Lanu herself remained calm, and refused to move an inch. Her eyes would occasionally flash, sending out invisible waves that knocked back any that would dare approach her. She looked around some more, and finally saw Zinx hurrying back and forth, desperately trying to stop whoever he could from fighting. This only caused more problems, as whenever he did stop one combatant, another would take advantage of the opportunity to cut or slice into them. Zinx would barrel forward, stopping the killer in their tracks, which only left them open for another attack. It was the angriest she had ever seen him. Seeing the otherwise calm and placid storn in such a state was too much, and she turned her attention to her father. Anzinius was laughing, relishing the chaos. He was also slithering away, hiding behind his throne, and eventually the bodies of his storn soldiers as they swarmed in to protect their emperor. He was easy to track however, thanks to his lavish violet robes and their long, shining coattails that trailed his every move. Without a second thought, Zzira dashed in, weaving between bodies being flung back and forth. She locked eyes with her father, who, for the first time in perhaps Zzira's entire life, looked shocked and worried. The look of fear reminded Zzira of the look on her mother's face as she was exiled, forced to leave and die in the wastes. It was a memory Zzira always tried to forget, but it came back to her in that moment, filling her with a blind rage. In a single, swift motion, she swung her left arm forward with enough force to nearly break her stinger from her arm, and her weapon found its mark—dead center in Anzinius's chest.

The look of fear turned to dread, and his face began to turn pale as he coughed up yellowed blood. He tried to speak, and tried to reach up and for his daughter, but could do neither. His body became languid, his movements weak and sputtery, before falling to stillness on the rocky plateau floor. Zzira broke off her stinger, leaving it in her father's chest. She looked up to see countless eyes all staring at her.

Maybe this was all that was needed, Zzira thought, doing her best to try and distract herself from what she had just done. *There's no reason to fight anymore, not with Anzinius dead.*

Every storn screamed, crying out louder than Zzira thought could be possible for a storn. She had to cover her ears again to keep the pain from splitting her skull. The screaming continued, even as the storns threw themselves into fury and back into battle.

"Wait!" Zzira screamed. "Wait! Stop! Your emperor is dead! I am Zzira Kul, true heiress to the storn empire! I command you all to—"

A sharp pain in her leg stopped her as an abandoned stinger fell from above, cutting her open. She kneeled down to grab at the wound, only to find herself being pushed aside by another weighty punch. Instinct caused Zzira to react instantly, and she was now locked in combat with her own soldiers.

It was easy enough to move and dodge everyone's attacks, even with her injured leg. Yet her thoughts were consumed with a silent dread. The situation had grown so beyond her, and there was nothing she could do aside from fight for her own survival. The sky grew dark as the reinforcements of both sides flew in, only adding to the chaos. The swift movement of a storn in the cloud of madness caught her eye, and she could see Zinx still trying to stop whoever he could from fighting, but to no avail. She had to turn away for a moment to deal with a few attackers, consisting of both storns and ptomeras. She made quick work of them, and looked back, only to see that Zinx had disappeared!

Where did he go? Zzira wondered. *Lanu? Can you hear me?* There was no response. *I don't know what to do... What am I supposed to do?! Lanu... Zinx... Please... Someone...*

Great winds began to sweep up the field. Many dark clouds, seemingly coming from nowhere, began to fill the sky. The fighting continued, and everyone seemed to be ignoring the anomalous calamity looming above them.

Zinx! Zzira thought to herself as she looked up in awe. *That has to be him!*

The wind grew more intense and bodies were beginning to be flung around. It made it difficult to fly, and a number of careless soldiers began to find their wings twisted and their bodies going limp as they fell to the ground. Thunder cracked the air above. The sea began to push back and forth, crashing against the heightened walls of the plateau. All of this was ignored, and the intensity of the storm continued.

Zinx...

Mist and smoke began to swirl into concentrated cones that reached down and touched Ozairos. The boom and whistle of twisters slicing through water nearly overtook the sounds of screams and carnage. The water itself was being flung with such force that mere droplets flew hard enough to injure many, and even punctured holes into a number of wings. This too was ignored, and soon everyone was surrounded by what could only be described as an apocalyptic scene— pure malice and anger seeping out from nature itself to add to the bedlam.

Zinx... I'm sorry! Please! Please stop! This is only making things worse!

The dark shadow cast upon the violent horde was such that the world was nearly black. The sounds of wind and water crashing was enough to drown out anything and everything. The rising calamity reached a fever pitch, its fervor enough that Zzira wondered if the planet itself would be torn apart. And then, silence.

A great opening broke through the black clouds above. A piercing ray of golden-olive light reached down to touch the many bodies below. Something massive and weighty cast a great shadow within this ray, as if the sun itself were being denied entry into the world. The sounds of wind and water thrashing about had been replaced with an ominous, almost alien buzzing hum that tickled the ear and rattled the heart. All were forced to stop and look above, though none could comprehend what precisely they were seeing.

Someone cried out, as if a reflex had taken over their body and was forcing out what everyone was thinking in that moment:

"I-It's him! It is Him! Buuziliel is here!"

A quick, sharp gasp swept through the horde, and all called out in frightened unison:

"Buuziliel!"

CHAPTER 31

THE GREAT, UNHOLY MASS THRUST ITS massive wings back, and then forward, and blew away the clouds themselves, revealing the clear sky, as well as its full form. It was an impossible amalgamation of elements that were at best contrasting, and at worst contradicting. From below, one could not see legs, but instead a great, black puff of fur that bundled together like a buoyant cloud, yet reflected no light. His chest bore a similar enough anatomy to be seen as that of a storn, though many more muscles poked through the chitinous layer of skin and were hard cut, giving his midsection the appearance of a pale green surface of stone that nearly shined like gold in the olive sunlight. His chest was mostly covered in the finest lavender fur one could imagine, like strands of silk dipped in oil that glistened as they waved in the wind. This fur covered much of his shoulders and neck as well, though his long arms stretched out in both directions, far beyond any normal storn or ptomera's field of view could take in at a single glance. Each arm was lined with count- less rows of tiny stingers that never crossed one another, no matter how he moved. Between each stinger was a thin, thread-like whisker, each one bearing a unique color and pattern, forcing the eye to twitch in bewil- derment as they observed them, as if merely trying to look up and down the divine being was strenuous. His hands each bore long and delicate fingers that ended with equally long black nails that reflected little sun- light. Each pointed nail was so fine that one could feel their vision being cut by the mere sight of them, as if he could reach up and cut the sky through his will alone. His face was something that could not be parsed. It bore an expression, though its intent was unread- able. He bore two large, shining gold disks that phased through different colors as it reflected light, appearing more like portals into something menacing rather than mere eyes. His lips nearly disappeared into a thin, tightly shut line beneath a short, refined nose. He bore six antennae that jutted forth from the crown of his large head—three long, thin and cartilaginous strands and three longer, puffier whiskers. The antennae were equally spaced, and swooped back and above his head as they wrapped around each other, forming a sort of pointed halo above his head.

His wings were undoubtedly his most striking feature. They slowly fluttered back and forth, reaching out and into the horizon. Clouds were pushed back and forth and smooth waves formed and fell in the water. These were the instruments that most on Ozairos—storn and ptomera alike—thought of when considering their lord. It was impossible to tell just how many wings he possessed, with the only conclusion one could draw upon viewing them was that it was too many. Seemingly infinite sheets of thin and lightly colored membranes shot out into the distance. The light filtered through them, and as they moved the world below flashed with a dizzying variety of glowing shapes and odd colors that moved and mixed and fled past one another, as if painting the world. They were long, and thin, but also somehow soft looking and round. They moved so quickly, and yet the hum and buzz they produced was almost pleasant to the ear, as if wanting not to disrupt the natural peace of the natural world below.

All eyes were on their lord. All hearts were stopped and all stood and sat with bated breath, caught between astonishment and fear as they anticipated what might happen next.

Lanu was the first to act, turning to her soldiers, and with a single look, all knew what to do—and they kneeled.

Zzira took notice of this, and turned around to face a horde of her own soldiers standing not too far behind her, all of whom looked on, mouths agape and eyes wide as they took in the full beauty of Buuziliel.

"Kneel, you fools!" Zzira barked.

The many storns all looked at Zzira in confusion, almost as if they didn't recognize her. Surely they still did, as she was their dead emperor's daughter, the one living storn with any true claim to the throne.

"I said kneel!" Zzira shouted again, this time her voice loud enough that its echo rivaled the ominous buzzing hum of Buuziliel's wings.

The storns were initially shook by the outburst, but quickly followed her orders, and lowered themselves to the ground. Only the empress and the princess remained standing among a sea of hunched bodies.

Lanu flapped her wings and rose, daring to approach the monstrous figure. Many gasped as they witnessed Buuziliel begin to move as well, and the two began to ascend upward. Zzira, more curious than frightened, quickly flexed her own wings and hovered above. She turned to her soldiers and gave a final order.

"All of you remain kneeling. No one is to bother us, lest you risk the wrath of Buuziliel himself."

A few storns nodded, and even a number of ptomcras looked over and seemed to agree. Everyone lowered their heads and looked to the ground. Zzira couldn't help but grin, finding a strange satisfaction in barking orders once again. She turned her attention upward and flew after Lanu and Buuziliel, who had since disappeared into the clouds high above.

It took a fair bit of effort on Zzira's part to break through the mountains of clouds that had appeared with Buuziliel. Most dared not to fly so high, for the air was thin and everything was cold. Normally only the most experienced and fit of flyers could go so high, and fortunately Zzira was one such storn. It was impressive to her that little Lanu could manage this flight as well.

Zzira finally broke through the layer of clouds, and found herself among the clear space above them. She could see two figures hovering not too far away—one was Lady Lanu, looking at and down toward a cloaked, pale figure who seemed to be looking downward. The two were not speaking, presumably sharing their thoughts with one another through Lanu's psychic abilities. It made sense, as the air was thin enough that saving every breath was crucial. Zzira pushed forward and was within speaking distance of them before long.

"Ah, Zzira, I am glad you are here," Lanu said. She seemed quite pleased with herself, a stark contrast to the dour looking figure across from her.

"So… what do we do now?" Zzira asked. She couldn't help but wear a worried look on her face. She could feel her lips clenching, and her brow furrowing deep lines into her skin.

Lanu turned her attention back to the stranger before continuing: "Zinx—or Cynkz, I should say—possesses a number of exceptional abilities. One of them is the ability to compress time itself within a small space around him."

"What?" Zzira looked at Cynkz, who remained unresponsive, before looking back at Lanu. "What does that mean? I don't understand."

"I hardly understand how it is possible either," Lanu said, "but essentially, he can force time to move at a heightened pace. It used to be limited to merely his perception, but he has grown proficient enough to affect other things as well, much like his shapeshifting has grown to affect things beyond his person. It is how he can manipulate nature itself, and create storms out of nothing."

"That sounds amazing, but what does that have to do with anything? Did we succeed? Did this all work?"

"There is a final thing we must ask of Cynkz, a finishing touch that will mark this day as one to be revered, and one that will force a union between us all—storn and ptomera alike. Cynkz will essentially embrace me, and speed up my pregnancy. He will lower me down, and you will guide me and my child safely below. My child's mixed heritage will be considered the result of Buuziliel himself signaling a union of storn and ptomera traits. This will be the beginning of a unified future."

"That is…" Zzira paused, her eyes darting about as she pondered Lanu's words. She looked at Cynkz worriedly, something that Lanu seemed to take notice of.

"What's wrong, my dear?" Lanu said. "The hard part is done. You are free to claim the storn throne, and we can easily command our people to stop fighting. My child will be accepted, and you will be free to live as you wish. We have won."

"We only won through deception," Zzira hissed. "We won through deception, and by forcing Cynkz to commit an act he plainly stated may have dire consequences. I suppose I am just as much at fault. I fell back into old habits and started the fighting, something that Cynkz wanted us to avoid. We both owe Cynkz more than an apology. We could never even begin to hope to repay him for everything he has done for us, and what we put him through. He would have every right to deny us this plan of yours, and fly back into the cosmos, leaving us with nothing to show for it all—"

"It is fine, Zzira," Cynkz muttered.

"Zinx—I mean… Cynkz…" Zzira stared at the stranger, perhaps for a moment too long. She could not find the appropriate words to express how she felt at that moment, but she forced herself to say something anyway. "Are you really okay with all of this? Is this what you wanted? Could you ever forgive us, or even me, after all of this?"

Cynkz closed his eyes, hiding them beneath the brim of his sharp cap, though he let out a quick chuckle and a smile. "It is fine, Zzira. I only wished to help. I suppose, if nothing else, I have done that. If this truly does make the fighting stop, and peace may be found on Ozairos, then I have done well, regardless of what anyone thinks of me."

"Why do you do it?" Zzira asked. It was an instinctual burst, as if something else had forced her to say it. "Why do you put yourself through this? What is in it for you? Are you truly that selfless? What is there to gain in all of this—for you, I mean?"

Cynkz went quiet, though he finally looked up and to the sky above. He peered right at the sun itself, through a harsh squint that said his thoughts were somewhere else.

"I have an old friend waiting for me back home," Cynkz said through a smile and a shrug. He turned to look Zzira in the eye before continuing. "I still owe him a worthy souvenir, and have yet to find it. What in the world would an imp of all things want as a souvenir anyway?"

"I have no idea what an imp is, but if this imp is your friend, I am sure he would appreciate anything you brought him."

"I sure hope so."

Lanu took in a deep breath, letting her presence be known: "I suppose we should hurry then, and get this done. We shouldn't keep our people waiting for too long."

"Wait, what will you do after this, Cynkz?" Zzira asked.

"I will have to leave. I will have to answer to many powerful beings for all of this. I do not know what that will entail, but I would like to move on."

"I guess I will never see you again. It was… It's been so fun with you around. The world seemed so small, and dark, and limited before. Getting to transform with you, and getting to peacefully travel for the first time, and even getting to experience a new culture, of all things… I cannot say thank you enough. Without you, I may very well have merely ended up in a grave, or locked away to give birth to new soldiers whose lives would have meant less than nothing. And to think that I was so curt with you when we first met…"

"Ah, think nothing of it." Cynkz shrugged again, and waved dismissively. "I had just as much fun. It's the little, fleeting moments of peace we share with each other that makes it all worth it."

Zzira could feel a wet warmth building up in her vision. She hated crying, but something forced her to. She didn't want to leave Cynkz with a final view of her face looking distraught and ugly, and she instinctively flew in and hugged the little po tightly. She could feel him patting her softly on her lower back, just beneath her wings so as to not interrupt them. A final breath and a bit of sniffling helped Zzira to recollect herself, and she slowly let go and hovered away to give him space. The two shared a final, warm smile.

"I am ready when you are, Cynkz," Lanu said.

Without a word, Cynkz hovered up and above Lanu. Through a puff of colorless smoke, his cloak reached out and split, forming a dark orb that cradled Lanu. Lanu could be seen closing her eyes and curling up just before disappearing behind the opaque vessel. Cynkz took in a long, deep breath, and the orb slowly turned and shifted, reflecting very little light in the process. At first nothing stood out. Yet the more Zzira looked on, she began to notice something at the curved edges of the orb. She squinted, and could see faint traces of distorted light flowing around the orb. The sky and clouds behind this light appeared to move and bend with it. It appeared to pull in whatever was behind it, like a painting whose edges were being curled inward. Zzira knew not what to make of the phenomena, but she was entirely transfixed, and unable to look away. Her trance soon broke as the orb began to slowly—painfully slowly—descend back down and through the clouds. Zzira gave Cynkz a final glance, but his focus was entirely on the orb, almost appearing as if his consciousness had left his body. Not wanting to interrupt him, Zzira flew down ahead of the orb and guided its descent.

It took a fair bit of time for Zzira and the orb to finally break through the thick layer of clouds, but eventually the lime green ocean came into view. The plateau, the Gnorel Basin, was just below them, and as they drew closer Zzira could see hundreds upon hundreds of faces looking up at her. All were still kneeling, and all were still in awe. It appeared as if the orb would soon land on the table used for the summit. Zzira noted the blood and broken bodies covering the table, and decided to hurry down and make space for the orb. She dashed in and began barking orders, and both storn and ptomera alike were compelled to follow them. No one dared to defy a gift being lowered down by the will of Buuziliel himself. It only took a few moments for the space to be cleared, and all soon waited patiently for the ominous orb to finally reach its destination.

The otherworldly construct stopped just short of colliding with the glassy surface. It paused, and then burst into ashen smoke, finally revealing its contents. Lanu could be seen still curled up, and defying gravity for a short time among several plumes of steadily dissolving smoke. She appeared disheveled, and trace amounts of fresh blood stained her body and robes. She appeared exhausted, yet relieved as she took a much needed breath of fresh air. Cradled within her arms was something odd, and tiny. It smelled strange, as if a mixture of bodily fluids and something sweet, like a newly bloomed flower or fruit. No one knew what to do or how to react, but all reacted with similar shock when faint, infantile cries rang out. As the cries continued, the small, tiny, wet and fleshy thing in the empress's arms began to move, reaching out with tiny clawed hands toward nothing in particular. Several curious onlookers crept in, and upon closer inspection the truth of the situation became apparent. It was a newborn child, one that possessed faint traces of both storn and ptomera features, bearing tiny, rounded stingers and sharp, colorful and thin wings that the infant's underdeveloped muscles could barely move. Several ptomeras moved in to hold up the empress, doing their best to clean her up and cover her and her child up with whatever rags they could find. Zzira looked over to a few nearby storns, snapped her fingers and gestured for them to assist. The storns, without a second thought, followed her orders, and even assisted a few ptomeras in lifting Lanu and her child up carefully to settle her in the cushioned seat of the throne she had been carried in on.

Zzira looked on to see storns and ptomeras talking amongst themselves. Eventually these conversations began to bleed over into one another, and everyone was freely talking with one another, without discrimination. Zzira found the scene surreal, but understandable— their "god" had just presented himself to them, and allowed them to witness firsthand a supposed "holy birth." It made sense that they would at least be willing to stop for a moment and try to make sense of it all. It was something simple, and something small, but it was a start. Zzira lamented the work ahead of her. It would be challenging to change the minds and perspectives of an entire nation, but part of her looked forward to it. It felt good to finally be in charge of her own destiny, without her father or anyone else bearing down on her. She was finally free to live as she pleased. Why not use that freedom to do something productive? Why not begin to mend relations between her people and the ptomeras? It would be nice if she could freely visit the ptomeras again, and sample more of their culture, and it would be nice if she could bring back bits of their culture for her people to learn from. Perhaps it was too much, but it was worth a shot in her mind.

Her thoughts quickly turned back to Cynkz. As everyone settled and began to prepare for their long flights home, Zzira felt compelled to see something. She knew it was foolish, but she had to at least try. She desperately wanted to see the stranger again that had helped her through so much. She flew up and back into the clouds, this time moving much faster, and taking little care for the cold or the thin air. It was not long before she had returned to the empty space above the clouds. It was not long before she realized that she was alone. She looked around, knowing it would do no good, but she felt compelled to try anyway.

"Cynkz? Are you..." Zzira stopped herself. She closed her eyes and tried to picture the stranger one last time. Somehow, despite seeing so little of it, the stranger's true form occupied her thoughts more than anything. She thought of his warm smile, which forced her to smile in response. She opened her eyes again, taking in the precious view of the fluffy mountains of clouds covering Ozairos. She looked on for perhaps a moment too long, and finally decided to return to the world below, disappearing into the mist beneath her.

CHAPTER 32

ALONE, DARK CLOAKED FIGURE CUT A harsh line through the olive green sky.

He flew alone, and his mind was blank, as if refusing to dwell any longer than necessary on past mistakes and regrets. There was nothing to fill his mind, save for the whip of his cloak against the wind as he flew ahead. He wanted nothing more than to be alone, but he knew that sooner or later he would need to confront the Omun. With his job seemingly done, he was certain they would address him first, so why not make the most of his solitude before they happened along?

Cynkz...

It was Anim. It was appropriate that Anim would be the first to greet him. He was the first to greet him in Omundisia, after all. For reasons beyond him, Cynkz's mind remained blank. He felt compelled to keep moving forward, as he always did, and maintained his flight. He didn't mean to ignore the Omun, but he was still struggling to come to terms with everything.

Cynkz? Cynkz, please listen to me…

The voice's tone only grew softer, and sadder. This was enough to finally compel Cynkz to stop, giving Anim his full attention.

"Thank you, Cynkz," Anim said, now choosing to speak more directly, rather than to invade his mind. "We must discuss what just happened. You accomplished your goal, ultimately, but your methods were—"

You! How dare you!

A familiar, bitter voice cut through, hammering violently against the inner walls of Cynkz's mind.

"You do not need to scream into his mind, Siar'C," Anim said. "You may address him appropriately—"

"How *dare* you!" Siar'C screamed. "We allowed you access to our realm! We allowed you to move and operate freely among our domain! Among our universe! We only asked one thing of you, jester! The audacity to mimic the image of the Creator himself! In a bastardized form to stop a single, measly conflict!"

Cynkz hung his head low, and spoke softly: "Siar'C, I am sorry, I am—"

"Of all the things you could have done! Of the limitless possibilities available to you, you chose to mimic the image of a god! You have imprinted a false image of the Creator upon an entire people! Upon *my* people!"

What do you think the consequences of such a careless act will have on them?!"

"You don't need to yell at him, Siar'C," Anim said, though his voice was meek.

"Quiet, Anim," Siar'C snapped. "I am discussing matters that pertain to my world, and its people. I have little patience for your pathetic arbitration!"

Cynkz wanted to speak, to at least try and defend his case. Unfortunately his mind was immediately filled with a number of new voices, each one piling on top of the other, and crowding out the rest:

Cynkz! What happened?!

I came as quickly as I could. What went wrong?

Cynkz, my lad! What is all this chaos?
Why is Siar'C so angry?

C-Cynkz? What happened? Siar'C has been s-so upset, his rage drowning out Omundisia itself.

The voices continued. Anim and Siar'C only added to the madness, filling Cynkz's mind with countless voices that all demanded to be heard. His head began to hurt, as if something were pounding away from within. He clutched his head, grit his teeth, and attempted to make sense of it all, but couldn't. The voices continued, to the point where they became unintelligible. It was merely a stream of scratching hisses and booming shouts rolling over each other again and again and again until his senses became numb, and all that was left was a boiling frustration that quickly rose through his body and eventually let itself out in a savage roar.

"What did you want me to do?!" Cynkz shouted, screaming at the top of his lungs so that his hoarse voice echoed infinitely past the horizon of clouded mountains. All finally went quiet, finally giving Cynkz a moment to think and speak. "It is so easy to sit back and criticize. What would you have me do, then?! Are all of you so useless that you can only sit back and watch me struggle?! Only to barge into *my* mind and scream at me when I do not perform perfectly?! I managed things as best as I could! What more do you want from me?!"

A short silence filled the air. Siar'C was the first to speak: "You have done many good things, Cynkz. This is undeniable. But you exist in a realm far beyond your own at our behest. It is a privilege that we Omun have ultimately granted to you. This is a great risk to us all, as your very existence in Omundisia, and your acquired knowledge of the many worlds beyond, could very well go against the Creator's wishes. Everything we have allowed could very well conflict with the Creator's vision of existence itself. We allowed you to more or less operate freely, and we only had but one request—to always honor the Creator, his image, his vision, and to never jeopardize that."

"So what should I have done?" Cynkz said, swinging his arm sharply through the air, barely containing his rage. "Should I have merely allowed your people to kill each other? Should I have merely allowed them to doom themselves to death and annihilation?!"

"Even if every one of them did perish," Siar'C continued, "they would have an appropriate afterlife to look forward to, not unlike your Potarium."

"And they should be fine with eventually learning that they are merely meant to bide their time in the afterlife?" Cynkz snapped back. "They should be fine with the knowledge that they would be unable to birth new souls? That their future is ultimately limited? That they should just reach the end, and then what?!"

"Existence is a privilege," Helon said, as calm as ever. "It is a beautiful thing that all should be grateful for."

"I didn't ask to exist," Cynkz said, retreating into his cloak to look back downward, his vision filling up with countless piles of light green fluff which made up the clouds below. "I never asked to exist. I never asked for the unholy union that was my birth to occur, yet here I am, burdened with the responsibility of things so far beyond me. Staying in Dulrot was not enough. And I could never truly fit in with the good po of Potarium. Perhaps I had hoped to find some solace in Omundisia, and perhaps I foolishly thought that I could find my place among the stars, the one constant that has followed me since before I lost my memories. Yet even now I see that may not be the case. I grow tired. For the first time in my everlasting existence I truly am tired. Everything that I have done, all that I do—it is never enough. Despite everything, I feel no closer to reaching a greater resolution, to finding any point or purpose in all of this. I enjoy doing good, I truly do, but what is any of this really doing for me?" Cynkz chuckled, as the words of the most unlikely person came to his mind. "I remember Harquin venting his frustrations,

I remember him stating a cold, harsh truth to me—
we po are all, in fact, dead. I have witnessed countless
worlds now, all of whom continue to exist, and get to
reap the benefits of life itself. We po, however, our time
was cut drastically short, partially thanks to my very
existence. I do not think there is anything I could ever
do to truly make up for that. I thought that, if I could
at least question the Creator himself, and get an answer
for why specifically all of my people needed to die, and
if there was perhaps something I could do, something I
could give to make amends… I knew it was a long shot,
but it was easier to barrel ahead, carried by whimsy and
the possibility, however small, of finding that answer,
than to merely sit back and dwell on what could be.
Even after all of this, I have no more to show for it all
than when I began. Even if I returned to Potarium…
would they even remember me? Would they care? It
has been so long now."

"I suppose we are, in all honesty, in no position to
ask anything of the Creator," Anim said. "Not even we
Omun can ask, let alone demand anything of Him."

"We are most certainly not in any position to ask
anything of Him," Siar'C said. "The privilege that is
our existence is only because of Him and His power. It
is His right to decide what knowledge we are and are
not privy to. There may well be a good reason as to why
you need not ever know why you were born, or why it
needed to result in the loss of your world."

"I refuse to assume such," Cynkz said. "I would
much rather have a proper answer. I had hoped that
working with you all would help, but I suppose I
was wrong."

"I was the first one demanding you be sent back home, jester! Perhaps if the others had merely listened to me, we could have saved you so much time and anguish, and saved me the trouble of risking His wrath by allowing you to act as you have!"

"True, Siar'C, but even you began to change your tune once you came to terms with the idea of me assisting you, of doing your dirty work for you."

"Who are you, a mere mortal soul, to accuse me, an Omun, a true herald of the Creator, of anything?! You could have said no at any time! You could have refused me, or Anim, or Carros, or Jio-Mol, or even Helon, or any one of us! Face it, jester, you saw just as much use in us as we did you! Do not try to act as if you are somehow purer than us, or Him, as if you are without self-interest!"

"I suppose we are all scoundrels, in a way," Cynkz said, turning his head down and leering from beneath the thin brim of his cap. "For all of his faults, at least the Munder King was not afraid to act, to actually do something of his own volition, and even stood by his mistakes to the very end. His convictions remain even now. My conversation with him proved as such."

Siar'C huffed, barely restraining himself from shouting more. "This is pointless. I may as well be trying to explain mathematics to an infant. Just know that your actions here may well have doomed the very souls of every storn and ptomera on Ozairos, and perhaps even future generations as they learn to revere the false image of their lord. Take that knowledge with you for the rest of time."

Cynkz merely lowered his head. He refused to look at the sky, and wanted nothing more than to cease talking to the stars any further. He was unsure of what else to do.

"Ultimately, we cannot allow this transgression to go without consequence," Helon said.

"What will you do then?" Cynkz asked, still refusing to lift his head. "Destroy me? Banish me to some dark pit somewhere? Somehow I doubt you would merely send me back to Potarium."

"No." Helon's voice was resolute and stern. Her once normally smooth and fading flair had vanished beneath an authoritative tone. "In truth, we do not know what to do with you. We have discussed much regarding your circumstances, and will have to discuss even more in private. We must consider our actions carefully, as Omun are not meant to pass judgment or enact punishments."

"So what am I to do in the meantime, then?"

I do not care what you do, Cynkz, but you cannot stay here." Siar'C's bitter tone had returned in full force. There was particular inflection added to the sound of the jester's name being spoken, something that Siar'C rarely did.

"So I am to just wander the cosmos aimlessly while you all bicker amongst yourselves?"

"That is… a harsh way to put it, but… I suppose that is for the best, at least for now." Anim seemed somber, barely able to let out his words even as he spoke them.

A heavy sigh slipped through Cynkz's thin lips. "At least I will finally get some peace and quiet."

And indeed it was quiet. The Omun were unresponsive, more than likely already gone and back in Omundisia to argue amongst themselves. Cynkz looked around, taking in the vast sea of mountainous clouds adding texture to the otherwise flat, plain olive sky. It was as beautiful a sight as any in nature could offer, and he could no longer appreciate it. He had grown tired of Ozairos, and slowly drifted up and away, and back into the darkness of the cosmos. He made sure to move in the opposite direction of the sun, and away from its light. He was tired of seeing that, too.

Once above the world of Ozairos, he noted how cold it felt. He had felt the all consuming frigidity of space countless times, to the point where he had grown more than accustomed to it. He chuckled, thinking it humorous that such an extreme thing never bothered him much before.

All alone and in the dark, he instinctively pulled out the thread once again. Despite being such an amazing thing, he would often forget he even still possessed the object. As he twirled the sliver of divine light between his fingers, he noticed that he could not appreciate its beauty either. He thought back to when the thread seemed to lead him forward, in some cases even pointing his way forward. He remembered that it was merely Krull prompting him forward—another Omun leading him by the nose toward some unknown objective. Cynkz, for the first time, was grateful that the thread was unresponsive. He was grateful to have complete say over his actions moving forward. Even if he chose to do nothing at all, at least it was his decision alone, unsullied by any outside influence.

Cynkz eventually put the thread away, deep into a chest pocket and out of sight. He looked on, relishing the cold. He wondered what direction he should move in, and decided on a random patch of dark space between a number of distant stars. He took in a deep breath, never questioning the possibility of such an action in space, and burst into ashen smoke. His head rested atop a large, obsidian orb formed of the same material as his cloak, and he set off toward nothing in particular.

PART 5

MEMORIES

CHAPTER 33

BACK TO THE COSMOS.
That appeared to be the way of things beyond the realms of po. It was, if nothing else, his way. If only the universe weren't so vast and quiet and lonely, and if only his mind were lost on other things, he may be able to appreciate its silent beauty in full.

As much as he tried to get his mind off of the Omun, at least for some short while, everywhere he looked, his vision was filled with stars. Gleaming, twinkling specks danced softly across every inch of the dark canvas before him. It didn't bother him as much as he thought it would, for the natural universe was far more comforting than the strange inversion forced upon the senses by Omundisia. The darkness compelled his mind to quiet, and finally allowed him to rest, even as he thoughtlessly drifted forward.

Despite his constant stargazing, he had come to regret never sparing much of his free time to studying astronomy. Even his knowledge of astrology—essentially stories explaining the many shapes and formations the constellations provided the po on any clear night—was mostly second hand, merely things he had heard in passing as others spoke amongst themselves. He always appreciated these stories, but knew that they were lacking in anything concrete. He was left to experience the universe with ignorant eyes. There was nothing else he could do but pass by countless phenomena, and appreciate their brilliance and strangeness.

Sometimes the usual pitch black canvas would fill with color. Within these colors many things could be seen, most often great gas formations. The gas appeared thick, almost solid in a way, and would gather together in the strangest ways. Sometimes they would form rows of great pillars, other times they would swoop down to bowl together into massive basins, from which new colors, and new materials could be seen slowly drifting out from within, like dust flying off of a shaken brush.

Farther along, he noticed the tips of many colorful strings of light. Each strand was impossibly long, and thin and wispy, not unlike thin hairs poking through the void. Or perhaps they more resembled faint threads caught in a soft breeze. Nevertheless, it was enough to catch his attention, and thus prompted him to venture closer. As he approached, an impossibly bright light began to burn out everything else in view. The many colorful strands of wispy light began to take on order, bending and curving into neat lines and loops that went in and out of the bright center infinitely. This center soon revealed a perfect orb, not unlike the many stars that he had seen up close, and at its edges a burnt orange ovaloid reached out. Countless little things, impossibly large and impossibly far away, gave this shape texture, and seemed to burn away into nothing as they faded into a beam of light that reached out infinitely from the center orb's poles. When close enough, the phenomenon appeared to divide the universe itself in half, as if a blazing hot knife had been taken to the abyss itself and sliced right down the middle. Strangely, there were no other stars or planets anywhere nearby the phenomenon, and faint traces of an uncomfortable warmth could be felt from even millions of miles away. He decided it was best to leave it be and drift in the opposite direction once he had gotten his fill of it.

Many nebulas began to expose themselves the more he traveled. Nebulas were a thing he knew, mostly thanks to Fiddle's curiosity about them, and his regular inquiries as to their origins whenever he came across a learned po in Dulrot. Nebulas were the imp's favorite things to watch in the cosmos. He loved their many colors, and all the odd, wavy shapes they would take. Even now, the drifter looked on and took note of the many nebulas before him, trying to think of what his old friend would equate each one to. One large mass, representing a messy, oblong shape of burnt sienna, probably would have been equated to a crushed almond. Another glance over revealed a giant sheet of greenish, bluish, perhaps turquoise mist. Fiddle most definitely would have equated that one to squashed bug. Farther along, the drifter noticed a circular, ice-blue mix of material that spread out into a border dotted with gold and green and white material.

It reminded him of an eye, a ruptured pupil peering back at him from the universe's edge. Fiddle would have loved that one in particular.

His thoughts slowly drifted to Kadd, and the many beautiful churches in Potarium. He remembered how well he and Fiddle got along. He smiled, and was grateful for the solace it provided. He wondered what sorts of jokes the two shared with one another even now.

His thoughts drifted further, and he thought of the bouncy, redheaded woman, Pairne.

Pairne A'Byrne…

He was relieved he still remembered her name. He wondered if she still remembered his name. He knew that, if nothing else, Fiddle would never let her forget it, but he wondered all the same.

He thought further, and remembered the dark haired woman from his earliest memories. He remembered Orilay, and inevitably the poem, of which its true meaning he still could not determine on his own:

Every star
Near and far
Waits for us
To just
Reach out
And accept them…

For the first time, he didn't want to dwell on the poem, or its meaning. His mind moved to other things, to Munderworld, to the abyss crowning the realm, and to Potarium and the great dark sea bordering the city. He thought of the po, and their long lost world, and the many worlds he had visited thus far. It was surreal to reminisce on the many worlds, and how the weight of life and death affected each of them. Without Peara, the old po world, they had no such worries, and could happily stagnate in their massive, but limited numbers in heaven. It was such an odd collection of thoughts and things that described the many unique traits of each realm and world. It was impossible to draw any greater conclusion about it all, and what his place could possibly be in all of it.

Even now, he thought of how weightless he felt in the cosmos, how weightless souls in the afterlife were, and how much heavier everything felt when a life was on the line. The many still living worlds he had visited thus far were still blessed with that feeling. If only the po could still appreciate such things.

Though he wondered if that was a good thing. There were indeed some who still appreciated and thought of such things, po such as Harquin, and Yla. Though the Sisters of Elm must have still appreciated such things as well, as they continued their work even into the afterlife. How many souls have they assisted in Munderworld? They seemed at peace with their thankless task, if nothing else. Perhaps it was easy to bear such a burden so long as the sisters had each other. If only Yla had been content with such things. Perhaps the damage done to Potarium could have been avoided. Though Eshra'Tel would still be alive, and the many souls he harbored would still be trapped within his evil core. He couldn't even begin to fathom the chaos the evil eyed Omun may have caused the universe had he been left to his own devices. All that Cynkz wanted to do was help out and explore, and to satiate his never ending curiosity. It seemed preferable that one with simpler, nobler ambitions had been permitted to move on into the universe. Though he wondered if, despite their dark ambitions, if Harquin and Yla were right to be angry with their situation. Not that it justified their actions in any way. He still felt some guilt over being partially responsible for the calamity. He dreaded how much worse he would feel if they had succeeded.

Such thoughts and regrets began to weigh down his mind. He pushed everything to the side to relish the peace and quiet of the cosmos.

A distant moon, barely in orbit of a lone, gray planet, caught his eye. The moon too was gray, though in the light of a distant star its dust nearly shined silver. It seemed as good a place as any to finally set his feet down on stable ground, to stretch his legs and stop drifting for a moment.

Though something else caught his eye, something that startled him for how different it appeared. It was something tiny, bearing a strange, reddish color. It almost appeared fuzzy, but it was difficult to tell from such a distance. It moved and bounced around haphazardly, the way a child might as it explored somewhere new. Cynkz wondered if it was his mind playing tricks on him. Or perhaps it was his powers acting strange and beyond him. It would not be the first time they did so. Yet he knew he could not ignore it, for curiosity was a most intoxicating thing, and curious he now was.

Cynkz finally drifted down to the moon's dusty surface. In a burst of smoke, his orbed form faded into mist, and he set foot on the celestial sphere. The soles of his feet pressing into the soft grains felt oddly satisfying. He began to walk, taking note of each footprint he left in the ground. Without any wind to disrupt the grains, who knows how long his imprints would remain. How long would this insignificant piece of history stay? Would anyone else ever see it? Could these very tracks outlast even him?

He finally noticed that his trademark smoke had never fully ceased. He walked carefully, making sure not to disturb the moon's floor too much as he moved, yet a thin layer of ashen mist seemed to follow him, and covered the ground all around him.

Are my abilities acting up again? How strange... At least they are free to do whatever they please here—who else could they possibly disturb?

"Cynkz! Hey, Cynkz!"

His heart jumped! He could have sworn he was alone, yet something, or someone, called out to him. Its voice was sharp, high pitched in tone but somehow gruff, as if long lived.

"Cynkz! I know you can hear me!" The voice called out again. It was much closer, and the fluttering of tiny wings could be heard fast approaching from behind.

The jester finally turned, and instantly met eyes with a small, scruffy red creature.

"It's me! Fiddle! You haven't forgotten me, have you? It hasn't been *that* long."

Cynkz continued to stare, bewilderment overtaking his features. He looked the creature up and down, and noticed much of his smoke still settling all around. It had to have been one of his illusions, perhaps his powers had grown in their ability to act out of turn. His illusions never outright spoke to him before, and as such he knew not how to respond.

"I know for a fact you haven't forgotten me. Look! I'm even small again! Just like I was all those years ago!" Fiddle reared himself back, smiling his usual wide, yellow smile and thumbing at his loose, furred skin like the collar of a shirt.

Small again? What? Cynkz looked on for a moment longer, then took in a deep breath as he turned away. "This has to be a trick. Perhaps I am slowly going mad from the isolation…"

"Hey! I didn't come all this way to be ignored!" The imp riled himself up into a furious ball and hurled forth, colliding with the back of the jester's head. Cynkz nearly fell over, and watched his trusted, pointed cap fall slowly and smoothly to the dusty floor of the moon. Cynkz stared at his own hat as if he had never seen it before. Before he could even reach to lift it, the imp scurried past him and did it for him, even going so far as to dust it off a few times with his tiny, clawed hands before presenting it to its original owner.

"Sorry about that," Fiddle continued. "You know, I figured I would need to knock some sense into you, but I didn't think it would be literal."

"Um, thank you, Fiddle…" Cynkz reached out, and weakly grasped his hat and took it from his old friend. The imp seemed to watch carefully, taking notice of the jester's languid motions.

"Did I wake you up or something?" Fiddle said. "You seem kind of tired. And mopey. Always so mopey, every time I see you now, I swear."

"No, I mean…" Cynkz slowly returned his cap to its right place, and looked on toward the stars. "Well, even if you are an illusion, I am glad to see you again, old friend, whatever form you take."

"Pah, I am no mere illusion, but I'm not supposed to tell you too much." Fiddle rocked back and forth, circling his body as he waved dismissively.

"The Fiddle I know would not be able to do that. Talking and revealing secrets was one of his favorite pastimes."

"Hah! Nice try! But my lips are sealed! You'll just have to be happy enough that I'm here to cheer you up and cheer you on."

"Cheer me on to what, I wonder?" Cynkz finally smiled, though faint it may be. He had not enjoyed such a conversation in too long, he felt.

"I don't know. I just know that you'll be back soon, and we'll all get to sit around and listen to your stories forever."

"We?" Cynkz raised a curious brow at the creature. "I never figured my illusions would be capable of expressing camaraderie, or even acknowledging one another."

"I am not—ugh!" Fiddle pouted, swinging his little limbs futilely in the air.

"Well, illusion or not, I am glad to see you again, Fiddle." Cynkz gave a smile and a bow before turning, as if to leave. "I should continue, I would rather not stay still for too long. The least I could do is explore the cosmos a bit more."

"Is that all? Truly?" A warm voice echoed from the peculiarly stubborn plumes of ashen smoke covering much of the moon's floor. Cynkz glanced behind him, and saw a man in shining, violet robes, a beaming white smile contrasting his tan skin.

"Hello Kadd," Cynkz said, "or, illusion of Kadd, I should say…"

"He thinks we are merely illusions?" Kadd shifted his attention to Fiddle, scratching his chin with a light finger.

"Yeah, he doesn't get it yet," Fiddle huffed.

"Well," Kadd took in a deep breath, and looked back at Cynkz, his features nearly glowing as he faced the light of the distant sun, "I suppose we can work with that for now."

"What?! No! I want him to know I'm real!" Fiddle exclaimed.

"Now now, Fiddle, Cynkz has clearly been through a lot. We were summoned to help him, and give him at least some much needed comfort so he can reach the end," Kadd said.

"That may be a tad bit of an understatement, old friend," Cynkz said, keeping his head low and his attention forward.

"What's wrong, Cynkz? Please, you can share anything with us," Kadd said, as soft and warmly as ever.

Cynkz paused for a moment, long enough to make Fiddle impatient as he twitched in the air. "I made a mistake. And I believe I may have done all of this for nothing, or that it will ultimately lead to nothing."

"How so?" Kadd asked.

"I only wanted to help. I only wanted to stop the violence, and the fighting. I have thus far been to so many worlds, perhaps too many. So much time has passed, and I have witnessed so much happen. I have spoken with the stars, I have seen countless different races, alien peoples and civilizations, each with their own interpretation of the universe, of Paithos, their own forms of birthing life and bearing death… Time moves so strangely for me now. The past, regardless of its recency, appears as little more than a faint and distant memory, one that I can hardly maintain, as if grains of sand slipping through my fingers. The future is a constant surprise, and forever a chaotic unknown that requires constant, stressful adaptation. The one thing I could depend on for stability—the present— now passes so quickly that I can hardly perceive it. When I look back on things I have done, it is almost as if it were someone else. Instinct has driven me to move forward, and instinct drove me to commit a great sin—imitating a false image of the Creator. The Omun have cast me out of Omundisia, and cursed me to wander the universe until they can decide on what to do with me. Paithos remains silent, when my ulti- mate goal was to bring his guidance back. I am no closer to the answers I seek, and I even wonder if the good I have done for countless other worlds will mean much of anything in the future. What I do know is that the false image I created may very well have doomed countless souls to worship something wrong. I only wanted to help, but I do not know if I have done much of anything, in the grand scheme of things."

"I see you are the same as I remember you, then," Kadd said.

Cynkz, now curious as to his supposed illusion's accusation, turned to meet eyes with the man. It was then that the jester noticed his long, dark and sharp shadow cutting a deep line into the vast, dusty silver landscape. "What do you mean?"

"You go on to commit great acts, to help others, and you still refuse to take solace in it. I have never met someone who could be described as possessing crippling humility, but you may be the first."

"Hmm…" Cynkz didn't know what to say, or even what to think. His old friend was correct, but it was all that Cynkz had known, and how he had carried himself for eons. Did he need to change? Was change necessary? Was it hypocritical for him to instill change in so many others whilst refusing to change himself? Perhaps change was primarily a choice, for each individual to make themselves. Perhaps he was merely presenting the question to others, and as for himself, he chose to stay the same. Though he wondered if this was the right choice. It was often easier for him to push such thoughts to the back of his mind and continue moving forward, letting curiosity guide the way.

"If there is one thing I can tell you, it is this," Kadd looked the jester right in the eye, making sure that his words were being considered, "we are all on journeys of our own, Cynkz. All po souls are destined for Potarium's shores. Even the po once trapped within the dark star Eshra'Tel are enjoying a peaceful afterlife, thanks to you. I imagine that this truth extends to all worlds, and all souls throughout the universe.

Whatever damage you believe your actions may have caused—if any at all—any lost souls you come across will each go on a journey of their own, and find their way to the light. That is the ultimate goal of our lord, Pathos. The dark compels us to journey forth, and his light guides us to a proper destination."

"I remember, I think…" Cynkz said, scratching the sharp point of his own goatee as his eyes looked about, observing the many glistening grains of sand caught within his long shadow. "I remember reading an old book you had in your home. I remember a page within it bearing a single phrase."

Kadd rested his arms within his billowing, violet sleeves and smiled: "'Light guides, darkness compels.'"

"I wish I knew how to read," Fiddle muttered.

"Well, there is plenty of time for you to learn, little one, once your patience allows you," Kadd said.

Cynkz smiled. He couldn't help but be happy to see his friends in good spirits, even if they were mere illusions, some excess of his strange abilities. "I am glad to be able to remember you two so well. Though I would not be at all surprised if you two had long since forgotten me, as well as the rest of Potarium, by now. It has been so long…"

"I haven't forgotten you!" A lilting, accented voice rang out from another plume of smoke hidden in plain sight. From within another shadow bounced forth. A bright young woman, her auburn hair shining in the distant sun and her freckled face rounded with a wide smile, sprung forth.

Cynkz had no time to react. Within moments the woman had leaped forward and into his arms and embraced him. For a moment it felt as if time had stopped. He knew it was just an illusion, but he couldn't help but feel warm as a jolt of ecstasy shot through his body. It felt far too good to be hugged by a loved one, illusion or not. The woman eventually took in a deep breath and pulled herself back to look at him, her ice-cold amber eyes staring into his.

"It has been too long, Cynkz," she said, still smiling, and squinting ever so slightly as the sunlight bounced off of her freckled face. "Do you remember me?"

Cynkz was caught in a state of perplexion, but managed to eventually respond. "Pairne?"

She gasped. "You *do* remember! Even after all of this time!" She pressed her head into his chest and hugged him tightly. Cynkz normally had no trouble discerning his illusions from reality. For whatever reason, his conjurations felt cold and heavy, at least initially to him. Yet here, in her arms, he felt nothing but warmth. Perhaps his abilities were merely becoming more convincing?

"It's so great," Pairne continued. "It won't be long now, before you're back, and we can all finally relax and listen to your stories and be together again."

"Together again..." Cynkz pulled back, unable to look Pairne in the eye, a now worried expression now on her face.

"What's wrong?" Pairne asked.

"I know better, but still... It stings a fair bit knowing you are all merely illusions. It would be nice if we were all together again, because... we are not actually together here now. None of you are actually here..."

"I *am* here, you idiot!" Fiddle screamed, letting loose his frustration. "Do I have to hit you again?!"

"Fiddle, we were warned of this," Kadd said, "we just have to be patient. Everything will become clear soon enough. There's no reason to be so angry."

"You know…" Cynkz turned back around, face toward the distant, pearly sun, eyes toward the countless stars nearly covering the whole of the black canvas of the cosmos. "The Omun have told me much about the universe, and how things work here. Even light itself requires time to travel, and from far enough away, what you see are not in fact living stars, but instead their remnants. Many of the stars you see here, even now, are not actually there. They are merely illusions cast by the fading light of dead stars. Dead stars, faded light, mere illusions… Echoes of the past… I grow tired of looking at things which are not truly there, a constant reminder of long lost memories…"

A slight scuffling of feet could be heard dragging through the lunar dust toward him. "Cynkz… We're not… Just please, don't give up, and just know that we are, in fact, still waiting for you," Pairne said.

Cynkz remained quiet. He spoke the truth, and was indeed growing tired. He refused to look back, not wanting to acknowledge the illusions anymore. Yet the smoke remained, and even seemed to move and settle with a mind of its own. It slowly slithered forth, and bundled together into a final cloud a fair distance in front of him. The way the light filtered through the smoke seemed to cast odd shadows around, and Cynkz wondered if his mind was playing tricks on him. Still he looked on, as if trying to find some meaning in it, when a new shadow began to form within. It was a tall, svelte form, with long, jet black hair that reflected the light brilliantly, and a long and flowing dress that seemed to disappear into the mist itself. The form, now clearly a woman, moved smoothly as if on water, as if a ghost merely floating on the edge of existence. The woman finally stopped and looked back at Cynkz, two diamond-blue eyes now peering into his soul.

"Orilay!" Cynkz's reaction was guttural, as if forced upon him by someone else. He couldn't help it, and he slowly leaned forward and began to walk toward the apparition.

The woman looked back at Cynkz, never blinking, never flinching, and smiled softly: "You're almost there, Cynkz. Just a little farther. You will have plenty of time to rest, soon enough."

Cynkz was stunned, and stopped in his tracks. *What should I say? What does she mean? This has to be another illusion, but...*

The woman turned to fully face Cynkz, and looked at him expectantly. It was as if she were inviting him to come forward. Without a second thought, Cynkz finally sprang ahead, yet no matter how quickly he moved, he never seemed to get closer to her. Eventually the woman slid into the mist. Cynkz finally reached her, but found nothing but moon dust, and smoke that began to fade into nothing. He stopped and looked around, only to find that he was finally alone.

They're gone... But then again, they were never really here, were they?

He looked to the ground to see a number of footprints and tracks. He could hardly tell the difference between his own footprints and those of his illusions. The once placid, flat plane of beautiful moondust had been thoroughly shifted and disrupted. That was all he ever was, the more he thought about it—a disruptive force that seemed to leave messy tracks wherever he went. He also noticed the cold again. He missed the warmth, but not if it meant indulging in mere illusions. True warmth, and a place of true belonging, was nowhere in sight.

He stood and stared, perhaps for too long. The thought of where he should go next crossed his mind, yet the answer remained just as illusive. A near imperceptible warmth caught the edge of his cheek from far away. At first he thought it was the sun, but he noticed it pulling him from a completely different, seemingly random direction. With nothing else to go off of, the jester finally lifted himself off the lunar ground, taking great care to not disturb the peaceful planet's surface anymore. He slowly stretched his arms forth, and in a puff of smoke, his cloak formed into a comfortable black orb for him to rest in. He closed his eyes and set forth toward the tiny warmth in the distance.

PART 6

UHDIN

CHAPTER 34

Hello, wanderer…

A NEW VOICE PIERCED THE DARKNESS. He felt as if his body had fully adapted to torpor, and it was easier to sit for a moment and relish the quiet.

I am sorry, Cynkz, but I must awaken you.
I only need you for a moment.

Cynkz… Ah, that's my name… His mind shifted from his own thoughts to that of the voice in the darkness. It was old and gruff sounding, and also sad, yet surprisingly light in tone. It was the sound of an old relative, one who had experienced such atrocities that he never shared with anyone else, and covered the trauma with a thin veneer of joviality. It was the sound of a piece of metal equipment that, for all intents and purposes, worked perfectly fine, yet it grinded and scraped with a weary, tinny frailty that exposed its true nature. Despite its affable sounding nature, there was an undeniable sorrow that supported its tone. It was somehow sweet and sad, all at once.

Cynkz picked himself up, his stiff neck creaking like old wood as he lifted himself from his black cocoon. A puff of smoke, and the obsidian orb was gone, exposing the jester to the stars and their light. He had apparently drifted close to a calm, orange star. It was a shade of orange so bright, it nearly appeared as the reflection one would see on the edge of a gold coin. The star gave off a thick warmth, as if the arm of a loving friend had wrapped itself around him, and refused to let go. Cynkz found himself drifting in the infinity of space, yet felt as if he were being held, or even coddled.

I only meant to take a short nap... Perhaps I was out for longer than I intended... Cynkz thought, stretching thoroughly and quickly scratching his head as he did so.

"You were asleep for quite some time," the voice said, now speaking in a more easily perceptible form. "I meant to get you here sooner, but I have grown old and weary, and without Omundisia, it took some effort and time to bring you here as quickly as I did."

Cynkz had grown used to his mind and thoughts being exposed, though it always seemed to come with at least a tinge of discomfort. This was perhaps the first time that the effect was soothing, even welcoming. As his eyes finally adjusted, he noticed that the star speaking to him was actually quite dim, at least compared to every other Omun he had seen up close. Though a dim Omun was still blinding, forcing the jester to at least squint as he attempted to face the celestial entity reasonably.

The voice continued: "I have heard much about you, dear jester. Your exploits have reached to the far corners of the universe—an impressive feat, considering its scale represents infinity itself."

Cynkz finally gathered himself, took in a deep breath, and spoke: "A pleasure to meet you, dear Omun. I feared I may have drifted into some nova or other such celestial hazard after sleeping for so long. I appreciate waking up in your warm embrace. Erm, what should I call you?"

"I am Guronimhal. Though most simply call me Guro."

"Guro! I know of you! You are currently the eldest of all living Omun! The others, they—ugh…" Cynkz's shock caused a reaction his body was not ready for. He could feel his tired bones stretching and creaking in ways they were not ready for yet. He quickly felt a sharp pain in his back and reached to rub it, though it did little good.

"Ah, my apologies, Cynkz," Guro said. "Here, give me just a moment to help you."

The light reached forth, and the universe went white. It was only for a moment, but it was enough to consume Cynkz entirely. An undeniable warmth welled up from within, and oozed out from every pore. A final deep breath rejuvenated him, and he was healed.

"Thank you very much, Guro!" He didn't mean to yell, but Cynkz's excitement got to him. It felt good to be moving again.

"It is the least I can do, especially considering what I am about to ask of you…"

"If you have truly heard about me," Cynkz said, looking down, as if in shame, "then you know I may have made a huge mistake during my latest venture. I do not know if I am fit to help any more worlds."

"I know of your transgression, and I do not care," Guro said, his voice now adopting a more stern tone, weighty and authoritative.

"Truly? Do you not fear that I may bring upon the Creator's wrath by accident?" Cynkz said.

"What difference would that make to me? I am on the verge of death—true death. We Omun do not reform in an afterlife, the way mortals do. Our consciousness, as well as our bodies, split and scatter to add to the mass that constitutes the rest of the universe. I am on the verge of this very process."

"I see… How much time do you believe you have left?" Cynkz asked.

"I'm not entirely sure, though not long. We Omun, we possess incredibly powerful cores, of such weight and density that they could destroy worlds by their mere presence. Such a burden is easy to bear, when young and full of life, when your fire burns bright and energy seems to flow through you without a second thought. This energy is needed, to keep flowing, to keep moving, in order to maintain itself. Even we Omun do not possess unending energy. With every passing moment I can… I can feel it slipping away… I am forced to sit and watch as the remaining few traces of life disappear into nothing, spreading into the void. But that is not what truly bothers me…"

The Omun paused, as if ruminating over something. Eventually Cynkz grew curious, and worried. "What is it, great Omun? What more could trouble you?"

"It is my people, the poor souls I watch over even now, of the planet Uhdin. When I am gone, they will certainly perish. If I had to guess, I may only have a few thousand years of life left. And my dear children, the uhd… I dare not even attempt to imagine the terror they will face as they are brought to an abrupt, violent end, forced to wither away in cold and darkness… as they are forced to accept extinction…"

"Is… Is there anything I could do? Is there any way to delay this fate? At least until I can perhaps find the Creator? Perhaps I can in fact bargain with Him and—"

"Cynkz… Death is a natural part of life. All things must reach their eventual end. We Omun, we possess such vast amounts of energy, of matter, stardust—the very building blocks of the universe. It is not fair for any one of us to hoard such things. As much as I dread my inevitable destruction, I understand its purpose, and understand that it is necessary for future worlds, future Omun, and future life to be given a chance to be born. I doubt that you would be able to bargain for that to change."

Cynkz sighed, looking down in defeat. He looked at the many stars filling the void, their distances impossible, the space between them all incalculable. He wondered how many of those stars were Omun, and how many feared this same scenario. He was fortunate, then, that his immortal soul allowed him to persist. He was dead, but still ultimately free to move about and express his will. The Omun bore a heavy burden, indeed.

Cynkz lifted his head, flared his cloak, and did his best not to fall too deep into melancholy. "What can I do for you, then? How can I help you? Is there some giant monster I need to deal with? Some natural calamity threatening to tear the continents apart?"

Guro laughed heartily, in a way that reminded him of Jio-Mol's trademark boisterousness. "No, no, nothing so dire or urgent, thank the Creator. Though my time is limited, I want to make the most of every moment, I want my people to have every possible moment to live and be free, to enjoy what time they have left. In my old age, bursts of my remaining life force shoots forth. These flares are beyond my control, and they whip out violently into the abyss. Worse still, these flares, these wild strings of solar energy, can cause such damage to the worlds they come into contact with. Look to your left, far into the distance, if you will."

Cynkz turned, and saw several planetoid masses spread far apart. A few were crumbling, though one stood out—a small red and gray orb that sat not too far away from a nearby turquoise planet.

Guro continued: "That is the last of Uhdin's moons—Irros. Those red streaks you see swimming across its surface are not natural, they are the result of my flares whipping the planet over the centuries. There were other moons, but… they eventually crumbled, and many of their fragments flew to Uhdin. Most burned up in the planet's atmosphere, but some did not. Such meteor showers have been the source of much prophesying, and many stories, for my people. They have watched my light shift in hue over generations, and that too has been the source of many ominous tales and prophecies. I never wanted to see them suffer, and I wished that they did not have to worry about such things, especially in their final hour."

"How dreadful…" Cynkz turned back around to face Guro. "I am sorry, Guronimhal."

"It is fine, Cynkz. But now, I offer you a proposition—you may stay in my world for as long as you please, if you will answer my call before the next flare up. I fear it may be the final flare, and the worst yet. I will summon you sometime within the next couple hundred years or so, and we will deal with it then. For now you may rest, and do as you please."

Another world… Another death of a planet… Cynkz couldn't help but think of his own world. He thought of the po, and wondered what went through their minds as they witnessed their end. He remembered Pairne's personal account of it all, and how a frightening, blinding light had merely taken them. He wasn't sure if he could handle seeing it happen. At least he didn't have to experience Peara's destruction firsthand. Could he handle growing attached to another planet, just to see them destroyed? Cynkz knew he couldn't handle it, but even more painful would be leaving them, and Guro, to suffer completely, and alone. He never abandoned the po in Munderworld or Potarium, and there was no reason for him to abandon the uhd, or Guro. Even if all he could do was lessen the pain, for just a moment, that was something, at least.

"Will you do it?" Guro asked. "I fully understand your trepidation, and no one would blame you for turning your back to us. You have done so much already, and thanklessly, I might add—"

"I will do it." Cynkz spoke with such resolution that even the star he spoke to heeded his authority. The jester had made up his mind, and there was no use in pretending that any other choice mattered.

"So be it," Guro uttered. He sounded sad, as if pitying the need for one as highborn as he, a celestial being, had been humbled, now on the verge of begging a mortal for help. Cynkz knew that Guro knew that the jester did not think any less of the celestial, but the feelings of shame remained. Cynkz too shared in this shame, knowing that whatever help he provided would not prevent Uhdin's ultimate fate. But it was all they could do, for the time being.

"What can you tell me about Udhin? I suppose I should learn as much about your world before I take residence there," Cynkz said.

"Uhdin is… a peaceful world. Its people are peaceful, they are… these little, wonderful balls of blue quills, that swim through the air and glide through water. The water is thick, the air is crisp and cool, the trees bend and stretch and wind in all sorts of directions, weaving harmoniously through rivers and mountains, bridging nearly every element of nature together. Well, everything except for the clouds, which seem to always be just out of reach. The clouds themselves are light and wispy, like streams of colored cream diffused over a broad, blue canvas. The sky is constantly filled with these fast moving, waving clouds, and they often filter my light in ways that even now continue to surprise me. The shadows themselves cover the world in many light colors and hues. No two days look the same on Uhdin. The uhds have been content with this world for eons, and live only to hunt and bask in nature's glory. They are simple people, with very short lifespans, and thrive on familial bonds. They undergo intense pair bonding. They have spread all over the world, and their populations have filled out nearly every continent."

"It sounds lovely," Cynkz said. "Though… I imagine that there are at least a few who do not get along with everyone else? Every family has its black sheep, after all."

"Yes, well… You are not wrong…" Guro seemed to hesitate. Though Cynkz noticed the occasional flick and twinkle of his light from the star's edges. "I know where you could begin, dear jester. There is one uhd, a young hunter named Ferin who is estranged from his family. Perhaps you could befriend him? Lead him down a better path, one where he freely socializes with others of his kind? Who knows, he may very well start a family of his own eventually."

"That will do," Cynkz said. "You can send me now, if you wish—"

"Wait, just one more thing. My power wanes, but I am still a capable Omun. I could give you a glimpse of Potarium? I know it has been some time since you have last seen it."

"I…" Cynkz paused, and lowered his head, shielding his eyes from Guro's light. His curiosity burned nearly as bright as the star in front of him, but he was just as worried. If Potarium had truly forgotten about him, how painful would it be to see it? Though it was just as painful to remain ignorant, to constantly wonder what the answer to that question was. Perhaps, even if his worst fears came true, at least he would have some closure.

"I do not think they have forgotten you, Cynkz," Guro said.

Cynkz looked up, eyes wide and nearly burning as he stared at the star. He finally squinted and smiled, slightly covering his face from the bright light speaking to him. "If that is true, then I have to see it. Please, Guro, let me see Potarium, just one more time."

"Very well. Calm your mind, and I will show you as much as I can."

Cynkz closed his eyes, yet Guro's light only grew brighter, piercing the darkness. All became white, and Cynkz's mind now looked over a familiar landscape. The great marbled sky took up most of his view, as well as a golden tower reaching up from beneath it at the center of a massive, pearly city. The golden tower—or the Hand of Po, as he remembered it being called—seemed larger and more ostentatious than ever. When before it was little more than a massive, golden brick, it now stood as a more appropriate symbol regarding its name. Its shape was smoother, and rounder, and its once blank golden walls now held countless waving curves and lines instilled in its sides, each a small crevice that made use of the harsh shadows provided by the light beaming down from the marbled orb in the sky. They were presumably written huums, and Cynkz wondered if they too sang sweetly in the passing wind. It was undoubtedly Potarium, the same city he once knew, though a number of things had changed.

The city now possessed a number of manmade rivers and lakes, with constant streams of glistening dark water from the ocean itself. Towering structures were neatly placed at key locations across the city, giant aqueducts acting as bridges for the city's water. There were more gardens, and even a number of gigantic waterfalls that poured even more water down into meticulously crafted and winding canals that led much of the water back to the ocean. There were many more trees, with leaves mimicking the trademark golden grass and leaves that shimmered like starlight as they waved in the wind. These trees covered much of the city, giving an almost cozy atmosphere to the once wide open streets. Cynkz wondered if they still held parades the way they used to. Surely some of the trees would get in the way of their attractions?

Something else that caught his eye was how much taller many of the buildings were. When he was last there, it was easy to sit at nearly any point in the mountain city and get a good view down and toward the ocean, with nothing other than the handful of giant holy flags to obstruct one's view. Many great pillars, expressing all manner of colors and shapes and twisting golden and pearl filigree, now stood out from the city and high above many of the trees littering Potarium's streets. Many of these buildings had spaces set specifically on top for po to travel to and gather, to get an even better look than Cynkz ever could from the ground. Most of these colorful buildings possessed hanging gardens, which provided countless flowers and nests for the many hummingbirds that still flew through the air, coloring the otherwise bright white sky with a variety of hues. Farther down the city and on its coast, Cynkz noticed a number of watermills channeling even more water throughout the city, as well as many po still manning the ships and others still tending to these new structures. The docks themselves were practically drab in comparison to Cynkz's memory of them. The place seemed livelier than ever now.

Cynkz noticed the puppets in the city, many of whom were being moved around and seemed to be making a number of the po laugh and cheer. It was surprising, considering the incident he and Fiddle caused. He would not have been surprised if the po never wanted anything to do with them again.

Except the puppets were moving of their own volition! And in fact appeared more lifelike than ever, and seemed to look considerably like imps.

Wait! Those are imps! The thought pierced his mind, and things became more clear. Countless little red and scruffy bodies flew about the city, in and out of trees and back and forth between rooftops. Many of them would even gather together to carry po and glide them across the cityscape. The po and imps were actually getting along quite well. Fiddle seemed to be doing a good job making sure everyone got along, imp and po alike. Cynkz couldn't help but be proud of his old friend.

There were many statues that now decorated the streets, at least what streets Cynkz could see from the bird's-eye view his mind was giving him. His mind ventured down, as if following these lines of statues, each one depicting all manner of po and knight and warrior and even imps carrying works of art and pottery followed by carved trails of silk and robes. His mind's eye brought him back to the golden tower's main entrance, as well as a new entrance just beneath it that led to a wide set of stairs leading deep underground. Cynkz thought he had once joked about growing tired of descending into darkness, but curiosity overpowered all in his mind, and in the tunnel he went. It wasn't long before the reflective light from above, seeping in from many meticulously laid cracks in the underground's ceiling began to reveal the way. The wide steps went far down into the darkness, and possessed shining, golden rails with countless branches and leaves hanging off of them. The sound and smell of fresh water brushing past began to fill the air, and more waterfalls could be seen in the distance. An elaborate, underground grove possessing all manner of plant and tree and docile animals and fruit and vegetation decorated the grassy interior, whose walls were lined with even more waterfalls that disappeared into the dark ceiling above. Strangely, there were no statues, save for one—a giant, golden structure that seemed to sit at the center of the grove. Many po could be seen going back and forth, and one po walking up the stairs, chatting with a group of nobles and holy men caught Cynkz's eye.

Kadd! Indeed, it was his old friend, his smooth tan skin contrasting against his bright wide smile as he relayed jokes to the others following close behind him. There was no time to stop however, and soon the violet robed po and his entourage disappeared up the steps, while Cynkz continued down.

The great statue sitting in the center of the grove was surrounded by tinsel weed, and many feathers from the rainbowed hummingbirds as they moved to and fro. A single po woman and an odd looking, short and hunched man sat at the base of the statue. Each of them were looking up at the statue as they spoke. The woman was instantly recognizable—it was none other than Pairne, wearing a shining dress of her own, silvery in color and lined with crimson huums sewn into every available space. The short, hunched man next to her was more difficult to parse. He wore blackish-purplish robes, and was nearly covered from head to toe. He appeared to be speaking with Pairne, and whatever they were discussing seemed to amuse her to no end, as she wore a perpetual smile on her face, only occasionally covering it up with a light hand to excuse her laughter. It was good to see that she was enjoying her time.

Cynkz looked up to the statue, and was at once bewildered, and embarrassed, at what he saw. It was a towering structure that at first appeared to be gold, but upon viewing up close and from a different angle, was actually a strange, pitch black material that reflected the light perfectly, giving the structure its initial golden hue. It depicted a lithe figure, adorned in a long, flowing cloak that spread out and around his form like great wings. His sharp features compliments his sharp and pointed cap, and a square jaw nearly pointed down, leading the eye naturally to his impressive musculature, which was defined well enough that it cut harsh lines in the shadow of the cloak. He looked down at something, a smaller figure—a compact, yet equally muscular imp whose fur was smooth and shot back and out, almost creating a majestic mane that flowed past two long, beautifully curved and pointed ears. He looked positively noble, reaching up as if not toward the jester, but something greater, higher even. The imp possessed a somewhat forlorn look in his slightly squinted eyes, as if possessing some greater burden that he was hesitant to bear, but knew he must.

If not for his current, incorporeal state within a vision, he would have instantly thrown his face into his palm, to hide from the shame. Though a small part of him felt tickled, and he couldn't help but chuckle at the absurdity of the construction.

His eyes went back to the woman and the cloaked man, still laughing and talking in the garden's heavenly light. Something about the man was interesting. A key feature of Potarium was its healing waters. The time a wayward po would spend drifting through a haze as the dark ocean's waters pulled them to the heavenly city's shores was meant to act as a sort of healing baptism. How and why would a po remain in such a wretched state? Surely, if the healing waters are meant to rejuvenate po, bringing them to their physical peak, it would not leave any poor soul to hobble around like an old crone with a bad back?

Except… the man's humped back seemed to flutter beneath its cloak ever so slightly. Upon further viewing, an unnaturally long nose poked forth, and inhumanly sharp and yellow teeth glowed from a partially hidden smile. The man reached out, and elongated, black nails glistened in the light from the digits of a reddish-brown hand, an unusually hairy hand that appeared more like fur than anything.

By the Creator… Is… Is that Fiddle?!

It was, without doubt. A final flick of the short man's gestures revealed two comically tiny black wings fluttering from his back. His posture was still poor, but not so much from a hunched back as it was his wings poking out from behind him. Fiddle had indeed grown. Cynkz had known the imp for some time. Fiddle did mention that he was the eldest imp, though Cynkz merely thought that it was the imp making up something to brag about. Was it something to do with Potarium's waters? Did it also have an effect on the imps as well? The effects of the waters did take a long time, and perhaps the imps needed an exceptionally long time to grow. Cynkz thought back to the moon where he confronted the illusions. The illusion of Fiddle mentioned something about "being small again." How would Cynkz know that? He was certain it was merely an illusion of his creation, but he had no idea of Fiddle's current state. Did he now possess some ability for clairvoyance? Cynkz was part Omun after all, so it would not be unheard of.

He had seen enough. Cynkz decided that he didn't want to spend too much time in his own mind, ruminating on things he could never find the answer to. He closed his mind's eye, and with a deep breath, he returned to darkness. A long, soothing exhale brought Cynkz back to the great orange star in the cosmos.

"It appears your people are doing well," Guro said.

"Yes, yes they are..." Cynkz scratched his chin, then looked ahead. "Thank you, Guro, truly. You have done a great favor for me."

"Think nothing of it, great wanderer," Guro said. "If you are ready, I will send you to Uhdin. If you wish, you may seek out Ferin, and assist him."

Cynkz smiled, flared his cloak, and gave a final bow. A bright flash reached forth, and the jester was gone, and the cosmos returned to silence.

CHAPTER 35

TIME FLEW BY ON UHDIN, AS IT SEEMED to do everywhere else.

Cynkz still had trouble maintaining his perception of the present. Time went by so quickly that he would often stop whatever he was doing to try and reminisce on recent events. Fortunately for him, there was no great or urgent dilemma troubling the world, and it was easy to find time to get away from it all to think back on his time on the alien world:

It felt nice to arrive at a new and peaceful world, without any greater calamity threatening it, or its people. It meant I could take my time, and fully appreciate a new world in a way I rarely could.

I was grateful to be blessed with the gift of flight, or else I might have been forced to spend the majority of my time on Uhdin climbing desperately along the many winding trees and struggling through thick, syrupy rivers. Guro's description of the strange world was not misleading in the least.

I still worried about my perception of time. The present still moved far too quickly for my liking, but, if nothing else, I was still fully capable of remembering the past, even if I did not necessarily remember experiencing it.

I still remembered my first meeting with an uhdinian.

To the unfamiliar eye, he was little different from most other uhdinians. He was a small bundle of dull blue quills. Not much stood out, save for the poking out of a stubby snout and large, round eyes that shifted between a deep brown and milky white depending on how the light shifted upon them. He possessed the usual thin, ropy limbs that hardly stood out from his quills when at rest, but made their presence clear when moving, When uhdinians wished to move quickly, either as the climbed a tree, or cut through the thick water, or made use of hidden flaps of skin to glide through the air, their quills would pull in and back, giving them an attractive, streamlined look. Despite the creatures being no larger than an average child po's hand, they moved quickly, and could cover large distances in a short time, and Ferin was no different.

The most impressive feat was their ability to utilize their quills as disposable weapons. They could pluck them to use as makeshift knives, or flex them to dig into the ground or aid in climbing otherwise slick surfaces, or even use them as arrows for their well crafted bows. They were excellent hunters, and once again Ferin was not unique in this aspect.

Unfortunately, Ferin was young and impatient, and would make mistakes when hunting. He had apparently made enough mistakes to be banished from his tribe. His youth and good health allowed him to enjoy this time alone, but it could not last forever. He, like all living things, would eventually grow old and weak, and suffer a quick and unmerciful end at nature's hand if he continued as he did. Worse still, he would do so alone, with neither friends nor family to give comfort. Sometimes this was just the way life ended, and nature took no prisoners. Though Guro hated to see this play out every time it did. It was especially tragic to see someone so young be so at peace with such an end.

It was easy enough to track him, to disguise myself as one of them, and to offer my aid. Eventually he learned to sit still and be patient, and his hunting prowess improved tenfold. A few tricks and plays later, and his tribe was given an opportunity to witness his skill, and he was welcomed back with open arms. I even witnessed Ferin as he found a mate, a female uhdinian named Nura.

That was nearly 200 years ago, and yet I could recall it as if it just happened moments ago, as if I watched another's experience of it. I could still remember the smell of sweet water running beneath our feet, and the flaky bark that split beneath our claws as we worked together. I watched him grow old, settle down, and pass away in a humble little hut on the edge of his village. I remembered the feeling of urgency as I had to constantly change my disguise to not give away my alien origin, adopting new uhdinian forms of different ages to replicate their aging.

It felt as if I needed to change my disguise nearly every day. Uhdinians have tragically short lifespans. I decided to keep an eye on Ferin's family. It was the least I could do, acting as a sort of guardian angel for them. It was easy enough to adopt new disguises, and to come in at opportune moments to become a family friend. The hardest part *was coming up with new names for each new disguise—Sinx, Rinx, Hinx, Tinx, I eventually had to get creative and began to just make names up. Darrin, Gehler, Velios, Zutrin. I eventually grew tired of that too, and just settled on my original name, which appeared to be just as odd here as it is with my own people. I suppose some things are just destined to be.*

Whenever I took a moment to gather myself, and to recollect on my fondest memories on Uhdin, it seemed as if it was with a new generation.

In a way it was nice, as I was granted many opportunities to babysit young uhdinians, a task that I grew particularly fond of. Being surrounded by a large gathering of uhds, young and old alike, all huddled together and snoring the night away… I was often reminded of the warm huums the good po of Potarium often shared. It even had a similar effect of causing me to tear up at the most inopportune of times. It was a similarly loving warmth that staved off even the coldest of nights.

I mostly made a living teaching other young uhdinians how to hunt. This was a skill I learned from watching Ferin. He was a harsh critic, but I am grateful he was. It made my own teachings easier to communicate. Though I could never bring myself to be quite as… abrasive as he could be.

Whenever I needed a break, I would disguise myself as an uhd with a peg leg, or a scarred eye, or some other disability. Normally such deception would bother me, but getting a generation or two to sit back and rest felt nice. With the extra free time, I would mess around with various tools and crafts. Uhdinians were indeed a very simple people, and anything that was not directly related to hunting was necessarily crude—doors, stairs, wheels and containers, even their very homes were shambly at best, though they made good use of the many large and winding tree trunks. There was plenty of space for everyone. Though even simple concepts, such as levers and pivots, were beyond most uhdinians. The children were quick learners, however, and would often ask what I was doing, and pick up on things rather quickly. Over time my crafts and ideas began to spread, it seemed, and it was not long before other uhdinians, both young and old, began to experiment with the concepts. It was all very impressive to see.

These basic advancements made it easier for them to lift and move materials, allowing them to build higher into the trees. They began to build crude watermills and windmills, which were mostly used for simple things such as moving and filtering water, or rotating wooden sifters that would parse the many grains and small foodstuffs they would store. These advancements took generations to actualize, but to me it seemed to happen overnight. It was bewildering to say the least. If nothing else, I was grateful that I could have a positive impact on a world without having to face some giant monster, or go trudging through some volcanic wasteland, or having to argue with royal families or deal with some mad despot.

Ferin's family had grown very large, very quickly. Despite his importance, his name was all but forgotten a mere five generations or so down the line. I still remember the looks of confusion and bewilderment the last time I brought him up. The fact that none of them knew who I was talking about was a shock, to say the least. I was grateful that Fiddle, and Kadd, and Pairne had at least remembered me.

As time passed, and Ferin's family grew, so too did stories about the sun. Stories of the sun's changing color and occasional flares had been passed down through the ages. Apparently the sun had once been a bright, lime green color, then slowly shifted to a pale yellow, and eventually settled on its now dull (if pleasing, at least in my opinion) orange shade. Most saw it as an omen, a sign of the end times. I hated to see these stories being shared with the children. Try as I might to assuage their fears, they always persisted, even until their final breath. I made it my personal mission to deter the other adults from sharing such stories. I did not care if it was a tradition of theirs, I hated to see the young uhdinians wrought with fear that would continue through their entire short lives.

Something that helped was to watch Uhdin's last remaining moon, Irros, late at night. Sometimes when the moon was full, and several of the fragments of other long lost moons were visible, their combined, reflected light would cover the usual crystal blue nights with a warm, pale sheen caught between green and gold. It was fun to sit out late at night and share stories with the family, listening to them all speculate as to how and why the moon did what it did.

It was around the ninth generation that I noticed I had completely lost track of time. I did not mind, however. I figured that when Guro needed me, he would call, and there was no use worrying about it. Though I know I should perhaps be distancing myself from this family, considering my final duty may leave me unable to return. Should I be growing so attached to a people whom I know I might need to leave behind?

Even now, this ninth and largest generation… I knew everyone by name.

For instance, there was grandpa Eein, a seventh generation descendant of Ferin. He was quite cranky, and possessed Ferin's temper and impatience, though he softened up quite a bit when around his wife, grandma Liyalin. She was the best chef in the family, and the first uhdinian the children would run to for hugs at any gathering.

There was Ser, Eein's son. He was quite strict, much like Ferin was, but acted as a sort of bedrock for the family. Whenever there was trouble, and I was not around, he usually stepped up to deal with whatever the problem was. There was his wife, Kailt, who wanted as many children as possible. Even now she believes her half dozen is not enough.

There was Pater, Ser's half brother, who had long since moved out of the main tribe to settle his own village. He wanted to build a large home for his wife, Ehl. The two argued frequently about the move, but she softened up to the idea once they began having children of their own.

Gatty, Judin, and Mono—Pater and Ehl's three children. Gatty was the oldest, and often fought with Mono, the youngest. Judin, being the only daughter, would often butt in and mediate between the two. Ehl found it adorable, and would often share stories with Cynkz concerning the trio working out their problems with little debates and conversations. Uhdinians squeaked a lot when flustered, and this quirk was only exacerbated by the young ones who would do it excessively. It was cute, if a bit grating at times.

An interesting fact I learned was the origin of Mono's name. Apparently it is an old uhdinian word that translate to "sun" or "old sun."

Oh! Ser and Kailt's children, how could I forget?

They had many children, and even I struggled to keep track of them all.

Ora, the eldest daughter and first born. She seemed to like cooking, though Kailt often wondered if she was just copying her mother and grandmother.

Uhl, the second born and eldest son. He loved to fight and hunt, and was actually a bit of a bully until Ser set him straight.

Til, the third born. He loved to break things apart. Ser has tried to get him interested in building, but he only seems to care for destruction. Kailt is not too worried about it, however, thinking it merely a phase.

Beahil, the fourth born. She was born underweight, and is still rather thin for her age. She also took a while to speak. Kailt dotes on her often, and I often come over to make sure she is eating well and exercising regularly.

Vad, the fifth born. He looks up to Uhl and Ser with such reverence. He wants so greatly to be a "big and strong hunter" like them. Ser was much more strict with Uhl after Vad was born, not wanting him to be a bad influence.

Ihd, the sixth born. Many considered her the cutest of the bunch, save for their final child. She had just barely started to grow out of her baby coat, so she still looked quite fluffy in comparison to the others. She constantly followed Vad and Beahil around, much to their dismay.

Finally there was Han, still an infant and a source of infinite amusement to Ihd. Ihd would sit close by and watch Kailt nurse the infant, constantly asking questions about the infant, where he came from, and why he had yet to begin speaking. Poor Kailt would get so exhausted that I wwould have to intervene and practically drag Ihd away so she could get a moment of peace.

Speaking of which, Kailt's brother—Quio—also had a child. Quio used to despise Ser, and before either of them had children they would fight often. Kailt would ask me to intervene regularly, and I did, not wanting anyone to get hurt. The two seemed to calm down once they became fathers.

Kahrn, Quio's wife, had many health problems. She was an old friend of Ehl, Pater's wife, and a friendly acquaintance of Kailt. Kahrn never thought she would have children, but she and Quio managed to have one. Miraculously, the birth went well, and their child exhibited no serious health issues of her own. I was even present when Kahrn gave birth. Needless to say, the process was no less uncomfortable for uhdinians than it was for po. I was grateful that I did not have to bear that burden, at least.

Quio and Kahrn actually gave me the honor of coming up with a name for their daughter! I was shocked. It was never something I thought I would be in a position to do. For as much as I have experienced, this one stands out to me above all others. I wracked my brain trying to think of something, but an old bit of uhdinian trivia came to mind, and I found the perfect name—Poro, ancient uhdinian word for "little star." Thankfully, Quio and Kahrn loved it.

I never learned the old uhd language, not fully, but many of its terms were short and simple, like many good things. I always enjoyed that.

Slowly, over time, and as my most recent disguise "grew older," much of my time began to focus on Poro. She was a tiny thing, and took a long time to begin speaking. This, in combination with her being an only child, meant that she had fewer opportunities to socialize. She was quite shy and reserved, and struggled to convey her feelings. It never bothered me, though. It just required a bit of patience.

She would eventually get her point across well enough. I made sure that every conversation of ours ended with her laughing, or at least smiling. Some would say children were simple, and that making them smile was easy. It was not so much simplicity, as it was purity, in my opinion, that made them what they were. I would love nothing more than to be able to share such experiences with the other po. I wondered how long the good po of Potarium have gone without experiencing a child's joy?

I knew that Guro would summon me soon. I knew that I might very well never come back. I only hoped that Poro would forgive me for leaving…

A pale, golden moon watched over the family tree. All were sound asleep, save for a single, dark blue bundle of quills who sat atop a thick, dark bundle of winding tree trunks and branches that formed an alcove high above. From within it was easy to forget that the ground even existed. From within, a clear, open view of the shining moon beaming against a dark, star-filled sky was all there was.

The stargazer was particularly fond of this spot. The uhdinians had learned to carve deep, thin canals in the many thick trunks, allowing the river waters to inexplicably run up and through them. There was a constant, soft sound of water brushing past all around. The true purpose of this marvelous little engineering feat was to provide a regular source of water into their homes, like a form of naturalist, primitive plumbing. Though he merely enjoyed the ambience it provided as he did his usual stargazing.

A new sound began to trickle in from below and behind. It was the sound of tiny feet tapping against grainy bark, and leaves rustling as they were pushed aside.

"Uncle Cynkz?" A quiet, mouse-like voice pierced the ambience.

"Poro? It is late. You should be asleep with the others down below."

The little, frayed bundle of quills yawned. Each spike flexed and stretched out as Poro reached up to cover her mouth. She tried to get a good look at Cynkz, but instead instinctively brought her hand up to her squinting eyes to rub them. It was already late, and she more than likely exhausted herself climbing up to the top of the family tree on her own.

"I just wanted to know where you went," Poro mumbled. "I got up to use the bathroom and you weren't huddled with the rest of us."

Cynkz, now looking over his shoulder, smiled warmly. "It is alright, Poro. Want to look at the stars with me?"

Poro yawned again, too tired to do much more than drag herself forward. She dropped down, nearly throwing her head onto Cynkz's lap, though her head remained turned to look up through the opening in the ring of leafy branches above.

"You always sneak away to do this," Poro said. She began to adjust her body, digging her head deeper into Cynkz's thigh and curling up. "Doesn't it get boring?"

Cynkz began to run his sharp nails through the girl's quills. "No, not really."

"I don't see how. Stars are pretty, but they don't do anything."

"Well that is not true, Poro."

"What do they do, then?"

"They tell stories."

"What?" Poro turned her head to look up, her furrowed brow betraying her incredulity. "No they don't. Stars don't talk. They just sit there and twinkle."

"You can tell a story without speaking," Cynkz said. "Stars twinkle when they are trying to tell you something, trying to tell you their stories."

Poro huffed as she turned her attention back to the night sky. "Pfft, sure, sure."

"It is true!" Cynkz had to contain his excitement. Sounds traveled far in the open air on Uhdin, and he didn't want to disturb the rest of the family.

"That's silly. Prove it then."

Cynkz looked up through the leafy opening. It took him a few moments to decide where to begin. He even began to worry if Poro would be asleep by the time he made his decision, but he could tell when she was actually asleep, and when she was pretending. The little uhdinian waited patiently for him, and he finally found the perfect bundle of stars to begin.

"Look there, Poro." Cynkz leaned forward, nearly pressing his arm into the little one's cheek so that his arm would provide a clear line to a spiraling bundle of stars, eleven in total, that spun around twice before trailing off to the east. "Do you know that constellation?"

"Hmm… Maybe…" Poro uttered. She was never good at hiding her anxiety, especially when she didn't know the answer to something. Cynkz found it best to merely lead her to the answer. She was more than capable of pondering its meaning on her own.

Cynkz continued: "That is the Great River Basin. Far to the south on an old continent, many believe that the first uhdinians rose from that basin. They managed to crawl across vast open plains and found refuge in the oldest and largest oaks Uhd has to offer."

"Do the rivers come from the ocean?"

"Well, technically most rivers come from water descending from a high elevation to a lower elevation. Gravity causes water to naturally flow down and into things."

"What does any of that mean?"

"Water drips down from high places to low places. The water collects and moves, forming rivers and lakes."

"Oh."

Oh… Poro would always respond that way to things she sort of understood. She would respond that way when she wanted to move on to something else.

Cynkz slowly moved his arm down and westward. "Look there, see those two stars sort of separated from everything else? They make a single line sort of pointing down?"

"Yep."

"Do you know that one?"

"I know the big one it's a part of."

Cynkz smiled, bringing his arm back down to rest his hand on Poro's head, rubbing some of the softer hairs remaining from her baby coat. "That is the

H'Dah Sh'A. An old, old word meaning 'connection' or 'the great connector.'"

"Pfft, I guess every constellation is a 'great something.'"

"Well I think they are all great. That one in particular is meant to represent how the first uhdinians began to notice how all things connected, how all things came together to form something greater."

"Great, great, greater, great."

Cynkz chuckled, which always made Poro smile, as she did then. Seeing her smile only made Cynkz laugh more, and this cycle would sometimes continue for minutes on end. Poro was too tired at the moment to engage in such frivolities, and merely rested her expression, keeping her gaze forward. She seemed to be anticipating something.

"You know what that constellation is connected to, right, Poro?" Cynkz asked.

"Yeah!" Poro lifted her head slightly as she pointed a tiny claw to another bundle of stars just a bit lower. They began with a single star that connected to five more stars beneath it. "That's the Hand of Dah."

"That's right. Do you know what that one is meant to represent?"

"A hand, duh."

"Well, yes, but…"

Poro chuckled, her warm breath whisking the top of Cynkz's thigh and her head slightly bouncing in his lap.

"The Hand of Dah," Cynkz continued, "is supposed to represent how the old uhdinians began to reach out to one another, and form connections, and establish tribes, and work together. They literally reached out to one another and lifted one another up."

"It sounds pretty great."

"You jest, Poro, but it has remained an important symbol for all uhdinians."

"Exactly, it's a great symbol."

Cynkz couldn't help but laugh along with the young uhdinian, lightly tapping her head as if to mimic chastising her. It only seemed to tickle her as Poro laughed further. Her exhaustion caught up with her eventually and she settled down.

Cynkz took a moment to look around, and settled his eyes on a new bundle of stars, far away from the previous constellations. "Look there, at those five stars forming an x. I know you know that one."

"Uh… nope."

"Poro, I know you know."

"Nope. Please explain."

Cynkz sighed, a playful breath filtering through a soft smile. "That one is part of a family. It represents the father. That single star in the middle is the center, the bedrock, and all the other stars around it connect both to it and each other, forming a stable stone."

"Just like dad."

"Just like dad…"

Cynkz stopped to think about his own father. Even now, Krull sat at the bottom of Munderworld, acting as a sort of bedrock for the abyss. Though he wasn't sure if that was something to be admired.

"How come you never talk about your family?" Poro asked. She asked that often, and Cynkz often answered the same way.

"Because I never got to know them," Cynkz said.

"That's sad," Poro muttered.

"It is alright. Besides, you all have become my family. That is more than enough for me."

"Yeah… What about the mom stars?"

"Well first you have to talk about the stars connecting them." Cynkz slid his arm to the right, pointing at three stars forming an open triangle shape. "That one represents flow—the flow of life, of rivers and water, of the exchange between peoples and the connections we form—"

"Great connections."

"—and just past that, a little farther to the right—those six stars that loop around and end at the bottom—you know that one."

"It's the mother."

"That is right. And you know the star that they end on?"

"The North Star."

"Exactly right—"

"And then there's the baby stars beneath it."

"Well, technically it is called the child—another six stars making two neat little rows that criss-cross—"

"Criss-cross, apple sauce…"

Poro was reaching her limit. Cynkz could always tell, because her breathing would slow down, and her wide eyes would squint, as if she were trying very hard to maintain focus, to keep herself awake, to no avail. Normally she considered her worlds very carefully, but the more tired she became, the more her inhibitions would slip away, leading to her blurting out whatever came to mind. When she was really tired she would begin to merely repeat the last thing she heard.

Cynkz wanted nothing more than for the little one to rest. How much longer would the uhd have? Even if he did help Guro, how much longer could the star persist? Would Poro be forced to her very existence upended within her lifetime? Surely the uhd have their own afterlife, but that is not something that should be forced prematurely upon anyone, least of all the innocent child resting in his lap.

A voice pierced his mind, one he had not heard in centuries, but one he recognized as if he had heard it just yesterday:

It's time, Cynkz.

Cynkz's heart weighed heavily in his chest. He didn't want to disturb Poro, who was on the verge of finally sleeping.

Just a moment, please, dear Guro, Cynkz thought.

The voice replied, his voice as warm as ever:

Of course. When you are ready, come to the sky, and I will summon you.

Cynkz smiled at the stars, then turned his attention back to Poro. She had her thumb claw pressed lightly against her bottom lip. She used to suck her thumb, and did so for quite some time, until one of the other children made fun of her for it. She put in much effort to avoid the habit, but when she was truly tired, and comfortable, she would nearly revert to her old habits.

Cynkz ran his claws softly through her quills once more: "Poro, do you remember the old poem I taught you?"

"Yeah… the one you like to say in old talk?"

"Yes, that one. Can you repeat it for me?"

Poro huffed again, barely able to hold off her exhaustion. "It's just gonna… make me fall asleep."

"You need to sleep, Poro," Cynkz said. "It is late."

Poro sighed, then finally began mumbling beneath her breath. At first her words were little more than slight whimpers and noises, sounds she made to keep herself awake. Eventually her words focused into something concrete:

Eiti poro,
Ni uhn ro,
Wel fur rus,
Ti jus,
Zeeya tuo dascet nuo…

Cynkz smiled, but stayed quiet. Poro's breathing finally slowed, and her thumb dropped from her lips as the side of her palm landed on his thigh. He brushed her quills, slowly, several times more.

"Goodbye, Poro…" Cynkz whispered.

Doing his best to not disturb the little one, Cynkz lifted her head ever so slightly off of his thigh. He pulled himself from beneath her, gathered a neat bundle of leaves, and set her down. He stared for a moment to ensure she was still asleep. He stood himself up, took in a forlorn breath, and drifted off into the night. He couldn't help but notice how much colder the world became the farther he drifted away from Poro. He thought he had gotten used to the cold, but apparently not. It was a bitter chill that slowly ran through his body, and seemed to slow him down the further into the night sky he went. He couldn't even bring himself to look back at Poro, or the alcove, and once he was beyond the clouds, he could justify that there was no reason to look back anymore anyway, and let momentum carry him on.

CHAPTER 36

SOMETHING WAS WRONG.

Cynkz had grown used to being transported by the Omun. Normally it was little more than an instant blip of blinding light that overtook his senses. It was overwhelming, but usually over before one could even notice.

This was different. Cynkz could actually "feel" himself moving through the light. The process seemed delayed, or perhaps slowed down. His senses remained, and a constant, warped pull seemed to drag them all toward something. He could see traces of things moving at his side, out of his way and behind him, at a speed that was nigh incomprehensible. It was as if planets and stars and meteors had been reduced to dust, mere black specks smearing quick streaks across a pale void. The shadow of something massive looming ahead caught his attention. He was fast approaching Guro, and he worried he may soon be thrust into the star! Cynkz gasped, his shock cutting the void with a piercing echo that seemed to get Guro's attention. Within moments, everything stopped, and the familiar darkness of space filtered into view. Cynkz sat, stunned, sitting in some indeterminate space between Uhdin and Guro.

Cynkz... I-I am sorry... I can hardly... ugh...

"It is alright, Guro," Cynkz said. "How are you feeling?"

I feel better, now that you are here, but... ah!

Something whirled in the distance, a great stream rising like the arm of a titan from behind the star. It burned a harsh line in the cosmos, and flung itself forward! It was so fast that there wasn't even time to think—only instinct and reflex saved him as he darted to the side, barely missing the heated stream. Another warmth caught his back, and again his body acted before his mind as he missed several more streams. The assault finally ceased, and he took a moment to breathe and gather his bearings. He looked back to the star to see its silhouette—a once perfectly round and shining sphere—now a mess of chaotic lines and threads fraying at their edges in all directions. While Guro maintained his usual pale orange sheen at his center, every edge now glistened a sickening reddish color, like veins which had just ejected blood. He thought he could hear the star's faint breathing, as if his lungs, if he had any, were struggling to keep up.

This may be the end, Cynkz... I can hardly maintain my form. My power wanes. And my people... they may be rendered to darkness soon...

"Guro, please! Just hang on for as long as you can! I will help. I will do whatever I can to ease the pain, or look after Uhdin. I would transform into an Omun myself, if need be."

Ha! Haha… Heh… I appreciate the sentiment, Cynkz, but I know that, as great as your shifting ability is, that it has limits. That you have limits, and it has been unfair of us all—even Paithos—to put so much onto your shoulders.

"I do not care about any of that, Guro. You need help, Uhdin needs help. We need to find a way to—"

Cynkz… It is fine… I merely ask this final favor of you. Please… intervene if any of my streams, my flares, would assault Uhdin. I may not perish immediately after this, and Uhdin may at least be granted a few more sunrises.

Cynkz gazed at the star, perhaps for a moment too long, long enough for his eyes to begin hurting. He thought of everything he had done thus far, and how he felt no closer to achieving his goal of bringing back the Creator's guidance. What more could he have done? How else could he have gotten His attention? If he had played his cards differently, would Paithos be here now, perhaps ready and able to assist the poor star? If Cynkz could at least talk to Paithos, maybe he could bargain with Him. Though he couldn't help but think of the last time he tried to merely get different parties to "talk" with one another, as he remembered his frustration with the storns and ptomeras of Ozairos. He wondered if that may have set him back in some way, if what transpired on that world would haunt him forever.

You must learn to stop blaming yourself, Cynkz…

Cynkz perked up, eyes wide and taking in the full glory of Guro's light. Every now and then he would forget that the stars were privy to his thoughts, and his feelings.

One mistake does not make a man. Neither does two, or three, or a million more. We all could do better, and it is in that striving for something greater that we become better, that we become good. You are more than worthy, Cynkz. None may take that away from you— not po, not Omun, not even Paithos.

A familiar warmth welled up inside Cynkz. It was the same feeling of warm honey filling up from bottom to top that he experienced in Potarium. The same warmth he felt as he huddled around the children who slept so peacefully at night on Uhdin. The same feeling that forced his eyes to tear up, just enough that the droplets would seemingly move on their own, drifting away from the warmth of his body to crystallize in space, and eventually fade into nothing, as if they were brittle diamonds melting into snow.

There was little time to ponder such things. As Guro gruffed and groaned, more flares began to shoot up and out from his core. Molten threads flew all around. Most merely disappeared into the far reaches of the galaxy, though a few flew frighteningly close to Cynkz. One stream seemed to hurl itself past his left side, slower and weightier than the others. It cut a harsh line right toward Irros, Uhdin's final moon, and broke in two as it came into contact with the planet. Irros has a thin atmosphere, almost unnoticeable, but it was there, and it reacted in kind as a bright red streak bore into the planet's surface, scarring the small gray orb with another mark.

Cynkz was awestruck. It was the first time he had witnessed such a level of devastation. He had witnessed storms and eruptions and earthquakes, he had witnessed wars and armies, but never anything on a planetary scale. It was almost impossible to even comprehend it, as it was so overwhelming. His sharp eyes quickly shifted over to Uhdin, the still peaceful little blue ball spinning by itself in space. He could see the faint outlines of the many continents on the planet. He could see precisely which one he had spent most of his time on, where Poro still lived. Guro's light was shining brightly over the continent. It must have been early morning, wherever Poro was at that moment.

I wonder if she is at least having a good day...

A rattled gurgling sound rumbled from behind. Rather than phlegm and flesh, it sounded more of stone and fire crashing against itself. Guro was having a fit, doing everything he could to maintain himself, but to no avail. Another violent cough led to a burst of light that ejected forward, and straight for Uhdin. Cynkz, again only keeping speed through instinct, without thought, spun himself around. With a flick of his wrist, a massive burst of colorless smoke exploded forth, revealing something long, shining and scaly, reaching out to block the radiated light. The maneuver was successful, but the pain was undeniable. It was enough to force Cynkz to immediately recoil his transformed limb back into smoke. The overwhelming burn now scarring his arm pulsed violently in the freezing vacuum of space. It was as if a thousand needles had been thrown into his arm, as if a million tiny, wet fangs had found their way into his flesh. He was tempted to rub the burns with his other hand, only to stop himself at the last moment, realizing it would only make the sensation worse. He could sense that Guro was calming down, and had something to say.

*For—... Forgive me, Cynkz... I never
wanted to hurt... anyone...*

"I-It is fine, Guro—"

Before Cynkz could finish, Guro flared up once again, heaving in uncontrolled outbursts of coughs and spurts as more fiery limbs waved out in all directions and at lightning speed. No fewer than perhaps ten or twelve streams—it was too quick to count them all—shot out, and four of them seemed to attract one another, and flew in a warbled arc that dared to edge Uhdin's rim. Cynkz grit his teeth, and spun in the void once again, whirling plumes of smoke, and once again shooting out massive shining, scaly limbs. Whatever Cynkz was transforming into appeared to have no basis in anything alive or natural. It was pure instinct taking over, leaving any strategy or tactics behind him; there was no time for anything else.

More heat collided with the glistening, iridescent scales. Many bits of scale and flesh instantly burned to seared crisps that flew off into the abyss. In that moment Cynkz recoiled his limbs once again into smoke, and then to himself as he curled up into a ball, trying everything he could to not let the pain overwhelm him. He was reminded of the burning pink mist deep in Munderworld's belly. He had hoped above else that he would never have to experience such a thing ever again, yet here he was. Things had a cruel way of coming back full circle in the universe, it seemed.

The cold of space, if nothing else, did well enough to numb the pain after some time. That was odd to Cynkz, how quiet things had gotten. He had hoped that Guro would speak more, to give him something else to focus on as the pain slowly—very slowly—calmed. When he was finally ready, Cynkz stretched out to turn around and face the star head on. Before he could speak, he found himself without words once again. Guro's once spherical core was now jagged, his edges frayed and pulsing and swimming in all directions. His pale orange hue had deepened, and reddened. Streams of fire burst and flowed like the excesses of a steaming pustule, unbound by wind or gravity, free to let the vacuum of space take it wherever whimsy would allow it. It was as if a web of bright, radiant puss were flailing in and out of the burning star, a woven tapestry of light, like a lattice pattern that was being crudely woven into the black cloth of the cosmos. Each stream burned a new, nonsensical pattern into Cynkz's eyes, and yet he could not look away. Such grand horror demanded to be observed, pain be damned.

C-y-y-y-y-y-n-n-n-n-k-k-k-k-z-z-z-z-z-z…

The voice was faint, but sharp. It cut into his mind and knocked him out of his stupor, and brought him back to the present. It took him a moment to rest his eyes, letting the burned lines fade away before gathering his senses.

It was then that Guro released a final flare, a last spasm that seemed to take everything out of the star. Every burned line, ever frayed edge, every molten limb, every ounce of energy within the star seemed to expand and shoot outward. Cynkz was presented with a light that consumed all, as if the natural cosmos were being phased into Omundisia, or perhaps that Omundisia itself were spilling out of the star to cover the universe. He could hear the star's lamentations shrieking just behind the blinding wave.

The way the many flailing threads of light weaved through and in and out of each other reminded him of the last apostle he saw in Munderworld. In the otherwise tepid and peaceful realm of Dulrot, the ethereal creatures stood out, clashing purposely against the otherwise plain purple land. He remembered its form vaguely resembling a sea creature, and the way its many fins and scales seemed to harness the otherworldly light.

That's it! An idea snapped the jester's attention. He thought of the limbs he had been instinctively creating, and how the loose scales would fly off as they deflected the molten light. It was painful, but it seemed to work. He could not directly bear the star's excesses, but he could deflect them.

All of this occurred within moments, and the growing flash of light was upon him. Cynkz turned himself around, and thought hard. With all of his focus, his concentration, he assumed his largest transformation, taking full advantage of the vacuum of space to allow for a form uninhibited by weight or gravity or land or sky. He thought of a rather peculiar fish he had seen in the dark ocean in Potarium. Most creatures needed to be fished out of the ocean deliberately, but there were a few exceptions, including an evolved fish that appeared to jump out of the water and glide for vast distances. Cynkz assumed their long and tapering form, and their beautiful, filtering wings. He took on no less than sixteen wings, eight on each side, and each one larger than Irros itself. The edges of each wing possessed small, hook-like scales that hung off and dangled like charms, flailing back and forth to deflect even more of the blinding wave. His back possessed the same sharp fins, and his body was thick, though it tapered down to a fine point as it ended in an even larger, sharper tail that cut the light like a needle through cloth. His scales were each a massive plane of thick, curved, and glass-like material that burned, but did well to deflect as much of the oncoming light and heat as possible. The creature's streamlined form curled slightly forward, acting as an aerodynamic lift that allowed much of the wave to slide up and off, and away from Uhdin.

The pain was immense, and sustained itself for far longer than anything he had felt before. It was enough that he lost nearly all feeling in his body, though he could still feel slight traces of heat and cold whisking off of the edges of his skin and wings. It felt as if someone with lava covering their palms were slowly squeezing his head into mush, and melting something heavy into his back, and that his limbs were being slowly burned away, turning fleshy fingers into muscle, and into bone, and into nothing, before moving on to the rest of his body. He had been nearly blinded by the onslaught, but he kept his eyes on Uhdin, and noticed the frightening, whip-like shadow he had cast upon the world.

He could still see the tiny little continent where Poro stayed. Aside from some clouds moving over it, the land and the world seemed entirely untouched.

The light seemed to slowly fade away, and the normal dark of the cosmos returned. Though his dark shadow remained over Uhdin, and seemed to be taking over everything else. It was not long before everything in sight slowly faded to black, and all that he had left were his thoughts, and the ever present cold of space.

PART 7

PEARA

CHAPTER 37

ALL WAS DARK. ALL WAS GONE.
Yet his thoughts remained.

He felt a great sense of calm as his thoughts drifted through the darkness. The pain was gone. The burning heat was gone. Even the frigid nothingness of still space was gone. He was almost comfortable, wherever he was. His senses were robbed of him—neither sight nor smell nor sound aided him. Part of him worried if the star's assault had rendered him to a pitiable state. As frightening as that conclusion was, he quite liked the peace and quiet it offered.

Though his sense of touch seemed to remain. He could feel something pressing softly into his back, particularly into the back of his head, with his voluminous hair acting as a pillow.

More than that, he could feel something running through his hair—soft fingers combing through each strand, taking great care to keep them straightened, and to not disturb his peace. With not much else to focus on, he began to notice a rhythm to the brushing— one, two, one, two, back, and forth. Back, and forth. It was akin to the swing of a pendulum in a clock. The rhythm actually possessed a slight musical flair to it. Images of simple metronomes began to fill the void in his mind. He couldn't help but wonder as to the purpose of such a thing.

He also noticed the sound taking on a sort of echo. It filled the void with an ominous, yet soothing hum. It reminded him of Omundisia. Thankfully the darkness was a much lighter assault on the senses. The invisible metronome of the void ticked back and forth, and something else caught his ear—the trickling of warm honey as a motherly hum began to trail the satisfying tick-tocking echo. It reminded him of the huums the good po of Potarium would sing. It was a voice he could recall, from a time long lost. The name escaped him, and just as his frustration began to simmer, the voice sang into his mind, a voice that could be felt, more than heard:

> *Every star*
> *Near and far*
> *Waits for us*
> *To just*
> *Reach out*
> *And accept them...*

"That voice..." Cynkz muttered. He could speak! He even caught himself off guard, though his voice felt strained, and echoed meekly into the void.

"Well hello to you too, Cynkz."

Cynkz's tired eyes, heavy blankets dragged over his eyes, shot open as quickly as they could manage. He looked up to see a woman coddling him, her arm still moving back and forth to stroke his hair. He noticed her hair draping down and around him like two black curtains that had been parted for a show, as well as two ice-blue eyes looking into his. A warm smile greeted him.

"You've been asleep for quite some time," the woman said.

He couldn't believe it. He refused to believe it, even then, as he stared into her eyes. He wondered if he was dreaming again, or perhaps the thread was filling his now empty mind with visions.

"This is as real as anything else, Cynkz," she continued. "You can relax."

His heart skipped a beat. He knew the feeling of another's watchful eye peering into his mind all too well.

"Oh, ah, my mistake," she said, pulling herself back slightly to scratch her head, as if embarrassed about something. "I can see your thoughts clearly. I'm sure you're at least comfortable with the idea, thanks to the Omun. The good news is that you can relax fully—you don't even need to speak! Just let your mind do the talking."

Orilay…

A thousand thoughts began to spill over in his mind. His mind began to tear itself into a frenzy as he tried, and failed, to focus on something, anything, that would make for a good starting point. He had long since wondered about the woman, but never considered the possibility of meeting her. He didn't know what to say, or think, more accurately.

"Cynkz," the woman could hardly speak through a series of giggles, seemingly finding much enjoyment in the jester's pondering, "you can relax. There is no pressure. In truth, you could merely sit and wait until your soul has been reformed. You take an exceptionally long time to heal, it seems."

Cynkz looked around as best he could. He couldn't move his head much, but from the edges of his vision he caught glimpses of little lights gathering together, at first moving quickly before slowing to a crawl as they clumped together around his body, or where his body should have been. He could see that they were sitting on a hill, with soft green grass swaying gently in a breeze. Try as he might, he couldn't see where the grassy plain led to, as it appeared to merely fade into some corner of the cosmos.

"I suppose I can start by telling you where you are," Orilay said. She continued to stroke Cynkz's hair, and looked up to the sky above. "We are at the center of all things. The center of the universe, essentially. We currently sit in the midst of the first light, within Paithos himself—the source of all existence. It is from here, from Him, that all things originate, and that all things are connected."

Within Paithos? So… is He here?

"Yes, well, sort of. It's difficult to explain." Orilay took a breath, and turned her attention back to Cynkz, never stopping her combing of his hair all the while. "He is not a simple being, a mere person that you can just walk up to and speak with. Paithos is…

omnipotent. He is all things, and everywhere, all at once. And he communicates with us, with the universe, through light."

Much like the Omun, and how they operate through light in Omundisia...

"Precisely! Still as sharp as ever, jester."

Jester...

"Oh yeah, that was a long time ago, wasn't it? Back when Peara still existed, back when you were still alive. So much has happened since then... Do you ever miss Peara?"

I hardly remember it...

"I know, and yet the few memories you have of Peara provided the basis for your visions, thanks to the thread, and have stayed with you all this time. I am honored to be among those ancient memories."

Memories... Visions... The thread...

"Oh! The thread! Wait, it's here somewhere." She turned her attention back to the stars. The sky was filled with them, and each one was moving, back and forth, as if in rhythm with the ticking hum of the void. Countless twinkling specks swayed to and fro, fading in and out of sight, over and over again. It was like watching a slow heartbeat breathing life into the abyss. Finally, something caught her eye, and she reached up, inexplicably catching a tiny strand of light that should have been too far away to merely reach and grab. She pulled it down, and revealed the familiar sliver that Cynkz had carried with him for so long.

"It's quite remarkable, isn't it?" Orilay held the thread just above Cynkz, twirling it back and forth between her pale fingers. "I noticed that the thread had been tampered with, just slightly. See?"

She spun it around again, and from seemingly nowhere, the thread cast a great shade, a dark blank swimming over the light forming Cynkz's body.

Orilay continued: "Paithos saw Krull's message. To think that he would do this, just to relay three simple words across the cosmos. Perhaps he didn't even think you would make it this far? Or maybe he did. Who knows what the Munder King is thinking when he does anything."

... What does it say?

"Oh, right... It merely says... 'I am sorry.'"

Cynkz wasn't sure what to think of it. His mind remained entirely blank for a time, something that Orilay seemed to take notice of.

"I suppose it's a tad disappointing. It's nothing so grand as an adventure across the universe, no? But... this means a lot. I also must suppose that you are due some answers, you of all po deserve to know *why* this means what it does, and to learn of the reasons behind Krull's banishment, and Peara's destruction."

Cynkz didn't think he was ready for such answers. He anticipated that, no matter what justification was given, that he would not deem it appropriate for taking away an entire world's future, an entire people's future, and all seemingly with his existence as the catalyst. Though who was he to judge a god? Who was he to judge a being so far beyond what a normal being could ever hope to comprehend? To judge something or someone who commands existence itself. He, a mere mortal being who was just as fallible as any other? Perhaps there was no better course of action than to hear Him out, though he appeared to need to speak through Orilay. He wanted nothing more than to hear Orilay speak some more.

"The Creator—Paithos—He can see all things, all pasts, presents, and futures. Every living, and non-living, thing in this universe, as they live and breathe, create tiny echos that reverberate into infinity. Paithos can easily watch and track these echoes, the way we would watch the ripples of small waves in the ocean. He can see where these echoes will go, where they will end, and what effects they will have on every-thing else. This is how he manages the universe, and guides all things to work and live and exist in harmony. If you have ever found yourself recalling the strange way things sometimes just 'work,' well… that is His influence ultimately. What makes this complicated is another core tenet of his creation—all sentient souls must be granted the freedom to choose as they will. No one is controlled, but their actions, and the conse-quences thereafter, can be easily followed, and thus He can alter his machinations in accordance."

I am not sure I entirely understand…

"Ah, sorry… It is all a bit strange, I know. It took me quite some time to even become able to listen to His voice, let alone understand things the way he does. All things exist for a reason, and affect everything around them for a reason. Without at least some guidance, and some purpose, everything would fall to chaos, and inevitably fall to destruction."

Destruction… Just like Peara…

"Yes… Peara… Your birth, Cynkz, carried great significance. You were never meant to be born. It should not have been possible. Yet… somehow, beyond all possibilities, Krull fell in love with a po woman, and had a child. Do you remember your mother's name?"

Ystara…

"A lovely name. Maybe it's not so surprising that an Omun would fall for her?"

Where is she? Is she still in Munderworld? I hope not…

"No… She is… here, exploring new worlds on her own. My beloved, Fraderiche, he is here… too…"

Something began to rumble beneath Orilay's voice. It was as if something ethereal, something powerful, something greater, were now speaking through her, and their voices combined to echo into the void with a heart-rending vibrato. It was no longer just Orilay speaking. Something, or someone, was aiding her, to speak to Cynkz in a voice he felt trembling from within him:

All things exist in a state of flux.

Souls are akin to pendulums, each one managing the delicate balance between life and death.

One's actions—their choices—are what drives their momentum. When one dies, this pendulum—their soul—rests where their owner decided to leave it, be it in light or shadow, and thus they are judged.

As light guides, darkness compels us, and back and forth the pendulum swings.

All pendulums are meant to find a final resting point.

"All po souls are destined for Potarium's shores."

I can both see and foresee these swinging pendulums, and the many echoes they create as they wave against the invisible walls of existence. I can weave these echoes, their movements, their fates, between one another, so that all may go about their lives in harmony.

Infinity is but a frame for me to direct the turning of countless gears and the perpetual motion of innumerable pendulums.

You, however, are a bit different.

Your pendulum swings slowly and constantly between light and dark—its weight-stone caught firmly between two opposing states. This is reflected in nearly every facet of your being—your ivory skin and ebony hair, your sharp features and soft expressions, the brilliant glints that reflect off of your pitch black eyes, even your oft cold attire betraying your warm and welcoming demeanor.

Even now, the thread you have carried with you for so long—a once pure sliver of divination altered, forced to cast a great shadow. Yours is an existence that defies existence itself. It is one that should not be, yet must be, at the same time.

As a result, your actions create dark echoes that cloud out all others. I cannot foresee what you will do, and thus the actions you take ripple forth in unseen waves, blinding me to my own creation.

It was exciting at first, I must admit.

I watched with a new sensation, with gripping anticipation, to see what one free from all things would do, and what effects it would have.

I watched you grow. You learned to love, and to get along with others, and the importance of sharing your warmth with others. You went so far as to infiltrate a foreign kingdom to sway for the protection of your family and homeland—the little grassy country of Hirlwe, where your then sickened mother laid bedridden until the end of her days. Your pendulum was slowly inching toward the light, and I could see again.

The pendulum began to swing back, however, as you fell deeply in love. It was with a woman similarly enchanting to the one who seduced a star. Yet this woman was forever beyond you, and, for the first time, you were truly dissatisfied, and refused to accept things as they were.

Your pendulum swung far back into darkness as you attempted to force hers to swing in your favor. The damage was immense. It led to her beloved's death, to her running away, the illegitimate birth and short life of their one and only child, and to the distraught king of her nation choosing to fan the flames of war.

The dark echoes of your treachery began to ripple forth into devastating waves that threatened everything. What glimpses I could see of your world's future—and perhaps that of other worlds—was dire. For the first time, I acted out of fear. I confronted Krull, who refused to atone for his actions, and Eshra'Tel, who took glee in an opportunity to vie for more power. I refused to break a core tenet of my creation—that all things must be allowed to exist, in some form or another—and merely banished them.

But that left you, and Peara.

I could see the dark future looming ahead of Peara, and, perhaps in haste, and in fear, I lashed out, and mercifully basked the world in destructive light. What po that remained would be judged and set to take their own journeys through the afterlife.

But what of you?

At first I was unsure of what to do with you, or what effect your very existence may have. All things must have an appropriate beginning and end, and all ends must lead to new beginnings. Everything in my universe is precious, and nothing may be truly wasted.

Yet, for the first time in my existence, in all of existence, I was unsure of what to do.

Perhaps… giving you a second chance was the only conclusion that made sense. Indeed, you did not choose to be born, or to have such a burden placed upon you. I merely planted the seed of change by letting you rest in Dulrot. I let you be reborn fully, though still maintaining much of your old self.

And then, I merely waited and watched, as I continued to wonder what you would become.

I must admit, I grew worried when your first true friend upon reawakening was an imp, of all things… I began to wonder if I had made a grave mistake in letting you continue as you did.

Yet something deep within me was intrigued. I continued to wait, and to observe, and let you do as your will would let you, perhaps for no reason other than curiosity.

As you began to have a positive influence on the imp, a creature of pure darkness, my worries began to fade, and I could rest comfortably in the knowledge that something good could be born from it. I am glad that I was right.

Just as I expected, your actions, the swing of your pendulum, began to affect everything.

Sometimes it made things better, sometimes it made things worse. What I noticed, and what solidified my thoughts, were your constant efforts to swing your pendulum back to the light every time it flew to darkness. Back and forth did it swing, yet you always found the strength to strive for something good.

I listened patiently to the beating of your heart, the ticking of the clock as the pendulum swung back and forth. It was then that I knew I had succeeded, and I could leave you be.

And even now, I, the source of all, have to ask for your forgiveness. I left my many children, my many loyal wards to fend for themselves. You did much to help in my absence, and for that, I owe you everything.

I regret acting so hastily. I regret taking Peara before its time. I even regret leaving you to deal with such hardships, but I had to be sure of your intentions.

I owe all that is and all who breathe an apology. Even Krull. I know that we had our differences. But I see now that he did not deserve his fate. Love is a power that operates beyond even Omun. Who am I to say such a thing should not be allowed?

What say you, Cynkz?

"I say…" Cynkz finally had the strength to speak, though his words were faint, and the action required struggle. Still, it felt wrong to not answer in such a way. "Just… Please, help the eldest star Guronimhal. If nothing else, spare him and his world from sharing the same fate as Peara. I know that I am in no position to ask anything of you, great Paithos. But I beg you, please, just save Guro, and Uhdin, and Poro…"

All went quiet, save for the familiar ticking hum of the void. Cynkz looked into Orilay's eyes, whose consciousness appeared to be elsewhere. Paithos, if it was in fact Paithos speaking with him now, seemed to be ruminating over something in silence.

Already done.

"What?"

You have been asleep for some time. During that time, I spoke with every Omun, across the entire cosmos. Your actions have… given me a new perspective. There will be many changes to come. Perhaps… Omun should be given a choice, just as much as anyone else is given a choice to live as they please.

I wonder if a more… unified cosmos would be beneficial. But such a thing would require time, far more time than any one Omun could hope to endure. Thus, for the time being, I will be guiding the Omun, and extending their lifespans indefinitely.

"So Guro lives? And Uhdin is safe?"

Yes.

"That is a relief…"

Is that all? There must be more that you want?

"I never did any of this for myself. I only wanted answers, and to help. I believe I have helped a great deal, and now I can finally satiate my curiosity."

Surely there is more that you want?
I can sense it within you.

"Well… I do not know if it is my place to ask one such as you of anything…"

You deserve it, Cynkz. You may ask
me for anything, and I will grant it.

Cynkz sat in silence, and thought. He thought long and hard, longer than perhaps necessary, but part of him was still afraid to ask. He thought of the po, and their stagnation. He thought of Krull and his banishment. He thought of the many worlds he had traveled to, and the weight of life and death that added so much meaning to their existences. He thought of how many lives were enriched and given even further meaning in their families, and their children, and the future children they would bear. He thought of Poro, and how much of an impact the little Uhdinian had on him in such a short time. It was something he wanted all po to experience.

"If I may ask anything," Cynkz said, taking in a deep breath as he prepared his request, "it would be for Peara's restoration. It would be to give the po a second chance, the same way you did for me.

If that is what you wish… Peara would need an Omun,
however. Would you be willing to fill such a role?
"Me? An Omun?"

It was something he had never considered. He admired the Omun, and appreciated their role in the universe. Is there a more glorious position in the universe than to be a literal, shining star? But he thought of Krull, and what happened to him upon committing a great sin. He thought of the Omun who were forced to sit back and watch as their beloved people tore themselves apart. He thought of Guro, and could not imagine the pain and the heartache he must have felt as he believed to watch his final moments pass, to witness the slow, frigid death of his beloved people. He could not imagine having to sit back and wait for death, to watch as innocent faces were forced to bear witness to oblivion. Paithos may have said changes would be made, but the thought of such a fate even being possible filled him with dread.

I sense apprehension within you. I do not blame you, star traveler. I only wished to extend the offer to you, as an honorific.

"I thank you, Pathos, but I must respectfully decline. I am truly honored, however."

What is it that you want, then? Truly?

There is no reconciliation too great, nothing that could truly make up for what you have done, and what you have gone through...

"I merely wish to fit in. To have a place I could truly call home, and a people I do not feel estranged from."

I can do that, and more. But it will take time.
Not that you need worry yourself with that.
Soon, you will rest, and all will be right.

"Hmm…"

"Is that all you have to say? Just 'Hmm?'" Orilay said, her eyes shifting back to focus on Cynkz, showing that her consciousness had returned.

Cynkz nearly jumped. He more than likely would have, if he were in any state to do so.

"Ah, my apologies," Orilay continued, "sometimes I get a little too comfortable with letting Paithos take over."

"I see…"

Orilay leaned over, cradling the jester's head. "Ystara, Fraderiche, they are here, exploring new worlds on their own. When Paithos first destroyed Peara, there were a few select souls whose destinies were so closely tied to yours that he didn't know what to do with them. He offered them a choice to settle with him here, and wait in peace. Of course, who could turn down such an offer?"

"I see…" Cynkz muttered.

"You know how the Munder King would threaten to 'wipe' those he didn't like from existence? In truth, nothing is wasted in Paithos' universe. Such individuals are merely returned to the Creator, to be judged and set along their own path."

"Hmm…"

"I already know what you're thinking. You wish to see them? Ystara especially? Though she may not be ready to leave."

Orilay turned her attention to the sky again, looking intently through the many shifting stars. Cynkz enjoyed the quiet. It gave him a moment to just appreciate the view.

"Oh!" Orilay exclaimed. "There she is! Hold on, just a moment."

Orilay reached up, and once again plucked out a light from the cosmos. She gently dragged it down and held it just above the jester. It was then that Cynkz noticed the thread had drifted a fair ways into the distance, like some wayward dust that had nearly been forgotten about as one cleaned a room.

"There she is," Orilay said. "She found a pretty world this time."

Within the light, one could see glimpses of a world, one that even Cynkz had never seen before. He could see endless plains, where the grass was tall and soft, and reflected an inexplicable warm orange hue. The clouds were mere streams of soft yellows and goldenrods swimming across the sky. At the center of it all was a woman, an older woman with pale skin that reflected much of the orange and golden colors around her, and had long, pitch black hair tied into a loose ponytail that reflected little light of its own. The wind pushed the world about with a gentle breeze, and she seemed to be soaking it all in, taking in every comforting moment as if it were the best she had ever experienced.

"You will get to meet her again, in due time," Orilay said, noticing the joyful tears welling up on his face. "Paithos is already working to set things up for you and the other po. She, and every other soul, will be offered the opportunity for a second chance at life on new Peara—hey! That's a name now, isn't it? New Peara…"

Cynkz sniffled, just a bit, and found the strength to answer back: "Yeah… I like that name too. It is nice and short and simple, like many good things."

"You've said that many times before, silly jester, you can't fool me!" Orilay's light teasing forced a big smile on Cynkz's face, which caused her to smile just as wide back at him.

"It might help you to know," Orilay continued, "that my beloved, Fraderiche, the duke… He has forgiven you." She took her hands to the jester's hair again, combing through it impulsively.

"Oh…" That was all Cynkz could say. It was a relief, certainly, but he still held on to some guilt about the duke's situation.

"It was so long ago. And it took the duke many years to come to grips with it all. But in a way, he was happy, as your meddling—as he would call it—allowed him to meet Paithos directly, and to reunite with me here. We have spent much time here, together, and with Paithos. We too will probably, eventually, return to Peara. I would very much like to meet my father and mother again, and would love to reunite with my daughter."

"Your daughter?" Cynkz asked, his brow furrowing, his concern palpable.

"Yes… Fraderiche and I had a daughter. She was born not long after you both died. It was after I decided to run away… I regret running away, I really do. My poor father… I saw you two meet up again. It was… an interesting bit of drama to watch, if nothing else."

"Yes… I do not blame him for hating me," Cynkz said. "I do not blame him at all."

"I'll have to thank him for forgiving you. Also, I should thank you for helping my daughter in Munderworld. Orla was always a feisty one. You did a good job helping her calm down—"

"Orla?! She was…" Cynkz paused, his eyes now wide and fixed on Orilay's. "I knew there was something about her. I am glad that I decided to help her."

"And to think—little Fiddle wanted to abandon her, but he ended up growing so close to her! What a silly imp."

"Yeah… Fiddle is quite silly indeed."

"You might need to apologize to him once you're back. He was so animated when he finally got to reunite with him on that moon, and you kept calling him a simple illusion! What a shame—"

"Wait… so that… Those were not illusions?"

"Of course not. Paithos offered them a chance to see you one last time before the end of your journey. It had to be brief, and he warned them that you were not in the best place at the time, but they didn't care. They each jumped at the chance to see you again, even if only for a fleeting moment."

"Oh… I see…"

Orilay smiled. "You and Pairne make a cute couple. You're silly, always worrying about her forgetting you. There was not a single day where she didn't think of you. Do you know how many suitors she has turned down in Potarium? None of the other po interest her the way you do."

Cynkz chuckled, enough so that he could feel it rippling throughout his still reforming body. "I suppose I am grateful. I never tried to be so interesting."

"That's the best part!" Orilay exclaimed, nearly bobbing Cynkz's head off of her knee in excitement. "You don't even have to try. You make it all seem so effortless."

Cynkz gathered himself, and looked Orilay straight in the eyes: "Orilay. I truly am sorry. I know it was a long time ago, and I believe you when you say the duke has forgiven me, but… what I did was still reprehensible. I never wanted to put anyone else through such hardship. Even now, your father, Burlowesque, must be worrying about you, and you have spent so much time away from your daughter…"

"Cynkz, it's fine, really. You can't beat yourself up forever, you know?"

"Yeah, I know, but still…"

"It's fine. Everything worked out in the end. You did good, Cynkz, better than anyone else could have."

Tears began to well up once again. Cynkz smiled wide, pushing his cheeks up into his eyes, the tight balls the only thing keeping streams from flowing down and onto Orilay's lap. "Thank you, Orilay. That means a lot."

She looked down at him, her smile warming him thoroughly. He looked back up at her in much the same way. He noticed that her dark hair nearly blended in with the dark space behind her. If not for the pearly, speckled reflections beaming off of the edge of each strand he may not have even noticed them at all. She appeared to be one with the cosmos, at least from his view below.

"Oh, one more thing—the thread." Orilay reached forward, once again ignoring space itself to grab the familiar sliver of light. She twirled the light between her fingers, and whipped it around into a crude sphere. The sphere spun and twinkled, and eventually an opening warped at its center. A flash of light blinded Cynkz, just for a moment, and a simple, light-infused ring descended slowly down and toward Cynkz's chest. He instinctively reached up to catch it, making use of his still gradually restoring strength. Its design resembled an intricate series of woven threads, locked into a perfect circle. It was not unlike the rings the Sisters of Elm wore, though its craftsmanship far exceeded theirs. In a strange way, he almost preferred the textured charm of the sister's rough hewn jewelry.

Orilay reached out and held Cynkz's hand, closing her hand over his, and his over the ring, blocking out much of its blinding glory. "Give this to Fiddle. Muns were never meant to be judged, and thus were immune to the thread. Though Paithos is now curious about them, the imps in particular. Seeing how well they have gotten along with the po, this could have grand implications on all of existence. Why does everything have to be so far apart, anyway? We are all connected, why not let all life get the chance to experience what the rest has to offer?"

Cynkz stayed silent. He wasn't sure what to think of Orilay's words, if they were even hers. She seemed to be more privy to Paithos' plans than him. There wasn't much else for him to do than to hear them out.

The ring almost seemed to have a life of its own, like a warm heartbeat massaging his palm as he gripped it.

Its pulse, a soft warmth swaying in and out, was like a faint breath washing over his skin. It reminded him of Poro as she laid on his lap, her faint breaths skimming the top of his thigh as she drifted off into her dreams.

"She saw you fly off, by the way," Orilay said, whispering. "She thought it might have been a dream, but when you left, and never went back… Well, no one believed her anyway. She held onto the poem you taught her for her whole life. She even taught it to her children. I think she may have had eight or so. They've all grown now and have spread out to the far corners of Uhdin, and started families of their own. Everything you do seems to create soft, warm echoes that go out into eternity. I'm glad that you turned out to be such a good influence."

"There is nothing else quite like it," Cynkz whispered back, though he kept his eyes on Orilay's hand, still holding his, and barely keeping out the bright light seeping out from within their grip. "I wish all po, all souls, could get the chance to experience it…"

"I can see you're getting tired." Orilay brought her hand down, running them up Cynkz's shoulders and to his hair, coddling his head in her lap. "You know that poem isn't actually a poem, right?"

"Then… what is it?"

"It was part of an old hymn, an old song from long before our time. It seems even our ancestors were enthralled by the stars, and would create their own stories. Heh, what's the deal with stories, anyway? Why do they bother ending? It's the journey that counts, right? So why not just keep adding on to those old stories and songs? Let them continue forever?"

"The destination is just as important."

"Really? How so?"

"The destination gives purpose, and the journey provides meaning. Beginnings and ends… Both are needed, and both feed into each other…"

Orilay chuckled. It was a light and tinny sound, like stardust echoing faintly through water. "You're just saying stuff now. You should rest. I can sing you the full hymn? Maybe it'll help you sleep?"

"I… Part of me does not want this to end."

"The ending is just as important though, right?"

Cynkz chuckled. His too was light and echoing. It sounded as if it came from somewhere else, from somewhere far away.

Orilay continued to comb his hair. "Just relax. I'll sing you the whole thing. Try to remember it this time, okay?"

Cynkz closed his eyes. Somehow, the stars remained in his mind's eye, filling the dark with countless shifting specks of light that ebbed and flowed in front of him. He could hear Orilay take a final soft breath, and she began to sing:

Every star, near and far, waits for us, to just, accept them.

*Every place, and every space, gives us
room, for warmth, and hymn.*

A twinkle in the dark,

A streak in their arc,

When stars shoot by, they paint the night
sky with a playful whim.

With time, we learn, to love, and spurn,

We live, we laugh, we cry, we yearn,

To share in the warmth, through huum
and through Him.

We grow weary and old, life may
seem dreary and cold,

But a single spark,

Ignites the heart,

And we remember that our time need not be grim.

All we need to do, is see past our woes,

Because for you, the universe throws,

Hints of brilliance,

Of warming transilience.

Every star, near and far,

Waiting to embrace us,

If we only, accept them...

CHAPTER 38

A SOFT BREEZE CARESSED HIS CHEEK. At first he thought it might be her hand, but the faint whistling of wind rustling through tree leaves above brought him back to his senses.

He took his first breath, filling his body with new life. It was as if it had been his first breath in eons. He could feel his back pressing into something, heavy and soft.

He opened his eyes, and looked around. At first the world was a blur, but soon his vision adjusted to the new light. He could see that he had been asleep on a gently sloping hill in a meadow. He could finally move. He felt well-rested, though he could hardly remember his dream.

That wasn't anything new to him. It was not often that he remembered his dreams, though something about his most recent one stood out to him.

The thread! Wait a minute…

Cynkz pushed himself up and leaned forward. Something small and round could be felt sliding through his cloak, and over his clothes. A bright light soon settled at his side, revealing a small, glowing ring. He could recognize the ethereal object. It appeared to be made of the same material of the thread. He soon remembered looking up at the stars, and Orilay.

I guess that was not a dream… Or was it? She told me something before I left…

Cynkz gathered the strength to pick himself up. He grabbed the ring and pushed it deep into a chest pocket. It was dark outside, yet inexplicably bright, the way a full moon might illuminate an otherwise gloomy landscape. The stars seemed to be hiding partly behind a new light that poked through the many openings of the trees above. It was somewhere ahead, peeking through the many trees. He could feel the tempting pull of curiosity weighing heavy on him, and without a second thought, he stepped forward and up, as if preparing to fly.

Except he couldn't! He tried several more times, and only ended up lightly stamping the ground around him. That too caught his attention, and he looked down, expecting to see deep holes carved into the soil from his excessive, otherworldly weight. Instead, he noticed his steps had hardly disturbed the grass beneath his feet. At first he couldn't believe it. His inconsistent weight was no longer a concern! For once, he didn't need to put extra thought or worry into his mere presence. He smiled wide as he set his feet down and apart, and set himself at ease.

"My feet… They do not sink anymore! I can just… relax…"

Something sharp caught his ear—something, or someone, was coming in fast from beyond the tree-tops! His startlement was quickly interrupted by the emergence of several beady eyes, all bearing down curiously from red furred heads and small, plump bodies that seemed to defy gravity as their tiny black wings carried them playfully to and fro. There were only three of them, none of whom Cynkz recognized, but they seemed to crowd together in a way that took up much of the airspace above. They were most definitely imps.

The leader of the troupe hovered forward, bringing with her a burning question as she squinted toward the jester.

"Who the heck are you?" she asked, her voice light yet husky. "Were you talking to yourself just now? You're kinda weird."

Cynkz couldn't help but chuckle at the small creature. "Hello there, little one. My name is Cynkz. What is your name?"

"Cynkz? *The* Cynkz? The legendary munder vassal?" The tiny imp seemed intent on making her incredulity as palpable as possible, going so far as to lean forward and squint sharply as she scratched the tip of her bony chin. "I've heard lotsa stories 'bout some guy with that name but… Nah, I don't buy it. You know the great Fiddle doesn't like cheap impersonators, right?"

"The 'great' Fiddle?! Ha!" Cynkz laughed, more heartily than he had in ages. He could feel a slight pain from the act forcing him to lean over and hold his sides. The imps seemed confused more than anything, with their leader looking particularly displeased.

"Oh boy, Fiddle's gonna have a field day with you," she said, crossing her arms and shaking her head at the poor fool before her.

"I think you are right, little one." Cynkz caught his breath, and stood himself upright. Once settled, he looked back at the imp hovering above. "Still, you have yet to tell me your names. I am curious if the 'great' Fiddle has kept to his usual naming conventions."

"Well, I don't know what that's supposed to mean, but I'm Chorale. The two behind me are Quart and Trill. Say hi to the weird guy, guys."

"Hello! I'm Quart." One nearly jumped up in his cheer. He held his tiny arms out and waved them playfully back and forth as he hovered in the air.

"Hey… I'm Trill." The other seemed more reticent, seemingly anxious to focus on anything else. He nervously fidgeted with his dark nails, picking at them shakily.

"You know," Quart said, "he does kinda look like the guy in the statue.

"Nonsense!" Chorale exclaimed, turning around to wave dismissively at her friend. "The guy in the statue was way bigger. He had more muscle, a more square jaw, the hair was nicer too—it almost flowed like water. His hair is just, well, hair."

"But look at his clothes! It's accurate down to the teensiest, tiniest, silliest detail!" Trill shouted, letting his excitement get the better of him. "Even the hat! Most impersonators get that wrong. His looks appropriately weathered, though well made."

"Pfft, whatever," Chorale said, nearly hissing over her shoulder at her friend, "if anyone would know, it would be Fiddle, the eldest and wisest of imps."

"Those are some impressive titles," Cynkz said.

"Well, he has earned them," Chorale continued. "Both he and the jester—whose glorious image you are impersonating—swooped through darkness and heaven, confronted the Munder King and, with his help, were able to begin finding all of the lost imps, all bazillion, quintillion, bajillion of us—"

"You're just making up numbers," Quart chided under his breath.

"Nu-uh!" Chorale snapped.

"Can you take me to him?" Cynkz asked. "I would love to see him."

"I suppose… He's farther ahead, trying to gather as many lost po and imps together as possible. With New Peara still forming, he's ordering the sentinels around to make sure everyone stays safe in the meantime-"

"The sentinels?!" Cynkz's shock seemed to catch all three of the little imps off guard. "So even they're getting along, huh? I have truly been gone for a long time, it seems…"

"If you say so." Chorale turned and beckoned for her companions to follow her. She began to drift ahead before looking back over her shoulder at Cynkz. "Come on, I'll show you the way ahead. I'll take you right to Fiddle, even, so he can figure out what your deal is."

Cynkz smiled. "That would be lovely."

The jester took in a deep breath, flared his cloak and pressed forward, following the little imps as they all disappeared into the light beyond the forest, ready for what may come.

EPILOGUE

M ANY YEARS HAD PASSED SINCE THE great reformation. Many new souls have come and gone since then, and the po have adapted well to their new world. Mun and po alike seemed to have adjusted well to the new world, and even the many sentinels were given time to appreciate life on their own terms, though most chose to do what they were always meant to do—to watch over and protect the po. They too were subject to the slow entropy of time, and all but one had turned to dust, their souls returning to the afterlife to continue their eternal duty.

The last sentinel shambled through a peaceful meadow. His tall, gaunt and bony figure traipsed through the woodlands with a lightness and deftness that one would never expect from such a thing. To see an imposing, statuesque warrior, still clad in his old robes and carrying an impossibly long spear shifting quietly through the trees without so much as disturbing the chirping of its many birds and insects—many po equated them to divine beings themselves. Though the sentinel himself preferred to not be seen as such—he was content to merely be seen as a helper and servant of po.

He had been tasked by a desperate young po couple. Their one and only daughter, after an argument, had run off into the forest. The parents suspected she had a favorite spot, though they were only aware of the general area. The night was young, and the moon shone brightly. Krull's restored light lit the world well, and did much to guide the path forward as the sentinel shambled forth.

His thoughts turned to other things as he pressed forth. He knew he was at the end of his life. With every step, more of his body broke away—tiny grains of dust and sand falling to the wind, akin to the erosion of a stone or marble statue. He had witnessed the great reformation. He had witnessed the first po settling the lands of New Peara. He had witnessed the burning horizon of the new world settle. He had seen the legendary jester spirit return to the po, and reunite with the eldest of imps. Even now, he basked in the once fallen Munder King's light, his true role restored as the Omun of po. He had witnessed the life and death of many po, and of his brothers. Hundreds of years had passed in the blink of an eye, yet he looked forward to reuniting with the others in the afterlife. He had heard many stories about Potarium, but had no experience of the place himself. He looked forward to it. It was enough to ease the pain of his deteriorating form, if nothing else.

He could see something rustling in the brush ahead. He heard the giggling of a small child, and something else accompanying her. It seemed as if they were playing. Not wanting to frighten the child, the sentinel moved calmly, though he made his presence known. A step forward revealed a young girl with hair as dark as night, that reflected the slightest red hue in the light. She was playing with a tiny, infant imp. She was climbing on several large rocks as she tried to keep up with the infant mun, who had no trouble flying through the air, playfully weaving back and forth and laughing all the while.

The sentinel couldn't help but smile. The two children finally noticed, and whipped their heads around, looking on with small, shocked faces at the statuesque guardian. Their shock settled once they realized it was just a sentinel.

"Oh, it's you," the small girl said.

"Your parents sent me to find you," the sentinel said, his voice gruff and strained, sounding of gravel dragging across a water-beaten rock on an ocean shore.

"I figured they'd do that..." The girl looked disappointed, turning her eyes away form the sentinel's.

"It's alright," the sentinel continued, "they don't know where your favorite spot is. It's still your little secret."

"Really?! Nice." The girl's face lit up. The sentinel couldn't help but laugh, watching the young po get so excited.

The girl looked at her new companion, then back to the sentinel. "I found an imp! She was just sitting over in the woods, chewing on some rocks. I think she likes me, but she's really young. I don't think she even knows how to talk yet."

"Well, give her time," the sentinel said. "Before you know it, she'll be talking your ear off."

"Yeah…" the girl stared at the sentinel, seemingly taking in his shambling appearance. She seemed both worried and awestruck, and at a loss for words. She furrowed her little brow, and scratched her tiny round chin, when an idea popped into her head. "Hey! Wanna see my favorite spot? I know it's supposed to be a secret, but… Well, I was gonna show it to the little baby imp anyway. Why not show you too?"

"Hmm… I would like that. Lead the way, little one."

"Here, I'll help you."

The girl pranced toward the sentinel. She reached out with a tiny hand, and the sentinel felt compelled to reach down and lightly clasp it. His hand was far too large for her, so the girl settled on merely gripping the tip of his forefinger. She gently pulled him ahead, and called to the imp to follow. The trio eventually disappeared into the brush, and were lightly traipsing through the woods.

The girl led the sentinel through several groves, past many trees, and even over a calm river that glittered in what moonlight seeped through the treetops. It was not long before they found themselves overlooking a secluded cliff that seemed to grant a view of the entire forest. A few scant lights of a town miles away could be seen, but not much else. It was little more than a patch of grass, yet it gave perhaps the best view of both the world below and the night sky above.

The girl, growing excited, began to pull harder. Once the sentinel was at the center of the patch of grass, she let go and ran to the cliff's edge to take in the view. The imp followed close behind, and appeared equally enthralled by the scenery. The sentinel, growing tired, sat himself down, a great gust of wind from his sheer size and weight washing over the grass, and clouds of dust shooting out in short poofs that quickly faded into nothing. The girl noticed, and ran back, crawled over his leg and sat herself in his lap, nestling in the middle of a bundle of his robes that covered much of his crossed legs. The imp followed the girl closely, but not before grabbing some grass and flowers to chew on, and even kept her eyes on the night sky ahead.

The three sat in silence for a while, soaking in the tranquil scene. The sentinel sat impossibly still, the girl breathed quietly, and the imp made hardly any noise as she chomped away. The stars themselves perhaps made more noise than they did, as they tirelessly twinkled and danced in the cosmos above.

"Rackel, what happened to the other sentinels?" the girl asked.

"I suppose they had fulfilled their duty, and were ready to move on," Rackel said.

"Why are you still here? Don't you miss them? Your brothers?"

"I do, but I know I will meet them in another place, in a world beyond this one."

"You won't go, will you?" The girl pulled her head back to look up at the sentinel, her face sitting in the shadow of the creature's large snout hanging far above her. "I could use another friend."

"You just made a friend, didn't you?" Rackel smiled, and turned his attention to the tiny imp at their side.

"That's true," the girl said, "but she needs to learn to talk. It would make things easier. It'd be nice if I could just tell her to not chew something bad, without having to actually chase her down."

"Does she have a name?" Rackel asked.

"Not yet. I haven't thought of one," the girl said. "Dad plays the flute. And his dad played the flute too, as well as his mom. Apparently my great, great, great… uhh… great… grandpa played many instruments, but he really liked the flute, as well as those weird ring things."

"Well, he was a jester, after all," Rackel said. "It makes sense that he would play many instruments."

"You got to meet him, right? What was he like?"

"You'll get to meet him eventually," Rackel said, turning his attention back to the stars.

"But I wanna know all about him! I've heard stories, but you actually got to meet him!" The girl seemed to be getting restless, her agitation causing her to bunch up the sentinel's robes even more.

"Well, this was one of his favorite things to do—to get away from everything and watch the stars."

"Really?! Why's that? He liked stars, and even talked with them, but… I don't believe it. It sounds like a silly bedtime story or something."

Rackel sighed, through a soft smile curling up the corners of his snout. "You'll just have to see for yourself then."

"I guess… Still need a name…" The girl looked to be in deep thought, darting her eyes around and scratching her tiny chin. "What am I supposed to call her? Impy? Fuzzy? Toothy? Flutey? Flutesel?"

"How about Flutelle?" Rackel said.

"Flutelle… That's so pretty! I love it. But maybe I'll just call her Flutey for short. I'd ask for her opinion but, well…" She looked over to the baby imp, who had found another rock to chew on when the other two weren't looking. She looked at the imp with a playful disdain. She seemed anxious, wanting to tell the imp to stop, but held herself back, perhaps knowing how futile it would be.

"Why are all of the imps named after music stuff, anyway?" she asked.

"Perhaps it's because we enjoy listening to them?" Rackel said, hunching over as more of his body deteriorated, leaving small piles of sand and dust that the girl had yet to notice.

"Well, they do make a lot of noise," the girl said, keeping her eyes on the imp. "Though I've never found them annoying."

"Heh, just like good music, I suppose." Rackel's voice grew more gruff, sounding as if stones were slowly tumbling out of a bag or barrel. He began to ooze sand from his face, and one stream fell from the tip of his snout and right in front of the girl. She stared, looking confused at the sand pooling between several folds of grayish robes just ahead of her.

"Is there really an afterlife?" She asked worriedly. "Are you going to be okay? Why do… Why do you have to go?"

"I believe… it is simply that you no longer need us. You po have adapted well to this new world. Perhaps we are simply needed elsewhere?"

"But… I don't care about what anyone needs. I want you to stay with me. And Flutelle. You know about my secret spot, so you can't go."

Rackel chuckled, sounding of pebbles being juggled around as more of his body fell to grains in the soil. "I promise I won't tell anyone about it. Your secret is safe with me."

"I guess you could tell great, great, great… um, super great grandpa about it," she mumbled.

"Hmm, I could do that, but… I think I'll just let you tell him yourself."

A soft breeze washed over the horizon, gently pressing against the sentinel and dragging away several waves of colorless dusty waves into the wind. The girl watched, and Rackel watched her. She seemed to only partly understand what was actually happening. She also appeared to be getting tired. He wondered how much of this she would remember in the morning. He figured it would be best to just comfort the small girl as much as possible.

"Promise me you'll go back to your parents, and apologize?" Rackel moved forward more, nearly covering the small girl in a looming shadow.

"Yeah, I will," she said. "But I wanna stay with you for a little longer."

"That's fine. If you fall asleep, by the time you wake up, I'll be a nice, soft pile of ash and cloth—the perfect bed for one to sleep beneath the stars on."

"Okay... Flutey?" She called out to the baby imp, whose tiny jaw was now slacked. They appeared to be getting tired. "Flutey? Come here, we can cuddle and sleep. I'm tired."

The imp seemed to ignore the girl, or perhaps she was too tired herself to notice. Or, more likely, the imp still did not fully understand language. Rackel mustered what little strength remained to lean over and tap the small, infant creature on the shoulder with the crumbling tip of his nail. Flutey perked up and looked back to see the small girl reaching out to her. She finally understood, and lazily drifted over to settle in the girl's embrace. Not wanting to cover the girl in more ash, Rackel leaned back, giving the two an unobstructed view of the moon and stars.

"Will I get to meet them? Cynkz and Fiddle?" the girl asked as she curled up into a warm ball in Rackel's lap. The imp had already fallen asleep, and the rhythm of her breathing appeared to be lulling the girl to slumber as well.

"Of course," Rackel said, sitting straight up, and keeping his eyes to the sky, even as his body ccrumbled more and more to the ground. He was practically little more than a torso, an arm, and half a leg sitting in a pile of dust, but he did his best to curl into a comfortable form for the girl and the imp.

"You'll get to meet plenty of nice relatives," Rackel continued, "and you can ask Cynkz about the origin of your name."

"Poro is a weird name," she said.

"It's a nice name," he said.

"My name is weird," she said.

"Poro is a sweet name. It means 'little star' in a foreign language," he said.

"You'll be there, right? You'll wait for me in the next world?" Poro said.

"Of course," Rackel said.

"Pinky promise?"

"Pinky… promise…"

Rackel reached in, and held a crumbling pinky before the half asleep po. Poro reached up and lightly shook the finger, only for its tip to fall to dust. The girl joined the imp in a deep slumber, dreaming the night away on a sloping pile of gray robes and colorless ash.

ᴀᴜᴛʜᴏʀ ʙɪᴏ

KYLE SORRELL, ALSO KNOWN AS 'Pendoodle,' is a fantasy author based out of northern Florida. Having grown up with countless fantasy and sci-fi influences, as well as a lifelong obsession with video games, he loves to stitch together stories of odd elements dipped in the weird and the wild. Having been born on a naval base in a watery town in Japan, as well as growing up a multiracial child and working many different jobs—from assistant plumbing to theme park caricatures to truck driving—he has worn many hats. You can catch sneak peeks at his next crazy idea, or just the occasional illustration, at his personal website at pendoodlez.wordpress.com.

BOOK CLUB QUESTIONS

1. How far away from Potarium do you think Cynkz traveled by the end of the story?

2. Of the many worlds Cynkz visited, which one was your favorite?

3. Which of the other 3 main perspective characters were your favorite (Valk, Yuto, or Zzira)?

4. What was your favorite sentence or line of dialogue?

5. What surprised you the most in this story?

6. What do you think the people of Sihl's world actually looked like?

7. Did you believe it was merely Cynkz's powers creating the illusions on that far off moon?

8. What do you think Orilay's final song sounds like when sung in full?

9. What do you think Paithos meant when speaking of "bringing things closer together" at the end?

10. Were Paithos' actions justified?

11. What do you think Fiddle will think of the ring Orilay made for him?

12. How exactly do you think new imps are born?

13. What would you have named the baby imp in the epilogue?

14. Would you read another series by this author?

Discover more at
4HorsemenPublications.com

10% off using HORSEMEN10